THREE GRAVES

Sean Gregory

Sean Gregory

Bluemoose

Copyright © Sean Gregory 2021

First published in 2021 by
Bluemoose Books Ltd
25 Sackville Street
Hebden Bridge
West Yorkshire
HX7 7DJ

www.bluemoosebooks.com

The permissions acknowledgments on page 309 constitute an
extension of this copyright page

British Library Cataloguing-in-Publication data
A catalogue record for this book is available from the British Library

Paperback 978-1-910422-83-0
Hardback 978-1-910422-82-3

Printed and bound in the UK by Short Run Press

Cover image by Pushkin (www.instagram.com/pushkinism)

Photograph of Anthony Burgess © Mark Gerson /
National Portrait Gallery, London

For Rosie

When I hear a journalist like Malcolm Muggeridge praising God because he has mastered the craft of writing, I feel a powerful nausea. It is not a thing to be said. Mastery never comes, and one serves a lifelong apprenticeship. The writer cannot retire from the battle; he dies fighting. This book is another battle.

Anthony Burgess, *Little Wilson & Big God,* 1987.

Manchester

He flicks the pinched tip of his cigarette onto the Mancunian Way and watches as gobs of rain shoot it down. The taxi moves beneath new shafts of concrete that pierce the skyline. Overhead, neon illuminations advertise an asinine, gurning radio disc jockey. They can tear down all they want and build whatever they fancy to replace it, but Manchester can't shift its own smell, its own skin. It's all rouge and blusher on pockmarks.

The drone of inching cars, the drone of the city itself. He dreams of living out his life as an enigma, present only as two words on a dust jacket. *Apis Bombus.* The dense traffic parts, syphoned off towards Princess Parkway. The taxi circles, Hulme high-rises, Trafford mills, Church of St George, Potato Wharf, and on to Knott Mill. So much concrete, you sense it setting around your feet. The Manchester Evening News building, a busy bit of Brutalism on this Manchester morning. And there's John Rylands Library, Gormenghastic, hidden in plain sight. He taps the partition glass, *Anywhere here,* pokes a crisp five pound note through the grille and stubbornly waits for change. His feet hit the pavement with a crackle of broken glass.

We're just this way. It's a pleasure to have you with us, Mr Burgess. Anita, the assistant manager, walks slightly ahead, setting a pace she intends to be met.

A pleasure to be here. He stops to take in his surroundings, *This is all very impressive, I must say*, and starts off again to catch up.

They pass the tills and the recommendations. He scans the shelves, noting a new print of *The Sword of Honour* trilogy complete with Cyril Connolly endorsement, but can see no works of his own. Above, a sign directs shoppers. An arrow pointing up: Crime, History, Art. An arrow pointing right: Toilets and Fiction.

Burgess nods towards the sign, *That sounds a fair combination, doesn't it.*

Anita briefly assesses a sign she passes every single day.

Toilets and Fiction, he muses.

In a room off the main floor, tables have been draped in black cloth. Beside the entrance there are two piles of his new book, hardbound.

Can I get you anything? Anita smiles, checking her watch.

Tea. A good cup of English tea.

How do you take it?

Five bags, left to stew well. A drop, and I do mean a drop, of milk.

Another polite smile and she is gone. Burgess lights up, using the pot of a wax plant as an ashtray. A tall lad, with a look of Larkin about him, straightens out the stacks of books. He rearranges them, fanned across the table. Assessing his work, he tuts, stacking them once more. It is, Burgess thinks, incredible what people will do to occupy the mind.

Anita brings tea and he sups at the insipid brew; too much milk, not nearly enough tannin. They pride themselves on a good brew up here. In his experience, they do everywhere. Sitting alone, nursing piss-weak tea, he feels undignified and indignant. Too long out of England, too long out of the provinces. And now here he is, alone. Bloody publishers and their – he spits tea – marketing strategies.

Hello, Mr Burgess.

He can see, just barely, above a stack of hardbacks and paperbacks, the top of a man's face and head. A spire of words held stable by hands at the base and a chin at the apex.

What do we have here?

I was hoping if I got first in the queue I might persuade you to sign some other books.

With pleasure, with pleasure. Have you waited long?

Not too long, no.

The books, Anthony can see from a quick scan, have been arranged in chronological order. *Time for a Tiger* is set before him first, followed by *The Enemy in the Blanket*, *Beds in the East*, and so on.

They tell me, he says, distractedly thumbing to find the title page, *that if you sell these things they're more valuable if it's just the name. My name, that is.*

There's a sudden, almost violent stop. He holds out his hand to receive what he assumes will be *Devil of a State*.

I would never sell them.

Who's to say what the future holds? Burgess feels the weight of his own words, faced with the tower of his past.

I couldn't. The man appears to be playing out the terrible circumstances under which he would have to sell this prized collection.

Shall we keep going? A copy of *The Worm and the Ring* is placed before him. *Not an easy book to get your hands on. Where did you...?*

A place in Alnwick.

Alnwick, indeed. Well. He signs.

I enjoyed MF, the man tells him.

I'm so glad. Nobody else did. Only book I take pride in, as a matter of fact.

The collector seems to bite down on this admission like a fish on a hook. He studies Burgess' face, looking for a tell. *Is that true?*

True? There is scrutiny in the question, in the look. Is this a piece of valuable Burgess information? The book will have to be read again, will have to be put under significant examination, this statement in mind.

Is everything all right? Anita wears a smile only an imbecile would take at face value. A queue has formed and is becoming restless.

A collector, Anthony tells her, to clear up any doubt.

If I could ask you to keep it to five items, sir.

Just this one, then. The man takes a hardback from the pile and presents it to Anthony.

He looks it over, *This isn't one of mine.*

Could you. Please?

But it's not mine. I can't sign someone else's work.

Anita lifts up the remaining books, out of order, four in each hand. Flustered, the collector grabs them from her. Books slip from his grasp, from Anita's arms, falling to the floor. He's on his knees, cursing and scurrying to collect up the books and check their condition. The tower reformed, the collector raises it and himself up, saying, *Take good care of yourself.*

All the best, Anthony says.

Underneath his own name, he signs dedications to Sarahs, Brians, Ians; he shares best wishes with Dimitris, Dianes, a Roger. As he gets into the rhythm – flipping two pages in, asking for whom, and signing away – he has to remind himself to look up, that a connection, a real conversation, is what they have all queued for. A youngish woman asks how he finds Manchester now. He gives her the old eye contact, the rehearsed parted-lipped pause, and pushes his hair from his forehead. That's right, let them have some of that acerbic wit they've all come for.

Well, of course, my Manchester is the Manchester of internal segregation lines – class, race, religion. But today, the city is a united cause. God bless Mrs Thatcher.

They like that. God bless Mrs Thatcher. You could pay no attention to the papers, stay out of the country for years, and still rely on the collective resentment of the powers that be.

This, for instance, raising his hands up to the building they sit-stand in, *was part of Kendals in my day. A bazaar of household goods, soft furnishing, and electrical appliances. I was brought here on day trips, as a child, just as others were taken to the zoo. We'd wander the aisles, my stepsisters and me, staring at all those foreign objects. Now, of course, this is a home for books, which I think is a very worthy enterprise for a building. I like to think of bookstores and libraries as my second homes. A part of me always remains – as long as I'm still in print.* Very good, let them believe there is always a bit of him up north, even if the man himself is drinking Aperol cocktails on the Monte Carlo seafront. Book signed, the woman gratefully thanks him and moves on. Anita puts down a fresh mug of tea, the colour of the Bridgewater Canal.

How's your hand going?

Oh, my hand's all right, but I'm forgetting how to sign my name. I start writing the title and then it sort of slips.

Any Old Burgess, she says.

Yes, something like that.

You're our Jackie. An accusation. A disbelieving statement. Somewhere in there is a question.

Anthony looks up at an ancient man, a practically dead man, who peers back through sunken eyes. He knows this look well, this bloody Mancunian glare. Think you know something, pretentious bastard, it said. The words *bookstores and libraries are my second homes* repeat, growing increasingly louder in his mind. The undead is flanked by two others, all three dressed in shades of beige. Polyester coats, pockets torn, stained at the cuffs and neck. Man-made, then, not figments.

He holds his nerve. *I'm sorry?*

Our Jack. I'm your cousin, Bert. Albert Dwyer. This is our Agnes' 'usbint. The relic beside bows his leathery skull. A foolish gawper, more disturbed by the amount of learning that besieges him than this impromptu family reunion. Anthony nods politely and turns to the third of this timeworn triptych. A woman, rippling with layers of skin, beady eyes peering out. The fat softens her wrinkles somewhat, though it does nothing to hide her years.

And who, smiling at her now, *is this?*

Wull, our Agnes, in't it. Of course it is. *Do thee not 'member us, Jackie?* That fucking name. He had crossed continents to escape the smear of Our fucking Jack.

I'm sorry. It's, well, I wasn't expecting you. Should I have been expecting you? What did they want? Money, he supposed. But for what, why, was money owed? They could not expose anything he had not already revealed himself. Maybe they thought it only right the pretentious bastard should put his hand in his well-tailored pocket and draw out a few crisp notes for them what got left behind. That'd be right. Drag them down what thinks they're better than the rest.

Agnes saw it in't paper. You bein' here, like.

Well, I must say, he says, words failing him.

Our Jack! Our Bert whistles. Not impressed, mind.

Elsie died, Agnes pipes up. John saw the comic scene immediately. This geriatric woman (his very own stepsister!), reeling off every name of everybody she could think of that had died since the last time she'd seen their Jack.

Well, John says, *what a surprise to see you all. Bert, Agnes, ehm...?* The relic nods receptively to Ehm.

Shall we wait? Bert says.

Wait?

For you finishing? Tom's Chop 'Ouse is just round corner.

Aye, John says.

We'll get you a pint in, Jack. For old times and that.

Relic Ehm lights a roll-up and John watches as they drift in a cloud of smoke towards the Natural History department.

6

Apparitions spent, an unsigned book is placed in front of him. *And who are you then*, he asks, *me daughter? Some long-lost niece?*

What had they, he signs and hands the book over, come here for? Forty years must have passed, he flicks to the right page, since the last time he'd seen any of them. He had assumed, *Thank you for coming*, they'd all be dead by now. But here they had stood. The murmur in the room and the sound of the city outside start to converge to a dull tone, at 440 hertz. He grasps a book by the spine, *Who should I make it out to*? He signs, John Wilson. He stares at the page. Any old Wilson. The words are an aberration. John takes his pen and draws a picture beside the name – sunken cheeks, double chin, bags under the eyes, hair manic, swiped to the right.

I'll get a fresh one, Anita says in her cheery, not-cheery manner.

John pinches the top corner of the page and pulls, tearing the first stitch. He tears again and again – shred, shred, shred. John fucking Wilson.

Outside, Manchester rain runs as only Manchester rain can. Some of the staff have been coerced into giving him a nice little send off. One of them asks for a copy of *A Clockwork Orange* to be signed.

Anita hands him a branded Waterstones' umbrella. *You're sure I can't get you a taxi?*

No. No taxis. He waves her off and bids them farewell, walking down Police Street. The staff watch, some mystified, others suppressing laughter, as the old man of letters, one of Manchester's prodigal sons, struggles to lift his umbrella against wind and rain, dragging a suitcase behind him, off into the city.

Cut up with broken glass, his suitcase ricochets off uneven paving slabs. Everything seems too new – shops he doesn't recognise, restaurants recently opened – yet if he lifts his gaze above street level, the tops of the buildings are held firm in the past. He reaches Cross Street. To his left is the Cathedral, the River Irwell, and Hanging Ditch, where he once had a job playing piano. Before the war, all before the war. To the southeast, his childhood home, his school, the university he attended. Brunswick Inn, where his first symphony was obliterated in the Blitz.

He finds himself standing before the Chop House and three people he shares nothing with but bleached-out memories. There is money owed, he remembers now. One hundred pounds from Agnes Toilett, borrowed some forty years ago. Do they intend to get it from him today? What is the interest on a debt like that? They'll not get a penny from him. He crosses Cross Street, has to shift himself, the case clacking behind, to dodge the growing puddles. He is lost and not lost. The rain had been merely a prelude to that about to fall.

John clacks his suitcase into the City Arms. It looks familiar, but then pubs always arouse familiarity. He orders a pint and sees himself as a lad, sat at a table drawing pictures of barmaids, as his dad sits at the joanna and talks up his piano-playing skills. The beer is sharper than John had hoped for. The sides of his mouth seem to swell with every gobful. It is not good beer. Joe Wilson would start all confident like, pulling out sheet music he could hardly read to give a taste of his repertoire. He'd try to time it so he was having a tinkle on the high keys just as the landlord came through. *Lovely joanna*, he'd tell them.

Do you still have the old joanna? John asks the barman.

Not 'ere, mate. You must be thinking of next door.

I was sure my father played here; piano against that far wall.

Could of, he replies. *But Ah've never heard of nobody playin' pianna in here. You play?*

In my own way. I'm more a composer.

Oh aye, he says.

The landlord, I take it?

Dad is.

8

My dad too, Anthony says. *The Golden Eagle up Miles Platting.*

The barman takes a pack of peanuts from the rack, revealing the naked midriff of a girl, her head poking out above two packs of dry roasted. *Never heard orrit.*

Not any more, of course, Anthony says. *That's long over.* He wants to say more and hear more of Manchester, but the man, no more than thirty he guesses, looks uninterested. Time to sup up and move on. *Give me some of those nuts too*, he says. *Originally from Oldham, are you?*

You what?

Oldham. I can hear it in your voice. Flattened diphthongs.

The barman eyes him. *When I were little. Been here a few years now.* Anthony knows the look: who the fuck is this posh prick?

It strikes Anthony that the man is in fact a boy, Manchester being a hard city to grow up in. He now puts him at around fifteen, sixteen, pulled out of school to learn the family trade. *I must get going*, he says, though he doesn't move except to hand his empty glass over the bar. *How do you like growing up in a pub?*

It's alright, I suppose.

I remember the sound of several pianos all crashing along at the same time, three different pieces being played. He thought he'd written all this out of himself. *The regulars used to give me a penny; a shilling if I snuck down late enough. Here you go, Little Jackie. I used to run down the stairs first thing in the morning and piss in the men's trough.* A fresh pint is placed in front of him, he tastes it, much better.

We 'ad a jukebox for a while, the lad says, *but the regulars just complained about kids putting the same song on over and over again.*

The pub wasn't my father's, it was my stepmother's, which she inherited from her dead first husband. My father just worked there. You need a male presence, don't you?

The lad lifts the bar flap and goes off to collect empty glasses from empty tables.

My mother had died, John continues. *She died when I was very young.* He raises his glass to the Manchester dead. *She was very young too, though I didn't think that for a long time. The old die, don't they. It's not the role of the young to pass away.* No, he thinks, watching the lad feed coins into the fruit machine, youth has no interest in death. *I perceived in myself, when my wife died, a great loneliness. A loneliness left by her death. And, I thought, what loneliness have I carried all my life, brought about with the death of my mother. I was just a babe, just a small thing. I remember her, you know. I remember her lying there, my sister too. The hand of death can never be forgotten, even when you are so very young.*

John looks over the many spirits in their many optics, waiting to be poured, one measure at a time.

Part One

Kuala Kangsar
1954

Rahimah held her arms around the bottom of his ribcage. She pressed her soft skin against his nakedness and breathed gently. *Hold me, John*, she said. A theme began to play, music welled inside him, languid strings beneath a taut and anxious oboe.

I am holding you, he told her. It was a phrase he had taught her, but she had misinterpreted the meaning. *You mean*, he said, *make love to me. Rasai cintaku.*

Rahimah looked into his eyes as he laid her upon the rugs and blankets that made up her bed. Strings swelled, woodwind rose through the chromatic scale.

As he moved, Rahimah began mouthing words in Malay, muttering along with the motion of his body. *Teruskan. Jangan berhenti mencintaiku*, she said. Rahimah never spoke words like this, not to John. He had heard, at the outbreak of a fight, one of his pupils yell out *Aku akan bercinta dengan kekasihmu* and, not quite sure what the boy planned to do with the other's girlfriend, had extrapolated that *bercinta* was as close to fuck as the Malayan language got. The same word whispered from her lips, from his own lips; it got his blood up. The tempo increased. Andantino to Allegro, Allegro to Allegrissimo. Allegrissimo – Rahimah calling *cinta* on every exhale – to Prestissimo and, suddenly, to Larghissimo. And rest.

There was semen on the bed. He wiped himself with the thin white sheet, which shone bright with morning sun. Lynne lay beside him, facing the wall, breathing heavily through her mouth, a low sck-sck-sck-sckur of air running over the lip of her Eustachian tube. He let her sleep. She couldn't seem to get enough sleep since they had arrived in the East.

After dressing and making a cup of tea, John went onto the roof. He sat slurping tea and eating the few biscuits they had left, watching and listening to Kuala Kangsar rise. Hawkers arrived, just across the river. Trishaws ran suited officers towards the colonial offices. An abundance of life. A symphony in full motion. The whole town seemed held in by the surrounding trees.

They had been in Malaya for six months. They had been promised a house and were given rooms above the preparatory school. Lynne had raged against that, had taken it as a personal snub. It had been the same in Banbury, it had been the same on the boat from Southampton to Singapore.

Aboard the *Willem Ruys* there had been nothing to do but drink and wait for the damned journey to be over. John found himself conscripted by a man who gave his name as Ronald Roland. They were introduced one evening in the Captain's quarters, when John and Lynne were still on their best behaviour. Had he been born in Harpurhey, Ronald would have been a bare-knuckle fighter. As it was, there had been, John deduced, a lot of rugby in Ronald's life. The colonies were the natural habitat of men like Ronald Roland.

The only real man we have, of course, is Ben Britten, Ronald had announced. He talked loudly over the string quartet and pianist, gamely reciting Brahms' quintet in F minor. A discussion about what they would miss of Britain had become what was best about Britain, which had morphed into what the British did better than other nations. Ronald had almost single-handedly driven the conversation.

What do you think, John? asked Sandra, a typist from Hemel Hempstead. What does he think? John thinks anyone who considers Britten finer than Elgar beyond the pale. Never mind a man who thinks art runs across territory lines.

Here she comes, Ronald nodded. Lynne slid into a seat vacated by one of Ronald's associates, growling the last of a conversation she had been having with no one in particular. *Good evening, Mrs Wilson.*

You've missed dinner, John said, managing to defuse most of the irritation from his voice.

Not to worry. Well, Lynne made herself comfortable, *what are we talking about tonight, then?*

Music, Ronald replied.

John boring on again. She used Ronald's matches to light one of John's cigarettes.

Musical genius. Composers from across the globe, Ronald continued. *Plenty of Germans, Italians, few French, quite a lot of Austrians for the size of the place. Of course, there's no Chinese Beethoven, is there. Not many English either, mind.*

None that you've heard of, Lynne said.

You'd think if they had one, Ronald took a pull of his pipe, *we'd have heard of him, wouldn't you.*

Stupid thing to say, Lynne said. *So, what if there's no Chinese Beethoven? You think the Chinese are claiming there's no genius in England because our vases aren't up to much cop?* The music came to an end and, as the game demanded, the table froze.

My favourite is Debussy. Where's Debussy from? Sandra asked.

Frog, isn't he, Ronald said, clearing his throat.

Do I mean Debussy? Who wrote Thingy in Blue?

Gershwin, John answered. *Yank. I admire Philip Warlock; I had the chance to meet him in—*

What about Africa, Ronald? Lynne took a drag. *Any composers of note from the dark continent, you can think of?*

Piff, that'd be right. Ronald held his pipe up, waved it, then made a circling motion above the table. Across the deck, an Indonesian waiter bowed and walked to the bar. *What African has ever seen a viola, ha!*

15

Samuel Coleridge-Taylor. Lynne placed the name on the table for all to excogitate.

Well, yes. I mean. British mother though, wasn't she? Not full coloured.

John saw the sneer cross Lynne's face, knew she would quickly be at the throat of Ronald Roland.

Sod it. John stood, stubbed a cigarette and scraped his chair legs back. The whole table, Lynne included, watched as he marched over to the band. He arrived with urgency but waited patiently while they finished a waltz. As the pianist thumbed through sheet music, there was a long drawn out mime, John haggling a price for the piano from its player. The musician demurred, but John called a waiter over, more miming was performed, and all was settled. The waiter left, stage right, the pianist shook John's hand and followed.

John ran his hands up the keys, foot firmly on the damper. It was like a rolling wave breaking into shards of ocean spray. His fingers ran along again. He took a breath, gave his hands a gentle rub and rested them on the keys.

The little fingers on both hands strike in unison, three octaves apart. The sound is almost discordant, though they are the same note. The right finger strikes again, while the left hand moves to the centre of the keyboard, hits a chord and moves off. John's body sways, his hands shift like undulating water. Sharp raindrops strike the hardwood floor, others hit heavy into collecting pools. As he plays the pools deepen, the whole room being submerged in water. While the ship rocks, water flows from one side of the dance floor to the other in a gentle, growing wave. Each table is a rowboat, lost and turning on the open sea. The water level is rising, there are no oars and no direction to pull if there were. John himself feels the call of the below. It all ends abruptly.

Back on dry land, rain that had held off overnight began to fall in fat, sporadic drops. His shirt ran wet with rainwater and sweat. Swallowing the last mouthful of tea, John made up his mind to leave Lynne. He would marry Rahimah. He would convert to Islam if it would make the marriage easier. He wanted to become a Malay, to be a child of this soil. She would make him happy and he would set Lynne free. Today, he told himself, I will do it today. The thought of it reignited the melody, his Malayan melody. It would be written. He peered down to see the first lot of young boys rushing out onto the fields, shouting up to the rain as it fell heavier and heavier. Their mothers, like his own, distant memories.

In a half dream, children screamed out to her, children she could not see; babies trapped underground, buried alive. Her mouth so dry she could barely move her tongue. Her lips cracked. When she tried to lick them, she split the scabs. The glass beside her bed was empty and while part of her tried to rise up, another was stuck in a desert, alone. Somewhere below the sand were the bodies of trapped children. Lynne got down on her hands and knees and clawed and clawed. But it was no use. Grains of sand in her mouth, her eyes, she felt exhausted, struggling for breath.

Yusof, she wheezed. She could hear him singing softly. *Yusof*, this time a little louder. Lynne felt the world return – the walls of the bedroom, the mattress beneath her. She could hear him in the kitchen, already rattling pots and pans. Pulling herself up, back against headboard, she called again, *Yusof. Tolong berikan air.* Strange that water should be air in Malay. *Api* was fire, *angin* meant wind. She could not remember what earth was. Yusof came in, tutting at the state in which he'd found her. He placed a glass of warm water on the bedside table, took one more look around the room, and left. In the hall he continued to half talk, half sing to himself. Lynne picked up the odd word, *menjijikkan* and *memalukan.* Disgusting. Shameful.

There was a loud knock at the front door. She took a mouthful of water, allowing her tongue to bathe for a moment. Water ran over the ulcers that lined her mouth, sore to the touch. The knocking came again, louder still. When she ate, she would bite them, and they would bleed. On the third knock, Yusof finally made his way to the door.

Dia ada di sini? Dia ada di sini? came their little voices. It was the same every day. Some of the boys waited until John had left before building up the courage to come and see her.

Di luar, Yusof replied angrily.

Missus, one of the boys called, the others giggling. *You are—* He was interrupted by whispers. *You are,* he started again, *beautiful.* She could picture the red of his cheeks. Ismail, she guessed.

Yusof's sandals slapped against the tiles as he chased them from the door.

Apa yang berlaku? Mas asked, coming in.

Yusof followed, out of breath. *Setan kecil,* he replied.

Puan tidur?

Dia separuh mati, he replied, enjoying himself.

Yusof, kamu jahat.

Lynne followed some of it. Mas had asked if she was sleeping, Yusof had made some comment, had said she was dying or already dead, Mas had told him off. It was the same most mornings: the amah concerned for her mistress's condition, the cook revelling in it.

They were exact opposites, Mas and Yusof. One lived as an adherent to all the rules of her religion, country, and duty. The other lived by a code entirely of his own design, which shifted to suit his whim. He was in love with John, or at least that was John's contention. She listened to them smoking in the kitchen, Yusof spinning yarns for John, making out little of what was said except the repeated *puan* from Yusof's lips. John told her that it meant madam, but coming out of Yusof's mouth the word was coarse and accusing. And no matter how much John bitched and moaned about Yusof and Yusof's cooking and the noises coming from Yusof's quarters, he never once talked about getting rid of him. Lynne talked about it daily.

The door opened, Mas brought in a plate of sliced fruit and a glass of mango juice.

Good morning, madam. She helped Lynne to sit up and held the glass to her lips.

He said I was dead.

Yusof a bit cracked, puan. Drink, eat. You have a fever. Here, Mas pressed her fingernails into the purple flesh of a mangosteen. The flesh ripped to reveal the white fruit. Lynne held it in her mouth. It was cold and the juice ran sweet and sour over her tongue. She held it there for a long time.

Mas went about the room, picking up Lynne's discarded clothes. She bore a look of permanent worry, her eyebrows repeating the curve of her eyes, her lips forever pursed. John had hired her. *Our amah,* he had said, and they had not once called her housemaid. Lynne had grown a sisterly affection for Mas. Sisterly in that she both loved her and distrusted her.

Cup of tea? Mas asked.

Lynne nodded. When the amah had gone, Lynne climbed out of bed. John must have put her in a nightshirt. She peeled it off and looked at her body in the mirror. Youth had left her, but of course it had, she was thirty-four; how long was youth meant to remain? Her paleness persisted even in the heat. Ibrahim appreciated her whiteness. *Perak sutera pada keluli,* he whispered. *Sutera* she knew was silk. Even as they crossed the border of two languages, he made it seem so simple. He wanted her to be his wife. What would it take to leave John. She hitched up a pair of knickers, pulled her nightshirt back on and took her housecoat from the hook on the door.

At the bridge John stopped, as he always did, and lit a fresh cigarette. He looked over at the raging Kangsar River, the palms, the forest beyond. The rain eased, but water lapped at the apex of the bridge. He felt a dull sickness. He felt the water beneath churning, furiously shifting. It reminded him of the Irwell, that dirty slash of water that cut Salford off from Manchester. Manchester and Malaya. Kuala Kangsar and Kearsley, Cheetham Hill, Clayton.

> *By and by the Eldest Magician met the Man on the banks*
> *of the Perak river, and said, Ho! Son of Adam,*
> *are all the Animals obedient to you?*
> *Yes, said the Man.*
> *Is all the Earth obedient to you?*
> *Yes, said the Man.*
> *Is all the Sea obedient to you?*
> *No, said the Man. Once a day and once a night*
> *the Sea runs up the Perak river and drives the*
> *sweet-water back into the forest,*
> *so that my house is made wet; once a day and*
> *once a night*
> *it runs down the river and draws all the water*
> *after it,*
> *so that there is nothing left but mud, and my*
> *canoe is upset.*

He threw his fag end over the bridge and crossed the Irwell from Salford to Manchester.

And what will I do, John? she asked. It was raining there too, raining still.

He kissed her, Lynne's breath ripe with beer and pub food. *We'll be all right*, he said.

They walked up Bridge Street and stopped, appropriately, at the Bridge Inn. He brought over two pints of bitter. *You seem distracted.*

She took the glass and took a heavy draught. *My parents want me home.*

He drank, was about to demur, this was home, but he saw what she meant. *To Wales.*

Bombs on Manchester, she said, as a sort of answer.

It made sense. He was to enlist soon enough. *They've got a point. Why be here when you can be somewhere,* he tried to think of the word, *safer?*

She took his cigarettes from the inside pocket of his jacket and lit up.

What is it you want, Lynne? He felt this was a poignant moment, hoped she felt it too.

How should I know, she sighed.

The pub was almost empty, just a couple of blokes still in overalls throwing darts and the landlord tutting his way through a copy of the *Daily Mirror.* John felt a deep urge to get down on his knee. He wished he was already enlisted, uniformed and booted, hair slicked down with pomade. He would hear the swell of strings as he dropped, taking a ring box from his breast pocket, just below his name tag. Lynne's eyes would well at the sight of the ring, nothing too fancy – this was wartime, after all. He would kiss her, she would lean into him, his knee bearing both their weight.

Lynne took a ten-bob note out of her purse. *Get a couple more in, John.*

What about us, Lynne? She was about to reply, but John said, *How about we get married? You and me. The war might well be over by the time you go home and I get drafted. We could stick together. I'll get some work piano-playing, composing.* He thought she might interrupt, but she didn't. *And, and, we can travel, if that's what you want. Once your degree is done. It doesn't have to be in Manchester. I don't mind where we go. There's nothing for me here, not really, anyway. Nothing I'd miss that couldn't be replaced.* He was rambling, he knew.

Thank you. She put her hand on his.

For what? He suddenly felt very alone.

For asking. She stood. *I'm going in there,* nodding to the Ladies. *Get them in.*

John sat, note held loosely in his hand. It had been, he understood, a no. But she had not said it aloud. She would need time to think. There was so much to think about now, never mind proposals of marriage. Never mind love.

She came back, kissing him on the cheek. *You'll stand by me, then?*

Of course, Lynne. Of course, I—

I'm pregnant, John.

His mouth dropped; his pint almost followed.

Before you say anything, I want you to listen. She looked around to see no one else was. *I can't have my parents see me pregnant out of wedlock, but my dad would never forgive me if I got married without him knowing. The way I see it, the only option is for me to go somewhere else. Find a job or something like that. Deborah is up in Preston; I could stay with her for a while.*

This was all too much to take in.

I'll have the baby, then we'll see. I can't think of everything, but I can do what's best for me and it now.

The baby had been lost. Lynne had stayed in bed complaining of stomach ache, and when John came home she was drunk and struggling with the cap of a bottle of pills. She couldn't articulate in any way what was wrong, not to him. And when he grew impatient and told her it was always the bloody same with her, she grasped at her stomach in a kind of desolate ache. She beat her hands against herself, while John yelled, *What the hell do you think you're doing?* and peeled her hands back and up into the air. She raged against him, her twisting wrists held in his grasp, contorting her body to face him and screamed and wailed and showed him how it felt inside. She wore herself down until she lay on the living room floor, John still gripping her arms. Finally, he gave her two pills and a glass of tepid water with which to wash them down.

Mas brought tea, a damp copy of *The Times*, a fresh pack of cigarettes and the post. Lynne fanned out the envelopes. There was one from Hazel, her sister. The handwriting was angular, carved into the paper. She shuffled the letters back into a pile and picked up the newspaper. Days old, of course, but then Britain and Malaya were not on the same timeline; they received news from Britain's past, yet somehow Britain loomed in the distant future. Lynne flicked through the paper. Adverts celebrated the end of rationing. Christ, the war felt like another lifetime. Bombs falling on the grey bricks of London a distant cry from Communists firing from the greenery of Kuala Kangsar.

Lynne read with interest the testimony of Mavis Wheeler, charged with shooting someone called Lord Vivian. Mavis had found the gun in the luggage of an American colonel, who she was probably having it away with before the lord was on the scene. The colonel refused to remove his luggage from Mavis' house, so she took the gun to her cottage, where there was a schizophrenic on the loose, burgling houses. Mavis said, *I took it down because bricks had been thrown at the door and I was nervous because of so many cases in the papers of women alone being attacked. I thought if I had the gun there I could shoot it and frighten anyone if necessary.* A gun would come in handy, yes, should American soldiers come knocking. Mavis'd have to shoot. Have to kill them dead. She'd had an affair with this Lord, but money had been tight. She'd had to sack the hired help. They were living hand to mouth. Then one day she wanted him to read a poem but instead she shot him in the stomach.

Lynne laughed. It was a laugh that cut through everything, all the pain, all the fog, all the bloody mess. If I was to kill John, that's how I'd do it. Call him into the room apparently to read some sodding poetry and stick a bullet in him.

The trial was ongoing. The prosecutor asked her why police had removed her from the hospital after the shooting, calling her a 'nuisance'. *I don't know. Do you mean I made a nuisance of myself there?* Counsel began to put another question to her when Mrs Wheeler broke down. Her shoulders slumped, she dropped her head, put her gloved hands to her face, cried and sobbed, saying, *I was not a nuisance. I never was.*

But she was a nuisance, wasn't she? There was a trial and journalists, and no doubt photographers waiting in bushes, and there was a Lord shot. Poor Mavis, probably in prison now. Poor Lynne, sent off to rot on a penal colony. For all of the suffering Mavis Wheeler was likely to face, Lynne couldn't help but feel a pang of jealousy. The adverts for HP Brown Sauce, Ambrosia Creamed Rice and Andrews Liver Salts. The anonymity of London. She was less homesick now than she had been, but it still formed a void in the pit of her stomach.

Lighting another cigarette, Lynne picked up Hazel's letter, thought better of it and put it back on the tray, thought again and tore it open.

Dear Lynne, she read.

I have not heard from you since my last letter. I am unsure, what with the distance and all, whether you received it or not. Mum is not well, Lynne. I know that we have discussed this, but it is more serious now than even we thought. The doctors have told us Dad cannot cope. After a lot of talking, we have decided, for now, they will have to move in with us. We will have to find the room. There's no other option. You are too far away and unwilling to engage with what is happening to Mum, so me and Bill and even Ceridwen will have to bear the brunt. But we need to know when you and John are planning to come home. Mum might not have much time but Dad will need caring for when she's gone and

I can't do this all on my own, Lynne. He asks
after you and talks about you coming home. He'd
rather be with you than us, what with Ceridwen,
and Bill's job keeping us in Leicester. Anyway, I'm
sure you'll do whatever you want as usual. Just be
clear, I can't do everything while you and John do
exactly nothing.

Yours,

Hazel

Fucking Hazel. She should go home now, just to save herself from this pettiness. If Hazel wanted her back in Britain so much, she would have to put her hand in her pocket. Maybe, she thought, I could move in for a while, to get myself organised. She would share Ceridwen's room. Still only a baby, really, she wouldn't mind having her aunt to stay. Then Lynne would look for a house back in Tredegar, which her parents could move into too. She still had friends in Wales, people willing to help. But there was Ibrahim to consider. She would have to convince him to move with her.

In town John shared a *Selamat Pagi* with the kedai keepers and towkays. He turned up Jalan Kangsar, one of his usual detours. Outside Restoran Yat Lai, Rahimah was sweeping the step. She looked tired. Mat, her son, had been unwell and she had no one to help her care for him. The wives of divorce were treated cruelly on the peninsula.

John was beside her before she saw him. *Selamat pagi, sayang.*

She looked up from her work, neither startled nor happy. She really did look worn out. *Selamat pagi, terima kasih*, she replied.

John knew she wasn't fine, knew the work was too great a burden. Her towkay watched from behind the counter. He would not reproach John; John was one of his best customers.

Okay, okay, John tried to soothe her. He wanted to pull her closer; heat radiated from her small frame. Music returned, the theme that had played since he had arrived in Kuala Kangsar. He thought about his dream. He would end his marriage and start a new life that evening.

At the clock tower he met Yusof Tajuddin, a fellow teacher. Yusof had arrived at the school under the headmastership of a man named K.D. Luke and spoke wistfully of the Japanese occupation that had sent Luke packing. Yusof shared John's antipathy towards their now headmaster Jimmy Howell. John saw in Yusof a longing for Japanese internment.

Planning any insurrections today, John? Yusof lifted his umbrella for John to share.

A misunderstanding. John kept out from under the cover, enjoying the cooling rain.

Senior boys in the hall yelling 'merdeka' while brandishing arms. What is there to misunderstand?

A rehearsal for a play, nothing more. What Clarke saw was a scene from Shakespeare.

I wasn't aware Shakespeare knew any Malay.

They passed a white bandstand on which some boys were sitting, passing around a single cigarette.

Buat jalan ke sekolah sekarang, tuan-tuan, Yusof gently requested. John followed his meaning. It was time to move on.

Very diplomatic, John said.

You have to, Yusof Tajuddin confided, *find a balance between discipline and respect. Some of these boys will go on to be politicians, business leaders. Some even,* he pointed out one of the boys ahead of them, *kings.*

Ahmad?

Indeed, yes.

So are we, then, to treat all our students like kings or all our kings like students?

We are their schoolmasters, but Malay culture requires our respect.

You mean, my respect. As a Brit. As a white man. Orang puteh.

Mat Salleh, Yusof corrected. *Westerners.*

They crossed the road and followed the wrought iron fencing that ran along the playing field.

I think you should try harder, John.

Try, how?

I hate to think of your leaving.

The school came into view now. It looked, framed by the green of the tree-filled hills behind, recently carved from marble and fresh alabaster. Its orange roof shone, almost radioactive against the clear blue of the panoramic Perak sky. John was reminded of the White House, Mat Salleh's house. All those pillars, the grandiose uniformity intended to remind one of Vitruvius. It was, he had to admit, an intimidating sight. As grand as the Royal Palace he had seen on his first day in Kuala Kangsar, the building was a statement: this school is as good as any in the West.

Eton of the East, Yusof said, catching John's thoughts.

Malay College of the West, John replied.

On the school field a group of pupils was playing rugby. As they got closer, John saw Mr Howell in shorts and long socks, calling after the boys with an accentuated Welsh baritone. *Get into it, lad. Drive. Bloody drive at them, then.* The boys, well presented though the rain persisted, barely a grass stain between them, moved with grace in and around puffing Jimmy Howell. Jimmy to his friends; Jimmy to John, at one point. Not for some time now. Not since the rumours of John fraternising with the locals got back to him.

Howell looked over as three boys fell to the ground, their pristine white shirts turned slick brown and dark green. *Get off him, Abu, you bloody clown. Azlan. Azlan, get up. You're not shot, lad. He barely touched you.*

Jimmy had taken John under his wing, introducing him to the drinkers at the Idris Club. It was the only respectable drinking establishment in the town, the rest belonging to Chinese proprietors. John had quickly had enough of British men regaling each other with stories of Britain. There had been words and perhaps – it was hard to piece the night together – a punch thrown. Howell had informed him he was barred from the Idris for a month. They had never gone back.

He and Lynne wanted to experience what it was to be Malay. Ironic that their guide should be a seven-foot white policeman called Donald Dunkeley. Lofty to his friends, Lofty to John.

The rain began to fall heavily once more. John lifted his satchel above his head. Howell blew hard on a whistle and checked his watch. *Right you are, lads. In for showers. Quick, quick, then. Wilson,* he called, jogging exaggeratedly over to John and Yusof. *Wilson, a word.*

Good day, John, Yusof said.

Indeed. Thank you, Yusof.

Howell jogged past to the gate and John went to join him. *Good morning, Mr Wilson.*

Mr Howell.

Just wanted to check in. All that bother.

Yes. John would rather Howell had not known about all that bother. *Water under the bridge.*

Were it so, Wilson. I've had a word. Can't have these lads getting above themselves.

Above how?

Self-rule Abu was yelling about, wasn't it? 'Merdeka'? They should be sodding grateful, so they should. All we've done for this country. He had a habit of talking like this.

It was nothing. It's good they express themselves.

Express? You'll have them running a-bloody-mok. I've written to his parents. 'Merdeka', indeed.

There was an awkward pause and John said, *It means 'freedom' in Malay.*

I know what it bloody means, Wilson, Howell said.

Don't do that. Don't tell his parents, please. He's a good boy, good grades. He only did what I asked.

Accused the British of keeping his people down? Told you he'd like to kill every white man in Malaya?

I asked for their understanding of Julius Caesar. Abu offered a reading the other boys could understand. Caesar representing the British, and Brutus the Malayan people. It was a well put—

While holding a makeshift sword. Mr Clarke thought he was about to strike you down.

I was playing Caesar. In context, it was all—

I'm not interested, Wilson. Howell went quiet. He had already written the letter; he hated wasted time. *He's a good scrum-half, I'll give him that. Be a shame to drop him for disciplinary matters. Right,* he started to walk towards the school, *on your head, Wilson.*

John followed. Lynne had been on at him to speak to Jimmy again. In for a penny, he thought. *I've been meaning to ask, Jim, eh, Jimmy. When do you think other arrangements will be made? For mine and my wife's living situation, I mean.*

Leave it with me, Wilson. These things take time. He stopped at the main entrance. *Anything else, while we're at it?*

It's just that, it's Lynne. The boys are so noisy, and it was never the agreement we would live in the prep school—

Howell put his hand on John's back. *These things take time, Wilson. Bide yours, now, mind.*

I will let Lynne know you're dealing with it.

Jimmy patted John's back once more and headed down the corridor.

It was through Lofty that she had met Ibrahim. John had come home one night talking about a new friend, a man who could get them a car. Lynne had only half heard. Neither of them drove, what use was a car? A couple of nights later, they were passing the police station when John pointed to a man in sweat-stained police uniform on the other side of the road.

Don, John called over. *Don,* he took Lynne's arm and led her over, *I'd like you to meet my wife, Lynne.*

It's Lofty, Don said. *Pleased to meet you.*

Likewise. They shook hands, hers tiny in his.

We were just about to get a drink.

I know a place. Lofty stretched out his massive arm before them. *Follow me.*

In a backstreet kedai, Lofty rowed bitterly with the owner. *Just take a seat, I'll only be a minute,* he told them, turning back to continue the argument. John and Lynne stood by the door, John listening to the unfamiliar music playing on the radio.

Finally Lofty and the owner seemed to reach an agreement. He brought over three bottles of beer and ushered them to a table. *Eh, John, you couldn't get this one, could you?*

John drew out his wallet and removed what money he had. *How much?*

Lofty, belying his size, gently pulled a few notes from John's hand and gave him a wink. Lofty paid. John looked over to the owner, all smiles now, bowing delightedly at John and Lynne.

He's a bastard, Lofty growled, taking his seat.

Various acquaintances of Lofty's passed through, mainly other policemen, some British, others Indian and Tamil. Lynne was on fine form, ordering gin and tonics mid-sentence, mid-story, regaling Lofty with tales of London during the war and Manchester in her university days.

At ten o'clock, Ibrahim joined them, surprised to see a woman there. *This is John's wife, Ibra.* Ibrahim nursed his beer, making sure he was not caught watching Lynne. *I was just telling them about the car.*

Ibrahim nodded. There had been a lot of talk of this car. Lofty had been banned from driving police vehicles; one too many prangs after he'd had a skinful. Ibrahim had had to drive him around for the past two months. What money Lofty had, Ibrahim knew, had gone on the buying of booze and paying off debts for booze bought on tick. There was nothing left for either the purchase or running of a car.

I was saying, said John, *neither me nor my wife drive.*

You drive, don't you, Ib? Like a nice drive out.

Ibrahim mumbled in Malay, diverting his eyes from Lynne and trying to create space between himself and Lofty's massive frame.

Lofty moved in, tight to Ibrahim's ear. *What the fuck are you going on about?* His breath hot and heavy, thick with cadged cigarettes and warm beer. *Mujhe yah chhod do, alright.*

Lynne waited expectantly for whatever might happen next. Still inches from Ibrahim's face, Lofty wiped the residue from the corners of his mouth and planted his empty bottle on the table. He gave his friend a robust pat on the back. *Adhik peene!* He called, standing, towering over the group.

More bottles were ordered, more money taken from John's wallet. The alcohol had loosened Ibrahim up. Lynne asked to see his hands, moving her own over them.

Powerful, she said, smiling. *John's got teacher's hands,* she ran her fingers over calluses, *his are prettier than mine.* He did not understand a word she said; he would have listened to her all night. Her husband did not seem to notice, or to mind if he did. But Ibrahim pulled his hand away when John started to sound out a loud, aggressive tune, arms flailing like he was stirring invisible spoons into invisible pans.

Give it a rest, John.

A rest, semibreve, then, dat, dat, dah, da, da, dah. He continued, verbosely, correcting himself, mimicking brass and violins.

Apa ni? Ibrahim asked Lynne.

John twatting around. Lynne and Ibrahim politely smiled at each other. She turned and watched her husband, glaze-eyed. *He thinks he's Elgar.*

31

Lofty leant in, *What's this he's singing?*

One of his little tunes. Ignore him, he'll stop in a minute.

No, I quite like it. He a music man then, is he?

He is, Ibrahim tried to think of the English and came up short. *Mrtakon se baat kar rahe.*

Lynne turned to Lofty. *What's he say?*

They watched John waving his lit cigarette like a wand. *He says, he's communing with the dead.*

At Lofty's insistence, John had hired Ibrahim as their driver. He would drive them to Ipoh and Taiping, where they would go to the casinos and cinemas. Some days the four of them would take drives out with a picnic to share. There was no doubt it was dangerous, but Ibrahim seemed to know the roads and had friends in the surrounding villages. Then John started a book club for some of his colleagues at the school. This was followed by Malay lessons for John and English lessons for the Malays he had befriended, until it seemed like he had to be somewhere every night. Ibrahim would drive Lynne to the cinema, where he would wait and return her back to Kuala Kangsar where they would meet John for a nightcap. But there had been a problem with the car one night and Lynne didn't make it to Ipoh.

She was flattered, really. A handsome police officer, albeit transport police, attracted to her. Not merely attracted, in love. Or so he had told her. Who could tell whether the words that left a person's mouth articulated what they had in their heart? *Saya sayang awak.* She knew what the words meant, but what could they mean to her? When he said them, she made him repeat again, slowly.

Saya, Ibrahim pointed to himself. *Sayang,* he placed her hand on his chest. *Awak,* he held his palm out towards her.

Then he said, *Aku mahu menolong kau,* and repeated the movements. He was drunk. In Lynne's experience, drunk men were always ready to talk about love. They had shared a bottle of gin and a couple of bottles of beer, bought with the money

John had paid him. He stared at her with such urgency, it made her breathless.

Balik rumah sekarang, she said, in what sounded like thick valley Welsh, against his Malay. It was time to go home.

But he didn't move, just repeated, *Saya sayang awak.*

Yes, yes, she agreed, climbing from the bed.

Listen, he said sternly. *I love you.* He was like the little boys who came to her daily with phrases learnt in English to impress her.

Just take me home. Rumah, Ibrahim, rumah.

Like a child, he had done what he was told.

Inside his classroom the boys waited patiently. They were used to John's lateness and thought it some kind of test. They looked sullen, but then they always looked sullen. Abu, however, looked ready to go again.

Right. Well, John rolled his sleeves further up his damp arms, *I feel we should recap on yesterday's – I will call it what it was – performance.*

Some of the boys glanced over to Abu.

Julius Caesar. The great Bard, Shakespeare. I asked you all to consider how Shakespeare writing in Elizabethan England about ancient Rome could tell us something about today, in 1954, here in Malaya. Now, he strode back and forth before the boys, *you were not too forthcoming yesterday, until Mr Bakar was a little too forthcoming.*

Sir, Abu reacted immediately.

Who else, other than Mr Bakar, has an opinion?

John scanned the room. No one, it would seem, had an opinion.

Well, he continued, *do we agree with Mr Bakar's analysis? Caesar represents the British and Brutus represents the people of Malaya? Do you, Sabit?*

The boy thought long and hard. *Maybe.*

Maybe, he says. Well, gentlemen, that has cleared that up then, hasn't it? And what about you, Wathiq, do you agree with Mr Bakar's reading of the play?

He too thought long and hard. *Caesar wants the people to be happy.*

Yes, go on.

But he also wants to have all of the power.

Like the British, do you think? Is that what they are interested in?

The boys all turned to Wathiq. *I don't know. My father says the British have done many great things for Malaya, but there is no more for them to do.*

I want to study law in England, Ahmad chimed in.

Which will be made possible because of Britain's presence in your country?

I think maybe, yes.

Anyone else?

When Caesar is killed, though, the people all fight each other. Go on.

Brutus and Mark Antony were friends but then they become enemies. Brutus is punished for what he did and the man, the poet—

Cinna.

Cinna, he is killed, even though he did nothing.

Are you saying people may be hurt if the British leave?

The boy thought, is that what he was saying? *I'm not sure.*

The British hold us back. Finally, Abu had heard enough. *Of course they do.*

Ah, Mr Bakar, would you like to come up and speak?
No.

Come on, you can take the class from here.

The boy looked around at his sniggering classmates. He reluctantly got to his feet and slowly made his way to the front.

Now, what were you saying?

We are held down by the British forces. Malaya should be run by Malayans. It is our country.

So, you don't think Britain has anything to offer your country?

This is not the point. We are second-class citizens in our own country, unable to rule ourselves.

You believe Brutus was right to end Caesar's reign then, whatever the cost?

There should be no oppression to any Malayan.

Oppression, John laughed. *Look at you boys. Sons of lawyers and doctors and businessmen. Some of your fellow pupils will be rulers of this country one day. You have no idea about oppression—*

No, Abu cut him off, *this is the point. If we are the sons of affluence and we are under the control of outside forces, then all the people of Malaya are oppressed.* He looked at John. *While the British ruling class takes riches from our lands.*

John bridled. *You'll not put me in that bracket.*

You are a colonial.

I am a teacher. Listen here, he stood, *I went to school with boys like you. Boys whose mam and dad would furnish them with new satchels, new shoes, new shirts, fresh haircuts. Never-need-for-nothing sort of lads. You pay for the privilege of a decent education, whereas I had to work for mine.*

The boys shuffled in their seats. Abu did not move a muscle. *You think we don't work?*

But where's the desire? The need to learn and create, to take knowledge and do something with it? You boys will always have it easy. He had said too much and was grateful Abu was no longer in possession of that wooden sword. *I just mean, you cannot know what real oppression is.*

Or you cannot understand what our oppression is, because you believe the British have a right to be here.

We've got off track here. Back to Caesar.

And now you want me to be silent because I do not agree with you.

35

No, not at all. But this is a lesson on Shakespeare and on Caesar.

Which we are forced to learn by our British oppressors, using their tongue and not ours. Kanak-kanak Malaya hendaklah dibenarkan bercakap dalam bahasa mereka sendiri.

Sit down now, Abu.

Kami adalah masa depan Tanah Melayu, anda adalah masa lampau. We will chase you from our lands and be rid of the British. Merdeka!

Some of the other boys were fired up. They began to bang their desks.

Merdeka! Merdeka! they chanted.

Now, now, boys. Abu, back to your seat.

Abu did what he was told, banging his desk as he sat. *Merdeka! Merdeka!*

The classroom door opened and slammed shut.

What in the name of all that is holy is going on here? The chanting stopped, the banging stopped. Jimmy Howell stood, face beet red, in front of the class. *Never in all my years as headmaster of this school, in all my years teaching, in fact, have I heard such a racket. Mr Wilson, would you care to explain? Perhaps there are a few boys here we would be better off without.*

Howell was trembling. Outside the classroom, other teachers peered in. John felt the sweat dripping down his back. The boys stared at him, all except Abu. Abu looked down at his desk, resigned to his fate.

What was it Ibrahim had said? *Aku mahu menolong kau.* She knew *aku, I.* And *mahu* was *want.* What did he want? Lynne needed a drink. She was starting to sweat, and the doctors had told her she must remain hydrated. What time was it? Early still. Jesus, she spent every day waiting for it to come to an end. The kettle whistled and Mas brought fresh tea.

Terima kasih, Lynne said. *Thank you.*

Sama-sama.

What is, she pursed her lips to pronounce the word, *menolong?*

Mas looked at Lynne with sad eyes, *Menolong?*

Yes, Lynne said. *What is the meaning?*

Menolong, Mas said, miming something Lynne couldn't quite understand. *Menolong,* she said again, raising her arms and waving, waving as if drowning.

Help? It means help?

Help, yes.

He wants to help me, she thought, and looked around the room at her sad little life.

From the kitchen came the wail of furious Yusof crying out, *Tak ada kentang, tak ada daging lembu.* The heavy front door opened and Yusof called, *Puan, I go,* slamming it shut.

Yusof cracked, Mas offered, going out again to clean the hallway floor.

Too bloody right.

Puan need help? Mas asked, very softly, like a mother.

No, Lynne said. *Not for me.* A charged silence sat between them, Lynne caught sight of Hazel's letter in the corner of her eye. *But what about you, Mas? What news do you have?* Lynne asked, thinking of Mavis Wheeler.

My son, Reheeq. He...

But Mas did not need to say any more; Lynne remembered. *Reheeq* – Mas smiled to hear Lynne say his name – *today's his promotion. I forgot; you should have...* She searched for the words and saw her opportunity. *Take the rest of the day. Be with your son. Pergi. Balik rumah.*

Puan?

Saya pergi. Finished, Lynne said. She gave Mas a wide smile.

Mas frowned and pointed at the floor.

Oh, leave the bloody floor. Go, Lynne snatched the mop off Mas and threw it into the pail. *Go.* Mas' eyes dropped. *Please, go and spend the afternoon with your son, with your family. Please.*

She held Mas' slight hands in her own, which felt enormous, cumbersome.

Okay, puan.

Terima kasih, Mas. Lynne felt herself welling up.

Mas looked deep into her mistress' eyes and saw that there was a kind of finality to those words. *I leave you,* she said.

Lynne stood, unsteady, and walked to the bathroom. She checked the bowl for snakes and scorpions, then sat and stared at the wall. A lizard, which had been there for a few days, held a frozen pose on the door frame. She peeled the tissue paper from between her legs, pink and wet. It had got better these couple of weeks. *Drink water,* the doctor told her, and she had. Plenty of tonic. It was all anyone could do in this climate to drink enough. She'd learnt this lesson over and again, since the day they had been delivered into Singapore.

They had been on the boat, an endless voyage, and then Lynne had woken in a stark white room. That's about right, she'd thought, dead. She had lain in a white-sheeted bed stood in the middle of a row of white-sheeted beds. The air smelt of nothing; not a single other soul alongside her. Memory crackled and fissured, a wireless shifting through the static between stations.

A Chinese nurse blinked into focus. Blurred and faded, expanding and contracting, she held a vast crimson rose. White walls framed the white clad woman and petals of red. She held it in both arms, taking some of the weight with her hidden torso. Lynne had heard about the wildlife of the East, but what she saw then was the magic of the East. Cool air blew over Lynne's naked legs. Dragons, no doubt, were drifting on the breeze which so comforted. The body and mind must acclimatise to talking reptiles and elixirs made from tigers' spleens; fat men, bellies painted gold, atop puffy clouds like night watchmen on chimneypots in the war. The old life, the sure footing of Europe's pavement and stone, of the Welsh soil which had always held her feet to the ground, was gone.

The nurse was speaking to someone else, just out of view. Lynne tried to shift her body, watched as the nurse turned to hide the cumbersome flower before leaving the room. Flowers of the East, Lynne thought.

A doctor stood at the foot of the bed. *How are we today, Mrs Wilson?* She heard a faint whiff of South Wales under his affected Oxfordshire. *You've given us all a fair old fright, I have to say.* He thumbed papers held in a buff-coloured file. Blighty came back into the room, into her life. He took coy, lascivious looks at her naked skin. His top button held his Adam's apple firm, a choke chain, his large face balanced on top.

It's so sad, he started, *the decline from a sheltered and provincial childhood to a non-life.*

Lynne couldn't speak, couldn't breathe.

Blackwood, I know it well. Lynne saw her nakedness grow and amplify.

I see it so often nowadays. Women getting fat on pints of beer, neglecting to do the washing-up or dusting. Allowing themselves certain adulteries. He watched her carefully, as the nurse reappeared and shook out a fresh sheet over Lynne's body.

Lynne's crisp lips peeled apart, her tongue unfurled like butterfly's wings from a chrysalis. She gratefully accepted the glass the nurse held gently against her bottom lip. The liquid turned baked sand to supple wetness.

This isn't Banbury, now, he chided, *and in your state, one had better remain hydrated. And not your sort of hydration.* He went on, *I've examined you thoroughly. I know what's what here, you know. I've seen it all before.*

But I'm better now.

You've lost a lot of blood. Secondary dysmenorrhea. He reeled off the menu. *Excessive uterine muscle contractions which cause cramps, hormonal changes, mood swings, vaginal bleeding.*

She knew all this, had had this for years, since the war. Since the American GIs had followed her from the pub. There'd been blood, alright. Dysmenorrhea. It sounded like one of those words John used a little too loudly in conversation.

The bleeding has slowed now, but not stopped. He placed his podgy hand on Lynne's foot and gave it a rub. Lynne caught the sympathetic eye of the nurse, who shrank from the doctor's speech.

They told her she was free to leave as soon as her husband returned to collect her. He arrived sometime the next afternoon, smelling of spirits and sweat. John kissed her on the cheek and clasped her cold hand between his hot fingers. Without a fight, without a word, John drew the curtain around the bed. Lynne remained still while he raised the sheet from her and rolled it down to her feet. He lifted her body forward, which held itself limply, head facing down. The rags placed between her legs were crisp and white.

She folded tissue paper into her knickers and collected herself. They had both promised to drink less; she had promised not to drink at all. The promise ebbed in the heat and the sheer fucking boredom of it all. The whole thing would play out again, Lynne finding herself back in a hospital bed, shamed by doctors because she should know better.

She pulled out a choice of dresses and placed them on the bed, a plain white one with a single flower embroidered on it, another of emerald and jade, and another with a Henry Moore print. From a shoebox beneath the bed Lynne counted out 300 ringgit, thought better of it and took 500 ringgit, thought better still and took 800 ringgit. It was more than she would need for a day and nowhere near what she would need for any longer. Where the hell would she go? She could disappear into the forest, to be captured by communists or aborigines. They could get the train to Singapore, she and Ibrahim. She could go to Penang and get on a plane. Lynne put clothes and the money into a wicker bag and set it in the hallway.

In the bathroom Lynne pulled the white dress over her head. She checked her teeth, yellowy and browning at the edges, in the gaps between. Foundation fell into the cracks of her skin and filled them. She touched the marks left by teenage acne and remembered briefly an early morning walk to school with Hazel and her father. She ran her thumb and index finger down either side of her nose. Her father had called it noble, but on a woman a noble nose is a blight. No, I will not have it. For once, that voice can be silenced. Her hair down, greasy, she patted some talcum powder into her hand and ran it through. A bit of rouge, a bit of mascara. It would feel good to get dressed up for once. She looked handsome. Ibrahim would think so too. She would have to find him. The most obvious place was the police station, but that was the nuclear option, meaning the fallout would be wide and unfathomable.

Lynne? Are you here?

Lynne watched the horror creep across her face. The bag in the hallway. The money tucked inside. She put her dressing gown over the pretty white dress, ran a flannel under the tap and wiped the rouge from her lips.

John was standing at the kitchen counter, slicing the chicken from yesterday. She could do with a drink.

I didn't expect you back, she said.

I fancied the walk. He turned, looked her up and down in a way that made her grasp at the neck of her dressing gown, and turned back to carving. *Up then, I see.*

I was about to... She went into the living room and poured the rest of the tea. Cold, but she drank anyway.

I'm making sandwiches. Where is everyone?

Out. Mas had to go and see Reheeq. He's passed the sergeants' exam. God knows where Yusof is. She closed the door between her and John, checking her dress was not visible under her housecoat, holding it tight against herself, a fist of material at her neck. John clattered about, humming the same tune he had been humming and whistling for weeks.

He brought in two plates and handed one to Lynne.

41

Never seems to be here when I come home. We are paying him, you know, Lynne. She ignored his bait. *This bloody place.*

Speak to Jimmy, if you're so sick of it.

I've been onto him this morning, John said, looking round the kitchen for something sweet. *Where's Yusof? There was a tin of peaches here yesterday.*

Did he say anything about when we might move?

He's looking into it. Bureaucracy, he reckons.

I can't stay here, John. The boys, they're—

What?

They're at it again. I've seen them. This morning I looked out of the window and there were three of them – dirty little shits.

What were they doing?

You know what. Pissing. Pissing off the veranda.

He went to the kitchen window. Sure enough, there were several boys, no more than six or seven years of age, cocks out, bare arses pushed towards the heavens, uncorking themselves over the balustrade. John watched them with something like awe.

They're at it now, aren't they? Lynne called from the other room.

He came in to join her. *They're just boys.*

They're disgusting.

I'll speak to one of the staff.

Again. You'll speak to them again. I hate it here, John. Please, speak to Jimmy.

I told you, I spoke to him already.

Speak to him again. You're too fucking soft.

John felt his blood rise. *Don't you bloody talk to me like that. Lying there in your sodding nightgown. You think I don't know what's been going on? I made it damned clear I want this sorting. Soft, is that what you think? You haven't asked me how my day has been, asked me nothing, just lying there feeling bloody sorry for yourself. And I know damned well why.*

42

He stormed out of the flat and slammed the door. It was treachery, was what it was. She had promised to try. He walked along the hall and came to the row of boys still relieving themselves onto the grass below.

Put yourselves away and get back inside, he yelled. *Sekarang, sekarang, sekarang!*

His shouting brought out Mrs Vivekananda, eating seeds from a small container. The boys pulled their shorts up and ran down the stairs and onto the field.

What's happened, John? she asked in a calm voice.

Anda tahu apa yang berlaku? Anak lelaki itu melakukannya sekali lagi, he replied. *Those boys have been exposing themselves, micturating on the veranda.*

They are young. We must give them time. What, she paused, *is micturating?* She looked in the direction the boys had gone and then towards the veranda. *Is Lynne not feeling well? We have not seen her today.*

She's fine. Sakit kepala.

She has them a lot. My sister has a remedy she swears by, I would be happy to—

Thank you, she'll be fine. Hydration, that's all it is. And a bit of quiet. Let them know they are not to expose themselves in front of my wife.

I'm sure this was not their intention.

Intent or not, let them know. And also make them aware that pissing, urinating, relieving oneself, micturating is prohibited everywhere except for rooms designated towards that end.

John left Mrs Vivekananda at the top of the stairs, steadily walking in the footsteps of the running youths. Jimmy Howell had given him what he had called a final final warning. Had said, *Mark me, and mark me well, you are on thin ice here, sunshine.*

He got to the bottom of the stairs before he realised he had left his dispatch case back in the flat. Sod it. Decisively, he about-faced and marched back up the stairs, Mrs Vivekananda still beaking at her seeds. John flung the door open, grasped his dispatch case, knocking Lynne's bag onto the floor, and slammed the door behind him.

He had twenty-five minutes before he had to be back. On the way home the speech he had composed for Jimmy Howell had been deeply apologetic, prostrating himself at the headmaster's feet. Now he raged against Jimmy's stupidity and the shit he must put up with.

He walked up Jalan Kangsar once more, to the Restoran Yat Lai. Rahimah held her hands against her stomach and kept her eyes low. John had never been entirely sure of the Malay College's policy on drinking during school hours. *Satu botol Tiger, terima kasih.*

Rahimah opened a large bottle of Tiger and brought it over. She moved away before he could thank her, before he could say what he had come to say.

Something was amiss. Where she had been warm, Rahimah was distant. The towkay was nowhere to be seen. He would be playing cards or dominos in one of the kedais. The place was empty except for her. He took a good mouthful of Tiger and got up.

Rahimah. Ada sesuatu yang salah? He knew damn well there was something wrong. She did not respond or turn around. There were plates and cups that needed washing. John was at a loss. He felt almost drowsy. *Sila bercakap dengan saya, sayangku.* But she would not speak, she would not talk to him. *Bercakap*, he repeated, standing at the counter, *speak*. It seemed to be a border he could not cross. Ridiculous. He banged his fist on the counter, *Cakap!* He knew it was madness. It would only be a matter of time before it made its way back to Lynne, or Howell for that matter. Well, it was exactly what he bloody well wanted. He had had to hear about Lynne's sordid little trysts. Sealey, Hughes, even Webb was rumoured to have had a go. If he had to deal with the ignominy of being made a cuckold, then she would too. *Cakap!*

Tolong. Tolonglah, Rahimah repeated, her back towards him. Tears, he could tell, were rolling. Her shoulders heaved. *Tolonglah,* she begged, blubbering.

He crossed the threshold and put his hands on her shoulders. *I'm sorry, darling.* She felt tiny under his palms. He had to bend to rest his chin upon the top of her head. She sobbed and inhaled as one, a shuddering noise reserved for children. In many ways she was a child. Pregnant as a teen, what did she know about adulthood? *It's okay. Baik. Baiklah.* He ran his hands down her arms, watched her wince as his hands reached her stomach and hips. She was skinny, taut. Her hair smelt of oil and Chinese spices. Her hands remained submerged in the washing up bowl. He dropped his hands into the water to draw hers out. With a soy-stained cloth he dried her fingers and palms. He bent down to kiss her lips. They had never kissed anywhere except in the confines of her bedroom. She instinctively pulled away but he held her to him and she did not fight. Finally he took his lips from hers. He wanted to look into her eyes but they were closed tight.

Kenapa awak buat begini? she asked. *Why are you doing this?*

He had often asked himself why. Why put himself and her through this? He didn't know, only that he had to. Perhaps it was fear of losing her. John kissed her again, more gently, on the lips. Rahimah fled through the backdoor and locked herself in the toilet before he had chance to see the towkay standing in the doorway. John could hear her weeping once more.

He greatly admired the Cantonese language, its rhythms and textures, though he knew not one word of it; however, as the towkay approached, both delighted and incensed, John got the sentiment: he was done for. Somewhere a voice inside told John not to play the part of exposed philanderer. The man continued to talk, pointing to the backroom, Rahimah still present through the sound of her tears, gestured to John, who had continued steadily back to his table, where he picked up the bottle of

Tiger and drank. The towkay began to hit the toilet door, still shouting. John had wanted to be caught, it was true, but now, in the act of being caught, he wanted nothing less. Rahimah would be the one to suffer. When the dust had settled and Lynne had chalked this up to John trying to even the score, Rahimah would be made to pay. And what of Mat? Not just a fatherless child, but a fatherless child whose mother had been caught with an *orang putih*. John's stomach twisted.

Money was always an option. You could buy someone's silence if you were willing to spend enough. He made his way behind the counter and into the backroom. The towkay was still slapping his hand on the bathroom door, held shut only by Rahimah's slight body.

John grasped the towkay by the shoulder, but the old man threw his hand off, shouting in indecipherable Cantonese. John would not be ignored. He grabbed him by the shoulder again and drew him round. The man was old, older than John by twenty or more years, and he was a good foot shorter, but there was a tension in him pent up over many years.

Please, I will give you money. I will give you as much as you want. There was money saved. It was not easy to spend money in Kuala Kangsar, even with the cost of the car, Yusof's and Mas' wages, a healthy social life, and regular money to Rahimah. His mind flitted to the box beneath the bed, all the money they had.

Okay, the towkay said.

John followed him into the cafe, where the man took out a pencil and paper and wrote *10,000RM.*

Ridiculous. 10,000 ringgit was something like £1,500. John grabbed the pencil and scratched through the figure, writing underneath *500RM.* The towkay laughed, put a thin grey line through John's counter offer and wrote his own: *10,000RM.* They continued to strike through one figure and replace it with another. John working his way steadily from 500RM up to 2,000RM, the cafe owner crossing out each new sum and writing *10,000RM.*

By the eighth time, John had had enough. *I could buy this fucking place for that. Here.* He wrote *2,500RM* and circled it several times. *Enough.*

The towkay took back the pencil and began to write *10.* John grabbed the pencil and threw it into the street. It was after one o'clock. There would be no money to give if he lost his job.

I've tried to be reasonable. If you don't want to be reasonable, then so be it.

John took out his wallet and left 320RM on the counter. *That will have to do for now,* he said, pointing to his watch, pointing at the door. He collected his dispatch case, the towkay cursing behind him, Rahimah still in the toilet. How long could she wait there? It would be busy soon, the locals taking their lunch after the midday sun had passed. Maybe Rahimah would have more luck bartering with him.

Lynne sat in a kind of stupor, swilling cold tea to dislodge claggy white bread. Knickers, bras and ringgit notes lay strewn across the hallway floor. In a panic, she put everything back as it had been – clothes in the wardrobe, passport in the drawer, and the money in the shoebox. It had started to rain again and Lynne opened the window wide, allowing the rain in, dappling her legs, the edge of the bed and the floor. She sat waiting for whatever would happen next. She realised she had spent months in a state of flux, a curdle of anticipation and despondency. The packet of cigarettes on her nightstand was empty. Lynne crushed the packet and coaxed herself from the bed and out of the bedroom.

Making her way down the stairs, she heard crying. The desolate sobs of a child.

Ibu, ibu. In the kitchen she took a fresh packet from the middle drawer and lit a cigarette. She poured tonic into a fresh glass and took a soothing draught. *Ibu,* the boy called in staccato. *Mum.* Lynne checked the hallway again. There was a fifty ringgit note by the side table she had missed. *Ibu,* he called. *Ibu, tolong.*

She was sick of the weight of others hanging from her – she felt she would soon be torn apart. John on her back, arms around her throat; Ibrahim on her front, arms around her neck; this boy, *Ibu, tolong, ibu*, trying to grasp her leg. Her mother and father's heavy presence everywhere she bloody went. Could she not just have some fucking peace?

She pulled the door open. *What? What is it?*

He stood, head down, bobbing upwards with every heave and then slumping once more. *Saya mahu ibu saya*, he cried.

I don't know what that bloody means.

Tolong, Tolonglah, he wailed.

Where's your teacher? Guru? He reached his hand out towards her, she pulled away. *You mard arse. Go and find guru, go on.*

Her words excavated a deeper sorrow within him. He was shaking, almost fitting, hyperventilating. Lynne held the door in front of her, a kind of shield.

Hey, hey, it's alright. Hey, stop it now.

Ibu, he managed in between desperate gulps for air, *ibu*.

His hands rested on the door; he was exhausted. Lynne bent, let the door fall open and caught him, his arms around her neck, elbows quivering on her collarbone.

Right, alright. There. Alright, she said. She meant to keep her distance, but he was in her arms, his small frame against her own. His legs wrapped around her hips. He buried his wet face into her shoulder and caught his breath. *Okay, you're okay now.* She pushed the door to with her foot and leant against it.

Ibu, saya mahukan ibu.

Ibu, Lynne repeated. *Mum.* Her hand ran through his thick hair. He smelt sour; she put her nose into his hair and took a long breath. *Ibu.* The heaviness reached her throat and before she could do anything to stop its trajectory it was in her mouth, forcing its way outward. *Ibu*, she found herself repeating again and again, until it became a metronomic sound, along with the rocking of her shoulders and the rocking of the boy. He buried his head into her, she into him. His small hands ran through her hair, both for comfort and to comfort. *Mum*, she gasped, and could not stop the tears and everything else from falling. She clung to him, squeezing, her back against the door, the door taking both of their weight and the weight of their loss.

Tidak mengapa. It's okay.

She had lost her mother.

Tidak mengapa, he brushed her hair with his hand.

She had lost her father.

Tidak mengapa, the boy had stopped crying.

She had lost her baby. *Tidak mengapa.* She had lost another and another. *Tidak mengapa.* There would be no children. Every morning she was reminded with red symbolism. This would go on now and forever. Daily reminders of loss, boys running in the hallways, babies in the arms of their mothers, the barrenness and flow of blood.

He pulled her head from his shoulder and held her hair back in his hands. His face red, his eyes swollen and wet. Lynne lowered him to the floor and he used his shirt to dry his eyes. She crouched so their faces met. The boy laughed, and so did she.

He was beautiful. She would have liked him to stay.

He had sheltered himself under the bandstand and by the time the rains had passed, it was gone one o'clock. He had forgotten to change his shirt, a daily ritual in the Malay heat, but the rains had washed him clean.

John sat on the toilet, his bowels responding to all that had happened. When he played back the scene now, he felt the threat of violence; he raged soundlessly at himself for his inaction, told himself he should have hit out with fists. He wiped. Had he not been a good man? A good teacher? He had sensed a growing grievance in Jimmy Howell from day one, who had warned John about fraternising with locals, who had warned him to drink only in the Idris Club, where decent British folk drank. John had gone with Jimmy to the club, had heard him hold court on what was wrong with the Malay people, what should be done about the Malays, the Chinese, Tamils and Indians. Jimmy had caught John leaving a kedai one evening and given him fair warning: *You've your reputation to think of, Mr Wilson.*

John emerged from the lavatory with his head held high, eyes wild with indignity. Walking down the corridor to his classroom he felt belligerent – a belligerent force in this sanctified space.

Mr Wilson, somebody called, their voice pitched too high. They coughed the last of his name and tried a second time with tenor and gravitas. *Mr Wilson.*

Abu held in his hands a box; John could see rugby boots and text books protruding from it.

Abu. Shouldn't you be in class?

I should, Abu said. His jaw was tight, his eyes wet and lips quivering. The boy held his head up to give the impression of poise, of dignity, instead making himself all the more childlike, a boy playing at adulthood. *Mr Howell has suspended me from school.*

Suspended or expelled?

This is to be determined, Abu said, taking breaths between each word so to keep his composure.

John trembled too. The classrooms around them were all but silent. Down the corridor he could hear Yusof Tajuddin dictating in his melodious tones. John tried to listen closer but could not make out the content. He found his hand ached from gripping the handle of his case too tightly. Abu shifted his feet and switched his left hand from under the box to the side.

He will not expel you, then, John said, finally.

And you?

John thought he caught a ripple of spite in the way Abu had asked the question.

I am on a last warning. A last, last warning, John said, hoping to lighten the mood. *How will it be with your father?*

Abu shifted the weight of the box. *It is my mother I fear. My uncle will not say anything; I carry the name of our family. If my father were alive...* He let the thought fade.

I didn't know, about your father. How did he—?

During the war. He was loyal to the British even after they had fled, even while the Japanese took Malaya.

John had started to walk towards Abu but stopped now, five paces away. *My father was Irish, my mother Scottish. The Wilsons know what it is to suffer under the heel of the British.*

John looked for some response in Abu, some fraternal recognition. The boy made his back taut and applied yet more defiance to his expression.

We are not at war, you and I, John said. *You are a fine student.*

You are a terrible teacher, Abu said. And then, as an afterthought, *You and your Shakespeare have nothing to give to the East.*

John became aware of a finality to their conversation. *It will not take much to change Jimmy's decision, I should think.*

He wanted... Abu started, finally putting the box down onto the parquet floor. *He wanted me to write a statement holding you responsible.* Without the box to carry he did not know what to do with his hands, shifting them from his sides to his pockets to behind his back. *He said I would not be reprimanded if I did this.*

I appreciate your loyalty.

Not loyalty to you, Abu said. *Contempt for him.*

I appreciate that almost as much, John said. *I did not betray you either, for what it is worth.*

Abu lifted the box up. He gave a nod which signified the end of their conversation.

Do not let your dislike of me or Jimmy Howell deter you from all the West has to offer. Read Joyce, John said, with utter sincerity. As Abu walked towards the main entrance John said quietly, *Merdeka.* If the boy heard him, he did not turn back.

He reached the rubber tree surrounded by an ornate fence. Beneath, a plaque declared in English and Malay that this was one of the oldest in the country. John read the Malay. The tree was nothing much to look at, trees surrounded the whole town, but the sentiment was clear: what was once British could become Malay. This tree, which represented a moment of great change and prosperity, was a British tree, brought from Kew Gardens. A great symbol of Malaya. It was possible.

Across the road a man leant heavily against a dust-sheeted Mercedes Benz. *British man. Hey, British man.*

John smiled politely and waved him off.

British man. Taxi? Where do you want to go? He heaved himself from his leaning position and threw his half-smoked cigarette into the dirt. *Show you the town?*

No, thank you.

Take you to Royal Palace. Take you to Ubudiah Mosque, he said, following John.

Tidak, terima kasih, John continued. *No, thank you.*

Take you to meet some local girls, British man.

Not today, Bukan hari ini, John said, and walked into the Idris Club.

Three Brits sat at the bar while a Tamil man cleaned glasses. John made his way towards them.

Good day, he said. *Anchor, terima kasih. And,* he added *brandy. Double.*

John sat in the corner, away from company. Two of the men wore linen suits; they looked like officials from a canned fruit company. The other peered over a week-old copy of *The Daily Mail*.

Did you hear about Philips? One of the linen suits said.

Philips?

Dan Philips, works for Heineken.

The third man folded his newspaper, *Dan Philips? I met him in KL.*

Car shot.

No.

Car shot, driver took a bullet.

When was this?

Last night, coming back from Ipoh.

How is he?

You know Philips, but the missus is in a state. She wants out. He came in last night, after the fact. Double brandies all round, of course. Left her to do the packing. Get it out of her system, I suppose.

Poor bloody Philips. How's the car?

Bit better ventilated. The other two laughed.

Dirty bastards. They're evacuating Vietnam, you know. Commies given the North. Give them an inch, I say.

How, John asked, *is the driver?*

The three turned around in unison. *You what?*

The driver, John repeated, *how is he? You said he'd been shot.*

How the bloody hell should I know how the driver is? He turned to the second linen suit, *Tapped.*

What did you say? John stood.

Go back to your drink, the *Mail* reader told him.

I said, the first suit continued, *you're bloody tapped. I'm telling my friend here how Philips nearly died and you're asking about some driver. Off your flamin' head, mate.* He turned back to the bar. *Darky lover.*

The other two laughed.

Come here and say that. John walked over and prodded the man in the back. *Get off your fucking stool and say that to my face.*

Steady on, pal, the second linen suit said, standing. *We're not after trouble.*

I'd say you are looking for bloody trouble. I'd say he's, he prodded again, *been asking for it since I walked in.*

Look, the second linen suit said, *we're just having a quiet drink. Norm goes home tomorrow.* Norm didn't look round.

Easy, old man, the *Mail* reader chimed in. *Let me get you another. Let's all have another drink.*

I'm not, said Norm, *drinking with no darky lover.*

John grabbed at the back of his jacket and pulled Norm clean off the bar stool. He had never been in a fight, not since he was a kid in Miles Platting. Not since they would gang up on him for going to a posh school.

Norm landed arse first on the floor. John felt a hand on his shoulder and lashed out with a fist. The *Mail* reader went down, clattering bar stools as he fell. John gave Norm a good kick in the backside.

Say it again, you English bastard.

Norm was struggling to his feet, his friend struggling to take it all in. The *Mail* reader dragged himself to his knees. John had hit him square on the jaw. He gave Norm another kick, and with that the second linen suit grabbed John by the throat and pulled back to have a good swing at him.

Knock his soddin' block off, Norm cried.

He was about to, his fist coming at John fast and true. John clenched his eyes shut and prepared for a punch that never landed.

That's about enough, I'd say.

John opened his eyes to see Lofty gripping the man's arm, his hand still balled in a fist.

He's the one that bloody started it, Norm yelled, clutching his rear end.

And I'm the one what's ending it. You, Lofty said to the man whose arm he held, *relax up, and sit down there.* The man obliged. Lofty turned to John, *How you going, Jack?*

John nodded but couldn't speak.

How's about we all sit down and have a drink, eh? Lofty picked up two of the bar stools and helped the suited man to his feet. His face was swollen. John had got him good.

You know him? Norm said, eyeballing John. Before Lofty could reply, Norm went for John, grabbing him in a kind of headlock.

Now then, now then, Lofty lifted the two men from the floor. *I should put one of you in the bloody corner.* He turned to Norm, *Sit. Right,* Lofty dusted himself off and turned to the three men, *which one of you is selling this car?*

Lynne lay in bed, still in her dressing gown, her pretty new dress hidden beneath. There was a knock at the door, followed by Yusof's tutting as he went to answer. Another boy, no doubt, looking for her to bandage a wound or clear up a graze.

Puan, Yusof said, just behind the door. *A man here.*

What man?

Brown man. He muttered something else under his breath.

Lynne took off her dressing gown and made her way downstairs. Yusof, wooden spoon in hand, watched Ibrahim intently. A stand-off. Ibrahim seemed impaired, as if Yusof had caught him off guard.

Sila, she said, directing Ibrahim to the living room before following Yusof to the kitchen, telling him to make two gin and tonics. He eyed her excitedly, already formulating his report for John. *Puan bring man here. Puan and him drink your bottles, tuan.* She returned to Ibrahim, still standing to attention in his policeman's uniform.

You know John might have been here. She sat and lit a cigarette. *You look well.*

He blushed slightly. *You too. I need to, but how to say? My wife, tetapi saya tidak tahu bagaimana untuk mengatakannya dalam bahasa Inggeris. My isteri. She –*

Just spit it out.

Saya mengambil isteri saya dan bawa ke Pulau Pinang kerana kami bakal timang anak.

You're going to Penang?

Ibrahim spoke quickly and went to the window, his back to her. Lynne couldn't follow; something about going away, something about his wife.

55

The doorknob turned, Ibrahim froze. Yusof gleefully brought in a tray of gin and tonics. He licked his lips. To be the instrument of John and Lynne's separation was a great ambition of Yusof's.

Go on, she said to Ibrahim. He watched as Yusof closed the door behind him. *You and your wife?*

Mahu timang anak.

I don't understand what that is. She could sense Ibrahim had hoped that she would make this easy on him. She would do no such thing. *Ulangi. Terangkan.* She took a drink. *Repeat yourself. Explain.*

Bayi. He folded his arms and rocked them.

A baby.

Yes, Lynne.

You and your wife are having a baby?

Saya cuba memberitahu anda, tetapi bahasa Inggeris saya tidak bagus. Saya tidak bermaksud menimbulkan masalah. Saya sayang awak.

She didn't catch it all, but caught the end. *You love me? You fucking love me, Ibrahim?* She raised her voice and he turned to the door that Yusof was almost certainly lurking behind.

He made his way over to her now, bending down, practically on his knees. *Tolong, izinkan saya membawa anda ke tempat lain.*

Take me somewhere? Where?

Somewhere. Please.

She made him wait, taking a mouthful of gin and smoking the last of her cigarette. *Fine. Have you got the car?*

He nodded. Lynne stood and walked past him. She felt his hand grip her arm. He pulled her towards him and kissed her.

Yusof stood at the kitchen door, half in and half out. He chose not to hide his look, and Lynne received it with a poisonous smile. To think he actually believed that John would throw Lynne out and take him in as his confidante. One day there would be a reckoning and it would not go well for Yusof.

In the car, Ibrahim was quiet. He made her sit in the back seat and drove with purpose, eyes on the road, only the quickest glances in the mirror behind. He had wanted to drive out to Kampung Buaya, but Lynne refused. There were communists in those trees. Better to be seen in town alive than found in the forest dead. As Ibrahim drove towards town, she could feel his discomfort. He took the first turn at the roundabout so as not to drive past the police station. Lynne wound down her window, lit a cigarette, and held her arm out in the afternoon sun. They would be noticed, of course, if they had not been already.

Ibrahim pulled up at a small kedai, far enough out of town. He got out and opened the door for Lynne. She was already lifting herself from the seat when he offered his hand. She did not take it. Ibrahim led, choosing a table away from the entrance.

Would you like coffee?

Gin. She called over to the young Chinese girl at the counter, *You have gin, don't you?*

Yes, yes, the girl replied.

And Anchor beer, Ibrahim added.

So, Lynne leant towards Ibrahim, *what are you going to tell me?*

Lynne. He took a deep breath, *Lynne, you and I can no longer be.* He wiped the sweat off his brow and exhaled. That was it. That was all he had come to say. A huge weight had been lifted and Lynne could tell he was pleased with himself. She took a deep drag and blew smoke towards the ceiling. He waited for her response. She waited for him to say more. Ibrahim lit a cigarette and tapped his matches on the table. Lynne waited. The cafe was empty except for the girl and two men playing Go in the opposite corner. The only noise the hiss of a bottle being opened, beer poured into a glass, the glass put down on a tray, the tray pulled from the counter, the girl's feet across the floor, a Go stone placed on the board.

For you, the girl placed Lynne's drink in front of her. *Untuk kamu*, and placed Ibrahim's beer on the table.

The girl went and the silence returned. Lynne drank quickly. If he was buying, she would drink as much as she could. One of the Go players started to mutter a repeated phrase. Lynne did not know what it meant, but the words somehow resonated. *Bù hǎo de xuǎnzé*, over and over. The player put another of his stones down but kept repeating the words.

Lynne? She had almost forgotten Ibrahim, sitting across from her, waiting to be absolved of all sins. *Lynne, please.*

What would you like me to say? She took a drink. *When is your baby arriving?*

Baby soon.

Yes, I know, when? Bila?

Saya pergi ke Pulau Pinang hari ini.

Hari ini? It hit her like a bolt. *You are going today?* Lynne finished her drink and called to the girl, waving her empty glass in the air.

The Go player continued with his mantra, *Bù hǎo de xuǎnzé.*

What are you hoping for, Ibrahim? Would you like a little girl? You probably want a boy, don't you, ay? Progeny to carry on the family name.

Saya tidak faham.

I know you don't understand. I would have liked a baby, you know. A little girl. You should see my niece –

Lynne, please. Saya tidak faham.

– just a wee thing. Beautiful, really. We tried, me and John. I suppose I'm too old now. Do you think I'm too old, Ibrahim?

Bù hǎo de xuǎnzé, bù hǎo de xuǎnzé.

I feel too old, that's the problem isn't it? You hear of these women who have babies when they're forty. Triplets, some woman had. It was in the paper the other day, did you see it? Could you face it, that's the question you have to ask yourself. Could you face the sleepless nights, the incessant crying, all that? You'll have to, won't you. Do you think you'll be a good father, Ibrahim? Do you think you'll give your son a good life? Well, you'll find out soon enough.

Ibrahim sat patiently. She dabbed her eyes with a handkerchief and listened, *bù hǎo de xuǎnzé, bù hǎo de xuǎnzé, bù hǎo de xuǎnzé.* There was nothing else to say. He had made his mind up, and Lynne had no ammunition to use against him that would not wound her too. The girl brought over a fresh drink, beaming.

Madam, she presented the drink like some rare flower.

Thank you, and then: *Could you tell me what he's saying?* Lynne pointed to the Go players.

He says, bad choice. He definitely going to lose. Mr Loo no good at this game.

Thank you.

The girl beamed, *Thank you.*

Boleh saya pulang ke rumah? Ibrahim asked.

After this. You can take me home after this.

Go stones were swept from the board. Mr Loo took a deep, rueful drag of his cigarette and placed a black stone on the board, beginning again.

Lynne and Ibrahim shared a table but occupied different spaces. She would wish him luck when he dropped her at home. She would wish him luck and wish to see him no more.

Hey British man, you want to meet girls?

The taxi driver had moved his car outside the club. *Beautiful young girls, British man.*

John left Lofty to deal with Robert Milton, the colonial officer who had been enjoying a quiet drink before taking the train to Penang, where he was to be joined by his wife. His jaw was not broken, but there was a great deal of bruising. Once Milton reported what had happened to his superiors, John would no longer be a British Officer. He would get a job teaching at one of the local schools. There was the Clifford School. He could speak to Mr Arumukham. Then he would tell Lynne he was staying indefinitely and tell Rahimah too.

Beautiful girl. Very pretty. Make you very happy, I think.

What a fucking mess. He took a pull on his cigarette. *Where? Not far. I drive maybe five, ten minutes.*

And what would John say when Mr Arumukham asked why John had left the college, why he was divorcing his wife, why he was converting to Islam?

No. No, I don't think so. You can take me home.

John brushed past the driver and climbed into the back, waiting while the driver heaved the door open and dropped into his seat. The car shifted to the right. John slid.

Pandu ke Jalan Istana, saya akan bawa anda ke sana, John told him.

You speak good Malay, British man, he said, setting off towards Jalan Istana.

Saya cuba menjadi lelaki Melayu yang baik, John replied, and saw it was true. He would try to be a good Malay. He would try.

Lynne? He closed the door and saw she was no longer on the sofa. *Lynne?* He called upstairs. No answer.

Puan has gone, tuan. Yusof came into the hallway, a wooden spoon in his hand.

Gone?

She just, he flicked the spoon about, *gone.*

Where's Mas? Is she with her?

A man came, tuan. Yusof was enjoying this. *Handsome, brown man.* Yusof put down the spoon and walked over to John. *He come and she go.* He put his hand on John's shoulder, massaging.

Not now, Yusof, for fuck's sake. Which fucking brown man?

There was a knock at the door. *Leave it,* John cried. Yusof ignored his tuan and opened the door. The taxi driver breathed heavily, resting his weight on the door frame. All those stairs.

Who is this? Yusof asked crossly.

None of your bloody business who this is.

John went upstairs and into the bedroom. The sheets were strewn, clothes everywhere. John tore at them, throwing dresses and blouses around. He checked the wardrobe. Well, she hadn't left him, not yet anyway. What bloody brown man? Someone who knew about Rahimah? Had the towkay talked already? Or had Rahimah told someone? There was, he knew, a brother. There was probably more than one. John checked Yusof was not watching – he had a habit of peering around doorways – and took *Hard Times* from the bookshelf. He opened the front cover to reveal a wooden box with an inner lid.

This man, John went back into the hallway, Yusof still looking the taxi driver up and down, *what did he look like?*

The handsome brown man? You know who. He is the one who drives the car.

I drive, now I want to be paid.

Quiet for a second, John told the driver. *Ibrahim? She's gone out with Ibrahim?*

Yes, with him.

She didn't say where?

She say not to tell tuan. She say she gone.

It all made sense now. *How long has this – Berapa lama mereka telah melakukan hubungan seks?*

Hubungan seks? Just hearing John say the words gave Yusof a tingle.

Yes, hubungan seks. Bloody hubungan kelamin. Bersetubuh. Screwing. Shagging. Fucking. How long?

Tuan?

The taxi driver was laughing. Yusof, for his own sake, managed to keep a straight face. A while, John thought, it must have been going on for a while. Those trips to the cinema in Ipoh, alone in the car for an hour either way. Always late, always with a story about flat tyres and Chinese gunmen. Lying bitch. Did Lofty know? Laughing at him behind his back.

British man, the driver said, recovering, *you owe me fifteen ringgit.*

No, no. We're not finished yet. Come on.

But tuan! Yusof called, watching John walk out of the door, the taxi driver lumbering behind. *Tuan, I make lobscouse.*

They turned off Jalan Kampung into a group of shacks. Some made of bricks with windows and doors, others made from wood, cobbled together out of whatever could be found. The driver pulled over outside a blue wooden one-storey house.

Her name is Gomati. She is – she was my sister-in-law.

Your sister-in-law? What is this?

Brother left. Don't know where. She need money. You pay me now. 200 ringgit. I wait.

Are you sure?

Yes. You finish, I drive you back. You help her.

Help, indeed. John went to the front door. His gentle knock was enough to push the door wide open. Inside there was a simple living space, a table with vegetables and two pans, large cushions on the floor, a rag rug. Out of another door a girl appeared. She was, John guessed, thirteen, maybe fourteen.

Selamat petang, John said.

Selamat petang, the girl replied. She came to the door, looked out, and saw the taxi. *Come. Come,* she said, leading John in, closing the door. *You would like a drink?* There was a bottle of cheap-looking brandy on a shelf.

Ya terima kasih, John replied.

She poured a large measure into a dirty glass and handed it to him. When he took the glass she moved her hand over his.

Very handsome, she said.

And you are very pretty.

He studied her face and she allowed him. Her skin studded with dark freckles, her lips parted and glistening. Her eyebrows thick, expressive. Her face and mood seem to change with every rise and fall of her brow. Her hand moved gently up and down his arm, slipping up the sleeve of his shirt.

Very pretty, he repeated. He took a sip of the brandy, raw in his mouth; the fumes curled up into his nose.

What would tuan like? I can make tuan happy.

He thought she was probably right. Though her face was young and her frame slender, her breasts were full. He watched, as she breathed, their rise and fall.

And what, John asked, *is the statutory age of legal consent in your country?*

The girl smiles, putting her hand on his thigh. Yes, he thinks. She runs her hand gently up his linen trousers, along the ridge of his thigh bone, and inserts her fingers between his. She places his hand on her waist, when he does not move it, she does, caressing her side. John is led into the other room. The bed is unmade, the room is sparse. She turns and stands in front of him. Only her arms and face are bare, but it is enough. Her body is supple, her eyes large and curious. She hitches up her long grey dress. Her legs, her hips, her waist, and those breasts. She runs her fingers down his chest and grasps the lowest button of his shirt, all the time holding his gaze. He is hard. Her hand brushes over him and he feels just how hard. Her eyes flit downwards, he thinks she might grasp him now, but she doesn't. She continues to fumble with his shirt button. An act of seduction becomes more focused, becomes a task. He considers the possibility that this may be the first time she has unbuttoned a man's shirt, her eyes fixed in concentration. Each time the button slips from her grasp, she begins anew with greater purpose. He pulls her hands away, down by her side.

Like this, he says, and opens the top button. *Like this*, the next, *like this*, another. He smiles, gentle, playful. *Like this, see?* The girl looks at the slice of white skin, white cotton curtains opening to reveal more. She steps away, her hands just where he placed them.

Like this. His hands sweaty, he fumbles and fumbles again. *Blast.* He grasps at his shirt, pulls it out from his waistband.

The material clings to his wet back. *Won't be a*, he intends to say second, jiffy, or tick. He sees himself now. Not his reflection but he sees what this is, a white man in his late thirties groping around in a teenager's bedroom. He stops fumbling with his clothing. He stops entirely. She steps forward, putting her hands on his.

John moves back, clearing his throat, standing in his stepmother's house, above the shop, watching the shop girl they had moved into his attic bedroom. He is eleven, she is barely sixteen. The girl had, on many occasions, undressed in front of him. She had been graceless where she intended to be sexy. She had told him not to look away, not to be embarrassed. He could not concentrate on any one part of her, instead his eyes shifted from the devil's door of her stomach and ribs, the soft brown curls that rippled from between her legs to the edges of her pelvis. She would drag the bottom of her greyish bed dress over her, clumsily groping around for the sleeves and collar. All the while his eyes fixed on the part of her enshrouded by hair and entirely unknown. And always, before her head reappeared, he would turn away. She would climb into her bed, turning the light out. But not tonight.

Do you not like girls, Jackie? she asks, lifting his bedding up and drawing herself into him. He grips the hem of his shirt, as she pulls at the band on his pyjama bottoms and plunges her hand in. He was bald, his groin ached, his penis spasmed soft to hard, capillaries opening, fear fuelled him; lust, newly felt, turned his stomach queasy. She cupped him in both her hands, repeating, *Don't you like it, Jackie? Don't you like it?* Then she took his hand and put it between her legs. *Do you like this?* He shuddered when his fingers moved through the fine hair, and again when he touched her moist skin and she pressed his taut fingers inside her. He lurched, pulling her hands off him and his from her. He thought he might be sick or black out. They were sure to come in, his father and stepmother. They were sure to see what he was doing.

She tries to kiss him on the lips. He is conscious of his hygiene. His teeth have not been brushed. He cannot see his fingernails, but he knows them to be thick with dirt, black-tipped. He has not bathed for two days. She puts her tongue in his mouth and he retches. I'm sorry, he wants to say. He wants to touch her again, he wants out of this room.

Do you not like me, Jackie? she asks, moving the sheets away to reveal her outstretched body. His eyes follow a plum-coloured vein running beneath translucent skin. The smell of sour milk makes him groggy. Her body so close and his stomach turns each time he thinks of touching her. If only she would take his hand again. He wants to say, I do like it, yes. I do like it. There are no words. He cannot help but look at that place between her legs.

You never seen a girl before? Never touched a girl before? She runs her hands down through her pubic hair and slides her index and forefinger down. She groans, *Like this*. He watches. She moves her fingers in a circular motion. *Like this*, sucking in the air and breathing it back out. His body contorts. The tips of her fingers disappear inside. His stomach aches. His hard cock shudders. He pushes his shirt further down into his waistband. The girl steps back. Her hands back by her sides, she appears younger, just a child. He steadies himself and grips the still-fastened button. I must go, he means to say, but says nothing at all. He drops uncounted ringgit notes onto the kitchen table and leaves.

The sun bore down from the clear blue sky. Her dress was wet with sweat. The road to the train station was dry and dusty. She walked alone, not a car passed. At the station bar she ordered a gin and tonic, drank it thirstily, and went to find what time the train to Penang was. She was an hour early. Sitting in the shade of the bar, she cooled down. The tonic water helped quench her thirst, the cigarettes calmed her nerves. A young British couple came in. Just back from a weekend in Kuala Lumpur, they told Lynne. They were from Worcester. His company had just won a contract to build for the British and they were going to be in Kuala Kangsar for six months. They told Lynne they did not have any children but hoped to one day. They had not been married before, no, they had met in the last year of school and had married two years later. No, they did not know her husband John, and no, they had not seen an Indian man and his pregnant wife on the platform. They apologised and said they had to meet friends in town.

The station filled with passengers waiting to travel to Taiping, Kamunting, Bagan Serai, Parit Buntar, Nibong Tebal, Simpang Ampat, Bukit Mertajam, and Butterworth. Lynne walked onto the platform. Ibrahim was carrying two heavy suitcases, his wife leaning her heavy frame on his arm. All the packing and planning on top of their soon-to-be new arrival. They looked a handsome couple. Her belly was round but perfectly in proportion to her shape. It would not be long, anyone could see that. Lynne watched as she gratefully accepted a seat from a smiling Malay man.

When Ibrahim saw her, Lynne thought he might collapse. His eyelids fluttered, his mouth tensed as with rigor mortis. He had been unhappy, she knew, and found solace and companionship in her arms. She raised her glass to him and pushed her way back through to the bar. The barman presented the bill and Lynne fished ringgits from her purse. She walked along the platform as the train pulled away, as Ibrahim looked from his window. The air had not yet cooled, though the sun had faded. She approached the ticket office, the light dropping a little more, to enquire about a ticket to Singapore. There was a sleeper train to Gemas leaving tonight. From there she could get a connection to Singapore in the morning.

Return? the man behind the counter asked.

Her mouth was dry and tense, her tongue as heavy as the weight on her forehead, the lamps overhead dimmed. *Single,* she said, but the man did not hear. Lynne cleared her throat, coughed out, *Single.* She took a handful of notes and pushed them towards the blank-faced ticket seller. *Single.* She held her eyes shut for a second, the light in the room suddenly radiating. *Single.* Eyes open, the man had left his seat. Her ticket sat on the counter in front of her. Lynne grabbed it and the lights in the office went out completely.

John walked up Jalan Raja Idris. He took a discreet look back and saw he was not being followed. The road stretched ahead. He knew there were a couple of little kedais round here somewhere. It was humid; he kicked dust up and it stuck to his clothing. He could just keep walking. The station was not far. A one-way ticket to Kuala Lumpur, Singapore even. He came to a small place with a large Tiger sign. Inside were four tables. Two Chinese men were sitting at one playing Go.

Selamat petang, John said to the girl behind the counter. He threw his dispatch case on one chair and himself on the other. She was in her twenties, dressed as close to the Western style as was acceptable. Her hair was twisted up, held with chopsticks. She nodded and brought over a menu, written in Chinese.

Tiger beer, he told her.

You are American?

British.

Oh, she said, and went to the cooler.

He quickly drank three Tigers and ordered another, along with some prawn noodles. He struggled with chopsticks, skewering fat pink prawns and crunching them down, rolling noodles around tightly held sticks and brought his mouth to meet them before they fell back into the bowl.

John took out his pupils' exercise books from his dispatch case. He opened one and tried to focus on English words in scruffy handwriting. The girl passed and John waved his empty Tiger bottle in her direction. He flicked to the back of the book and absent-mindedly drew a stave on the page. The pen stabbed between C and G in a loose circle. John hummed as he went. A Malayan melody, he told himself. The notes resembled a man, much like John, in Malaya. He drew ties between the crotchets and saw a scuttling movement, left to right. On the right-hand page John wrote: 'Victor Crabbe stood before his form and knew something was wrong.'

The image and the music sat well together. John drew out another few staves and continued the movement. A conductor, then. Waving his baton like a fiddler crab waves its right claw. Crabbe the conductor stood before his orchestra.

He saw now, very clearly, how the trouble he had had with the symphony could be resolved in literature. The various influences on Kuala Kangsar – Chinese towkays, Malay drivers, British officers, Indian workers – could be represented in a novel, rather than abstract notes on the page. Not that words were any less abstract than musical notes, John muttered to himself. Writing with words first would, he suddenly realised, act as the foundation for the final orchestration. To hell with *Julius Caesar* in Malaya, this would be *Ulysses*, Kuala Kangsar standing in for Dublin, literature as symphonia, but towards the creation of music.

The lives of the British characters moved in counterpoint to those of the natives – a different rhythm, an altogether different cadence. The Chinese and Malays were the backbone, the string section and brass, respectively. That would need to be worked on. There were the Eurasians to take into consideration. And the Tamils. The Tamils were the woodwind, he decided.

His bottle was empty. Where was he up to? The woodwind? Surely the woodwind must be the women, women of all races. Rahimah the flute, Lynne the oboe, this girl ignoring his call for more Tiger must be the xiao. There would have to be parts written for Chinese instruments, Malay instruments too. He would have to see if he could get his hands on a karaniing, Indian drums too. He wrote:

'The process of which he, Victor Crabbe, was a part, was an ineluctable process. His being here, in the brown country, sweltering in an alien class-room, was pre-figured and ordained by history. For the end of the Western pattern was the conquest of time and space. But out of time and space came point-instants, and out of point-instants came a universe. So, it was right that he stood here now, teaching the East about the Industrial Revolution. It was right that these boys too should bellow through loudspeakers, check bomb-loads, judge Shakespeare by the Aristotelian yardstick, hear five-part counterpoint and find it intelligible.'

John wandered back along Jalan Raja Chulan, aiming for home. The instrumentation would have to be carefully developed. As the words came, so too the correctness of instrument to part. It was coming to him in great waves now, as the river ahead rose up, as the rains fell in a great torrent.

He necked beer and looked around the kedai, the very same one Lofty had brought them to that first night in Kuala Kangsar. At the next table a group of Malays were drinking. Beyond them, young women, Malay and Chinese, were eating ais kacang and talking quickly over one another. John tried to focus on the rhythms of their speech, the melodies held within. Their voices ebbed and flowed. He turned to Abu's exercise book and continued to write, switching between musical notation on the left and words on the right. Starting from the back page and working in.

Like the Quran, John said, hoping not too loudly. *Like Analects*, he said, a little louder.

What are you writing?

John peered high up, leaning as far back as the chair would allow, and finally found a face, just below the ceiling. *Alright, Lofty, lad. It's a shim-phony*, John told him.

Lofty sat and took the book from him. *Looks like a story.*

It'sh a shtory and a shimphony.

Are you drinking both of these?

It'sh yoursh. I've got all thish. He took several notes from his pocket. *Have a drink. Have a drink,* he insisted, the bottle already firmly against Lofty's lips. *Have a drink with your pal, John.*

We'll have these and then I'll get you a ride home.

Bollocksh.

I'll get you a taxi. We'll just have these and one for the road. What do you say, John?

John climbed into the waiting taxi, was helped into a taxi just hailed. Lofty carried him, arms under armpits, and dropped John onto the seat. *I've got money,* John said, searching for ringgits. *I've got no money. Will you take cigarettes?* He held a sleeve of Victory brand over the driver's seat.

Lofty got out. Maybe he said something, some sort of goodbye, but John heard nothing. He was in a stupor, a reverie; he was in shock. Late became early, end seamlessly became beginning. The morning was setting in.

John focused again on a musical phrase. Pound, wasn't it, said poetry should be composed to the phrase not the metronome. Tick, tock, tick, tock. Time slipping away like rope between sweaty palms. How did that phrase go again? C to G, was it? A, shifting up one whole tone to B. No, no, it would have to be invented again.

John flicked through Abu's workbook. Try as he might, he was unable to fix his eyes on the notes on the page. Focus on the one theme for now, the one composition. Words blurred crotchets. Drunk John Burgess. Pissed-up Anthony Wilson.

Sekiranya saya terus pandu? The driver asked.

John ran his fingers along his unshaven chin. He would have to wash, change these clothes too.

You can pull over just here.

Manchester

What you havin', duck?
    Three bitters, pints. One gin and slimline, my dear.
The young girl, young but not youthful, puts her hand around the pump as though preparing for a bout of arm wrestling. She flexes each finger to form a solid grip. With a squeeze, her bicep swells, the sleeve of her t-shirt tightens, and she pulls a good half of bitter in one go. Another tug and the bout is won.

Anthony watches her fill three pint glasses in quick succession. He would like to feel her arm as it tenses. The lip of a hi-ball is thrust up to the optic, gin spurts into the glass. A wilted lemon slice is retrieved with metal tongs and dropped into the spirit. She hits the tonic bottle on the top of the bar, the cap spins off, bottle raised high above the glass and the foaming liquid poured with great drama. His mind has turned to music. She is Brünnhilde. Somewhere Siegfried awaits.

Cheers, Jack.

They raise their glasses. *Cheers*, Anthony says.

We wert sure y'd come, Jack. All them people waiting to talk to thee. Agnes read one of yours, which one was it, Agnes?

That one about him who was always on't crapper.

He knew it would come. Brünnhilde had put him in mind of his stepmother, her ghost haunted all Northern pubs, as far as John could tell.

An old one. The new one is about Manchester—

What w're he doin' on the crapper?

Christ, John thinks.

What d'you think he were doin'? Kind of daft bloody question's that? Bert shakes his head, shakes a bit more head into his pint.

T'were Madge who told me to read it.

Yes, well, I've written many books since Enderby, Agnes.

All that 'bout 'is stepmother. Got Madge awful in a state. All that smellin' of female smells.

As I say, an old book. John sups, planning to return to Brünnhilde for more beers and a bit of respite.

What d'yer mean, smells? Ehm says, finally with some semblance of a sentence.

I dunno. Ask 'im.

Look, John says a little too sternly, *it was a piece of bloody fiction. A poet who lives alone and hates the world. He hates every bugger, including his stepmother. I wrote a book about a teenaged rapist, am I one of them too? And another about Napoleon. I am no more Napoleon flaming Bonaparte than bloody Francis Xavier bloody Enderby. Now, another. Agnes, another. Bert, another. Drink up, I'm getting a round.*

He has to get out of here. This has been a mistake. He can see from the bar, Agnes' wheels turning. There was more than female smells, there were soiled knickers, crotch rubbing, uncontrollable flatulence. The dirty bitch was laid bare and given the full autopsy. Brünnhilde awaits.

Same again, my dear.

Remind me, she says, sassy, chewing on a chunk of pork pie.

Bitter, bitter, bitter, gin and slim.

Bitte, bitte, bitte, she mumbles under her breath, begging for fulfilment. But the Teutonic beauty is no more. She has morphed into Maggie Dwyer, her arms no longer taut but fat and rippled like rotten orange peel. A piece of suet crust protrudes from her gob, she scratches her arse through stretched-out leggings while waiting to get to the pump for more gripping and yanking. John recoils and heads for the gents.

He showers green tiles in green piss. Maggie Dwyer, 'mother' as they told him to call her. His father had first met her asking after piano work. John sat in the corner, sketching her bulbous frame, Joe and Maggie had got to talking about pub work and raising babes. She had three pianos that were all in need of a tinkle. He should come back that night, a trial, if you like. John assumed they would be walking on to other pubs, a bus into town, perhaps. But Joe dropped his lad off at home, and that was the last time he took little Jack on pub visits.

John saw nothing more of Maggie Dwyer until the day he was told to call her mother. Up until then, he had lived with his aunt, Ann, who he had taken to calling mother, or *muther* in the Mancunian. Ann had only agreed to care for John on account of the fact that Joe could not. They would argue, his real father and surrogate mother, but only when they were both in the house at the same time, which was not often enough to make life intolerable. Ann would be glad to see the back of Joe, and that meant seeing the back of John. Did she love him like a son? Doubtful. John was the walking reminder of a family tragedy. Ann could mourn Elizabeth's death, now she did not have to care for the child.

John and his father moved in with the Dwyers, above the Golden Eagle. Of a morning, John would rush downstairs, into the snug, and then into the gents to piss in the urinals. Dirty, Maggie called it, but it was no dirtier than anyone else doing their business there, or him doing his business anywhere else, for that matter. He liked to see how high he could go, putting his hand on piss-soaked tiles to get better purchase.

He had sisters now, Madge and Agnes. John tried to capture them in his drawings and they cried at the results. He would have preferred either one to be his mother. They were closer in reality to his memories of Elizabeth. Maggie Dwyer was something else entirely. She was hard. John thought a person could only love so much, could only care about so many people, and her quota had long run dry. She became his muse. In order to understand her, in order to find a way into her affections, he would draw her in minute detail. John pulled up a stool and sat in the kitchen, while she cooked mutton stew or meat and potato pie, and studied her. He drew her from every angle. He drew her thinner, and younger, and fatter, and hunched over with age. It became something of an obsession. In school, he would sketch her down from memory. None of this gave him any clues to the woman herself. It was as though they were living on two planes, offset by mere degrees. They saw the same world around them, the same people who inhabited that world, but they could not see each other, not entirely. What they did see was blurred, not fully formed. John grew to detest her acts. Wiping her nose on whatever was in reach, coughing with mouth wide, hand nowhere to be seen. Over the course of his childhood, the act of trying to understand and install himself in Maggie Dwyer's affections became the act of distilling his loathing of her. He noticed the rogue hairs growing from her eyebrows, fixated on the dirt beneath her fingernails. John found himself, aged no more than eleven, sat at the breakfast table, studying the contents of her ear. He was scolded for his lack of appetite.

He shook himself off, climbed the stairs, and paid for waiting drinks. They drank well of his generosity. John saw Agnes had become a sort of duplicate Maggie Dwyer. She bit down as she took swigs of gin and let most of what was in her mouth run back into the glass.

How's the wife, Jackie?

Very well, thank you, Bert. She'll be joining me tomorrow.

You'll 'ave to bring her round. I'll cook a dinner. Do you still like beef, Jack? Agnes turns to her own Jack, *He used to love a bit of beef when he were a kid, our Jackie. Used to suck all the juice out of the meat and then soak up the gravy. Do you remember doing that?*

I'm afraid we have plans. We must travel up to Edinburgh. More books to sign, more books to sell.

Ah well, Bert says, raising his glass, *cheers to you, Jack. And the missus.*

Out on the street it's still raining, which shouldn't be taken as some kind of comment on the city itself, this is just a fact of life; it rains everywhere. Anthony lights another cheroot and holds his umbrella high above his head. Where to now? It's still early. In fact, no time has passed at all.

He crosses Albert Square, each cobble an island in a vast network of rain-filled moats. He turns down the side of the town hall. The huge structure of gothic bronze weight bears down on him from the left; the murky white of the library bowing towards him on the right.

His dad used to take him here as a kid. They'd climb the marble stairs to the first floor, little Jackie holding his father's hand, looking up at the crests that adorned the ceiling. At the reception desk, his dad would tell him to have a good look around. *Make sure to remember.* He'd point out the pile of books at the end of the desk, the two women deep in concentration, the pillars that ran down to the ground floor. Once he was sure he had it all in mind, he and his father would start to walk. They passed row after row of books and row after row of seats. Readers reading, fixated in silence. They passed paintings and carvings and dedications. Huge oak doors that hid dark secret places.

The corridor continued straight, not deviating, not turning once. Little Jack would walk around with his mouth agape. He'd climb up onto the ledges to stare out at Manchester below, and his dad would help him down and keep him moving along this endless corridor. Until, by magic, they were back at the desk, the two women sat exactly where they had been, heads down, hypnotised by hidden books. He spent the journey home puzzling at how they had walked in a straight line, only to end up where they began.

Anthony climbs the twenty or so stone steps to the general reading section of the library on the first floor. His suitcase thud, thud, thuds against each stair, a hollow sound that echoes through the grand hallway. At the uppermost step he lifts his head towards the crest-lined ceiling, just as he remembers. The reception desk is still there, though the woman in attendance is younger and reads a glossy magazine. *Make sure to remember.* In the reading room, there are several people with their heads down, frowns across their brows. Anthony wheels his suitcase over to the desk and the receptionist nods in the direction of a rucksack and a couple of coats. His suitcase dispensed with, he passes row after row of books and row after row of seats. He would like to find something on the shelf he has not read in years.

How far, dad?

His father does not answer, but gives the boy's arm a gentle pull as they continue. From a door off the corridor a large man pushes out a trolley of books. The boy skitters to a halt. His long, slender child's face does not move, his almond eyes do not blink. The trolley trundles past, the librarian wheezing under the strain.

As Anthony moves, using the umbrella as a stick, he catches glimpses of the two of them, the boy's hand trailing against the wall, his arm permanently outstretched, the other hand gripped tightly by his father. He cannot make out the father; he sees only the hand that holds the boy's, his arm up to his elbow, the very edge of his shoulder and head, which leans to the right, a cap upon it.

The boy says, *What's in there?* But they do not stop, the man moves his son on. *What's this one?* The books are not there to be read, they must not be taken from the shelves. The boy pulls his hand from his father's and tries to climb onto one of the ledges. His dad stops, lifting him up to the window. Anthony could catch them now, could casually pass by. The umbrella takes his entire weight, he has to hunch his tall frame so its tip touches the parquet floor, so his hand can rest firmly upon it. The boy stares out at the wide world, the father only looks at the boy. He says, *Have you seen where we are?* The boy is too distracted with the world below to notice they are back at the staircase, back at the reception desk with the librarian reading her magazine, the page open on several images of Diana.

Can we go in? The boy asks, pulling towards the stacks.

No, not today, son. And the father starts towards the stairs, gently pulling his son away.

Joe would never let him look at the books, let alone take one out. The library was somewhere to get out of the cold. Downstairs you could get a cheap cup of tea and no one bothered you. They would wait until the rains had passed and then continue on their way. His stepmother would never bring him into the library. She thought there was something unseemly about public buildings, ironic considering her trade. Maggie didn't trust books, preferring to rely on rumour and gossip.

The schoolmen were schoolboys first, he says out loud, drawing the attention of the librarian. He fears she will shush him; he would have to retaliate. He stares at her. She peers over her glasses. Her hair is lank and asymmetric. If she raises her finger to her lips, he tells himself, I will strike her with this umbrella. She senses the threat, turning back to her magazine. He swipes at the handle of his suitcase and lets it clatter behind him as he descends the stairs.

The suitcase is theatrically taken from him on the stairs of the Midland Hotel by a man in a chauffeur's outfit. Another man opens the door for him, and one more asks him if he has a reservation.

I do, John tells him and is pointed towards the reception desk he had been heading to.

Good afternoon, sir. What name is it?

Wilson. John. He takes a damp handkerchief from his trouser pocket and wipes the rain from his forehead and fringe.

Buckets, out there, she says. The receptionist, hair dyed the same black-purple as aubergine skin, flicks through a box of index cards, putting him in mind of a dirty novel. *I'm afraid we don't have a Mr Wilson here, sir. Could it be under a different name?*

Of course, it is.

Burgess.

Anthony?

I – my wife booked under my working name.

Sorry to ask, sir, but do you have some kind of identification? Just for our records.

He takes his sodden passport from his sodden top pocket, *John Wilson* printed beside a picture some ten years out of date.

If you could just – he bends and places his suitcase flat on the floor and unzips the main compartment. From it he takes out a copy of his latest novel. He pulls himself back up, using the counter for support, and puts the book down in front of the receptionist. He opens the inside back cover to reveal a pugnacious portrait of John Anthony Burgess Wilson, eyeballing anyone who might doubt him.

I see. Apologies, Mr, eh, Burgess. I didn't recognise you.

That's because you don't know who I am.

She holds her thin-lipped smile firm. *This arrived for you.*

He takes the envelope, scratched writing, no stamp attached.

Should I get your case, sir? One of the bag handlers asks.

Terima kasih, Anthony replies and heads to the elevator.

They share a silent ride to the fourth floor. The boy delivers the bag and leaves tipless. Anthony rings down and orders a large gin and tonic, changes his mind and asks them to bring him up a bottle of their best cognac.

Alone, sat at the foot of the bed, Anthony opens the letter. A single sheet of paper, four lines set out like poetry.

> *We've reserved three graves for you, Mr Burgess.*
> *One for your body,*
> *one for your books,*
> *and one for your ego.*

Part Two

London
1968

A book of matches rested on a book of his own. His first, in fact: *Time for a Tiger*. Pristine condition. He blew smoke and the driver blew condensation. Strange that John, who had lived four years in the constant heat of the East, did not feel the cold. His hand tremored, the cigarette tip flitted back and forth, but he felt nothing. The car turned off the A40 and drove past the cricket club. No one around, of course. It was too late, or too early for anyone to be walking these streets. He ran his fingers along his unshaven chin. That would need doing. And he would have to wash, change these clothes too. They turned onto Bath Street, the Tabard ahead.

You can pull over just here. Foolish, reflex reaction at the sight of a public house. He could have told the driver to forget it but leant over to pay.

The window, the driver called back, without even a thank you.

Bollocks to the window, John replied, and gave the door a good slam.

He stood, fag in mouth, trying to force the paperback into his jacket pocket. He still had half a mind to return it to the shop in the morning. It would not be the first time he had returned his own books for beer money. There had been *Enderby*, written under the pseudonym of Joseph Kell, sent to him by the *Yorkshire Post* to review. He had given it a negative review and been fired when Kenneth Young found out the authorial truth. He had taken that *Enderby* to a Soho bookshop with several others. He and Lynne had drunk well on the proceeds.

Did he expect the Tabard to be open? Enough to try the door, certainly. He pulled his jacket tight and grasped the plastic bag they had given him. The paving outside the Turnham Green station, an ugly squat thing, was littered with rotting stems, leaves and petals from the previous day's flower sellers. Still in bed, John imagined. No one buys flowers at this hour in Chiswick. London is something of a dead place at this time.

He knew of a club where he would be given access to various drinks, but that would mean another cab ride, the long journey into the city. He looked in the windows of butchers and cafés and grocers. All empty. No one lives in a dead place.

At Chiswick High Road he waited for traffic that did not pass. He waited for a terribly long time, just watching the asphalt of the road, the fag ends and other detritus, pages of yesterday's newspaper, matches, bus tickets, a child's shoe lodged in the grille of a drain. How had it got there? Had the mother not realised? He picked the shoe up and crossed the road.

John tried another set of doors and found them, too, firmly locked. He placed the shoe at the entrance of the Baptist church. All houses frozen. The yellow of the bricks looked grey in the darkness, windows frost-glazed. He had often walked by here, jealous of the size of these places. Big three-storey townhouses, he pictured having the top floor to himself, a room for writing, another he could sleep in when writing got too much. He lit up, a speck of warmth in the fug. The white of the bay windows, like bandstands, like wedding cakes, like the pillars of King's Pavilion. He carried on, past Strand Antiques and the dry cleaners, on to Glebe Street, and, passing the dirty wooden garage doors, to home.

It wasn't his home, not in ownership anyway. Lynne had bought it with the money from her father's death. It was a Jones house bought with Jones money. She had not gone to the funeral; John had been sent in her stead. He had heard of voodoo doctors who, with just a few words, could put a curse on men that would kill them dead overnight. Her sister's words had cursed Lynne, and the curse of guilt had rendered her inert. She had lain in bed for two days on news of her father and could talk about nothing except for Malaya and that tape they had listened to, some three weeks after Christmas, of her poor dead mother and poor father, now dead himself, singing hymns of new life and rebirth. She imagined Hazel whispering as she passed the open coffin, *You decided to make this one, then?*

The temperature seemed to drop another degree but he stayed in the street looking at the bricks and mortar. The house in Etchingham was his, they couldn't claim otherwise. Fucking Joneses. Edward, before he was finally spent, would continually ask about his next teaching post.

No more teaching posts, John would tell him, *I'm a writer now.* And he would be looked over with narrow Welsh eyes, though the bastard was originally from Bolton.

Writing what? The conversation had to be had all over again, how John had written books and was continuing to write them, and he had been on the BBC, radio and television, to discuss his work. Even Lynne would tire of her father's reluctance to believe his son-in-law was an, inverted commas, author. He stubbed out his cigarette and put his key in the lock.

Haji barked shrilly, having been woken from deep sleep. The house was cold and dark. Lynne had called it their London bunker. It was a retreat for both of them. A retreat from the country of Etchingham for Lynne; a retreat from London society for John. No one came to Chiswick. He felt for the handle to the living room door and opened it, then switched on the standard lamp. The dog raised his nose, but not his mass, and sniffed at the air. The smell acceptable, he lay his head back down and slept. From the mat, John picked up a heavy brown envelope. Several four-cent postage stamps adorned it, along with his name and address. The handwriting florid, written in thick felt-tip pen. John feared envelopes such as this. They rarely contained anything good and, more than likely, contained death sentences.

He prised the now warped copy of *Time for A Tiger* from his jacket pocket, threw it on Lynne's armchair, and went to the bar. This was the one bit of house improvement they had made, an ornate glass-fronted drinks cabinet with sideboard. More of a cell than a bunker, John thought, looking at the wallpaper, its pattern almost completely dulled. He poured gin and walked the few feet into the kitchen to get a bottle of tonic. They had been cellmates here. No need for ice. Every venture outside the cell took all the plotting of a prison break. No need, for that matter, for tonic to be in the fridge. John tore a half-typed page from the platen and held it to the light, an unfinished review for the book section of *The Washington Post*. He crumpled the page and tossed it.

Dropping the glass onto the side table, he tore open a pack of Burma cheroots and chewed down hard, fishing matches from his pocket. He raised the head of the anglepoise lamp, straightening it so it loomed over him. The rest of the cell fell into shadow. *What have you to say for yourself, eh?* From the envelope he drew out a thick wedge of paper. On the front, written in his own cartoonish handwriting, *WILL!*, his name beneath. Beside it was a drawing, a child's caricature of Droeshout's Shakespeare. Big, bulbous eyes, triangle nose, excessive forehead, wisps of hair above and thin lips below, dog ears for hair. John flipped the page.

SCENE ONE

From a leather bag, a hand carefully draws
out a bundle of parchment, in raffish
calligraphy the title: A COMEDY OF ERRORS,
and the author's name: WILLIAM SHAKESPEARE.

WILL peruses his work. He rises from his
desk and leaves his house.

```
In the streets of London, MUSIC BEGINS TO
PLAY.

Will is greeted by the many people he
passes, wenches in bust-enhancing bodices,
stallholders, ragged children, and wealthy
courtiers.

                    WILL

Give the people what they wish: Something trite
                and tawdry,
            Balladry and bawdry -
        Give the people what they wish.

WILL continues on, through the streets and
into the GLOBE THEATRE.

                    WILL

    Give the groundlings what they crave:
            Bombast and unreason,
          Dog and bitch in season,
```

The word 'bitch' was crossed out. A note beside the line read: *Though the Bard should be bawdy, he should not be outright vulgar.* Skimming through, he caught flashes of red ink littering the pages. John fished out a piece of paper from the bottom of the envelope:

> *Dear John, I've had our script fixer take a look at what you sent. Look forward to seeing what you do with it. Time is of the essence! BC*

A fixer? He coughed, felt his throat tighten and coughed again. A fucking – he scanned, catching a red penned *dull* and *not believable* and *Shakespeare wouldn't say this* – fixer! Rage pervaded the tip of every nerve ending. These fucking Americans. *Hrrrkkk*, he tried to shift whatever was trapped in his throat. Throwing the script to the floor, he drained his glass and got up to pour more.

He drank, bent down, unscrewed the part-written *Washington Post* article, glanced at it, and screwed it up once more. He hawked and rasped, trying to clear his throat. No good. John took a mouthful of gin and directed it towards what was lodged there. He coughed and found he could not stop coughing. Spluttering, he stubbed his cheroot out on the space bar of his Olympia. The smoke stung his eyes. Haji stirred in his bed, whining and licking his teeth.

Jesus fucking Christ. He slammed his empty glass on the desk, trying to catch his breath. If he squeezed any harder, he knew, it would shatter into his palm and fingers. He would have to pick shards out and bandage himself up. John thought to himself, I would like to get into a fight. I would like to punch and be punched. These – he grasped the script from the floor again – fucking Americans. Did they not know who he was?

Sixteen novels in thirteen years, Bill Conrad had whistled.

Eighteen, John corrected. *I published two under the name Joseph Kell.*

Did you hear that? Joseph Kell! Bill called, delighted. *Who the hell is Joseph – never mind. Eighteen goddamned novels in…*

Thirteen.

Eighteen goddamned novels in thirteen years.

The women did not seem all that impressed. They were Hollywood women; eighteen scripts may have garnered more reaction, though it would have been fewer words, less work.

Delilah here, say hi, Delilah.

Hello, Joe.

It isn't Joe, darling, laughing, *this here is John Burgess. Delilah is quite the reader, isn't that right, sweetheart?*

Oh yes? What sort of things do you like to read? John took in her long miniskirted legs.

Mainly short stories. Do you know Borges?

Borges? Why don't we get a drink and you can tell me all about it?

He skipped to a scene between Anne and Will. Their son, Hamnet, has just died. Will sings him a song about ambition and legacy. Will is distraught, as is his wife. She says she would give her own life, gladly, that their child would live on. Beside these lines, the fixer had written *morbid and overwrought*. He also suggested the whole dead son business be cut entirely from the script. *This is a musical, Mr Burgess, not a tragedy.*

He cursed himself, not for the first time, for selling the rights to *Nothing Like the Sun* for a pittance. And not just that one, he had sold a job lot of novel rights to callous film producers. The money gone on two weeks in Marrakesh and two weeks in Tenerife. There was the mortgage to pay too, Lynne having spent the money on gin and cider. He had had to start from scratch and if he wished to be paid, he must genuflect to the Yanks and the Yankee dollar. They wanted a musical in the style of *My Fair Lady*. Shakespeare as a lovable rogue, somewhat rough around the edges but with a heart of poetaster gold. Anne would be his adoring wife, keeping the home fires burning for her adoring husband. Shakespeare would, perhaps, be a kind of Cyrano, writing poems that his shy Lord Southampton would deliver to a fair princess as his own thoughts and desires. There would be much made of this fair maid singing from tall towers, while Shakespeare whispered couplets to his kindly Lord below. He knew what they wanted all right, and refused to write it.

He had hesitated, in his London agent's office. The pen hovered. John knew his novels had cinematic quality, he had written them that way.

He said, *Perhaps we should rethink this. I have a feeling that—*

Christ, John, Lynne groaned. *Just sign the bloody thing. You have sown, now is time to reap.*

Had she really said that? It would be something of a coincidence, as John had been considering the possibility that Shakespeare had authored that very line in the King James Bible. Indeed, part of the libretto John had been working on would include the very phrase.

> *Be not deceived; God is not mocked: for*
> *whatsoever a man soweth, that shall he also reap.*

There was something of Shakespeare in those words. They did not exactly flow in Bardic iambs, true, but it shared something of the sentiment and the plot of *Measure for Measure*.

He thought of another possible plot for *Will!*: the newly crowned King dressing as a civilian and joining the Lord Chamberlain's Men – he had a particular scene in mind, Chamberlain watching a rehearsal of the play, demanding Shakespeare find someone with a more noble stature for the role of Vincentio. The role is cast, only the Bard recognising the true identity of James I. As director, Will teaches His Royal Highness a lesson about ruling and the King is forever in the writer's debt. It was not particularly bawdy, but subplots could be added. Perhaps Will would offer James lodgings above Mountjoy's shop of elaborate headpieces. There, in that attic room, the two could engage in royal buggery.

John had a good mind to write the whole thing and send it back to Conrad. *I await, with eagerness, the thoughts and suggestions of your script fixer.* He went back to the bar and poured himself more gin.

He fed paper into the typewriter. He wrote:

SHAKESPEARE sits at his desk, quill in hand.

Close-up on parchment. He is writing a sonnet, 'Let me not to the marriage of true minds' (116). There is a knock at the door.

WILL

Come.

BURBAGE OPENS THE DOOR.

BURBAGE

Sorry to disturb.

WILL

Burbage, come in. You are not disturbing much,
only the turning of my mind.

BURBAGE

That is the very reason I have interrupted.
You have been in here for days now. When was
the last time you ate?

WILL

I cannot eat. When my parchment is full, so
too my stomach.

BURBAGE

What is it you write? A new play?

WILL

A poem. A sonnet for my absent wife,
expressing my continuing love.

A PUB IN STRATFORD.

THERE ARE MANY MEN DRINKING AND MAKING
MERRY. OUT OF THE WINDOW, WE SEE A YOUNGISH
MAN PUSHED AGAINST THE SIDE OF THE PUB BY
AN OLDER WOMAN. THIS IS ANNE.

OUTSIDE, SHE KISSES HIM PASSIONATELY.

MAN

But Anne, what if your husband were to find out?

ANNE

He'll not know. All he knows and cares about
is London and London life.

SHE KISSES HIM AGAIN.

                        MAN

          Do you not love him?

                        ANNE

(laughs)

          Does thou speak of love, youngling?

                        MAN

               I only meant -

                        ANNE

     I know what you meant, daft lad. I love him
     for the money he sends and for the life he
     provides. And I love him for the distance he
               keeps. Come with me.

SHE LEADS HIM OFF BY THE HAND, THE TWO LAUGHING
AS THEY GO.

He had seen it with his own eyes, his wife and a nameless man.
It had been Lynne who had travelled south and found herself
accepted into literary London. His first taste was in a letter,
read on the toilet of his Warrington barracks, Lynne revealing
another extramarital dalliance; this time with none other than
Dylan Thomas. After lying about a dead or dying relative, he
arrived at Lynne's flat and found Lynne beautifying herself with
black-market make-up.

A party? I'm not going to a bloody party.

She pulled her stockings up, raising her leg high and
lengthening it.

Lynne, we need to have words. He still had his haversack in
his hand, standing by the bed in his coat and shoes, watching
Lynne parade around in underwear.

We can talk tomorrow. Come on, I can smell you from here. Get yourself cleaned up.

He had come to end it, to take back the ring and have her out of his life once and for all.

You, she laughed, fastening stocking to suspender, *so serious, Jackie. Poor lad.*

She ran her hand over his jacket, unbuttoning. He grasped her wrist and held it. *Pent up*, she said, kissing his cheek, catching the edge of his mouth. He imagined himself striking her, like in the films. She teased his jacket open and pressed her palm against the zip of his trousers. *Can I do anything to help?*

It had been almost a year since he had last felt her touch. There was a smirk on her face as she stood before him, bare-breasted, the curve of her stomach against the flat of her black suspenders. She kissed him again, John moving his lips from hers, her peeling his zip and reaching the tips of her fingers inside. *Poor lad*, she said again, holding his hardening cock through the sheath of his underwear. He could smell himself now, diaphoretic from the train journey, from the bus ride, clothes that should have been washed days ago. *Let's see if I can't help you relax.* She tried to guide him to the unmade bed but he held still, her hand tight around him, moving slowly.

I want a divorce.

Good Christian boy like you?

I'll not be made a fool of any longer. She unbuttoned him, pulled his underwear around his thighs. He dropped the haversack and grabbed at her left breast. *You make me a cuckold, Lynne.* Holding his cock, she shifted his hand from her body. He met her lips this time, tasting gin on her breath, feeling the heat of her breath is his mouth, feeling the surge growing.

I'll be good, she said, her tongue licking at his bottom lip. *I'll be a good girl.*

He grabbed her again, pulled her tight against him as he came. Lynne wiped her hand across his shirt and before he could lift his trousers she was fastening her bra and pulling a black dress over herself.

At the party, Lynne did no introducing and went straight to dancing in one of the parlours. She called John over, but he was in no mood for dancing, no mood for anything. What she yelled, he did not hear. He lost her in the crowd.

John wandered the house – enormous and ornate – catching glimpses of conversations about Sartre, Saussure, Jewishness and the rebirth of the British nation. There were many tall, elegant women, all, it seemed to John, holding court on everything from poetry to Peace of Westphalia. He had never been good around literary women. He had a strong reaction whenever he saw photographs of Virginia Woolf.

In the kitchen he found himself surrounded by the main members of this group. John recognised certain faces from newspapers and book jackets. T. S. Eliot, wasn't it, making vodka cocktails? He found a crate of Fuller's Chiswick Bitter and opened a bottle. Some of the men drank cans of Ballantine, an American beer. They swigged straight from the can and spoke in England's finest RP.

John felt a slap on his back. *Seen Cyril anywhere, old man? How would I know if I had?*

Well groomed, with sharply angled features and steely lips, he raised his idiosyncratic eyebrow, *Who've you come with?*

I'm here with Eliot, John lied. *And Auden.*

Auden is in America.

Well, then, he thought for a moment, *Thomas.*

You know Dylan?

Yes, we're very close. Like brothers, you might say.

You're lying. This was not said in censure, but enjoyment.

I, myself, am a poet of great note, John continued, not knowing what he might say next. *Are you a literary man?*

Not in the sense you mean. I fund literary men. Are you looking for funding? He drank from a Martini glass, keeping his eyes on John.

Certainly. Certainly I could do with a bit of funding. Certainly.

I've a new collection called, it came to him, *The Pet Beast, that I am working on. A stipend would greatly relieve me of certain financial responsibilities and allow me to occupy my time in more fulfilling endeavours.*

How much are we talking?

I shouldn't think I would require more than, he totted it up in his head, *twelve, maybe fifteen pounds a month.*

Very reasonable. He finished his drink, was about to speak again, when another man whispered into his ear. *If you'll excuse me.*

Of course. John watched him leave, relieved it was all over.

The man passed Dylan Thomas on the way out. *Your friend's just there,* he winked over at John.

Thomas came over looking for booze. *We've met?*

John knew he should be angry at this feckless poet who had had it away with his wife. *I don't think so. John,* he offered his hand. *I, of course, know who you are.* Perhaps he should have punched Thomas in his pudgy nose. *I'm a great admirer of your work.*

Very kind. Friends with Peter, are you?

Great friends. From school. But he felt no animosity.

Well, la-dee-da. Thomas poured wine into his glass. The two of them surveyed the room. *See anything you like?*

John nodded. *I'm on leave from barracks. I cannot stop seeing things I like.*

John saw Lynne enter, attached to a big-chinned man from the dance floor. He looked like an East End club owner or a Hollywood gangster, with mirrored sunglasses and camel-hair coat. His hair was slicked back, but kinked and uneven. It seemed they were arguing, but then she let out a raucous laugh. He filled their glasses with punch and Lynne cadged two cigarettes from a man who seemed pleased to see her. Lynne's friend placed his into a holder and bit down as he smoked.

That one? Thomas narrated, Lynne playing silly buggers, blowing out matches each time one was offered. *No, I'd steer clear of that one, if I was you. She may seem like fun from here but believe me.* He said no more. There was, apparently, no more to say.

I shall bear that in mind, John said. He watched on. Lynne was laughing, showing teeth, shoulders rolling. His wife, truly happy.

Thomas said, *So, what are you? Painter, philosopher, philanthropist, philander?*

A piano-player, he said. *And a damned fine poet.*

Indeed. Well, Thomas loudly cleared his throat. *If I can have everyone's attention.* And he did, immediately. *This is John. John what?*

Just John is fine, he replied, his voice a whisper.

Just John here is a great poet, the poet of our generation, I should think. What are you going to recite for the people, Just John?

The room turned in on him, unblinking eyes unblinking at him. Lynne had reduced her laughter to a titter but couldn't hold back when she saw John's terrified face.

Thomas said, *He's ruminating.* Then, whispering, *Just make something up, it's only for a laugh.*

I will, John cleared his throat, *I will recite,* coughed into his hand, *my poem*, took a swig of beer, *which is called* – expectant faces began to turn towards one another. John tried again to clear his throat, tried again to clear it with beer.

Bollocks, come on, Just John. Here, have a shot of this. From his jacket pocket he took out a hip flask. John shakily unscrewed the cap, put it to his lips and gave it a nervous jolt. Warm alcohol rushed through his cheeks, throat, ears, nose, to the top of his head. *Now,* and again loudly, *Just John will perform.* But Just John said nothing.

Let's have it, Jack, Lynne called over.

He screwed the cap back on the bottle, coughed a little more, and handed it back to Thomas, who said, *Well, Just John is just a little thoughtful this evening, but if I recall correctly, I can give you one of his finest pieces. Does it go,* he turned to John for confirmation,

> *There was a young lady named Bright,*
> *Whose speed was far faster than light;*
> *She started one day*
> *In a relative way,*
> *And returned on the previous night.*

Those assembled laughed, some applauding. *Applause this way, please,* Thomas said, patting John jovially on the back. *Just entertaining the troops, as it were.*

John picked up his bottle and nodded farewell. He made his way over to Lynne, who had draped herself again over the tall, handsome man.

Having fun? she asked.

Not particularly. And you?

Always, Jackie. She gave him a peck on the cheek. *I've got to pee.* And off she went, into the bowels of the house, John following.

He lost her down the hallway and continued to wander. There was no war on here, John realised. Theirs is a kind of dream world; they've been transported back to a London that never existed, where artists and flâneurs, like Orwell in Paris, write about empty streets and squares. Everything is a metaphor, all is present and all is lost. All the men have gone off to war, yet here are all the men, imbibing unrationed Yankee beer, raising glasses with soon-to-be-widows, who sup bitter gins with slices of unreal lemon. The whole bloody world could be on its knees and this lot'd still be mocking them that takes Nazism too seriously.

Idly complaining about what a bore it will be when they must return, cap in hand, to their dear old father to extract another few pounds of inheritance they feel they're long since owed.

John climbed the wide staircase up to the second floor. There was a kind of tuning up in his head. A piano ran through the Aeolian mode. He began to hum, wandering a long corridor. In various rooms he caught fragments of scenes: two men hunched over a desk with their backs to him; a woman reciting poetry alone; Yankee soldiers, cigars gripped between their teeth, playing poker; a woman quietly undressing on a bed, a man sombrely closing the door. The melody choked. He stood at the door for a moment, his hand pressed softly against it. Slowly retracing his steps, John attempted to regain the melody in palindrome. Down the stairs he went.

In the corner of an unoccupied room John found an upright piano. He tried to resuscitate whatever had stirred in him. The notes he hit rang false. There was too much thought, too little feeling. Debussy's *La Mer* and all of Stravinsky in gross distortion, reflected in black pools of stagnant water. He hit a couple of big, bawdy chords and closed the lid. On top of the piano sat several scores. From the pile he drew out *Lohengrin* and took it over the settee. Bottle empty, John used the lip as a kind of makeshift flute and attempted to whistle the Act I prelude. Deep breaths, long drawn-out blows. Ridiculous but amusing.

Are you having fun? John looked up at a brunette it was reasonable to describe as beautiful.

I'm, eh, yes, just haven't, he put the score down, *I'm rather tired after a long journey back to London.*

I had to get away for a moment. She placed a cigarette between her lips and raised a light. She looked, John thought, like Vivian Leigh. Or Olivia de Havilland. He wasn't sure which, but certainly one of them.

Yes. The same.

I'm Sonia. She sat beside him and held her hand out.

He took it. *John. Don't know anyone either?*

I know everyone. She said it matter-of-factly. *I work with Cyril.*

Yes, do you? It seems I'm the only person here who doesn't know Cyril.

How is it you're here then?

I'm with a friend.

Who? She blew smoke and eyed him suspiciously.

Dylan Thomas.

Bullshit, you are.

We're old school friends.

You don't sound Welsh to me.

I had it educated out of me.

Liar.

I am, he said. *But only when I speak.* John lit his own cigarette. He watched as Sonia turned in her seat, looking for an ashtray. Picking one up from the side table, he presented it like a waiter would present a tray of hors d'oeuvre.

Thank you, she said.

He held the glass tray between them and switched his legs over, so his knees were inches from hers. More de Havilland, on closer inspection. The melody returned, refreshed, in Dorian mode.

Excuse me, Sonia said, uncrossed her legs, stood, and left. It was to be that sort of night. No doubt she would be out there now, asking for help to remove someone who claimed to be invited, who claimed to belong. He supposed it was about time he find Lynne and get on with getting drunk and getting out of this place. He stood, brushed the ash from his crotch and bent to pick up *Lohengrin* from the floor.

Sonia was standing in the doorway with two glasses. From a cupboard at the far end of the room she retrieved a bottle of red and a corkscrew. The theme grew bolder, a single piano played with great verbosity and warmth.

You're going back in?

No, I was, just, he held the score up, *doing a bit of tidying up.* Sonia was the major sixth, shifting everything from Aeolian forbidding into rising anticipation.

Well, aren't you an excellent houseguest. Open this, she handed him the bottle, *unless you're leaving?*

John hurriedly threaded the corkscrew; a chord struck, the cork came in one fluid pull. He poured the wine into the glasses she held out, both of them still standing in the middle of the room.

Cheers, John. They touched glasses. The wine was good. John checked the bottle, French, Côtes du Rhône Villages.

Good, isn't it? Cyril has good taste. And the money to feed it. She sat on the sofa, straightening her dress. *What kind of man tidies up at a party where he doesn't know anyone?* She studied John's face as if the answer might be writ large upon it. *Catholic,* she finally pronounced.

Guilty, he said, not meaning to make the ecclesiastical pun. Sonia laughed and he acted along, the comedian pleased with his punchline.

If it makes you feel any better, I'm one of the guilty ones too. Educated?

Oh yes. A boarder of the Sacred Heart, Roehampton. And you?

I was instructed by the Xaverian Brothers.

Here in London?

Manchester, he said, though not enthusiastically.

A Northerner. I lived up north for a time. Liverpool. So, what has brought we two Northern Catholics to literary London during wartime, John?

He knew what the answer was, but it wasn't the answer he wanted to give. *Do you know Lynne Wilson?*

Wilson? Not sure. I know a Lynne Jones. Blonde, quite tall, pretty.

Jones, was it? *Yes, Jones, that's who I mean. What about you, Sonia, how did you—*

You're John! How exciting. You know, Lynne showed me some of your poems.

He blushed. *Well, I—*

No, don't be embarrassed. They're very good. Have you ever written for publication? With a bit of work, I think some of the ones I've read, what was it, she tried to think, *something about her heavy body?*

He knew the one. He had sent it to Lynne from Eye, Suffolk. The music playing in his head shifted into the scherzo. Two notes trilled as he spoke. *Now earth turns her heavy body about,* he quoted himself.

Yes, yes, that's the one. Lynne was very keen for me to read it.

I bet she was, John thought. Lynne would enjoy showing his literary scribblings to literary scribes. She must have hoped Sonia would share the joke with Cyril Connolly.

This was real schizophrenia. Part of him raged at Lynne for letting her drinking friends read their private correspondence, the part who must now recite verse. Part of him developed the cynicism of the scherzo into forward propulsion; this part would have kissed Sonia there and then. He hesitated, but began to recite.

He pictured the words coming out of Lynne's mouth, standing at the head of a table in the Fitzrovia, waiting for the laughter to die down before she recited the next gelastic line.

And before him, Sonia; her eyes softly shifted, as though she were reading from the page. Here was a beautiful, intelligent woman, showing interest in him and his writing. A woman who took his creativity seriously. Would she like to hear something of one of his compositions? The music forming as he spoke could be played to some degree of competence, if not completion. He angled his head to the piano in the corner of the room. *I'm afraid that's all I can remember with any confidence.* He picked up the bottle and poured them both a glass.

Do you have literary ambitions, John?

Sometimes, he said, hearing the vagueness in his voice. *I wrote a great deal in university. Poetry and prose, for the stage too. Music is my passion.*

You play?

The piano, yes, but composing is where my interests lie.

Like opera? You mean librettos?

No, no, the actual notes played by musicians. That's what I do, play in the entertainment corps, 54th Division. I haven't written much recently, not unless you include the knockabout tunes I write for the band. But, he shifted in his seat, straightened himself, *I have an idea for a piano sonata in E major. Something uplifting.* His heart beat in triplets. *I feel, don't you feel, what is needed is—* John was interrupted by a young man he hadn't seen before.

Don't mind me, the man said, *just looking for some paper. Every piece I find seems to be full of words.*

Have you met Lucian, John?

Pleasure, John said, Lucian said. A and B trilled in dunamis.

Cyril wants a portrait. He says I can have no more wine until I fulfil the commission.

Lucian rifled through piles of papers, all filled with big, grey blocks of text, anathema to an artist. Sonia got up to look too. She picked up *Lohengrin* from the top of the piano and flicked to the back page. She tore it, and the back cover, clean off.

Here you go, darling, she handed him the paper. All music ceased.

Sonia, he beamed, and kissed her on the cheek. *I'll do one for you too. Come and find me.* And he was gone. *Lohengrin* violated, John violated.

Incredible talent. You know who his grandfather is, don't you? Did you see the resemblance?

John didn't. He saw only torn staves and the ripped name of Richard Wagner. She was looking at him, he sensed. *A literary ancestor?*

Freud. Yes, Sigmund Freud. Lucian's at Goldsmiths. We're keeping a very close eye on him. Cyril's obviously looking to become part of Lucian's legacy early on.

What had they been talking about, John could not recall, all these torn sheets of manuscript still tearing through his head. He became aware of the rising silence in the room.

So, you work for Cyril. As his secretary?

Sonia stiffened. The word hit like fingernails down a blackboard. *I'm an editor. I select submissions, commission pieces, and edit what comes in.*

I didn't mean to—

Cyril calls himself the editor, but he's more a figurehead. No, that's not quite right either. Cyril is Horizon, but I make Horizon happen. If that's not too self-congratulatory.

I'm sorry, I just. Well, I have never been – never before, I mean – attracted to Catholic girls.

Sonia laughed, thinking this a joke, but saw that was not John's intention. *What a funny thing to say. Do you mean you can tell a Catholic girl because they are unattractive to you, or once you find out a girl is Catholic she becomes unattractive?*

I've always thought it a kind of incest...

John, you're pulling my leg, surely.

My stepsisters are Catholic, my stepmother too. My own mother, not known to me, also.

Well, yes, of course your relatives were Catholic. That stands to reason. Incest! What would you have done before the Reformation? She laughed at the very thought. *Considered all women your sisters and off limits?*

John felt the back pages ripped from him. Sonia said, *It's not your fault, of course, guilt laid on so thick will tend to pervade all spaces.*

She took a sip of wine, watching him as he watched her. There was a feeling of space and time shifting, their space closing, their time slowing, the space between them and the rest of the party expanding, time outside of the two of them practically frozen. *You said, 'never before.'*

I did. I did say that. A note struck with dampener down.

Lynne's not Catholic, then?

C of E. Welsh Presbyterian. One or the other, or they are the same thing.

I don't think she'd like to hear you talking like this.

No. She was right. *No, of course not.*

Sonia leant over and kissed John gently on the cheek. *You're very sweet,* and she left. He poured what remained of the bottle. It really was very good wine. He tried to conjure back the theme that had played as she spoke, but found nothing but final fading notes. Something had been stirred, though. Sonia had stirred something within him.

From the fridge John took out a jar of piccalilli and a packet of sliced ham which had turned. He tore the packet open and dropped the dried-out meat into Haji's bowl. He would have to go shopping. It was nearly 5.30am, hours before the shops opened. In the bread bin, bread had started to grow spores. He pulled out the few slices left and carefully removed the greenish mould from one piece. This he put under the grill. The butter dish had been left out; he caught a rancid whiff. When the bread was toasted, he smeared it in yellow relish and took a desperate bite.

His head ached. His bones ached, for that matter. Every bloody part of him wept and he could not sleep or think or stop fucking thinking and found himself again back in London, in Chiswick, yes, in the Globe Theatre in Baron's Court, in Fitzrovia, in the arms of Sonia Brownell, in the bed of his wife who had written to him to say it was over; while he had been away in Gibraltar she had found someone else, a journalist or some such, who she would now live with.

He entered the Bricklayer's Arms to find the two of them, Lynne and Sonia, deep in conversation. Lynne received John as though he had just popped out for cigarettes. A quick peck on the cheek, she told him she was in the middle of something, and shooed him off to get a drink. Sonia smiled casually. He held her gaze and thought he saw her blush. They had not seen each other for more than two years. She shone out as C, as he fought against Aeolian sorrow. No longer did she resemble a Hollywood starlet; she was far too much her own being. He bristled with jealousy, imagining what these years had been like for her, all these men who surrounded her; all their opportunities, while John had none.

A pint, John told the barman. He paid, lifted his drink, and surveyed the pub. At the other end of the bar were three faces he recognised, though only two he had met. The pudgy, punchy face of Dylan Thomas railed up at the thin, sallow face of George Orwell. Beside them stood Alf Jones, one of John's old friends from Peninsular Barracks, Warrington.

L-l-look who it is, Thomas said, as John approached.

John gave a wave and walked over, *Long time, no—* a young woman passed John, cutting him off and embraced the poet.

Martha, oh Martha, the poet laughed. *Several drinks for Martha,* he bellowed.

Alf turned his attentions from Orwell and caught sight of John standing, suspended in embarrassment. *Bloody hell, how did you get here?*

John regained his composure and made the rest of the short journey. *I could ask the same.* The two shook hands.

Are you out?

Me? No. A week's leave. I'm stationed out in Gibraltar. Yourself?

Finished up. I took one in the leg, in Anzio. Italy. We were bringing wounded off the beach. Fifth Infantry.

Nasty business.

You should tell me. Nastier than Gibraltar, I imagine.

How is it now? John nodded towards Alf's leg.

He lifted and gave his cane a wave. *I get by. My manners. Have you met Eric?*

No, no. John held out his hand.

This is John Wilson. John, Eric Blair.

Pleasure, John said.

Likewise, said Blair.

John's a – what are you now, John? He used to entertain us when I was stationed up north. Pianist and writer of amusing little things.

Well, John feigned shyness.

Whereas Eric here is a writer of unamusing big things.

That's your literary opinion, is it, Alf? Blair spoke distractedly, wielding a rolling machine and packing it with pungent shag. John took his Victory cigarettes from his pocket and offered one to Blair.

I prefer my own, thanks.

Thomas joined them. *Those pre-rolled sticks* – he took one and put it between his lips – *are a bourgeois conceit. We've met.*

Yes. John. Wilson.

Very well, Thomas smiled and drew his cigarette from John's match. *We are getting drunk, John. We are drinking to as many lost as we can remember—*

For God's sake, Blair interrupted, his voice blasted with static.

Certainly we are drinking for those we miss. Certainly. A toast. He lifted his glass. *More. More to drink.* And then,

There's a text and a photo, a garter, a drunk,

And a fair face you half forgot.

He clasped Blair's hand.

This is remembered when the veins are scrubby,

And the shellholed gums no longer pink.

Alf got more drinks and John felt part of something that was not war or waiting for war to be over. He surveyed the pub, heaving with drinkers, spotting Cyril Connolly and Maclaren-Ross and God knew who else. John listened as the poet spoke between mouthfuls of wine and spirits. He could look Thomas in the eye now, the sharp stab of adultery sufficiently healed.

One, one, one image make, make, he drank, *makes another, in the ordinary dialectic process.*

What did this mean? John was not sure but was glad to be privy to this conversation rather than barracks talk and the pros and cons of Billy Wright or the rise and fall of Rawmarsh Welfare FC. Thomas lost his thread, took a draught, caught it again and continued: *In a poem, one, one image breeds another.* John finished his drink and waved the barman over to buy another. He felt a hand slap his back.

Your round, John? Blair coughed heavily into his hand, *I'll join you.* He set his empty glass on the bar.

One pint breeds another, John mimicked in ebullient Welsh.

Blair ignored this and said, *Alf told me you write.*

I did. University magazine, that kind of thing. I'm more interested in writing music.

A composer?

Trying to be. The war has got in the way. The barman nodded at John. *Two pints.*

One for Thomas too, and Jones, if he's still present. Blair scoured the bar but could not see their companion. *Buy him one anyway, surely one of us shall drink it.*

John cursed quietly and counted pennies. Bloody writers on writers' salaries taking drinks from soldiers forced to live on soldiers' pittance.

What sort of thing do you write? Big symphonies for the big symphony halls, I suppose?

I've mainly written—

Not what this country needs. All symphonies are opulent. This is no time for opulence. And then, *I can't stand these places.*

Blair, suddenly gloomy, cast a glowering look over the pub, rowdy with literary jibber-jabber. John was about to second Blair's sentiment but said, *Why do you come then?*

It was a question as much to himself, though Blair was not to know.

I'm lonely. His words hung heavier than the cloud of smoke that rippled overhead. Heavier than London fog. John tried a few times to reply, to change the subject, to make his excuses and retreat. *My wife,* Blair continued, John already sensing the weight of the following words, *she died.*

I'm sorry, he was sorry, *to hear that*; he wished he hadn't heard.

Yes. She was a good stick. Blair coughed. *We adopted a son.* Oh Christ, John thought. *Now he has no mother.*

Out of the corner of his ear John heard Thomas reciting, *On almost the incendiary eve,* intertwined with Alf Jones' vivid description of the sinking of HMS Janus. *A Fritz X bomb.* They were only feet away, *When one at the great least of your best loved,* but Blair had drawn some kind of wall around them. *A Heinkel He 111.* He could simply turn away. *Who'd raise the organs of the counted dust.* He could find Lynne and tell her it was time to go – *deepest down shall hold his peace. That cannot sink or cease.* He could do these things. *She sank within twenty minutes.* He could simply say excuse me and walk away. *All but eighty dead. In many married London's estranging grief.*

My mother, John started, barely aware he was speaking, *died when I was just a baby.*

It's a hard thing for a child.

It is.

You miss her?

Jesus, let it stop. *He'll bathe his raining blood in the male sea / Who strode for your own dead.*

Yes. Yes, I suppose I do. Perhaps not her, her I do not quite remember, but I miss the idea of her, I miss the idea of having a mother.

I come to these things to find Richard a new mother. Maybe someone will marry me.

John lit a cigarette, Blair turned his handheld mangle. *Strange wounded on London's waves / Have sought your single grave –*

Ah, well, a stepmother is a very different thing to a mother. One cannot substitute the other.

In your experience.

Yes, I suppose, just in my experience. My stepmother wanted a husband, not a son. She resented the one for bringing the other.

And resented you too?

John nodded and heard, *Your heart is luminous.*

Yes, I will be clear. Thank you.

When Alf introduced us, John quickly changed the subject, *I thought he'd made some kind of mistake.*

Mistake? Oh, you mean Blair? No, no mistake. George Orwell is the name of book covers, Eric Blair is who I am.

Why the pen name, if you don't mind my asking?

Family. The Blairs would not like to be associated with poverty.

Perhaps if I ever publish a novel, I shall call myself Anthony Irwell, so not as to tar the Wilson name with success.

Irwell. Yes, very good. You write? They were here again, everything coming full circle.

Yes, John lied. *Do you have any pointers for a novice writer?*

Yes, Blair looked distracted, *head East.*

He patted John on the back, gave a short hacking cough, and took off across the pub to the table where Lynne and Sonia sat. John watched him arch his long body over the women, lowering his head towards their waiting ears. He found himself outside the crowd gathered around Thomas. Alf Jones was nowhere to be seen. John supped alone and cursed all those he had stood a drink.

Blair pulled up a seat between Sonia and Lynne. They laughed and he smirked like a child. He leant and whispered something into Lynne's ear. She moved closer, Blair's lips practically kissing her long neck. John caught on. Things on the Rock moved slowly, but here in London, Blair was working quickly. His son must have a mother and Lynne was without child. Irritation rose in his throat, like Blair's incessant cough. He strode over to the table.

This seat taken?

Blair raised his face from Lynne's well-groomed hair and said, *Ah, Irwell. Ladies, this is Anthony Irwell.*

We've met, John said, pompously. *We've all met, haven't we?*

Sit down, John, for pity's sake, Lynne slurred. She was drunk, John could see now, slumped against Blair.

This, John said, sitting, *is my wife, Lynne.*

Blair blushed, Brownell let out an involuntary giggle. *I had no—* Blair started.

No, I expect you didn't. John took his cigarettes out and watched this Eric Blair agitate tobacco into his roller. *Here,* John slid over his packet of Victory cigarettes. Blair coughed and continued to fidget with the contraption.

How are you, John?

Very well, Sonia. You are looking fine this evening. This was intended to antagonise Lynne, but Lynne was too drunk to be antagonised by anyone other than herself.

Eric suggested a nightcap at his place, perhaps he would be kind enough to put you two up.

Blair placed a perfectly cylindrical cigarette between his lips. *By all means. I'm not far. We can share a taxi.*

Out on the street Blair helped John get a half-sleeping Lynne into the cab. The driver was old enough to be Blair's father. He had been retired, but had started up again after the war broke out. He and Sonia had a long, drawn-out argument about the impracticalities of women becoming taxi drivers. Sonia telling him she would have no problem learning the Knowledge. John paid for the cab with a couple of packets of Victory cigarettes. They left with the driver tut, tut, tutting and carried Lynne up to Blair's flat.

Blair opened the door and directed John to take Lynne into the living room. The air in the flat was stale, as if it had been closed off from the rest of the world. John stumbled into the living room and dropped Lynne onto a nearby armchair.

Where's Richard? Sonia asked, from the hallway.

With Susan, Blair replied. *I'm making tea.*

Sonia came in and sat across from John; they both watched Lynne as she slept. *She's had a long day,* Sonia said.

A long night, I'd say. How do you know George Orwell?

John, I know everybody. Everybody of interest, anyway.

Of course you do. You even know me. There was far too much self-pity in that.

He asked Lynne to marry him. But don't worry, he asks everyone to marry him.

You?

Especially me.

But you've told him no. He felt a pang of jealousy.

Several times.

Blair continued his clinking in the kitchen, while Lynne snored softly on the armchair. John stood and approached Sonia. *I've thought about you a lot.* He waited for her to reply but she said nothing. *I've wanted you since the moment I met you, Sonia. I—* Lynne stirred, muttered something and fell back asleep.

John, please.

I've been so miserable on that fucking rock. You have no idea. You, thinking about you, is all that has kept me going. He had no idea where these words came from, but he felt compelled to make Sonia believe him. *Is there somewhere we can go?*

John– He kissed her before she had chance to say more, pinning his lips to hers and holding them there. He felt months of pent-up frustration so close to being released. Sonia pulled away.

I'm sorry, it's just – I intend to leave her, she intends to leave me. I had hoped, I still hope you will – he felt the heavy weight of these words on his tongue. *Fuck it all.*

Sonia poured herself a large brandy from the drinks cabinet and lit a cigarette. *I can't do this to Lynne.*

Do it for yourself. Do it for me.

John, it's not—

Blair pushed the door open, carrying a tray. He placed it on the table and swirled the teapot.

None for me, Sonia smiled, turning her brandy glass.

John?

Not for me, thanks. John crossed his legs so Blair would not see what was clearly present.

Blair placed a strainer on the rim of his cup and poured thick brown tea from the pot. John suddenly felt a deep desire to drink Stepmother's Tea. Everything rationed, there was so much to want.

On second thoughts.

Blair poured a second cup. *Milk?*

A touch. John received the cup with joy. It was thick as tar and lip-smacking with tannin. He lit a cigarette and blended the two flavours in his mouth. *Northern tea.*

There's a spare bed, Blair told him. *I've put fresh blankets down.*

Thank you.

The three of them sat in a not-uncomfortable silence. Lynne every so often interrupting it with a whinny or snuffle. John tried to catch Sonia's eye while she focused on her glass. Blair thumbed through a book on his desk and poured more tea.

What are you writing? Sonia asked.

Blair lifted two pages from his desk and held them aloft. '*Why I Write*', he pronounced. *The thing a writer should never write about. I am writing about writing.*

Can I read?

Only if you promise to keep your opinions to yourself.

Blair handed Sonia the pages. John saw the desk was covered in paper. Pages under ashtrays, on top of books, inserted into books, on top of cups and plates. The tea had made John incredibly tired. The day had been long.

Sonia laughed as she read. Blair pulled a face and said, *It's not supposed to be funny.*

But it is, she replied.

And why do you, John let out a yawn, *write, Eric?*

Because I am vain, selfish, and lazy. Blair said this as a joke, then took up a pen and jotted words down.

I should get some sleep, John said, standing. *This morning I was in Gibraltar. I was in a war, as strange as that sounds.*

Blair helped him lift Lynne into bed. The two men shook hands. *I'm sorry for all that*, Blair said.

John lay, unable to get warm, and thought about Sonia. Jealously pricked once more, the thought of Blair taking her to bed. He got up, ready to sit between them and talk until sun up, the time for sharing beds over. From the hallway he heard the sound of keys being struck. The rhythm of it was like Wagner, immediate and aggressive. He stood in the living room doorway. Amid a plume of cigarette smoke, George Orwell, alone, his back to the door, hammered at the typewriter.

John's eyes watered from too little rest. They had been open for some forty-eight hours. Now they bore witness to another morning, without the kindness of a restful night. He stared at the painting above the mantlepiece. Black and white and, he supposed, *surreal*. He had often tried to understand the composition, a horse's head in profile, some thick marks like hieroglyphs, a woman's face, who – if it were not for the inability of the artist – might have been beautiful. Lynne was adamant it be hung in the living room, not, as he had suggested, the guest bedroom. It had been a cherished gift, an Italian artist, no less.

He ambled through shop aisles with memories of rationing and bought more than he needed. For Haji, he purchased four tins of dog food. For himself, he bought a sliced loaf, a chicken, potatoes, carrots, a cauliflower, lemons, celery, butter, milk, potted ham, tinned garden peas, Colman's mustard, Rich Tea biscuits, Bourbon biscuits, tea, instant coffee, sugar, gravy granules, eight packs of Benson & Hedges, and a two-pint bottle of gin. The girl double-bagged his items and he paid with a cheque. He dragged the whole lot back, stopping regularly to catch his breath on garden walls.

Back home, he turned the tin opener over the lid of the dog food and shook the can until the glistening meat slid free and landed upright in the bowl, a perfect cylinder. He set the oven to a high heat and pulled the giblets out of the chicken. He peeled the butter wrapper and scooped up a good amount in his hand, which he inserted between the skin and the flesh of the bird. Clumsily, he rubbed grease into the meat, leaving big gobs of butter in places. He sliced a lemon and inserted it into the bird's skin. Potatoes were peeled and dropped into a pan. He did the same with the carrots and poured in tinned peas. Timer set, he put the chicken in the oven, opened a bottle of Bordeaux to breathe and made himself a large gin and tonic. He lit a cigarette and opened the back door. Haji, licking his chops, went out to defecate on the grass.

John fell back into his seat and spooled yet another fresh page. He stared at the pure white, the void. Nothing more terrifying than an empty sheet of paper. They had not parted, of course, he and Lynne. He reminded himself of that now. Sonia had faded from their lives. Other women had come and gone, women who represented an escape from the life he and Lynne had concocted for themselves. There were chances. By God, there had been some fine opportunities for separation.

Between Etchingham & London
1963

It was a chilly November morning. Lynne had sent him out, the clack-clack of keys against the platen driving her to distraction. Haji bounded expectantly on the lawn, followed by John, wearing his overcoat and the hat he'd brought back from Leningrad. He carried his Olympia into the garden, collecting the morning post along the way, and set his typewriter down on the garden table. Between bills and statements and the general clutter there was a letter forwarded from his agent. He was behind schedule with the Shakespeare novel, the quatercentenary of the Bard's birth being something of a fixed deadline. Were the publishers already demanding to see early drafts? He took a good mouthful of Stepmother's Tea and sliced the envelope with the butt of a teaspoon.

> *Dear Mr Kell,* the letter started. *I hope this missive finds you well. I am contacting you –* a woman's writing, it was clear – *in regard to your most recent novel, Inside Mr Enderby.*

He read the line again – *I am contacting you in regard to your most recent novel* – it made him want to write a hundred other novels.

> *I found it a most engaging novel. The reason for my getting in touch is I am writing an article for the Bompiani Literary Almanac, which will serve to offer some insight to the scope of English novels released this year.*

He was part of the scope of English literature, just as he had known all along. *I would be grateful if you would agree to meet me, so I may discuss your work, and future projects, for this publication.*

There was an address, *19 Elder Street, Stepney*, and a name, *Liliana Macellari*. He rolled that one around his head and over his tongue a good few times. *Liliana Macellari.* He put out his cigarette and folded the letter back inside the envelope.

John peered down at the words on the page. Young Shakespeare stood on Clopton Bridge contemplating what his future may look like to those who saw it as the past. It was schoolchildren hovering over a not-yet-dead poet's body all over again. The trick was obvious. William Shakespeare, some other Shakespeare's son, watching the rivers of time flow from the inception of Naseby to the near future of Tewkesbury to the unknown of the Severn Sea and the unfathomable of the North Atlantic Ocean. *Dear Mr Kell.* And what of John Wilson? Would his name float down the Rother and into future seas? *I hope this missive finds you well.* What of Joseph Kell and Anthony Burgess, the author skins he climbed into? *I am contacting you in regard to your most recent novel, Inside Mr Enderby.* How many of their works would survive? And who, in that dark and deep future, would connect the two writers as the one man? Would there be conspiracy theories about the origins of Joseph Kell's works? Scholars attributing them to the pen of Queen Elizabeth II, perhaps, or Lord Abergavenny? *I found it a most engaging novel.* No writer can write with future approbation in mind. Bricklayers, surely, did not anticipate their bricks to last nine hundred years. Bricklaying paid, so bricks were laid. Words paid, so words were written. *The reason for my getting in touch is I am writing an article for the Bompiani Literary Almanac, which will serve to offer some insight to the scope of English novels released this year.* To survive on through time as black marks on a white page. To continue on along the continuum, imbibed through the eyes of people from distant futures. But thoughts like these did nothing for the jobbing writer. *I would be grateful if you would agree to meet me, so I may discuss your work, and future projects, for this publication.* What price legacy when there is food to be put on the table? Reviews paid far more in spendable pound notes than literary craft. Novels paid little, so he knocked out novels. Three weeks' worth of work rendered some sixty thousand words and enough notes to pay off the gas, electric and mortgage bills. *Yours Sincerely,* only the independently wealthy, *Liliana Macellari,* had the privilege to write to further their reputation or in the name of *art.* If John had been the son of Leslie Stephen or had inherited the wealth of a merchant banker, he might have spent his time considering, rather than writing, literature. *19 Elder Street, Stepney.* But that was not the case.

He went in to the kitchen and filled the kettle. In the living room, Lynne was on the couch, cuddling one of the Siamese and nursing a glass of white wine.

Where are we on the house? he asked. The Chiswick house on Glebe Street had been purchased but there were matters for the estate agents to take care of before keys could change hands. They would squeeze another few drops from the Wilsons before the house became their own.

You've got the post, haven't you?

Nothing today. He could take the early morning train from Etchingham into Charing Cross. *I'm thinking of going in.*

Going in where? Lynne craned her neck to see him.

Into the city. See if I can get things moving.

You?

I'll go tomorrow. The kettle whistled. *Do you want one?* Lynne replied by raising her glass to her lips. He made his way back to the kitchen.

We could book a room, Lynne called.

John poured hot water over teabags piled at the bottom of his vat-like mug. *We?*

Go and see a show or something. Have a night on the town.

He stirred. *Can we afford that?*

Why don't you sell some of this lot? He peered through to the living room. There were review copies not only on bookshelves but on the dining table and mantelpiece. A pile in the hallway, more lining the stairs. They would bring in a few pounds drinking money.

He took his tea into the living room. *I only meant to visit the agent's office and see if I could gee this all up. I've got too much work on to go drinking in the West End.*

Lynne stood, the cat falling gently onto the carpet. *Just an idea, John.* She passed him and pulled the half-drunk bottle of Riesling from the fridge.

I've not said no. All I'm saying is, I've got a lot of work. Six reviews, an article for The Listener.

Forget it.

Lynne, don't walk away. If you... He stopped in the kitchen doorway. She refilled her glass. *If you really want to go, we'll go. I just thought, well, I thought I'd only be gone a few hours.*

Shift. She met him, her face lifted towards his. He could feel her warm breath. *Shift, John.* John stepped aside and Lynne took her full glass, the bottle in her other hand, and went upstairs. *I'm getting in the bath.*

John held the envelope to his mouth. He caught a scent, sweet and yet delicate. All that was required was a reply. A simple, *Thank you for your kind letter. I would, of course, be happy to discuss my work, present and future, at length. I am working on a novel currently, for the Shakespeare Centenary. Yours, Joseph Kell.* Nothing too strong, nothing too imposing. Was this how Joseph Kell wrote letters? He wasn't sure. Wilson would be more intrigued: *How did you find my novel, who else are you speaking to?* Burgess would be aloof; he'd pass it on to his agent. But Kell, he wasn't sure how Kell actually worked. It had merely been a name to cover the presence of Burgess, which was, of itself, a masking of Wilson. He rather enjoyed playing the role of Burgess. Kell was a paper name rather than a pen name. What were his politics, what had he read, what would he be writing next? How would Joseph Kell, only three years old, respond to Liliana Macellari?

John went back into the garden. He could hear water running, looked up to see Lynne dropping her nightgown and dropping the blind. He turned back to young Shakespeare, soon to make his trip to London, and started to type.

He came through the front door of Applegarth. *Lynne, I'm back.* In the kitchen he made two large gins. Haji fussed at his feet, waiting to be fed; Lynne was nowhere to be found. On the coffee table was a note, *Gone to Rose and Crown.* He fell into the sofa and drank bitterly. He had spent the entire journey back from London struggling with Shakespeare and everything he did not know about Shakespeare. Why had he been described as a schoolteacher, when there was no evidence of him ever being employed in such circumstances? Where the hell did he go between 1589 and 1592? He sank his gin and went into the kitchen to sink Lynne's.

He was not in the country, thus he was not accounted for. But where could WS have gone for three years? There was a boat. He boarded at midnight, escaping who knew what. The boat took him around the Bay of Biscay, where they docked in Tangier for a few nights, through the Strait of Gibraltar, resting at the Rock a day or two, and then into the Alboran Sea, the Balearic Sea, the Tyrrhenian Sea, and finally the Aegean Sea. Yes, John could see it all now. He poured another two gins, a force of habit. WS spent some time in Athens, where he was introduced to the story of Timon. From Athens he visits Ephesus in Turkey. Here he shares quarters with an Italian merchant who owes a great deal of money and wants only to escape home to his wife and sons. Down to the Red Sea, through the Gulf of Aden, and across the Arabian Sea, stopping briefly in India, and finally to Malaya or, as it was then, Tanah Melayu. Here, WS becomes a teacher to the children of rich Portuguese and Dutch traders. He finds himself infatuated with a Malayan women named Rahimah. No, Fatimah was better. She cannot be with him because she has followed Parameswara into Islam, but they cannot control their passion for one another. The moment they promise never to see each other again, the lovers are caught in a passionate kiss, WS's life is in danger. He absconds in the dead of night, his poems and plays safely hidden upon him in a brown leather satchel, and journeys back home. When he arrives back in London he falls ill; it appears terminal. A doctor gives him just a year to live, and WS, desperate to raise his family's status and the Shakespeare name, begins a crazed period of writing. He survives, but alas Hamnet, his boy child, does not. The legacy he has set about creating will be lost. But in these plays, WS comforts himself, the Shakespeare name will live on. Back in Tanah Melayu, Fatimah gives birth to a son she names Hajat.

The plot was sound enough, but John feared he did not have the time to write it all to a satisfactory standard. The novel must be completed by Shakespeare's quatercentenary or he would have to suffer the ignominy of having it published the year after all the Shakespeare celebrations had ended. Just getting WS to Greece would take five thousand words, the whole bloody thing was running away with him. He would have to write much in Greek and Latin and, by Christ, Cleopatra herself spoke Egyptian, Ethiopian, Hebrew, and God knew what else.

Beside Lynne's note was the day's post. An envelope that bore the sigil of the Inland Revenue, a couple of bills and a handwritten letter. He recognised the handwriting and blushed. Finishing one drink and starting the other, he tore it open. A flush of anger, of shame, of – it was all too much.

> *Dear Mr Burgess,*
>
> *I hope this missive finds you well. I am contacting you in regard to your most recent novel, A*

Clockwork Orange. I found it a most engaging
novel. The reason for my getting in touch is I
am writing an article for the Bompiani Literary
Almanac, which will serve to offer some insight to
the scope of English novels released this year.

I would be grateful if you would agree to meet me,
so I may discuss your work, and future projects,
for this publication.

Yours sincerely,
Liliana Macellari

He thought he might be sick. Joseph screwed up the letter, Anthony unravelled it.

The bitch. She's writing these to every bloody bastard bugger. I bet she's written one to sodding Muriel sodding Spark, an' all.

Don't be such a fucking kiddy. She clearly states she's writing to other bloody writers—

But you?

Yes, me. What the hell is wrong with me? I am a fine writer.

John was too drunk to stop them. Joseph and Anthony fought all night, raging about who was the better author, Burgess claiming it was he on sheer output alone, Kell sniping that productivity did not equal quality.

Lynne was dropped off by a taxi just after midnight. She came in, opened a bottle of wine, sat on the armchair, asleep in moments.

You sad prick, Kell.

Oh, piss off, Burgess.

John took control. He sat at his Olympia and wrote a letter. *Dear,* he wrote, *Miss Macellari. Thank you,* he wrote, *for your kind letter.* He would be happy to meet to discuss his work and help in any way he could. She may be aware that he had recently had a book published on the very subject of *The Novel Today,* which was its title. He suggested a place, time and date. *I am,* he wrote, *coming from Etchingham which,* she might not be aware, *is a town outside London.* There was the small matter of a new house, he informed her, he was purchasing in Chiswick, hence the place, in the afternoon, hence the time and date, which brought him to London. *If this is not convenient, then something else,* he wrote, *could be arranged. Although,* he wrote, *I so rarely find myself in London at present, what with the writing,* he wrote, *of a novel about Shakespeare set for publication in his quatercentenary year.*

She was late. The waiter moved between him and a young couple who talked first about how glad they were to be away from the baby and, from then on, about nothing but the baby. The wine was oily and tart; he decided he would order a fresh bottle before Liliana arrived. And then, as he had raised his hand to call the waiter, a woman walked in. Her hair was a rich black, like an obsidian mirror. She was beautiful, there was no doubt of that. He watched her take in the place, studious and precise. When their eyes met, he felt himself go to pieces, his hand still raised as if hailing her to him.

You are not, by any chance, Anthony Burgess, are you? she asked.

I am, he stood. Inside, Kell raged. *And you are Liliana Macellari?*

Liana. She held out her hand, firmly. John shook it weakly. Liana took off her coat, revealing a pristine white dress with a single flower running its length.

Please, have a seat. Let me take that. He snatched at her coat, and had it gently taken from him by the waiter, who pulled out a chair for Liana to sit.

Another glass, John said, shakily.

Of course, sir.

And another bottle, he added, draining what was left of the first.

By the time the waiter arrived with another bottle of miserable Greek wine, John had gathered himself. He would be Anthony Burgess, debonair and entertaining.

You have bought the house today?

Finalised today, yes. I picked up the keys moments ago. He jangled them in his hand.

How exciting. You will move from…

Etchingham.

From Etchingham?

No, I will keep the house. It has been good to me. In a writing sense, I mean. I have written several novels there. It is a quiet place. Quietness is required for the writing of novels.

But your novels are so noisy! She said it as a compliment. He took it as a compliment. *Riots and beatings and Russian parties and—*

Music.

Yes, lots of music.

You have read a number of my novels?

I have. Though not all, I am afraid.

And your favourite?

She sipped her retsina. It seemed she had never drunk retsina before. The pine flavour obviously did not agree with her. Liliana tried to close her nostrils every time she drank. *If I had to choose one, but I do not.*

Go on. For my own curiosity.

I loved A Clockwork Orange.

A minor work.

But with major ideas. Major statements about the world. She stopped, the waiter serving up their starters. A medley of Greek tapas. Taramasalata and pitta bread. Dolmades, like fat slugs marinated in their own juices. Keftedes Arni. Baba Ghanoush, which is not Greek but a welcome imposter.

Well, he said, *thank you for saying so. And tell me about your work at the Bompiani Literary Almanac, who else are you speaking with?*

Many. She put a dolmade in her mouth and chewed. *You will know them?*

I have my literary friends. John wondered if Shakespeare had ever eaten rice wrapped in vine leaves. He found it very easy to imagine WS sampling the foods of the world.

Muriel Spark. Have you read her most recent novel?

He coughed on his mouthful of pork. *I have.*

She is a great talent, I think. She chewed. *John Fowles. He is new.*

The Collector?

Correct. Yes. With her elegant hand she dabbed a slice of pitta bread into mushy aubergine. *Joseph Kell. He wrote a very funny book. But Kell is not very productive,* she continued, *two books in three years. Whereas you,* she made a sound and a gesture of an explosion, which put him immediately at ease.

Yes, well. A man must work to eat.

In that case, Anthony, you must eat very well. How will anyone ever keep up with you?

I'm not sure. He drank down half a glass of retsina. It really was quite awful.

What are you writing now, if you don't mind my asking?

No, I don't mind, don't mind at all. I'm writing a novel about Shakespeare, kind of a celebration of the man, joining the dots. More about the man than the myth, if you see what I mean.

He worked to eat. She bit into a meatball.

Exactly that. He has no sense of the Shakespeare we know now, the Shakespeare of the RSC. No, he writes plays because plays put food on the table, because plays are demanded of him.

And novels are demanded of you?

No, no. No one would mind very much if I never wrote again, I should think, but it is how I make my living. Now, at least.

Now?

Yes, I was, in another life, a schoolteacher, if you can believe it. I taught in Malaya.

You gave it up for writing? She scooped up the last of the taramasalata with the last piece of pitta. Refreshing to be faced with Italian hunger instead of British politeness.

I had a kind of episode. I collapsed in Malaya while teaching. They told me I had a tumour in my head, he pointed, *and just a year to live. So, I thought I had better start writing. I was under the impression a writer would earn much more than a teacher in a year, although that proved not to be the case.*

I would think there are very few teachers who have a house in the country and a house in the city.

I have no doubt about that, dear Algy. John laughed. Liliana did not, it seemed, get the reference. *I'm going to go ahead and order some more wine. This,* he held up his empty glass, *is not going down well.*

Don't order on my account. I cannot drink too much, I have work to do later.

He called the waiter over, *Can I see the wine list again, please? But this is a celebration, it is not every day I get to have lunch with a beautiful lady.* It was too much, he knew it was too much. The waiter returned with the list. John busied himself with it. *The Sancerre, I think.* It was by far the most expensive wine on the list, besides the champagne he toyed with ordering.

A very good wine.

Good wine, he quoted, *is a good familiar creature, if it be well used.* He lit a cigarette. *Apologies if I embarrassed you then, it's just being with you, an intelligent, sweet lady,* he was doing it again, *I'm just very pleased to have met you.*

You are very kind.

He had brought her back here, to Glebe Street. Entirely bare and entirely empty. He found, in the upstairs airing cupboard, some pillows and cushions. They opened another bottle of wine, bought from Kleftiko along with two large wine glasses.

So, Anthony, what is your Shakespeare novel about? I mean, which part of his life?

Centrally it is about his relationship with the Dark Lady. He thought of it now: have the Dark Lady come to WS, have Liana come to him. *While his wife is at home, in the country, Will falls for an exotic woman in London.*

I see. It is a romance? Liliana looked comfortable, lounging on cushions. John sat against the wall flicking ash onto the threadbare carpet.

Of sorts. It is about sex, so there is romance attached.

But not love? I get the impression you are suspicious of love. She accepted another glass of wine. *Those who do love are so often separated by death, in your writing, do you see? Mr Winterbottom killed by his friend who loved him; Beatrice-Joanna loves her son, dead; Alex, I think, loves no one, but loves the him now dead, the him that was free.*

He felt a hard lump in his throat, and sinew between his teeth. *I don't... There is very little a novel can say about love. Love comes at the end, if at all, as some kind of reward for the characters—*

And the readers.

Yes, yes, I see that.

Will your William find love in the end?

He crouched down, now, against the wall and smoked. There had been, from John especially, too much honesty. He had described, in great detail, the loveless marriage he persevered with. Liliana had recently divorced a writer by the name of Ben Johnson. John hated him with all of his drunken rage. An Italian Catholic divorce was no small matter, she told John, but sometimes you must do what is best for yourself. And, she said, she hated God. But this was after they had shared three bottles of Sancerre, when all nuance and specificity had gone out of the window.

He told her he could not bring himself to divorce. *Lynne would have to*, he remembered saying it, he said it out loud with only Haji to listen, *die for me to be free of her.* Liliana looked on him with pity. Carefully, she put her wine glass down and crawled over to him. She kissed him and, he remembered vividly, it was like being kissed for the first time. He felt faintly ridiculous, like one of these greasy-haired teens he saw necking outside confectioners. It wasn't long, though, before he had forgotten all about that, about the world outside. He delighted in kissing her. As she continued to talk about the indelible harm lovelessness could do to a person, John tried to put his mouth against hers, she pulled away but only to finish her point, which she had, by that time, forgotten.

They made love. Liliana set the cushions out, drunkenly, trying to create something approximating a bed. She laughed, bent over, on her knees, trying to get the damn things to go where she wanted. John attempted to help, just there, it had happened just there in front of where he sat now, tired and alone, beneath the place Lynne would hang her precious painting. He sat and watched the scene play out before him. Liliana pulling him towards her. This beautiful young woman pulling this ageing man on top of her, and inching down her underwear. There had been something thrilling about it. No, not something, everything about her was thrilling. Even in memory, it was all thrilling. She had made him feel, how to explain? It was like Jesus making the crippled walk again. Synapses fired that had lain extinguished. He had had, on a trip to Marrakesh earlier in the year, his first taste of opium, with William Burroughs, an American writer famed for opium-tasting. This was better. This was freedom.

John watched himself roll over, a cushion causing his back to arch painfully. He freed it and threw it across the room. *I have a confession to make*, John said, sitting now, stubbing a cigarette out.

What kind of confession? How had she made herself look so elegant, here on this derelict floor?

I, he lit a cigarette, then and now, *I write under a pen name, occasionally.* He took a drag and passed it to Liliana, remembered passing it. *I'm also,* he fastened his trousers, *Joseph Kell.*

Liliana laughed soft plumes of smoke. She coughed a little, took a sip of wine, and handed him his cigarette.

She stood over him. In her hand she held something. It was morning, the room illuminated by sun. He must have fallen asleep at his desk. What was it she was clutching?

What's the time?

Late.

He rubbed his eyes, *What's that?*

I was going to ask you the same thing. He saw now she held two pieces of paper in her hands.

Lynne? She left the room. He got up quickly. Dressed quickly. How much had he written last night? He checked his Olympia and found out. There was a simple explanation, he told himself, before telling her. It was part of the novel he was writing, a letter from Will to his Dark Lady. He said, *Have you been messing about with my work? I'm missing a bit of my work.* The words rang hollow. He said, *Did you take something from my room? I've got a deadline, Lynne.* He buttoned up his shirt and went down to the living room.

I would have sussed it out, you know. Even if you hadn't have left these lying round the house.

They weren't lying around, he said.

No, but you were.

Lynne, he couldn't help it, *a poor pun, even by—*

Don't you dare! She set upon him, pinning him to the wall. *Don't you dare start that linguistic bollocks with me now. This is deadly serious, John. How long has it been going on?*

It's part of my novel. My Shakespeare novel.

Bullshit. You don't bullshit me.

This was the first—

How long? She seemed like she might tear her hair out. Hers or his.

I am telling you that this was the first time.

A one-night stand? Lynne sought an answer in his silence. *No, of course not.* She read, 'My wife is ill, as I said. I cannot leave her.'

His stomach twisted. *Enough, Lynne.*

But she continued, *'I have dreamt for the longest time of leaving her.' Are you going to leave me?*

Isn't that what you've been waiting for? Isn't that what you've been bloody well hoping for, for Christ's sake? You've wanted to be free of me for years, Lynne. Years.

Free? John, look at me. Are you really planning on leaving me now? Like this? Alone? Alone in fucking Etchingham, while you fuck her in the house I bought – yes, I bought, with my dad's money. Have you gone mad, John?

I am not the only one who has been unfaithful.

That was years ago—

Now who's the bloody liar?

What the hell are you talking about?

Marrakesh. Don't roll your eyes at me. Marrakesh, I came back from a night alone, after you'd told me you were too sodding tired, and I come back to find you getting into bed with someone.

Getting into bed? Are you fucking mad? You are!

Just a kid, he was. A bloody, he felt embarrassed saying it, *gigolo.*

She laughed. She laughed and coughed; coughed heavily and had to sit down. *He was a member,* she cleared her throat, *of staff. A barman or something. I went down to get a glass of water—*

A bloody gin, more like—

And I, she tried to clear her throat once more, her eyes welled. *I collapsed, John. I'd been vomiting and you went off to get pissed up. I needed help.* She cried, her face still full of rage, her eyes pitiful with sorrow.

That's not... He tried to play the scene out again. Strapping Berber lad in a striped waistcoat, climbing into bed. Why the hell would he get into bed with his waistcoat on? Where had Lynne found him? It made no sense. *There've been other times, too many to mention.* He wished he could stop. Lynne sobbed weakly, she looked all but broken, yet he couldn't keep his anger in check. He could not, when asked, show her compassion.

You are a bastard. If you think you're going to leave me and shack up with her in my house – my house! –

Lynne—

– you've another think coming, Jack. You really bloody have. He winced, he couldn't help it, the name cut through him. *You think you're some kind of big shot, Jack? Been on the telly a few times and now you're summat special. Is that what you think, Jack, eh? Some kind of fucking celebrity! And you need a pretty new thing on your arm? Sad bastard, Jackie, you're a sad bastard.*

Lynne—

She call you Anthony? His face reddened further. She carried on, *Anthony's place in London, where we make love.*

Lynne, please—

Anthony takes me to parties, to restaurants. Anthony is a great lover. She drew closer to him.

Lynne.

Anthony – and closer *– tells me that he will take me to Rome, to America –* into his ear *– to Malaya.*

I said, I am sorry.

No you never. Say it now.

Do you think this is easy for me?

She whispered, *Do you think I give a shit?*

We haven't, but he found he couldn't say it.

Go on. She grabbed him, pressed her thumb and forefinger into his cheeks, and moved his face to face hers. *We don't fuck any more, is that it? Haven't fucked in you can't remember how long. Easy enough to blame me. How could you fuck me when*

I'm like this? Changing bloody bastard bloody pads every hour.
It was you who stopped, not me.

It was you, he said, his mouth held tight by her grip.

She drank heavily, the television up loud as punishment.
John trapped in his room. He would leave her, he knew that
now. Liliana had been the catalyst, the instigation he needed.
He began to plot. Lynne couldn't keep both houses, and she
couldn't move to Chiswick. It would be best for her if he let her
remain in Etchingham. He would take the London house and
they would continue in some ways as they had for years, John
working and Lynne being cared for. But not by him, not any
more. They would still be husband and wife. He would still want
to see her. Was that true? He couldn't imagine his life without
Lynne. But there was a better life without her.

He stamped downstairs and made a noisy gin and tonic.
Through the crack in the living room door he could see she
was watching some drama, an older man discussing melons
with a young woman. John went in and sat down. Lynne paid
no attention, exhaled smoke, inhaled Hock. He cleared his
throat, slapped his hand down on the armrest, farted loudly.
She continued to ignore him with utter conviction.

Glass drained, he got up with excessive grunts and barrelled
back to the kitchen. He poured and drank another gin and
slim. Humph, he dropped down into his chair. Lynne tutted.
He tried to catch her eye, watching for a change in her face,
while she stroked one of her horrible cats. He would take Sandy
to Chiswick with him. And Haji. Haji would need walks. Lynne
could barely drag herself upstairs to bed.

He wanted to tell her then and there. I'm leaving you, Lynne.
I'm going and there's nothing you can do about it, nothing at
all. There'll be no divorce, and you can stay here as long as you
want. I'm taking the dog and Sandy. Don't try to argue, I've
made my decision. I may move Liliana Macellari in with me.

We will make love, while you are here alone. What will you do when I'm not here Lynne? Drink, of course. No one to make you mutton stews or change your bedclothes, buy new bedclothes. You could move someone in, couldn't you? You've always been good at finding men to take care of you.

She had put on a lot of weight. Her hands were balloon-like, tight and fat. Her skin sagged in places, was taut in others. She was an old woman. A sick woman, it occurred to him. If he saw her on the street or in a pub he would wonder what she had, what sickness had taken her. Her sallow, jaundiced skin, bloodshot eyes, lips permanently t-t-t-trembling, her whole body in a kind of constant frisson. He drained his glass, she poured herself more wine, holding the bottle high by the base, patiently waiting for the very last drop to fall. John got up, quieter this time. He lit a panatella and went into the garden.

It was cold December. Horrible weather. Haji followed him out and pissed on the dormant rose bush. Just in his shirt, sleeves rolled, John shivered and chattered. Etchingham in December, not a place to be alone. She could cope. She would have to cope, there was nothing else for her to do but bloody cope.

He threw his fag end across the garden. *Come.* Haji followed him in. John made another drink for himself and opened a fresh bottle of wine, placed it gently on the coffee table. Lynne did not look, she fixed her eyes on the television screen and Harry H. Corbett. He looked at her again, searching for the woman who had betrayed him, that beautiful young woman who had made him a cuckold time and time again. Her eyes were wet, wavering, weak. He made his way upstairs and sat at his typewriter. The work would not wait. WS would find no solace with his Dark Lady. Sickness had already gripped him. Sickness would define his last days, not love or companionship. Sickness.

He ran his tongue around his mouth, the bitterness of gin, the sharp sweet of tonic, the dank of hours past. Downstairs, yawning, scratching at stubble and rubbing sore eyes, John went through his usual ritual of making tea and toast, letting Haji out to do his business on the lawn. He carried the tray upstairs into Lynne's room, placed it down and took in the image. Lynne, fully dressed still, lying on her side, clutching at her belly, knees lifting up towards her bowed head. Blood-stained and vomit-covered. Her face a mask of red and beige. Thickly caked, so you might be able to peel it back and have an exact replica of her visage. Blood-soaked sheets behind her, before her, encrusted from the waist down. He touched her arm, which was wet with sick, and gently rocked her. She began to cry, a child's cry, and baby's tears. John left her and went downstairs. The dial tone hummed, wavering as he kept himself upright. A panatella vibrated in his right hand, telephone receiver held against his shoulder; three matches spent before he managed to get the thing lit. He phoned Doctor Stinson, who did not answer at first.

There had been a second, in that rocking, before that crying, when he thought she was dead. What had he felt? Sadness, sadness for Llewela Jones, the girl he had met back in 1940 when she was just eighteen, who was now dead. Anger at his wife for letting this happen, for doing this to herself. Pain at the idea of having to sort through her things and throw things away and keep things because they had come to have meaning and value even though they were not his. Grief that Lynne was no more and that that was their last conversation, *Viewpoint* was the last television programme she had ever watched, Hock the last wine she had ever drunk, that she had eight cigarettes left in the packet when she went, that she was dead. And grief because she wasn't dead, she was merely dying still. Pain that it was not over and he would have to suffer at least one more morning such as this. Pain, real pain, that she had not made it easier on both of them and simply let it all draw to a close. Anger that she would not just fucking die. Sadness that he felt this way, that he had revealed these deeply held feelings when all he should have felt was sorrow, compassion and remorse.

The receptionist answered the phone on the third ring. John marvelled at the calm in his voice. It was calm enforced by his father, who had treated any show of emotion as a kind of hysteria. *Hello, yes, I've found my wife in rather something of a state, could I be put through to Doctor Stinson?* He tapped ash off his panatella. *Yes, well, there's been a lot of bleeding.* Pause. *Yes, I'll wait, thank you.* The doctor told him an ambulance should be called for. John duly hung up and dialled 999. He tried to clean her up a little. He used a flannel to wipe away the sick and blood from her mouth, cleaned between her legs. Under the bed he found the empty medicine bottle. Another empty medicine bottle. He hid them in the bathroom cabinet, told the paramedics nothing when the ambulance arrived.

Lynne lay silent but awake on the gurney. All those plans, he thought, all that thinking, it had been fantasy, a dizzy expedition into the mountains of possibility. At intervals she sobbed and the paramedic would try to calm her, rolling his eyes at his colleague. John hated the way he spoke to her, like she were some kind of invalid. Even when she asked questions, she was treated as though catatonic. John wanted to punch him in the bloody face.

She can hear you quite well, he said. *Why not answer her question rather than talk yourself in circles?*

Please try to remain calm.

I'm not bloody calm. John folded his arms, impotent. He scowled at the paramedic's receding hairline.

When they arrived at the Hawkhurst Community Hospital, doctors gathered and doctors murmured and doctors shook their heads. It was a much played-out performance, one John and Lynne had seen time and again. This was certainly not their first visit of this kind, not even their first visit to this hospital. She was wheeled into a little room, more like a bed and breakfast than a ward, and lifted onto a bed. The doctors followed, shaking their heads, muttering this and that about her general state.

And you say, one of them said, *you found her this way?*

This morning, yes. John watched a nurse insert an IV drip into Lynne's arm.

Just fluids, she reassured. Lynne began to sob again.

This isn't the first time?

No, but it is worse. Another nurse pulled the curtain around them. She took a pair of scissors and began to cut Lynne's clothes off. John thought he might be sick.

What medication is your wife taking?

I'm sorry, I didn't quite –

Who is your GP?

Could you – is there a chair?

What time this morning?

I'm just a bit –

Did you ring the ambulance straight – Please, I can't – Is this a regular occurr – Do you have in-house – I'm not feeling – Does your wife have an – Could I have a glass of – impolitic relationship with alcohol, Mr Wilson? Mr Wilson?

John woke up in a bed next to his wife. Lynne was a kind of grey, a sort of dirty beige. They had found, in the garden of King's Pavilion, snakeskin discarded from shedding. She looked the same colour, the same cellular appearance, as if her skin were being held up to the light, all blood and muscle removed. He felt queasy again. He pulled himself up and found he too had an intravenous drip in his arm. It was taped down well. Lynne was fast asleep. She would live, he felt it in his bones. Her behaviour, her actions would not change, she would continue to kill herself slowly, or not so very slowly, but she would live some time yet. The curtain had been lifted.

For so many years, John had somehow convinced himself her drinking was more personality flaw than addiction, more of an inconvenience than a death sentence. Lynne's bad behaviour was legend, yet he had denied himself the obvious truth: she was sick. She was desperately unwell. The blood, the constant stream. How many doctors had told him she must never drink again?

If she drinks again, she will die. He pictured them all, white gowned, lined up with clipboards, repeating the phrase in unison. He knew it was true, yet he also believed it to be hyperbole. His doctor in Brunei had said it. Lynne wasn't even his patient. That time she had fainted while visiting John. Another embarrassing episode.

A doctor came in, saw Lynne sleeping, and approached John. *How are you feeling?*

Somewhat humiliated, but otherwise fine. He hid the arm that held the cannula, embarrassed at the fuss he had caused.

Very good. Your wife, on the other hand. He turned his gaze to Lynne and shook his head. *There's no other way of putting this, Mr Wilson. If your wife drinks again, she will die.*

Yes, I see.

I hope you do. If you have any affection towards your wife, you will help her. I would recommend getting the house empty of all alcohol. If you want to help her, don't drink in front of her, don't keep anything in the house.

That seems a little excessive. I work from home.

As I say, if you value your wife's well-being, you will do this.

I was going to— John caught himself and said no more.

You were going to?

It's unimportant.

Please. The doctor sat on the end of John's bed. Both of them checked Lynne was still asleep.

I was going to leave her. Today. Yesterday. I'm not sure which one. We've bought a house in London, Chiswick. I was – There's someone else, might be someone else. The doctor said nothing. John waited for some kind of reply, the silence growing pregnant. *She tried to kill herself,* he finally said. *She's done it before.*

How?

Pills. Painkillers.

134

Most likely, she vomited them up.

She did it to get at me.

Mr Wilson, the doctor sighed, took off his glasses, rubbed his eyes. *Whatever your wife did last night was merely a punctuation, a sudden plummet on what is already a downward fall. Your wife did not try to kill herself last night. Try to understand, she is killing herself now. She has been for some time. But I think you already know that.* He put his glasses back on. *I'll ask one of the nurses to discharge you.* He checked Lynne's chart, made a note, and left.

London
1968

L ynne woke and felt at once better. She wanted tea and hot cross buns. Could you get hot cross buns in February, or was it too far from Easter? John would see to it, the shop around the corner did all sorts. If not hot cross buns, then teacakes. *John*, she called. She didn't want to get up. Today, she would have tea and breakfast in bed. *John*, she called again. This room, so bare. She had meant to get the place decorated. It had never truly felt like a home, just John's workplace with rooms attached. She shouldn't have bought it. For four months, she would not even acknowledge there was a Chiswick house, not after what he had done. John reacted badly, of course. Reacted worse when she told him she wanted the house to be exorcised. It wasn't a joke. He thought it was a joke, but it wasn't. Lynne was dead serious.

John, are you in? She couldn't hear the typewriter, she'd bloody be able to hear the typewriter if he was at it. Damned thing. They might buy some new curtains, get Terry to recommend a decorator and get the wallpaper done. She could get a catalogue from Laura Ashley. It was her house, after all. John wasn't interested in that sort of thing. *John, can you not bloody hear me?* She was losing her appetite for tea and toast, for hot cross buns. A headache was coming on, and that taste. *Fuck*, she spat. Meat extract, dirty Bovril drink. *John, please, John.* She tried to spit the taste from her mouth. There was water beside her, she drank and the taste only deepened. Nothing in her stomach but wine and a few chips, she could feel the acid lifting through her. *Jesus.* There was someone coming. *John.* He was at the door. *John, I need you.* She felt sure he was at the door.

She had bought herself a wig, which he thought preposterous. She didn't need a wig. But when she put it on, he was hit with the shock of it, the years rolled back. He saw time's effect on her only now when she suddenly looked like his Lynne once more.

You don't like it. She watched him in the mirror, his eyes wet, misty.

You look, he took a breath, *you look lovely, Lynne.* He kissed her on the cheek, her skin sallow and dry. *You look lovely.*

She smiled, she saw it was true. But he could not unsee what he had seen. The girl in the shop had shown her how to apply foundation. Not too much, you'll quickly lose sight of how much you've applied. Blend into the neck, she'd told Lynne, who looked at her sagging neckline. He watched intently, as if she were some magician and he had been permitted to see the trick behind the curtain. These moments of silence were as close as they came. No smashing of keys or glasses or smashing of words against the other's words. It felt good to have some peace between them.

She stood and lifted her arms. Silence. John had helped her on with her dress. Lynne had chosen the caftan; it looked like it had been sewn together from Van Gogh's Sunflowers. The canvas clung to her. She watched herself turning in the mirror, feeling a warm sense of pride move up and flush her cheeks.

Well, she said.

Very good. Yes. Very nice. And then, *I'll check the car is here.* He left.

She took two more pills and a good slug of gin to help them down. She made her way downstairs as he was putting his jacket on.

What do you think? he asked.

You look bloody awful, she told him, no hint of irony. *Who bought you that tie?* She lifted it to her face and flicked it away.

I like it.

At least get the bloody knot right. She pulled the thing off, John choking under the strain. *Bend down.* She threaded the tie and straightened it out. Her eyes twitched and blinked as she fiddled around his neck. Impatient, she pulled hard, the knot tight to his throat. *Done,* she pronounced. It was all wrong, but there was no time. John looked in the mirror, a bulk of a man with a schoolboy's tie.

They arrived to a great mob of flashing lights and yelling. Lynne peered out of the taxi window to see who they were shouting at. A couple posed, she seemed more accustomed than him. He was, from what Lynne could see, through the flashes of camera bulbs, a short, big-nosed man. The woman on his arm was blonde and angular. Long legs, a big bit of fur over her shoulders. She was not pretty, she was too provocative for that. Terry had come round and opened the door. He helped Lynne to her feet and into the lightning storm. She wanted to see this woman up close. Her hair straight, the roots showing, but not in a sluttish way. As Lynne got nearer, the girl draped her elongated arms over the short man's shoulders. His hair was scruffy, long sideburns, in the way men were wearing it. Quite effeminate, it seemed to her, but Lynne had seen some right brutes with similar styles. The girl turned and their eyes met. She gave Lynne a big, white-toothy smile. A glamorous smile. Lynne ran her tongue over her own teeth, touching the false tooth, and gave the girl a closed-mouth though fulsome smile in return. John pulled at her arm.

Come on, they're not interested in us.

She followed John towards the entrance. *Who is that, John?*

Polanski. He's a director.

And her?

An actress. She was in one of his films, I think.

Isn't she bonny.

They climbed the stairs, Lynne holding onto John, John holding on to the handrail. A slow ascent.

Inside there were a great many more photographers taking a great many more photographs of vigorous beauty. John sat Lynne down, lit her a cigarette and was called over to another table, all waving and gesticulating.

Champagne, madam?

Go on then. Another stunner, in a black waistcoat and blouse, placed a tall foaming flute on the table.

Enjoy your evening, the girl said.

Might as well leave a couple, save you coming back again, Lynne told her.

John was talking to two old couples, all nodding in unison, laughing politely as one. He was pointing in Lynne's direction, no doubt inviting them over to join them. She didn't want to speak to old people. She had no interest in old people, she never had. Using the back of her chair and the table, she eased herself from her seat. Lynne polished off her first glass of champagne and took the second with her, shuffling towards a table of bright young things.

Who are you lot, then? She sat in an empty seat.

They looked at each other, laughing slightly at this woman and her hairpiece. One of the women scowled at the man next to her and said, *I'm Mary, I'm a singer.*

You're Welsh.

That's right.

Are you very famous? The table laughed again.

I'm not sure, Mary said, thoughtfully. *Am I?* She asked the young man beside her.

I should say you probably are.

What about you? Lynne asked him.

No, I'm not famous at all, the table roared, even the pretty Welsh one.

Why do I feel like you're taking the piss? The table went quiet.

Another woman said, *And what about you? What do you do?*

Me? Nothing. I'm the wife of someone who does something.
She looked at the other women sitting at the table. *He writes books. Not very good books, but he's written a lot of them. He's over there,* she nodded behind her.

That's Anthony Burgess, isn't it? One of the men asked.

John, he's called. Or Jack.

They're making a film of his. The Stones are going to be in it.

Are they? How fab, the Welsh girl said to Lynne.

John came over and said, *Good evening, everyone. Lynne,* he placed a drink next to her.

Your wife says you're a writer, Mary said.

Well, I consider myself a composer who also writes books.

Lynne groaned. *Here we bloody go,* she said. The table laughed, John's face reddened.

He said, *Lynne, come and say hello to Angus. We're on this table here, look. Places reserved.*

It was nice to meet you, Mary said, as John helped Lynne from her seat.

You too. You're lucky, you know. Getting old is shit. She followed John over to their table, where writers were talking about writerly things. The waitress, unbidden, placed another two glasses in front of Lynne.

Angus was saying to the other old people at the table, *We really must get Tony to tell us about this big Hollywood thing he's working on.*

Tony, Lynne sneered.

John laughed him off, *No, no, no. I'm trying to present myself as a reputable writer, Angus.*

How much are they paying, eh? Who's in it? Tell us everything, Angus insisted.

Well, if he's doing that, Lynne finished another glass, *I'm going to have to get extremely pissed.*

She left John boring on about his Shakespeare musical. Who, anyway, would want to watch a musical about plays that had no music in them? It made no sense to her and sounded like it would be a bloody disaster. Why John had to get himself into these things she didn't know. He had more than enough on his plate, what with writing for all the different papers and working on his books and reading books for reviews. She made her way to the bar. A barman, shining up a brandy glass with a cloth, nodded towards her.

Free? she asked.

What would you like?

Gin. Have you got any Jenever?

Bombay Sapphire or Gordon's.

Double Gordon's and slim.

He made her drink without enthusiasm. If she'd been the actress, whatever her name was, Lynne was sure his service would have come with a song and a bloody dance.

Lynne? Lynne Jones?

Lynne recognised the voice; she turned and recognised the face. *Sonia Brownell.*

Orwell, Sonia corrected flatly, but smiled and said, *I recognised you straight away. Lynne Jones. Look at you.* Sonia meant it as a compliment, but Lynne felt horribly self-conscious. *How are you?*

Are you having a drink?

I'll have what you're having.

Excuse me, Lynne called over the bar. *Two of those.* He would never give that look to a beautiful woman, jumped-up little shit.

How long has it been?

I'd prefer not to know.

Twenty years.

We don't look that old, do we? Christ, we do. Well, there's nothing for it, then. She lifted their highballs and handed one to Sonia. *We'll just have to get paralytic.* They clinked glasses. Lynne watched Sonia take a drink. She'd aged well, considering everything Lynne had heard. Big drinker was the rumour. Bit of a state. There had been many occasions when Lynne had meant to make contact with Sonia. They had been so close for a while. She knew the reason. Even now the past was closing in on them.

Is John here? Or do I call him Anthony now?

Our Jack? Lynne did her best Manc accent. *He's over there with them. I'm sure he'll be over soon. Always had a thing for you, didn't he?*

Don't be silly.

Did you two ever...?

No! God, I wouldn't have done that.

What did they talk about now? Dead George? How's the kid, Sonia? What've you been doing these twenty years? Lynne knew most of it, the failed marriage to the homosexual, the affairs with whoever she could get her hands on.

So, tell me about yourself, Lynne. Where are you now?

Chiswick. Chiswick and Etchingham, Sussex.

Very nice. All that writing has done well for you then.

It's mainly mine. Parents dead. I was told to invest in property. What about you?

Oh, not far from here. I've a little place in France too.

Très bien. Très agréable.

Lynne listened distractedly. She drained her glass and placed it beside Sonia's. *I'll get us another.* She walked the few steps back to the bar, the surly bartender still polishing glasses. *Two more,* she told him. *This time, pour like you're not paying for the sodding gin yourself.* He picked up a metal spirit measure. *Not with that,* she shouted over. He scowled but did what she said. *Keep going.* He poured. *That's fine.*

Sonia laughed. *Lynne Jones.*

Wilson, Lynne sharply corrected, caught Sonia's stung look and let out a howl of laughter. *What's the point of a free bar if you're given Methodist measures?* They took their drinks and found an empty table.

You do look well, Sonia said, just to say something.

Lynne looked her old friend dead in the eye. She saw, underneath the mascara and make-up, bloodshot eyes and a familiar weariness. *I'm dying, Sonia.*

You're...

It's okay, you don't have to say anything. I don't know why I'm telling you. I've been dying for a long time now.

But you look—

That's kind of you. You were always kind. You weren't always nice, but you were always kind. She put her hand on Sonia's. Both shaking, their shaking cancelling out the other's. *And you?*

I'm tired. I've been putting together this collection of Eric's work. There's so many enemies out there, Lynne. They'd prefer me dead. I'm all that's between them and Eric. Vultures.

You need to take better care.

And you? Should you be drinking that?

We're celebrating. She squeezed Sonia's hand, *Old friends.* They touched glasses, Sonia on the verge, Lynne offering her a napkin from the table. *We're okay. We're fine.*

Had she ever been friends with Sonia? Who was to say now? Women like us, Lynne thought of the pair of them in their early twenties, vivacious, self-sufficient, and saw that women like them never truly had friends. No matter how many people orbited around them, a deep sadness, a deeper mistrust coursed through Lynne's and Sonia's blood. They had good reason to be friends. Both of them had been aliens in London, which made them both exotic to the rarefied world they had inhabited. They had been introduced as kindred spirits by Caitlin Macnamara, who thought them the only English women who had toured war-shadowed Europe. Sonia had travelled to Romania and Poland, where the war was already escalating, while Lynne had travelled with John a year later to Belgium, France, Holland, and Luxembourg. They talked about the threat that seemed to envelop the continent. Lynne told Sonia of the fear that pervaded France, Sonia recalled salivating Polish men who could not wait to conquer the world. Well, France had been right to fear and the Poles had merely caught a whiff of the violent fever that would strike out at them first. She looked at Sonia now and could see Sonia from then, from 1944, Sonia holding court in Fitzrovia pubs. Posh blokes in swanky coats made to look threadbare, looking to find out if Cyril Connolly would publish their bloody poetry. Buying her and Lynne drinks, chatting them up with their ever so well-spoken lines. And then that night. As soon as she thought of it, she was there, standing at that bar and him saying, *Evening, ma'am.* He leant into the bar so that their heads were the same height. *How are you this fine evening?*

Very well.

There had been other American GIs, they were everywhere, forever buying British girls drinks, fucking them while their British boyfriends were on the battlefield.

Who's next, the bartender interrupted. When a short, bespectacled man behind began to place his order the GI straightened up and swung round.

Hey, hey. Don't you Brits let ladies go first? His friends, three other American soldiers, crowded round the little man, who could only cower and say, *I didn't realise there was—*

Didn't realise. He turned back to Lynne. *What'll you have miss?*

Half a pint, Lynne told the barman.

She'll have a pint, the GI said. *Sorry about that. Some guys, eh?*

It's fine. Thank you. The barman placed her drink in front of her and she held out the money.

Can't have a lady paying for her drinks, can we boys? He looked for agreement and found three nodding heads. *Your friend don't want one?* He looked over to Sonia who was talking to two older men.

Not this round. Lynne took her drink and went back to their table.

Maybe we'll come and join you ladies, the GI called behind her.

Lynne sat, the two men said their goodbyes to Sonia and left. *Who's he?* Sonia asked Lynne.

Some Yank trying it on. Says they're coming over. Going to take us out, I reckon.

I'd like to see them try.

The pub was filling up. The great and the good of Fitzrovia. Writers, artists, curators from the British Museum, Lynne recognised nearly all of them, Sonia knew all of them. Sonia was about to face the now busy bar when one of the barmen set down two glasses of sherry. *From the lads*, he nodded over to the group of American GIs.

What do you think they want? Sonia asked.

They're probably asking the same of us.

The GIs, their names something like Hank and Butch and Johnny and Scotty, raised their glasses from the bar at the two women, who in turn raised their glasses back. They continued to stand them drinks. Two gins, then two ports, two glasses of white wine, two halves of bitter. The glasses were lining up around their table, the women not particularly keen on half of what had been offered. After two watered-down Scotches arrived, Lynne wandered over, glass in hand.

No don't, Lynne.

Thanks for this, she put the glass down in front of the group, *but I take mine neat.* They laughed. The broadest of them, hair slicked with pomade, turned and put his hand on the bar, creating a barrier between Lynne and the other three.

You want another?

Go on then. She turned to Sonia, winking.

Barkeep, the GI called, *another one of these things*, he held the short glass in his hand and rotated it, the spirit rolling around inside. *Neat?*

Neat, she replied. Lynne took a cigarette from a soft pack on the bar and waited for a light.

Neat, barkeep. Make it five of 'em. He lit her cigarette and stared searchingly into her eyes.

So, where are you lot from then?

Oh, all over. He laughed, his friends laughed with him.

Five glasses were placed in front of him. He slid one over to Lynne, *For you darlin'*, and drained another. The rest of the crew followed suit, downing their drinks, one of them coughing and spluttering, the other two grabbing at him, pushing and pulling him about as he tried to get his breath.

Cheers, then, Lynne smiled, necking her drink and sliding the glass towards him.

How about another? Invite your friend over too. He smiled his broad, American smile, revealing teeth he was clearly proud of.

You're not my type, Lynne replied, holding her ring finger before him. *And whisky's not my drink.* She returned to her table to a barrage of hoots and whistles.

Goddamn, these Brits are something else.

Sonia put her book back in her bag. *Do you have to?*

Just a bit of fun.

With them? I can't imagine any of them being much fun. Anyway, Sonia changed the subject, *Cyril and Stephen will be here in a minute.*

Don't you want to have one night talking about something other than bloody books and sodding poems? She looked back over at the GI, but he was no longer looking her way. The Americans had grown rowdy, jeered, pinned down the smaller one and forced a pint down him. He spluttered and gagged, but when they pulled him up he laughed along with the rest. *Your round,* she said, heading to the bathroom.

When Lynne returned there were two glasses of sweet Vermouth on the table. Sonia hadn't touched hers.

From the barbarians, Sonia said. *I told them I didn't want them, but he wouldn't let up.*

It was about 7.30pm. Uniforms and civilians, groups of people trying to have a quiet drink, while the Yanks bawled and catcalled.

A drink's a drink, Lynne took a draught of Vermouth. Not to her liking, she set it down. The GI watched her.

So, this is how it goes here, hey? What's wrong with these? He picked the Vermouth glasses up, spilling liqueur over his thick, hairy hands.

Piss off, now, Lynne said.

Just ignore him, Lynne.

Ignore me? Is that what you said? You drink at my expense and now you want to ignore me. No fucking way, lady.

Hey, Andros, one of the other GIs placed his hand on his arm, *come and have a drink.*

I'm having a drink, he drained one of the glasses and let it fall.

Lynne walked round the table to meet him. She was only a couple of inches shorter than him. *You go back over there with your friends. Go on.* She could see in his eyes he was drunker than she'd realised. He stared, almost through her.

Come on, Andy, man. Leave the girls alone.

Do what your friend tells you, Lynne advised.

Blinking, he seemed to come out of a trance. He looked at her closely, shifting his face towards hers. *Cunt,* he whispered; the word hit her like a smack. He turned his head as if to go and spat at her. Shock turned to rage turned to shame.

How dare you, Sonia was up, red-faced, as livid with Lynne as she was with the soldier.

Andros, he was pulled away and back to the bar. There was a dense silence, as though the stylus had been dragged from a record that played background chatter. One of the Americans was trying to get the others to leave. He was pushed away and fell into two men, tried to right himself and slipped, spilling two pints. Another man in uniform, English, his sleeve sewn with several stripes, made his way over to the other three and asked them to leave. They crowded around.

What the fuck d'you say?

Fucking limey.

Where do you get off?

You wanna piece?

The barman stepped in, *That's enough now, thank you, lads.* But he was turned on quickly,

I'm not your fucking lad, you piece of shit.

Now, there's no need for that kind of language. There's ladies here.

Fuck your snotty English bitches. Get your goddamned hands off me.

Others had stepped in. The GIs threw their glasses at the back wall, shattering bottles of Angostura Bitters and Stone's Ginger Wine. A few punches thrown, a few landed, they were ejected. The landlord locked the door, which was kicked and punched.

You motherfuckers. We're coming back to burn this shithole down to the fucking ground.

After a few minutes the door was opened, the GIs nowhere to be seen.

They treat London like it's a bloody holiday camp, Sonia said, setting down two pints of bitter, pushing away the sweet Vermouth. Lynne tried to hand back the handkerchief, which Sonia pushed away.

They're just drunk. Who knows where they're being sent off to tomorrow.

Sonia took a drink and studied Lynne. *Bollocks.*

Lynne glowered. The doors opened and in walked Cyril. Sonia stood and waved and budged Lynne up so everyone could be seated.

You remember Lynne, she said.

Of course, Cyril beamed his chubby smile. *Sorry for being late,* he kissed Sonia on the cheek, *Peter wanted to go through some things. Financial headaches he thought best shared. Busy, busy,* he said, smiling at Lynne.

Book reviewing for Queen and country.

Lynne, Sonia scolded.

You'd be surprised.

I wouldn't. Sonia held his arm.

What can I get you girls to drink?

A half for me, said Lynne, finishing her drink.

Gin and tonic, Sonia smiled.

The door went again, Cyril turned around, *Stephen,* and waved him over.

Sonia, good evening. Nice to see you, Lynne.

Right, drinks. Give me a hand Stephen? The two men went to the bar.

You're sleeping with him.

Shut up, Lynne, and then, *what are you talking about?*

The lispy one. 'Nithe to thee you.' And what about the other one? Fat Cyril? You having it away with him too?

You are coarse. She lit a cigarette. *Not that it's any of your business, Cyril and I are colleagues.*

Colleagues! He's your boss.

It's not like that. We enjoy each other's company.

Which means you are fucking Cyril. That Stephen's more your type, though. I can imagine you two at it.

Stop saying that, Sonia hissed. *Do you know his work? A great poet.*

He's queer, you know.

Oh, Christ, Lynne—

Look at him. Stephen had his arm around Cyril's back, nudging him as they spoke.

Well, Sonia watched on, *you should know.*

Meaning?

Meaning just that. Don't you worry about John on that rock with all those strong, handsome men?

Bitch.

Here we are, then. Cyril set down their drinks.

Cheers all, said Stephen, raising a wine glass. All raised their glasses.

Stephen was, Cyril said, lighting a cheroot, *just telling me about a new poem.*

No, no, no, Stephen demurred.

Something new? We'd like to hear it, wouldn't we Lynne?

If you fancy, Lynne replied, signalling to Cyril, who unpeeled a cigarette from his pack and offered it to her. *Why not?*

Well, I don't know if it's quite ready for public performance.
Come on, don't be modest.

Well, alright. Stephen took a drink, his lips dyed red and then pink again. *It goes like this,*

> *You dream,' he said, 'because of the child'*

Lynne watched Sonia watching Stephen, aware it was not sexual tension but a shared admiration she had sensed. She saw it now, as he recited his poem of entrails and blood streams. This was not the first time Sonia had coaxed words from Stephen in the Fitzroy Tavern. When asked by some Connolly hanger-on what she thought of another of his verses, Lynne described it as tepid. This was not. While other poets wrote of the vast cruelty of war, Stephen spoke of the imperceptible pain of womanhood, of having and losing a baby. Lynne sat at the periphery, aware it was all fakery. Drinks shared in a pub, performed gaiety while teeth itched at the anticipation of sirens and bombs and letters from the War Office, condolences for your loss.

> *'Baby,' her lips dreamt*

Go see the world, Llewela, her dad told her and she had gone to Manchester. The toughness of the city drew out her own toughness, impenetrable; only John had bothered to tap at the shell. Her dad told her to see the world and she had gone to London. She had sought out and found the literati and here she was, profoundly aware of her distance from them all. But where, she demanded to know, was she meant to go now?

Wartime London was purgatory. Lynne remembered her baby, the one they had lost. She remembered it as an ache, the ache endured. John would be discharged, the war would end, they would begin a family. She had made friends who might help John with his music career. He would want to return to the North; without any better ideas, she would follow. Stephen spoke of flesh, her flesh, and bodies.

> *Between their clinging bodies rocked.*

He took another deep drink of red wine and set his glass down.

Marvellous, Sonia said. She reached over a grasped his hand in hers. *Really, marvellous.* Cyril patted Stephen on the back and shook his head in something like awe. Lynne blew smoke and studied her nails.

Sonia, a smile fixed, her eyes cloud-covered, turned breezily to Lynne. *Pourquoi ne pars-tu pas si tu vas être si impolie?*

Moi? Lynne leant forward, responding with a toothy smile of her own and said. *C'est toi qui te ridiculises.* She looked Sonia up and down. *Stupide vache.*

Salope.

Lynne stubbed out her cigarette. *Connasse.*

If the two men spoke French they did not let on. Sonia, for her part, kept up the pretence of a jovial conversation in the language of love. Lynne walked around the table and bent to give Sonia a kiss on one cheek, *Bonne nuit, salope.*

Sonia replying, *J'espère qu'il jouit sur ta jolie jupe.*

Gentlemen, Lynne nodded, as they half stood at her leaving. She made her way through the pub and out into the pitch black of the London night. Taking a full pack of cigarettes from her bag, she lit and held a match to her mouth. The small flame captured the street in dull, flickering light. She started up Charlotte Street, cursing Sonia, herself, Cyril Connolly, and anyone else she could think of.

Hello again. The broad GI sidles up to her, placing his arm around her shoulder. *Should you be out here, in the dark, on your lonesome?* The three others walk behind at a distance, their laughter long silenced. *We could escort you.* He removes the cigarette from her mouth, takes a deep drag, and clumsily returns it. Lynne snatches it from her lips and tosses it behind her. *Hey, hey,* he draws his arm tighter around her neck, *what the hell's the matter with you?*

Lynne stops in her tracks by Colville Place, nearly tripping the GI, and pulls herself free from his arm. *Right, that's enough. You can all fuck off now.*

Is that right? The other three catch up but keep their distance. *And why would we do that?* He moves towards her, grabbing the back of her head. *Thought it was pretty funny getting us kicked out of that place?*

Get your hands off. It had nothing to do with me.

You fucking English. You want us to come and save you and you can't even say thank you. Go on, he grips tighter on her hair, *say thank you.*

Andros, let's just get out of here. There's a place around the corner–

We ain't going round the corner. We're going to her place. Isn't that right, what do you say your name was?

Get your hand off! He tightens again. *You're some tough specimen aren't you? Waiting in the dark for a woman, waiting to get her on her own. Real man, aren't you?*

Shut your fucking mouth. He pulls her into a side street, his friends looking wildly around to see if they've been seen.

Do you think I'm afraid of the kind of man who preys upon women at night? How could I –

I said, shut your fucking mouth.

– be afraid of such a coward as a man who would– He hits her across the face and she can speak no more. More shock than pain, more surprise than fear.

I told you, he strikes her again, *to keep your goddamned mouth shut.*

He drags her head sideways and hits her hard on the cheekbone. She feels her eye pulse and a surge of nauseous pain. There is something hard and small on her tongue; she presses it tightly against the roof of her mouth. Lynne tries to turn to the other three, if only so they have to register what is happening, but he grasps at her hair again and draws her to the floor.

She can hear, in the distance, his voice yelling about sluts and bitches and how he will teach them a lesson. Absolutely frozen and absolutely detached, she knows she should be angry, knows she should fight back, but the fight is going on somewhere out there, as she shrinks deeper inside. She rolls the tooth across the ridges of her hard palate.

He hits her harder on the side of her head. Her temple throbs. How will she explain this to Mr Jacobson and the women at work? It will take more than a bit of blush to cover up. What will Eddie say if he finds out? Or Herbert? They'll think she deserved it; women like her get what's coming eventually. *You treat men like you want them to hit you*, Eddie had once said. *I treat men*, she'd told him, *like a man would*.

She feels his boot against her ribs. She'll have to take a few days off. Maybe she can get some friends to bring some supplies, she can see the bare cupboards in her mind's eye. Molly will have to take care of her. After a few days, she can go back to work and tell them she'd fallen, something like that. She hears his heavy breathing some way off and turns away from it, bringing her knees up to her chest. There will be no more drinks or visits to London pubs, not after this.

He yells something and there are other voices too, American voices with their dropped *Gs* and pronounced *Os*. She tries very hard to listen to what he is saying, to listen closely. *Not my type, eh,* he says, and she can feel his fingers envelop hers, grasping to pry her hand open, gripping at her wedding ring. John. She will have to tell John. But what can he do all the way from Gibraltar? That isn't the point, she thinks, sensing the weight of the GI as he continues to pull and tear at her hand, John is her husband and he has a right to know what has happened. He wouldn't like them to have a secret like this between them. Her ring finger trapped in his fist, the other hand pulls at her wedding ring. She can feel the skin around her knuckle growing hot. She'd tried to take it off herself only a couple of nights ago but found she couldn't. Water retention, Molly had said with an air of knowledge. There's points in the day, she had continued, when your body expands and points when it contracts, like. It was nothing to worry about, she assured Lynne. But she did worry and she'd stopped having lunches, but still the ring wouldn't budge. As it won't budge now. He, the fucking idiot, pins her finger down and punches it, punching the pavement at the same time. He stands up, or is pulled up by the rest of them, and gives her a few more kicks to the stomach, one between her legs. Everything goes very quiet.

The world has got a lot more evil, she supposes. Death and death at the hands of another is all too common. Germans killing Brits, Brits killing Italians, Italians killing French, it is only a matter of time before any death is a justified death. They are all strangers in this new world that seems like it has such a short lifespan, that seems like it might be the death of them all.

She keeps her breathing shallow. The tooth must have been swallowed. Or spat out. Something inside, something like a voice but not a voice of sound, tells her she will pass out soon, but she tries desperately to remain conscious. He might come back.

When this new world is finally done with there will have to be another world to replace it. It might be, she clings on to her knees and on to consciousness, that the old world will return, even older, even more broken and banausic. No, there will have to be a real shift, a place arrived at by design, come about because it is a place where people want to live. She is slipping. Pain flushes through her, colouring her whole body at first red and then so bright it turns blinding white.

The shuddering grows, the sound of coughing swept towards her like a train through a brick tunnel. She woke with the feeling of water trickling onto her lips and down her chin. Lynne swallowed and coughed more. The parts of her that were not numb ached.

John? Lynne asked.

You're awake, came a voice, soft as cherry blossom.

Lynne felt the tears continue to fall. *This is it, isn't it?*

She waited for John now, like she had waited for him all those years ago, like she had been, it dawned on her now, waiting for him all their lives together. He had never really arrived, was always looking for a way out, searching for an escape, yet never escaped. He would be free of her now, which was perhaps what he had always been running towards. There was something interesting in that image, a man running away, unsure from what, but always carrying with him the very thing he sought to escape.

A nurse cracked the window and a cool breeze caressed sleeping Lynne's white-hot face. She woke to find the nurse standing over her, smiling. Where was she? Arrived in Singapore once more to make another go of it. I'll get it right this time, she tried to tell the nurse, but her lips were too dry, her head too heavy. The nurse placed the back of her hand on Lynne's forehead.

Singapore, Lynne managed.

What did she say? a male voice spoke behind the nurse. For a moment Lynne thought it was John.

Sounded like Singapore. The nurse leant towards Lynne. *Did you say Singapore?*

Lynne tried to speak. The nurse held the glass to her lips. She saw the man move towards the window and reach to pull it closed. *No, please,* she barely sounded.

She says, she would like the window open.

John? Lynne asked.

Your husband is not here. But not to worry, he will come soon.

Yes, the male voice confirmed, *we're expecting Mr Burgess to return for visiting hours.* He toned Welsh notes, within an English overture. *You've given us a fair old fright, I have to say.*

Lynne felt the sickening lurch of the Earth's turn. She knew that voice, she saw his physician's whites, knew the doctor who approached her now.

What is carefree and confident in our youth becomes stupid and vulgar later on, the doctor chided her. *I seem to recall telling your husband back in Singapore that one more drink might kill you. It seems,* she could not see his face but felt him eye her up and down, *you sought to put my prophesy to the test.*

Lynne began to cry. It felt like they crowded in on top of her. The nurse, dragging the bedsheet out from beneath Lynne; the doctor, continuing his monologue about Lynne's impending demise. Lynne craned her neck, but the nurse pushed her back against the rough pillows.

Now, Mrs Wilson, or is it Mrs Burgess now?

I want him out, she told the nurse, who strained to listen. *Get him out.*

More water? The nurse asked, holding the glass close.

Ching, Lynne whispered. She gritted her teeth, he continued to prattle in the background.

What's she saying?

Chu chee, Lynne breathed, again trying to sit up. *Chu chee.* She sounded the words like two quick exhalations. *Chu chee,* louder and louder.

It means, go out.

Chu chee.

Ridiculous, I'm about to examine her.

Chu, Lynne railed, *chee.*

The nurse pushed her back down, but Lynne fought this time, grabbing the girl's wrists. The nurse cried out, trying to hold Lynne down.

Lynne? Llewela? Lynne?

Lynne clenched her eyes tight and mustered up all she had left. *Chu chee,* she yelled once more.

Can't you give her something? A sedative, anything at all? The voice had morphed. She felt her body soften, felt the heat of an all-encompassing pain split into so many pockets of aching.

John?

Yes, Lynne, it's me. You're in the hospital. In Central Middlesex. He emanated gin as he spoke.

I thought I was, she licked her cracked lips, *back in Singapore.*

Singapore? It's 1968, Lynne. Wet your tongue, John said, placing a paper cup to her mouth. *That's what the nurse says.*

That doctor...

What doctor?

The one from Singapore, the one... she couldn't put the events in order.

Doctor Scott said he'll be with us shortly.

He and John spoke as if in another room, talking about a cadaver that had been dredged from the Thames, from the Mersey, from the Penang. She was no longer a patient but a death John must prepare for. The tests were in and the tests pronounced no more tests were needed. John listened attentively to the doctor and nodded. He did not interrupt or correct or question. After the doctor had finished, John took her hand.

They say it could be any time. They'll keep you comfortable, that's the main thing now. I should – he was preoccupied. *Is there anyone you want me to contact? Hazel? Anyone?*

Lynne shook her head. She took in the water he offered, it stung at the ulcers and sores. *The book.* She pointed at John. *Bring the book with you.*

She could have asked for anything and he would have brought it. He half expected her to tell him to bring gin, or white wine. He would have brought them to her. Doctors had been telling her the next drink would be her last for years now. It seemed apt that she would drink herself directly into the grave. What she had asked, was for him to bring a copy of *Time for a Tiger*, his first novel. She had asked him to read to her from it before, in Etchingham, when she had woken and found him in a bed next to her, the two of them incapacitated and she thought it might be the end.

Anything else?

Her eyelids grew heavy. He watched her sleep for a moment and then, on unsteady feet, left the hospital.

When she awoke, John was sitting across from her, flicking through a paperback. It looked brand new. Lynne tried to remember the parts she wished to hear and John tried to remember the page numbers. But it was no good. The new, collected edition had put all page references out of order and

Lynne was too weak to describe what she wanted. John turned pages until he came to the first mention of Crabbe's wife, Fenella. Though she was not exactly Lynne, she was certainly more Lynne than any other woman. He read:

> *Fenella, his living wife, would sleep on, long,*
> *killing the hot morning in sleep. She wanted to go*
> *home, but she would not go home without him.*
> *She wanted the two of them to be together. She*
> *believed her love was reciprocated.*

Lynne laughed a little at the word reciprocated; only John believed love could be dealt with in such terms. He carried on. She found herself ebbing and flowing with his voice. Some sentences she caught only the odd word, others returned her to King's Pavilion or to the kedai by the wet market.

One must love the living, she heard and crooked her neck to see her waiting parents. *She deserves whole wells of pity, tasting and looking like love.* The Malayan sun cut through London pea-soup and bathed her in a soothing light. She turned and saw that John had stopped reading. He had gotten old too, had she aged them both? He opened his eyes and smiled a half-asleep smile. Yes, Lynne thought, I'm still hanging on. He lifted her head and let water drip coolly in. He split a grape between his thumbnails and placed it on her tongue. She drained it of its pulp and juices, then weakly spat the seeds and skin onto her chin. John took a handkerchief from his pocket and wiped her.

John sat back down and found his place. *Victor Crabbe put on clean starched white slacks –*

Lynne coughed to get his attention. *What happened to her?* she murmured.

To Fenella? They're forced to leave Kuala Hantu. She and Crabbe are sent to somewhere else. Dahaga. He lifted the book once more, but she coughed again.

After that.

Well, I... They separated. Crabbe can't save her from drowning.

She died?

It's a test, to see if he truly loves her. She swam out and cried for help. Crabbe feared the water more than he feared her death. Fenella went home, Crabbe stayed in Malaya. He dies out there, drowning amongst the reeds.

She left him?

Rather good, I thought. Set it all up in one book, pay off in another.

And after?

For Fenella? Lynne nodded. *She went home,* John said.

Wales?

Fenella wasn't from Wales.

She went home.

Yes. Do you want me to keep reading? Lynne did not reply so he went on. She closed her eyes and saw John pulling on sweat-stained linen pants. Trying to keep quiet, he blundered around their small bedroom and kept her out of sleep's warm embrace.

She tried to stay focused on his voice. Lynne waited for the hit of nostalgia she was so desperate for. But as he kept reading she realised there was no sentimentality in John's words. This, she supposed, was no bad thing for a writer of serious novels. But even his beloved Joyce had sentiment.

She listened hard but her mind wandered to other points in time, her golden hair darkened at the forehead by sweat, her delicate white face dripping with sweat, the back of her frock stained yellow. She remembered the heat, the dry lips and dull headaches that came of dehydration.

Was there a way John could sneak something in, a bottle of gin, perhaps? Even a double would suffice. Just a drop to cool her down, to take this blasted migraine back a few notches, to give her some strength. He had most certainly put a few away before this visit. Maybe he could go out now and pick a bottle up, a quick taxi ride and he'd be back before visiting hours were over.

Get me something to drink, she told him. *Tall glass with ice and lemon. Ice and lime. Something refreshing.* He held a glass to her mouth and she tasted the bitter bite of gin diluted in the dull fizz of tonic.

That's, she gasped in the liquid, *that's it.* She bathed her tongue and swilled the ulcers in crackling water. She let it pour into her, gasping huge mouthfuls down, raising her hand to stop him from moving the glass away. Her thirst raged.

You know, that Khan man, the driver, is rather nice really.

No. She would not have said that. Not to John. Whatever Ibrahim had been, it was not really rather nice. He was there now, in the room. Ibrahim, tall and handsome, his full beard and piercing eyes, tinged with lime leaf green.

I only wish I could understand what he's saying.

She wanted to tell John to shut up, he was still reading, but feared any movement might expel Ibrahim's ghost.

Hantu hantu, she thought and Ibrahim smiled back, having exactly the same thought. The torrent of diluted spirit flowed through her; her hand, the ring finger, tapping the glass. Like one of those cheap novels about Cairo and what-not. She giggled a little, and Lynne remembered being that way, remembered how much fun she had been, how much fun she had meant to be. Her senses were overcome. Gin on her tastebuds, John's words in her ears, and beautiful Ibrahim stood before her. She should ask John to get him a Tiger. She looked at his full lips. He spoke some words of English. *Beautiful*, he said. She raised her hand from the glass and out to him. *Bloody beautiful.*

Manchester

T hree graves. He can't get the image out of his head. He takes a sip of brandy and its warmth radiates from the roof of his mouth over his shoulders and down his body. Were they dug in Moston Cemetery, beside the three graves that held his mother, sister, and later, father, or Southern Cemetery where, no doubt, there were plenty more of his relatives, distant and otherwise? The phone rings. He stubs his cigarette in the tray and picks up the receiver. *Hullo.*

We've got Mrs Wilson on the line for you, sir.

There must be some – Mrs?

Putting you through now. The receptionist's clipped tones replaced by the harsh tones of a bright ring. The telephone trembles against John's ear. He switches hands. Why would she call herself that, was it some kind of joke? A voice comes on the line.

I thought you might visit our little flat on Ducie Avenue.

No. That's enough now.

What was her name, that landlady who turned a blind eye to our premarital arrangements?

I said, enough. His words forced out through a tight Adam's apple, threaded through tight lips. *Mrs Tate.* He can't help himself.

That was her.

Please. His eyes well with tears of frustration.

What memories might await you there, John? Memories of me.

I'm sorry. He holds his breath.

Who can dismember the past?

The receiver rattles on the hook. What cruelty was this? He takes a cigarette, a lit match waving like some dancing firefly. He eyeballs himself in the mirror. Bulbous nose, thin lips revealing a row of lower teeth fading yellow into brown. Eyes, red-hued pools in a brittle, cracked face. An old man. He picks the phone up once more and dials down.

Hilton, he says. *London.* A slug of brandy, waiting for a connection. At the other end of the phone a man says, *Good evening, this is the Hilton, how may I assist you?*

I'd like to speak to my wife, Mrs Burgess. She is staying with you.

Please hold the line, Mr Burgess.

The phone makes a bleep bleep noise, G#. He hums a melody above it, dark, in the minor. *Dah dah, da da da, dah dah.*

Mr Burgess?

Yes, I'm here, yes.

Your wife is at dinner with your son, I am told. She has left a message, would you like me to read it?

Of course, of course I bloody would.

She says, I am taking Andrea for dinner, just the two of us –

Like when we were boys, Anthony mutters.

I'm sorry?

Go on.

She says she will see you tomorrow.

That's it?

That is everything, sir, yes. Would you like to leave a message yourself, sir?

Tell him, I'm sorry.

Him?

Andrew. He puts the phone down.

Death is in the air, her death, his own, chopped up into multiple caskets, and – heaven help him – Andrew's. Liana had driven him back from the hospital. When he saw the house, Andrew began to sob. She took his head from his hands and held it in her own. She tried to draw him towards her but he remained rigid.

I am sorry, Andrea, she said. Depleted, all she could think about was sleep, the fear that she would go another night without it, the fear of the dreams she would have, the fear that in sleep her son would be out of her control and free to harm himself once more. Her fatigue was so great she could not hold him, even while he was trying his best not to be held. Her eyes fluctuated between dull ache and stinging pain, the clothes she wore itched and irritated her skin, her veins rubbed painfully against the bones of her wrists.

Andrew refused to look at her. Every time she made her presence felt, unclipping her seatbelt, opening the car door, taking his suitcase from the boot, a wave of sorrow overwhelmed him. He wanted to be a child again, but not the child he had been, he wanted to become the child of the man of nineteen he was now, himself reset in a child's body; lost, broken, deeply in need of love and affection. When he was a child he felt none of these things, though he saw that the seeds had been planted very early in his life. Liana opened his door and said, *Come on, it's cold. Let's go in the house.*

He looked out at the yellow glow of the living room, light radiating from all those lamps his mother had filled the room with, casting a slow moving rotating shadow, like a silhouette zoetrope. Andrew said, *I don't want to see him.*

You don't have to see him, she said. But then, *I think you owe it to him to let him see you are okay.*

I'm not okay.

That you are home, then.

Tomorrow.

Do you want him to think this was his fault, is that what you want? He said nothing. *Is that what you want? To make him feel responsible for this?* Her eyes darted down to the

163

bandages covering the length of his forearms, her veins rubbed red hot.

I just want to rest. Please.

Fine. Let me help you. She held her hand out to him. Andrew gritted his teeth and lifted himself.

As they approached the front door, he said, *Tell him I just need to sleep. Tell him they gave me some heavy drugs.* Liana nods and opens the door.

She puts his suitcase down in the hallway and watches him start up the stairs, dead on her feet. She wants to follow him up, to make sure he is safe, but would have to crawl up those stairs on her hands and knees. Hand on the bannister, she is about to sit on the first step when he calls in from the living room, *Andrew? Liana, is that you and Andrew?*

Unable to work up even the energy to reply, Liana cries. She hangs there, her arms heavy, her hands dead weights, spine no longer able to hold her head.

Liana? Anthony walks into the hallway, a glass of wine in his hand. *Andrew, where are you going?*

The boy leans into the bannister, watching his mother's shoulders rock uncontrollably. She tries to speak, to say it's okay, my darling, our son is just a little tired from the medication, he is going to bed, let's go through. She inhales in three quick bursts followed by a forceful exhalation, the air refusing to get to her lungs.

Andrew? The old man looks entirely lost. He is helpless in these situations, his son knows. The three of them stand entirely apart, Andrew looking down on his parents, Anthony in the doorway, not sure what to say or do, hoping someone else will take control, Liana stuck, trying to breathe, knowing she needs to take a breath, unable to do anything but gasp at the air all around her.

Come on, come and sit, help me get her in here, Anthony is saying, looking for somewhere to put his wine glass. This is how it always is, the son thinks, climbing back down the stairs. The

164

two men stand either side of Liana and coax her towards the living room. As they walk, Andrew realises that Anthony is not holding her up, only walking beside her.

He sets his mother down in the armchair.

Anthony says, *I'll get her a drink. Cognac.*

She doesn't need a drink.

Of course she needs a drink, look at her. He is at the drinks cabinet, filling a large brandy glass almost to the rim.

Andrew says, *That's your answer to everything.* How stupid those words sound, how clichéd.

Anthony ignores him and holds the glass out for his wife. *Take this, drink this,* he says. *Take this, drink it.* Liana's arms are down between her legs, hands almost touching the floor. *Take this, take it and drink. Drink this. Take – Andrew please. Andrew, do something.* Her black hair, grey in places, obscures her face, her shoulders lift, one, two, three, then fall again, *Take the glass, drink the glass, take it and take, Andrew? Andrew?* The boy is watching his impotent father. He is determined to stand his ground, to resist. *Help her drink this, Andrew. Help her.* His old man's frame hunched over his inconsolable wife, he holds the glass in both hands as though for communion. He raises his wrinkled, rubbery head and stares at the boy, first the white wraps around his wrists, then his washed-out face. *I can't get her to take the glass,* he says.

She doesn't want it.

Of course she bloody wants it, look at her. Look at her there, now. Liana, can you take this? Can you drink this?

She doesn't want it.

Shut up, Andrew! Don't just stand there not doing anything. What are you doing?

Trying to help your mother, can't you see? Can't you see what's right in front of you? Jesus, boy. Drink, he bellows, *drink the bloody stuff.* And then he says, *You drink it,* holding the glass out towards Andrew.

She doesn't want it and I don't want it.

Take it, Anthony commands, shrilly but firmly. *Take it from me.*

The boy does so. He holds the glass at arm's length. Anthony straightens up, his hand on the back of the armchair, beside Liana's head. *Was it an accident?*

I can't... Andrew feels the tears well once more, but he is fighting them. If he doesn't speak, if he doesn't look at his mother or father, if he – the brandy burns and the burning quickly fades from his tongue – can only sleep.

Stupid thing to do.

Don't, Andrew snaps. He coughs brandy heat, stinging at the back of his throat.

This reminds me of when you were—

Stop, please stop.

Always one for making a show of yourself. We were worried about you. Your mother was worried sick.

Then why didn't you visit me? The brandy has helped, the brandy has filled him with warmth, he feels his chest expand, his cheeks flush.

I've been in too many hospitals. When you get to my—

Why didn't you visit me? Me. I'm talking about you visiting me, your son, in the hospital.

Anthony tuts, flicks his hand in Andrew's direction and goes back over to the drinks cabinet.

Come on. Come on, pointedly, *Dad. Why not? Why not?*

Anthony pours himself a large glass and says, *Have you ever lived with suicide? Every day surrounded, overcome by the threat of someone taking their life right there in front of you? All done just to hurt you, to punish you for something you can't change, you can't make better?*

Andrew takes a drink, the brandy running from the sides of his mouth. There is no amount of alcohol he could consume now that would be enough. *I didn't do this to hurt you. I did it because...* He cannot say it. His father says it for him.

You want to die? That it? You want to die, do you? Well, do you?

Andrew is filled with a reckless warm energy. He wants to throw the glass at his father's head, to scream and rage and turn this whole room over, to smash every bottle in that fucking cabinet, smash them over his bastard head.

No. I didn't think so, Anthony says. *Here.* He fills Andrew's glass.

I don't want any.

It will help you sleep. You want to sleep don't you?

Why are you like this?

Me? And what am I like? Eh?

He sips the cognac, cheap stuff, Andrew knew. *Let me go upstairs.* His whole body droops. *Please, Dad.*

Go on, then. Leave me here. Leave me here to deal with your mother. They look over at her, somewhat recovered, elbows resting on the armrests, head resting on her hands.

She needs to sleep too, Andrew says, softly.

Yes, no thanks to you.

Snap. *Fuck you, you fucking –* snap – *who the fuck –* snap – *I fucking.* He drains the brandy glass and drops it, drops it and listens to the dull thud of it bouncing on the thick carpet.

He goes, turning and leaving, climbing the stairs and locking himself in his bedroom, locking the door on the room they allocated him, a child's bedroom, though he never lived here as a child; the bedroom of a child that died from some sad, pathetic childhood illness, whose mother could not face packing up all her dead child's things. He lies on the bed, warm from brandy, thinking about the doctor's warning, thinking about the thinning qualities of alcohol on the blood, watching the pinkish blotches that spread out from the centre of his arms.

He finds himself reciting a poem, like an unbidden song that festers and repeats in the mind.

> *There were times, misunderstood by the family,*
> *When you, at fifteen, on your summer evening bed*

Believed there were ancient towns you might anciently
visit.
There might be a neglected platform on some station
And a ticket bought when the clock was off its guard.
Oh, who can dismember the past? The boy on the
friendly bed
Lay on the unpossessed mother, the bosom of history,
And is gathered to her at last. And tears I suppose
Still hunger for that reeking unwashed pillow,
That bed ingrained with all the dirt of the past
The mess and lice and stupidity of the Golden Age,
But mother and loving, ultimately Eden...

He had not meant to memorise the thing, but since his fifteenth birthday he had been trying to make sense of it, of why his father had written it for him. At least, that is what Anthony had told him. Years later, Andrew had found the very same verse in one of his father's books, one that predated his birth. This discovery only made the lines more intriguing. He hated each word with a blistering passion.

A weak knock at the door. *It's me*, she says. *It's me, Andrea.* He hates that name.

He unbolts the door and falls back on the bed before she has the door open.

Are you okay?

Yes.

What can I get you? Anything. What would you like?

I'm fine. Go and rest.

Your father, he finds it hard. He is not good at talking about these kinds of things.

But he will use it.

She sits on the edge of the bed, her hand resting on his calf. *Use it how?*

It's all fuel for him. I'll show up in a novel, some bit part, nearly dead, barely alive. He sits upright and says, *Fuck it. I'm already one of his minor characters.* He smirks, begins to laugh, a laughter that quickly shifts up the gears.

Andrea, stop it. Stop it now, don't be so stupid. He stands in the middle of the room, laughing, his mother sitting on the bed horrified. *Stop it, Christ, please, stop now.*

He manages to quell himself and say, *Alex, nearly dead, not dead, stupid kid. Then there's him, Dad and you in that book, he tries to kill himself too and fucking fails. That fucking poet of his tried to do himself in as well. That's it, isn't it? I'm a character in the latest novel, aren't I?* He begins to titter, holding it back with great seriousness, feeling another wave of brandy heat. *Shit. I am. So are you, Mum.*

Stop saying these things.

No, listen, it's true. He feels sick, the wave still washing over him. He sits on the floor, his legs straight out in front of him. *We're in one of his books. How else does any of this make any sense? I* – he hiccups, hot brandy rising up his oesophagus – *do I make it? Am I there, on the last page?*

Part Three

London
1968

*H*ello? Bill! Bill, it's John, eh, Burgess, John Burgess – – – *Fine, yes, fine thank you. And you? – – – Very good. Now listen, Bill, there's been – well, I don't know quite how to – I suppose I should just come out and – my wife, you see, I told you that she hadn't been feeling, all the blood loss, I don't know that I mentioned the blood loss, but, well, anyway, look, sorry, what time is it with you? – – – I didn't wake you? – – – Good, that's good. She's dead, Bill.*

He said it again: *She's passed away.*

The phone line was as dead as his wife. John said, *Are you there?*

What are you playing at, it was not Bill Conrad's voice, *going around telling people I'm dead?*

I'm not going around telling anyone anything. I told Bill, that's all.

Who the bloody hell is Bill? What business is it of his?

We're working together on the Shakespeare musical – I don't have to – He hung up. As the receiver hit the hook, it rang back into life.

Look, he said before the thing was close to his mouth, *you've got no fucking right –*

John? John, it's Bill. We got cut off. Awful news, truly –

They were far too liberal with their emotions, these Hollywood Americans, hence all of the bloody therapy. *No, that's fine. No, thank you for saying so.*

You must come out to LA. You don't wanna stay cooped up in London. Is it raining there?

He checked. *Yes. Just a light drizzle.*

You don't need rain in your situation. Come over here. Come and get some sun on you. He actually said *sun on ya.* John pictured him giving it the old golly-gosh clenched-hand gee-whiz arm gesture. Shucks, we'd be just delighted to have you come visit. *John? You there, John? I'll call back.*

No, I'm here.

What do you say? (Waddaya say?)

I've got to deal with a few things here. Deal with her, body.

Sure, sure. But when that's all been taken care of. John felt a sickening amount of empathy exuding from the speaker. *We'll take good care of you.*

You're very kind, Bill.

Nonsense. Call me and I'll get my girl to make the arrangements.

Okay.

You take care, John.

You too. I've – he stopped himself.

You've? John?

I think I've solved the problem of the Shakespeare script. It came to me tonight. No, came to me four years past. Shakespeare on the high seas.

John, I don't think now is –

A poetaster Phileas Fogg. There will be much opportunity for musical numbers, an Egyptian song with lots of Arabic scales and plucking lyres. Then on to Turkey, more sombre, sultry, men playing great big reed pipes, like didgeridoos, thick-browed women dancing, waving their arms in smoke rising from hookahs. He journeys to her, do you see? To his Dark Lady.

You get some rest, John. We'll talk all this through when you get here.

He clutched the phone, the disconnected tone shrill against his tired ear. Then, before she could speak again, he hit the

174

switch hooks with the base of his fist and dialled the number of Deborah Roger's office.

Deborah, it's John. I have some news, I'm afraid.

He told her everything. She was his agent, but she had known Lynne. She was kind, offering to accompany him to Applegarth where Lynne's possessions would need to be put away. And while they were folding dresses and underwear into cardboard boxes Deborah brought from the village shop, he asked her if she could find the address of an Italian translator who he had lost contact with four, maybe five years previously.

Anthony had suggested they eat somewhere better than the oily Greek restaurant of four years earlier. Liana booked a table at one of the few Italian restaurants in London that bore some approximation to the food of her homeland. She ate as much as she thought acceptable: calamari dipped in mayonnaise to start, alongside garlic bread, overly buttered but still delicious. For her pasta dish, she had seafood linguine, the calamari being so good the first time she wanted more. She broke soft pink prawns from their hard clear casings and pierced clams from their shells. For the main course Liana had sea bass with green beans, potatoes, and a thickly reduced ragù. Anthony ordered spaghetti Bolognese and sat spinning his fork for much of the time. They had coffee and Liana ordered two scoops of vanilla ice cream. Like all British, Anthony thought ice cream a thing for children, and perhaps the gap in their ages widened with each mouthful. As the waiter passed, Liana ordered a brandy. When it arrived she poured half of it on her ice cream. Delicious, truly delicious. She had not eaten this well in some time. Her fullness pleased her and she would have liked to go back to Martha's apartment and sleep awhile. But she had received and now she must give.

We should take a walk, she told Anthony, *along the river.* He was unsure but agreed and called for the bill. When it arrived, he studied it intently. She could tell he was *that* kind of writer. There was always someone else to get the bill, an agent, a publisher, a Hollywood film producer. What was he looking for in the list of numbers? Finally, after Liana had smoked one cigarette and lit another, Anthony paid.

Molte grazie, she placed her hand on his. *It was a lovely meal.*

They walked and she told him about life in Cambridge. She did not mention Paolo Andrea, at least, not as much as she normally would have, and she did not mention Stephen. Other things she failed to mention included the huge amount of debt Stephen had got them into, the fact that she had had to take on three lodgers to cover the mortgage and bills. Liana, instead, told Anthony all about the great work she was doing at the university and the beauty of Cambridge compared to London. She told him about the papers she was working on and the possibility of writing her PhD thesis at Cambridge. Hearing all this, removed from the daily grind of mothering a son and a man she had long lost patience with, Liana believed herself to be rather impressive. Impressive enough, at least, to feel no intimidation in the presence of the great Anthony Burgess.

They came to a pub and he insisted they go in. The British cannot walk for walking's sake, unless they are halfway up a hill surrounded by nothing. Why a city, which was built by men for men to walk through, cannot simply be a place to stroll, she could not understand. She felt too full to drink any more. They had had two bottles of Soave with their meal. But there was still some brandy warmth lingering on her tongue, so she ordered another. John drank his gin and tonic with great thirst. The brandy in the restaurant had been smooth and glistened with alcoholic heat; this one was all raw booze that made her mouth tighten.

Another? he asked, already standing.

No. No, thank you. I think I had better go. Liana stood but Anthony did not move, blocking her path.

But I thought we could – he indicated towards the bar.

I have to catch a train very early. My son, she said, with no further explanation. *Thank you for a lovely evening.* She kissed him on the cheek, gently but firmly moving him aside.

I suppose I could walk with you. He eyed the bottom of his glass.

You stay. It was good to see you again. Liana left, happy to be leaving. She was happy to be walking in the city alone, drunk and thinking warm thoughts of Paolo Andrea.

Liana! Cara Liana! He was not running, but the intention was there. She stopped, lit a cigarette and enjoyed this tall, cumbersome, but somehow charismatic man half-bounding towards her.

Mr Burgess, she laughed. In her mind, Mr Burgess was a sitting man. Sitting on television panels talking about this, that and the other, sitting at his typewriter writing all those articles she had been reading and, she could not get the image out of her head, sitting in a little toilet, distracting himself with poetic thoughts. He stopped so close that she could smell tobacco and meat on his breath; she thought he was going to kiss her. He did not, but he took her hand and they walked together.

Bad manners, he said by way of explanation. *It's being married all these years, you forget how to behave around women. It's easy to think of the correct way to behave when you're sitting at a typewriter. It has been so long since I've taken a beautiful woman out to dinner.*

Liana could not help but be complimented. *Truth be told, Antonio, it has been a long time for me too. With,* she added, *a handsome man.*

He convinced her to have another drink. They walked for a time, past the great landmarks of Parliament and Big Ben, which Anthony told her was actually not the name of the tower at all, but the largest bell within, which sounded E natural. They took a taxi to Fitzrovia, where, he told her, he knew a place that did a good bottle of Italian white.

By the time he brought glasses over, she was quite ready for a nightcap. Liana asked him if he was working on a new novel and he fell into character, explaining that a new novel was something like a pregnancy and gestation did not guarantee birth. She enjoyed the way he spoke. He started most sentences with an elongated *Well*, his bottom lip jutting so she could see the brown base of his front four teeth. He said a few words, *one has to understand* or *when you treat writing as a career rather than an art*, before taking a long, thoughtful pull on his cheroot, and making his pronouncement. It was not conversation as she knew it. She made her own promulgations, talking over him, and placing his gesticulating hands down on the table in order to make her point more clearly.

She enjoyed his company, his way of talking as if there were no doubts left in the world – *Well, of course, a man and a woman are designed to be entwined* – it was much how Paolo Andrea talked about the world he lived in. Whatever was unknown to Paolo Andrea was filled in by imagination, so everything fitted into a harmonious, sensical whole.

Liana had been talking about Paolo for half an hour. She could get like this, particularly when he was not close by. She could not wait, she repeated whenever she lost her train of thought, for the two of them to meet. There would be, she felt, an immediate sense of kindred spirit. Paolo, she told Antonio, laying her head on his shoulder, wrapping her fingers around his, had always been a musical child. Any record she would play, Vivaldi, the Beatles, Joe Sentieri, little Paolo Andrea would shift backwards and forwards in time with the beat. Liana, heaven knew, had no musical abilities. Paolo could hear a song once and sing the melody perfectly. Of course the words were not quite correct, he was only four years old for pity's sake, but the melody was perfect. Days later, weeks later even, he would be able to remember the tune as if he were singing along to the record itself.

You should hear him, she urged Antonio. *You should hear my little boy sing.*

When she woke up she was back in the Chiswick house. She dressed in her white cotton dress from the night before. High-necked, white with an embroidered rose covering the length of one side. Thorns removed, of course. She made her way downstairs and caught the odour of bloody meat frying. Uneasy, her head heavy, she pushed open the door to the living room. It was exactly as she remembered it. There were a few more pieces of furniture, a standard lamp, an uncomfortable-looking sofa, an upright piano, but nothing to suggest this was a place where life went on. It was as though four years had passed in the rest of the world, while time had been unable to penetrate this place. She had to remind herself that, between her first and second visit, a woman had lived and died in these rooms.

In the kitchen area, Anthony stood over a spitting pan, thick with coagulated fat, drinking noisily from a tea-stained mug. He whistled and waved his wooden spoon like a conductor's baton. What the hell was she doing here? He had, before passing out next to her, proposed marriage. *I'll take you to Etchingham*, he declared. *I will*, his eyes barely open, *take care of you, you'll see.* Then they had both slept.

Good morning, Antonio.

For a second it was as though he'd forgotten she was there. He wore a creased and stained shirt with baggy green trousers, carpet slippers. He put his mug down and wiped his hands on his trousers.

Buongiorno tesoro, he sang, happy, so happy to see her she could not help but laugh. *I've bought pork kidneys. Sit down, sit down.*

She sat at the Formica table, barely room for two, and watched him carry the pan to the table. Fat sloshed the kidneys around like rotting dolphin corpses rolling on the tide. Anthony clumsily dropped a kidney onto her plate. Oil splashed onto her

179

dress. He went back to get plum tomatoes, which bubbled and spat. He poured tea that ran like treacle. It was all she could do to breathe through the stench of overcooked meat, burnt fat and stewed tea. John could hardly contain himself, slicing into and chewing down on the rubbery meat, bloody grease smearing his plate.

Do you have coffee?

Just, he chewed, *tea.*

Liana lifted a piece of toast from a plate in the middle of the table and took a small bite.

Not hungry?

I'm feeling a little, she held her breath as a wave of nausea washed over, *delicate.*

I can make you a G&T? It would be no trouble.

She laughed, then saw he was serious. *No. No, I don't want anything like that. Just coffee. You don't have any? Not even instant?*

I don't drink it. I could go out? He put his knife and fork down, wiped his mouth with a napkin.

No, no. Just some water, then.

Anthony stood up and went to the tap. *I leave for America tomorrow.*

Yes, you said. He handed her a glass of warmish water. *What will you do when you are out there?*

They want to go over ideas for the Shakespeare script. Bill, that's William Conrad, he thinks we should see a green light soon enough.

You like being a scriptwriter?

I suppose so. He chewed his kidney thoughtfully.

But you are a novelist.

Novels don't pay the bills, I'm afraid. Not like movie scripts. I've already made more for this non-existent film than I did for the novel it was based on.

Yes, but, surely – the water was doing the trick – *surely, you want artistic fulfilment, artistic joy?*

Fulfilment, I get from composing.

Music?

I can play you something, if you like. He chewed rhythmically. *I thought we could go into town after this.*

I haven't any clothes. She looked down at the spreading stains on her dress.

There's clothes upstairs. You can pick out what you like.

She began to cough. Her throat tightened. She could feel something like sand in her windpipe. He tried to feed her water but she could not stop coughing long enough to drink. He slapped her on the back, too forcefully. Tears streamed down her face. What the hell was she doing here? She drank water and sealed her eyes tight.

I must go. I've got to get home for Paolo Andrea. He will wonder where I've got to. It's been lovely, thank you for a lovely evening. She kissed him on the cheek, saw he did not know what he had done wrong. She said, *Get rid of your wife's things, Antonio. If you want to move on, if you want your life to continue. My mother, when my father died, she kept everything. She is alone still.* She kissed him again on the cheek and left.

Are you my dada now? Andrea studied Anthony. His long, slender child's face did not move, his almond eyes did not blink.

That depends on you, I suppose. Would you like me to be?

Not really.

No? I don't blame you. Anthony drew out a page from the typewriter and handed it to Andrea. This page was full of rhyming words – *bum hum tum numb thumb sum gum dumb thrum drum.* Andrea did not recognise them but understood they were connected. Anthony went back to typing and Andrea went back to staring. *I had a wicked step-parent too, when I was about your age.*

What was he like?

She. This was my stepmother. She was not terribly kind to me. She had no time for children, especially not little boys who were naughty and not her own. She did not want me.

Is that what I am?

You're something different, Anthony said.

Do you not want me?

No, no. I'm happy you're here, Andrea. I love your mother and she loves you.

The boy looked quizzical. He took his page of rhyming words and sat on the sofa, running his finger over the print. *She's my mamma,* he said, finally.

And she will be my wife.

It was July, late evening sun stretched out the days, and they were something of a family together. Paolo Andrea had made many friends, Glebe Street being full of young families. He brought his own sort of joy into the house, which made it feel even colder, as if it sought to reject the boy. Anthony complained bitterly that the children interrupted him and his work. Paolo Andrea would lead in a steady stream of other children who asked if they could press the keys, as if he himself were pressing keys at random. *Bugger off,* Anthony told them. Paolo Andrea would not bugger off. He found Anthony endlessly fascinating. All that hair and those huge hands which turned like windmills as he spoke. When Anthony stood, Andrea would try to climb him. Taking big handfuls of corduroy, he pushed his heels off Anthony's shins and began the long ascent. *There's no reasoning with him,* Anthony complained, prising Andrea from his trousers and placing him back on the ground.

There's no reasoning with any four-year-old, Liana told him. *Be kind to him.* Anthony promised he would.

Liana found Anthony in the living room, hunched over his desk, searching through a rolled up copy of *Time for A Tiger.* She stood at the door, studying him, silent, sombre with cigarette and highball.

What are you looking for in there? She had startled him, though he pretended otherwise, discarding the book with performed disinterest and going the few feet to the kitchen, pretending he couldn't be seen while fixing himself another drink.

Liana lit a cigarette from his packet and picked up the book. She knew so little of her husband's time in the East, only that he had suffered some kind of seizure and had faced the prospect of an early death. While another might write their will, Anthony had written five novels and, to only his surprise, found they did not make an immediate fortune for his soon-to-be widow. But he had outlived her, and what money he had made, what money she had gained through the deaths of others, was all his now. Liana sat with her back against the armchair and began to read; Anthony, sitting at his typewriter, inserted fresh paper and began to type.

Why did Crabbe move them out there? Liana asked, accepting a glass of Frascati.

He sat back at his desk and lit another cigarette. *Experience*, he said.

Did he expect Fenella to go with him? Did he expect her to stay?

He had been working on a review of a book Liana had not seen him reading. Striking keys once more, he said, *She was his wife.*

Liana was struck by the simplicity of his statement. *I would not have gone.*

She did not look up but returned to fictional Malaya. A moment passed, the lighting of a fresh cigarette, and Anthony went back to typing.

She read with a translator's eye; it had ruined literature for her. Being a translator meant entering the creative waters of another writer and reaching your hands beneath to find how the undercurrents flowed. She had done it with Pynchon, had learnt his rhythms and ticks, transferring them into a new language. But more than that. A new piece of literature existed in the world, and she had been its creator. It was, Anthony might say, akin to the boatman giving passage over the River Styx; whoever stood on the bank of the far side was certainly not the same as had stepped aboard. The boatman had done more than hold the tiller.

In Anthony's novel, Victor Crabbe's first wife had drowned after their car had dropped into a frozen river; the Crabbe who had emerged, half-drowned himself, had not been the same Crabbe who had driven the car over the edge. Liana saw her husband was emerging from similarly cold waters. The experience left its mark on Crabbe. He was afraid to drive and afraid to swim, the two means of propulsion that had killed his wife. The second wife, Fenella, was apparently unaware of the nightly nightmares her husband suffered, reliving the death of the first wife. Liana was not. Anthony woke her up with a dead woman's name on his lips. She pretended to sleep, while he pulled himself from their bed and back downstairs, back for another glass of what had drowned Lynne.

The dead are dead.

Liana read and tried to see Lynne, to experience a real life from the illusion of the page. As she read, the sculpture of Lynne she pieced together fell apart and the façade of Fenella fell too. Fenella and Victor Crabbe were two sides of Anthony.

She read a passage in which Fenella saw others as mythological creatures – Prometheus and Adam and the Minotaur.

That was all Anthony. How many women of myth had he cast Liana as since they had met? She could not count.

Fenella trying to escape Crabbe, Crabbe trying to escape Fenella – it was as Freudian as Anthony claimed all life to be.

In his writing she saw greatness and she saw laziness. The greatness was undeniable, no matter how hard Anthony tried to deny it. But translation was not simply a case of weighing up the greatness of the writing, but its potency. As with all transplants, some would not survive the operation.

Anthony was ripe for translation. She read his writing as an attempt to translate itself, stretching beyond the limitations of English for something more. Anthony had talked about creating a new language, a pan-European language. She had read *A Clockwork Orange* and saw he was already writing beyond the borders of Europe. *Time for A Tiger* revealed he had long since left those borders behind.

Anthony was a work of English awaiting transition into a new tongue, a new culture entirely. Jack Wilson had become Anthony Burgess; the Northern accent had been, not lost, but carefully removed. Anthony Burgess' past did not begin in Manchester but in Malaya; in the act of writing, he too was written onto the page and into real life. Marriage to Liana would complete the task, it seemed. He would no longer be Jack at home and Anthony in public.

What is it you want to be, Antonio? she said.

He had stopped typing long before but still pulled a face, a childish face at being asked such a question. *I am what I want to be. And will be more so when we are man and wife.*

No, Antonio, I think not. A man who writes five novels in one year does not want to be a reviewer of other people's novels. A man who writes about Shakespeare and ageing poets does not want to be a Hollywood script writer.

He drew paper from the typewriter and held it between them.

What is it you want to say?

Say? He let the one page drift from his hand before picking up the heavy bundle sat on the desk. *I'm putting Shakespeare on the cinema screen. I'm earning a decent living. I write whatever puts food on the table.*

That's my point. She had risen as he lifted his unfinished script. The space was small enough that her few movements, two steps at most, became a confrontation. She stood over him.

You write so much, she checked her tone, even and calm, *but you have so much to say.* Anthony scoffed and she knew it had not come out quite right.

After a moment, he said, *I want to write a modern retelling of Oedipus and call it Motherfucker.* And then, as if by explanation, *After Levi Strauss.*

Why?

He lit a cigarette and held his empty glass out to her. *I want to infuse theory into a piece of literature. Music has theory at its core, it is inherent to the art form; why not the novel?*

Your friend Bill Conrad will not want to make this into a Hollywood movie.

I don't know. Sex and controversy sell whatever the form. Oedipus is ripe for Hollywoodification.

Let's leave London. She walked the few steps between living room and kitchen, poured him a fresh drink she felt he did not require, and went to the kitchen to grind coffee. She made up the moka pot, lit the stove, placed the pot on top. It was getting late and yet, as always, they were just getting started.

London is where my work is.

You are not a sculptor with masses of stone. The typewriter, cigarettes, paper, tools and materials can be carried.

It's our home. The dead wife's spectre circled the room once, before Anthony said, *You've just got here. And I've got too much work on.*

If we are to be married, to give ourselves a new beginning, let us begin anew. Take me away from here, Antonio.

Where would we go?

She was not ready to return to Italy. Italy was the patriarch whose power over her was still raw. She was not yet ready to forgive Italy. Anthony's French prohibited them from residing in France. There was America, but she had been there, had been married and divorced, been half destroyed by America. And Anthony would be wooed by movie executives, TV executives, he would be writing commercials for washing powder within a month. Germany was out of the question and Spain was the gateway to Gibraltar; the war was still a bitter taste for him.

He had gone back to his typewriter, back to his reviews or his screenplay. The moka pot shrieked. Liana let it.

She lit a cigarette and went to the back door. Paolo Andrea was outside, naked, chasing Haji. She checked for faeces on the lawn and came back in. The pot began to splutter and spit. From the cupboard she took an espresso cup and poured frothing coffee into it. She took a sip. It had been a long night and the day had started slowly, meaning Paolo Andrea had become a frenzy of energy. They had spent the day in the park; he had met her lack with an abundance of movement and words. She had had to drink a glass of white wine with lunch just to get through it.

Anthony had gone into town to meet his agent, Deborah Rodgers, and his new accountant. There were reviews to deliver and new books to collect. Anthony was his own cottage industry, working to several deadlines. His energy, his movement and words, could make her head spin too.

Liana took her coffee into the garden. Paolo Andrea was making holes with a stick, the dog watching eagerly.

Do you like it here?

He stopped and stood up. *Are we going home?*

This is home, she said, had said a hundred times. *But we could go on an adventure. How does that sound?*

Fun. Just us two?

And Antonio.

He went back to digging, prodding and striking at the earth.

You and he will be good friends, Andrea. You'll see.

The front door slammed. She kissed her son's forehead and went into the house. Anthony stood in the doorway sweating, shirt soaked with sweat. Liana made him a gin and tonic, chipping ice into his glass.

The Inland Revenue plan to take all of my money away, he said.

What are you talking about?

He clutched an already crushed envelope. *Lynne had some money, they want all of that. Death duties, death tax. Then there's this money from Bill Conrad, they want that as well.*

She approached him, reaching for the letter. He pulled back, burying it into his trouser pocket.

What does your accountant say?

He says, get out of the country. That's what he says. He tells me that I should do what everyone else is doing and tell this blasted Socialist, Communist government to go directly to hell.

It's fate.

Fuck fate.

We will escape to Morocco. Or Peru. We will fill suitcases with bank notes.

I've been to Morocco, he said, fishing the letter from his pocket. *Lynne fucked an orange striped bellboy in my bed.*

Anthony took the drink and sat miserably in the armchair. *Malta,* he said. *It's in the sterling zone.*

Malta. She thought for a moment; she knew nothing about Malta.

Stop looking so bloody pleased. He drank and lit a moist tipped cigarette.

Come into the garden, Liana said. *We can tell Andrea the good news.* She went outside.

Anthony remained, still sweating. He could hear mother and child, both in fits of youth. The house would have to be dismantled. Both houses sold. He looked at the front room that Edward Jones' death had procured. There had never been any bloody money. But now there was a poxy sum they would come for it, every single sodding penny. All he had wanted was to carry on, a new wife to wash away the pain of a dead one.

188

The ceremony had been simple. He was a widower, after all, and a Catholic one at that. Archbishop Dwyer – his distant cousin-in-law – was, John felt, watching. Liana was an aggressively lapsed Catholic and a divorcée to boot. No, nothing too elaborate at all. A quickie in the Hounslow registry office, and then a decent meal somewhere nearby. The registrar, a man of John's height, John's age, had presided over matters with little interest. Liana winced when asked if she would take John Burgess Wilson as her lawfully married husband. Liana did not want to marry a John Wilson she had barely met; she wanted to be Mrs Anthony Burgess. It was, Anthony assured her, just a detail. They were Mr and Mrs Burgess from hereon in.

Anthony sat in bed and watched Liana take off her clothes. He felt a kind of sickness, not unlike hunger, not unlike being caught in a lie. They had lived in Glebe Street together for several months. A new wife in the house raised the spectre of the dead one. Lovers had been fair game. Lynne had, he was sure, had several men in their marital bed, but was never so indecorous as to marry one of them. Liana watched him through the mirror of Lynne's vanity table and smiled, her torso glistening, her breasts full. He started to salivate and worried he might vomit.

Antonio? Liana looked on with a wife's concern.

I'm fine. I just need something. He did not say what; he did not know what. Anthony put on his dressing gown, newly bought by Liana, and went downstairs. After pouring himself a large glass of Frascati, he lit a cheroot and went out with Haji into the garden. Life in sin; prenuptial sex was like the dress rehearsal, married life and marital intercourse the performance itself. He thought about this metaphor and blew smoke. It did not stand up to interrogation, there was no audience present. There had been, though, an audience that morning, and marriage vows hinted towards what wedding guests were implicitly bearing witness to, when the couple had and held one another, loved and cherished until – he threw his smouldering fag end into the long grass and lit another.

As he locked the door the phone rang. It was late, past midnight. Bill Conrad, no doubt, ringing to give his congratulations from Hollywood. Anthony picked up the telephone.

Burgess, he answered. The line crackled, went dead, crackled again. *Bill? Bill, is that you?*

Who is she?

No. He would vomit. *No, I'll not have this.*

Who's that little slut, John? That little bitch you've brought into my house. I told you, I wouldn't stand for it. Using my house, bought with my dad's money, for your depravity. And the child, who is the child?

He's mine.

Are you fucking him too?

Enough! Enough of this. You are dead. You are no longer my wife. You are dead!

Get them out. Pack their things and—

He put the phone down. Beads of sweat ran from his top lip to the lip of his poised glass. He saw off the Frascati and poured more. Perhaps it was Hazel, getting some sort of revenge on him for moving on. The niece, Ceridwen, had pulled faces, refused to attend Lynne's funeral, would not look him in the eye. Youth could be cruel. The voice had sounded youthful, Lynne from twenty years previous. He lit another cheroot and went upstairs.

His heart still thumping, he opened the bedroom door and found another woman lying naked on top of the bedsheets. He half expected to blink and find Lynne there, blink again and find her cadaver, blanched of colour and life, drained of blood, hollow cheeked and dead-eyed. He pressed down hard on his eyelids with his thumb and forefinger. His mouth was dry, brow wet, heart throbbing.

Antonio, Liana sighed, tired and a little drunk. *Come*, she tapped the space beside her.

He stubbed out his cheroot and took off his housecoat. He took off his pyjamas. His heart picked up with every button he unfastened. Be-beat, b-beat, b-ba-b-ba. He was hard. He felt young and on borrowed time, all at once. He climbed, not next to her, but on top of her. This was his wife now. This was new life, a new life had been bestowed on him.

He kissed her lips, all garlic and wine and she kissed him back, sleepily. Holding himself above her he took in her body, the curve of her breasts and hips, the slenderness of her waist, her elegant arms. *Be quick*, she whispered. He kissed her breasts and placed his head between them, hoping his heart rate would fall. She wanted him. She was his wife and she wanted him. He felt like an adolescent. Fifty years old, gripping his penis and trying to guide it into his new wife, this beautiful woman. She took him in her hand – he shuddered – and guided him inside. Her hands on his hips, she pulled him towards her. He saw himself from without, a child watching the hired help touch herself. He remembered Rahimah, her beautiful tanned skin, biting her lip while he was on top of her.

Liana said, *Yes, like that. Make love to me, Antonio.* She moaned, her eyes closed the entire time. He felt himself within her, how she controlled his movements, the sensation of it all through his body, all over his skin. This is too much. Lynne would – Lynne is dead – Lynne could not – she would not stand for – she is dead and gone – she will have revenge – there is no revenge, she is dead and buried – she was – she is – she was – she's gone – this is life – this is my life now – this – this – this.

He fell beside his wife. She licked her lips, touched his leg with her hand, and rolled over, immediately asleep. His body continued to pulse, shots of electricity racing through his capillaries, through his pulmonary system. His left arm tingled. Downstairs, the telephone began to ring. He closed his eyes, naked and shuddering. They could not stay here. The ringing continued. If they stayed, they would never be free of her. He would never be free of her.

Anthony pulled the sheets over him and thought of Will travelling to Malaya. The vastness of the world, so many routes of escape.

Europe
1968

A nthony was suddenly struck with a melody, a theme that
rumbled just as the engines rumbled below. The sea had its
own music, its shifting tempo, waves of undulating bass and the
treble spume, like shimmering bells. He attempted, watching the
coast of England gently slump below the horizon, to match the
music in his head to the libretto he had been writing. Nothing
fit. This was not the music of a Hollywood showtune, this was
something far more onerous, more profound. The sea wind
picked up, the waves following suit. He leant over the barrier
and down into the wash below. There, he heard strings murmur,
pulling this way and that, the sea drawing him in, *Join us.* It
was the music of dread. All he had tried to bury was making
its way up in sonata form. There was no money. There was not
enough to pay for plane tickets. Liana had expected flights from
Heathrow, perhaps even First Class. He tried to get the money
together, but how little there was to go around. It was Terry who
had suggested a camper van. You've got to take into account the
resale value, he said, and Anthony had.

When the Dormobile arrived, bought on tick, she said little,
just: *You expect me to drive this thing?*

*It will give us time together, just the three of us, as a family.
This is the beginning of our lives together. It would give me time,*
he said, *real quality time with Andrea.*

They did not talk about it again, though he felt her
resentment begin to build as they queued to board the Channel

ferry. She would forget all that once they disembarked. And while the debts were never far from his mind, at that moment, looking out at the waning English coastline, his head swam with music, besieged with strings and brass and woodwind and percussion. He went back to the van to write all this down, pulling out drawers and opening cupboards to find his music manuscript. He scratched the first few notes. They needed money. He winced at the thought of having to tell Liana the man she had married was, in fact, a poor writer, that her bag contained not just the deeds to the new house but every penny he owned. He put away music and wrote a letter to Professor Louis Rubin at UNC Chapel Hill to ask if there was any teaching available. English writers could command a decent salary in American universities and none of it would have to go to Deborah Rogers. Agent's fees would be the end of him.

In Paris he posted his letter; his palms had grown quite sweaty with the deceit. Liana, armed with her newly purchased Zeiss Ikon Contessa, stopped at the windows of Parisian art galleries, pointing out and photographing particularly interesting pieces. One look at their price tags would send him into partial paralysis. He would then denigrate the piece as badly composed, a crude imitation, or simply not to his tastes. They left Paris distanced, one a liar, the other doubting her critical eye.

From Paris they headed southeast, vaguely in the direction of Troyes. Liana drove and navigated. Paolo Andrea swung between the front and back seats, depending on what piece of scenery caught his attention.

Anthony sat in the back and wrote, continuing with *Will!*, picturing himself following in the Bard's footprints, albeit chugging along in a beige and burgundy caravan. Will had become a kind of Quixote, Anthony a kind of Sancho Panza. The rain pelted down, ricocheting off the metal roof, snare raps interrupting that damned piccolo theme he just could not get out of his head. He still felt the swaying of the English Channel that was no longer beneath him.

He wrote a large set-piece scene: Will leaving Gibraltar and his Gibraltarian lover, a black-haired mystic who had had a vision of his wife and his brother, Richard, in a lovers' tryst. Will stands at the front of the ship and asks God to put a curse on Anne Hathaway. A storm breaks out, like nothing any of the mariners has seen before. The sailors sing:

MASTER

Boatswain! Boatswain! The sea is upon us,
Speak to the mariners: Fall to't, rarely.

BOATSWAIN

Heigh, my hearts! My hearts, oh cheerly, cheerly!
Yare, take in the topsail, yare tend the whistle!
Blow, til thou burst thy wind, our seabound
missal.

WILL

Pry, I'm to assist, tis my fault the sea
rages.

BOATSWAIN

You? A poetaster, can thou write pages,
To quell the mighty sea beast beneath us?

WILL

I can hand a rope, the mast I can untruss.

BOATSWAIN

Make yourself ready in your cabin, Will,
For the mischance of the hour, if it so hap,
if 'tis God's will!

There were certain rhymes that were not too pleasing on the ear, but once they had been Hollywoodified, with American twanging Elizabethans, it would do well. The crew and poet were surely drowned but the following scene revealed their ship washed up on the shores of Algiers. He made a note in the directions that an albatross should fly over just as Will woke, still gripping the ship's wheel. He had saved them all from certain wreck and when the men came too, they celebrated Shakespeare's name, singing:

MARINERS

We were shook, our lives we feared
Thank the seas for Shakespeare!

The rain was coming thick and fast now. The tarmac beneath, the road ahead, set a rhythm and pace which demanded to be matched. The rain continued to fall, crack crack crack, peppering the Dormobile. Anthony pounded at the keys, clack clack clack, more words than he had written in a year.

The storm passed, but the storm of metal kept apace inside their mobile home. It took several minutes for Liana to realise the exhaust pipe had fallen off, the clattering of keys sounding much like the clattering of car parts on the autoroute. She ran out into the rain-soaked night to retrieve it, still hot to the touch, from the roadside.

He sang Berlioz from Lyon to Montelimar, and now they were reaching the Southern coast, he had started on Satie. Paolo Andrea stared with open-mouthed wonder as Anthony began to parrumph Milhaud's *Provence*. Ba da pa da dar dah! He would strike the keys in time, accompanying himself with great vigour.

What is he doing, Mamma? Paolo Andrea asked.

He's making music.

It was not long before the boy joined in. He learnt the bassoon part of *L'apprenti Sorcier*, parp-parping away with such confidence that Anthony was able to provide accompaniment, filling in string and brass sections. Paolo Andrea had never heard the music before and had no notion that it was in fact written for a hundred musicians with instruments rather than dah da dahs and bla bla blas. The boy had an ear, Anthony thought, and he set about trying to teach him the whole cello part for Saint-Saëns' *The Swan*. Paolo Andrea quickly grew bored by Anthony's insistence that he listen carefully and copy exactly. Liana enjoyed hearing them play together. Even living in such close quarters, man and child kept each other at arm's length; yet in all of this blaring and warbling, the two seemed to have found a connection.

When they arrived in Avignon, Anthony collected up all the books he had finished reviewing and the three of them set off to find a bookshop. Anthony posted the copy he had produced, some twenty reviews, as well as a further letter to Professor Rubin, suggesting he could come for the spring semester, listing a range of courses he could teach: the works of Shakespeare (of course), Seventeenth-Century Literature, British Literature, Post-1910 Poetry, Contemporary American Culture and James Joyce. Anthony explained he expected to be in Malta by December and gave his new address: 168 Main Street, Lija, Malta.

In the bookshop, the owner, a hunched myopic man, questioned the value of English books he had never heard of. Liana pushed him; she explained, in a cocktail of Italian,

French and English, that she was a literary agent, that the bank had closed and that they would not sell these books, which represented the best of contemporary British literature, were it not for the dire straits they found themselves in. She got a good price, tucked the francs into her passport and put it in her bag alongside the wad of sterling notes; all the money they had.

They spent the afternoon on the banks of the Rhone, drinking Châteauneuf du Pape, sampling Racket and Pieds et Paquets, Liana photographing Anthony as he reclined, glass in hand. She took pictures of Paolo Andrea as he undressed and clambered to the riverbank. They watched as he pissed in a vaulting arch into the Rhone. The locals stopped and gasped. Anthony saw the boy's slash hit the river's flow and felt a terrible foreboding.

He turned to a couple of elderly women stood on the bridge. *Il est fou*, he told them, nodding towards the child.

Liana shook her head. *Il est four*, she corrected.

As night drew in, they walked back to their temporary home. When it came into view, Liana cursed its very wheels, gears and gearbox. Andrea, tired from a day of swimming and singing, tripped and scraped his legs. Anthony cursed him, Liana cursed back, and a young man who had been following, unseen, snatched her bag and ran into the shadows. Her blood already hot, Liana flung a weeping Andrea into Anthony's arms and gave chase.

She would beat his head with a rock should she catch him. She yelled, *Stronzo!*, bearing down on the thief's heels. She would crack his skull in two. She would pierce his throat with her fingernails. He turned down an alleyway and she turned down after him, but too late. She had lost him. *Vaffanculo!* she cried, *Vaffanculo!* she raged. He had taken everything. All of their money, their passports, and all of the documents pertaining to the house. *Vaffanculo, stronzo!*

She took her time returning to the van. Anthony was sitting on the step with Andrea asleep in his arms. Once he had been put to bed, Liana begged her husband to put an end to this nonsense. They could fly from Marseille-Marignane to Malta. They could sell the van and use the money for a hotel, for the plane tickets. They would need to travel to Nice for new passports and Anthony would have to contact his bank to have money sent. If he was so serious about their new home, what was the delay? If he was determined to see Italy, Liana was willing to drive to Turin, after which they would fly from Torino-Caselle. But he would hear none of it.

Anthony's temporary passport proclaimed, unlike the boy's birth certificate, that Paolo Andrea was the son of Anthony Burgess. Or rather, the son of John Wilson who was, to some degree, still alive in the world. Without her passport, Liana would be crossing from France into Italy illegally. With his passport, Anthony was able to withdraw money from the bank, and buy bottles of Côteaux du Tricastin, Rasteau, and Lirac.

There is wine enough in Italy, Liana cursed. And so there was.

Piedmont, Lombardy, Emilia Romagna. Anthony wrote a bawdy ballad, with Will necking soothing carafes of wine, wrapped in wicker. Brunello, Carmignano, Chianti, Bolgheri. Will read poems to the beautiful women of Florence, who stole from him all these sonnets only to encounter Will once again in an Arezzo taverna.

Liana had reacted to the road in the same manner a man lost at sea reacts to salt water. That she no longer felt ashamed when she kicked out her husband and son so she may use the vehicle's chemical toilet was, in itself, a matter of great shame for her. She had long ago stopped putting on make-up. She would go days without changing her clothes. None of this mattered, but Liana had not agreed to travel the length of Europe to piss into a plastic bucket. It was like some kind of magician's trick; Anthony seemed to be living in luxury, drinking fine wines and smoking expensive cigars, while she and Paolo Andrea made sandwiches from stale bread and hardened cheese. Anthony ate these with delight, exclaiming that this was true European food.

She fell into a kind of delirium, getting into the driver's seat each morning and simply pointing the van in whichever direction took her fancy. From Venice she drove west to Padua. It was only when he realised they were travelling back into Verona that Anthony tried to draw his wife from her trance.

This thing will destroy me, she told him. Paolo Andrea lashed out with his feet at the glovebox, an act of solidarity.

The quicker you get us to Malta, the quicker you can get out of the bloody thing, Anthony snapped, counting stolen and spent pennies in his head. Liana snarled back, but she knew he was right. They turned on to the A22 and started southward once more.

In Bologna Anthony used a public phone to call Deborah Rogers.

I'm glad you've finally made it to Malta.

We're not in Malta. We're in Bologna. He could hear a hand muffle the mouthpiece on her end and cotton-wool expletives.

Anthony, she said calmly, *you're expected in LA in two weeks' time.*

I will be in Malta.

They've green-lit the Enderby project. You're expected to deliver a completed script.

But I'm working on the Shakespeare script.

Which you're also to deliver in two weeks. She was breathing heavily. He sensed the receiver was shaking in her hand.

Well, how the bloody hell am I supposed to write two bloody scripts at once? What the hell is going on there? It took her a long time to reply. He was worried his money might run out. *Hello? Deborah? Can you hear me?*

I can hear you, yes. Anthony, the fee has been agreed and wired to you. I would suggest you make the best of this situation. Could you stay in Italy and write? You can always come back to London and work here. She made it sound so simple. They had been travelling for weeks and yet he could be back in Chiswick in a few short hours.

No, no, we're not coming back. I'm working well on the road. Leave it with me. And you're sure the money has been transferred?

Very sure. How is Liana?

We're all fine. We're all extremely happy. He hung up and went back to the van to open another bottle of wine.

Anthony set about working on two scripts. *Will!* was nearing completion, the Bard having arrived in Malaya only to almost immediately begin his return journey. The second script, based on Kell's book *Enderby*, would be mainly written inside the chemical toilet cupboard, Anthony thinking this approach close to method writing; it may also aid excretion.

He rang Deborah again, from a bar in Faenza, and arrangements were made for him to fly back from Malta to London and from London to Hollywood in ten days' time. This he kept from Liana.

Anthony had not been told what to expect, but whatever he had expected was not this. He thought these might be the maid's quarters, that they were here to pick up a key or drop something off. Liana's mother was a Contessa; these were the rooms of a pauper. Her mother, the Contessa, was old but still striking. Her greying hair was wrapped in an elaborate Italian braid, entwined like rope, pinned tight to her head. Her clothes were much like Liana's, modelled on Chinese Communist attire, though the Contessa's outfit was dappled with paint of many different colours.

Liana introduced her mother to Anthony as *Maria Lucrezia Macellari, Contessa Pasi della Pergola*. The Contessa mouthed her name along with her daughter, nodding with satisfaction when her full title had been announced.

Molto piacere di conoscerti, Anthony recited, holding her frail hand, scaly with dried paint, and smiling absently.

È questo l'uomo a cui è morta la moglie? La donna a cui hai dato il mio quadro?

She had said it quickly but even Anthony had picked up on *morta,* dead and *moglie,* wife. He turned to Liana to translate but she was scowling at her seemingly innocent mother.

Ora lei è la sua defunta moglie e tu sei la moglie in vita, her mother continued, her face warm and smiling.

Defunta moglie, dead wife. *Moglie in vita,* living wife.

You have the painting back now, the Contessa nodded, turning from her daughter to Anthony and back again. The painting still hung in Chiswick, neither of them willing to take it from the wall, take it with them to their new home.

Mamma, Liana said, clearing her throat. She shifted slightly to reveal the small boy who clung to her wide denim culottes. He pulled at them like a curtain, covering his face. Liana, gently as she could, peeled Paolo Andrea's hands from her and moved him out before his grandmother.

The old woman held her venous hands to her thin, wrinkled lips. Tears wetted her arid skin.

Say hello to your grandmother, Andrea, Liana sang, though Anthony heard the anxious tone she sought to hide.

The boy's eyes began to well too. They all stood there for an uncomfortable moment, Andrea's lip quivering.

Una foto! Liana called, moving her husband, mother and son together in a huddle. S*orridete!* They did not, for their own particular reasons, smile.

Venite, venite, the Contessa clucked, and led them into the living room, a little place with a farrago of furniture and mouthfuls of dust for all.

The walls were filled from floor to ceiling, it seemed, with paintings presented in elaborate gold-leaf and artless plain wood frames. Anthony moved away from the conversation and towards the largest of these paintings. Lynne had been given a painting much like this in Chiswick; she was taken aback by such generosity. He and Liana never spoke of it again.

His wife and her mother spoke in rapid, dizzying Italian. He made out the repetition of Paolo Andrea's name but little else. Each picture was different but contained the same young woman at the centre. He had seen her before, in a photograph that recently adorned his mantelpiece and was now in the hands of some Avignon thug. This was Grazia, Liana's sister. She shared the same striking brown-black curly hair as Liana, but there was an innocence in her eyes, absent from Liana's. This was the blessing of youthful death. Liana's sister had died in a skiing accident some years before; her mother had not overcome her grief.

Objectively, the paintings were terrible. The composition was all wrong, buildings simply disappearing into the background, surrounding figures seemingly made of driftwood and wire. Yet as he studied the largest of the paintings more closely, Anthony couldn't help but be drawn to the beauty of this young girl, almost always in the same pose, always with saltwater eyes. He moved from painting to painting. Grazia in a ballgown, horse-riding, reclining by the pool, hugging Liana, kissing her mother's cheek, standing by a gleaming new car, sitting at a restaurant table, surrounded by other people all looking at her, in a bridesmaid's dress, at the beach, her hair in a dramatic beehive, laughing in a rowing boat, one oar floating away, smiling intimately into the camera, her hair as it had been when they first met, sitting outside a bar, bottles of beer filling the table, standing next to a tall off-duty police officer, Ibrahim no doubt on the other side of the lens, sitting in the window of an airport terminal, waiting to fly from Malaya to Borneo, sitting by a water fountain in Rome with friends, holding John's hand on their wedding day, he in uniform, posing with the Bedwellty School Ladies' Hockey Team, meeting the prime minister of

Kelantan province. *Antonio, why don't you come into the garden?* In her skiing outfit, goggles on her forehead. *Yes, darling. In a second.* As a child, sitting with Liana outside the church they had passed on the way. As a baby, swaddled in her mother's arms.

He found himself turning on the spot, his breathing shallow and quick. Drinking a glass of wine, a half-pint of beer, swigging straight from a bottle of Tiger. He saw what this place was: a shrine. Endlessly smoking cigarettes, in each and every painting, grey brushstrokes blended with the bright background. The Contessa, Havisham-like, lived in her daughter's tomb.

Lynne loved that painting *What a nice gift*, she had said, holding Liana's hand, *and you say it is by your mother?* No. No, that wasn't how it had happened. He felt drunk, drowning. Strings started to swell, the swell of a cyclone. Horns stabbed, Lynne's eyes were everywhere, her lips, her – snapping snare hits, snap, snap, over and over – he tried to get his breath – ba dah, ba dah, da dah – falling into a dusty armchair. The room spun. They had come to a stop, yet his mind and body told him he was still in motion. He felt the rumble of the road beneath him now. Motion for him always carried with it music, and this was violent music. Anthony held his eyes tight for a long time, placed his hands over his ears. He waited until he could no longer make out her face in the blackness, until the sound had quelled to a dull background hum.

I am opening prosecco, Liana said, passing her clenched husband and going into the kitchen. The idea of bubbles horrified him.

Anything still? He called after her. *My stomach,* he said, blinking back into the room, his eyes averted from Lynne's visage. From the kitchen came a cork pop. Liana walked in with a tray of glasses and an opened bottle.

You look sick, she said to him.

A brandy, anything?

I have poured you a glass of Galliano. Come out. She continued out into the garden. He cursed her under his breath and followed.

The garden was a few potted bushes and plants on a thin balcony. Contessa Maria was making a fuss of Paolo Andrea, tears in her eyes, chanting, *Paolo mio Paolo, Paolo mio Paolo.* The boy smiled, though Anthony could tell he was unsure of this woman and this place. He did not want to explore; the rooms were cold in every way imaginable, but he did not want to stay here, with this woman who seemed either mad or a child trapped in an old woman's body.

Paolo mio Paolo, the Contessa kept repeating, holding the boy's face vice-like in her hands. His bottom lip started to go again.

Anthony drained his liqueur, just what was needed, and said *Andrea, why don't you go and see if the Bedmobile is okay? Bring back a bottle of wine. Red.*

Liana tutted at this, *He is just a little* – but she saw her husband's intention. *Yes, you go and check for us, darling.* Andrea pulled away from his grandmother's hands that grasped after him as he went inside.

Lui è bello, Maria said, tears in her broken eyes.

Mamma, Liana warned, but the sobbing had begun. And then the accusations. Why had her only daughter, her only living daughter, left her alone for so long? How had she kept her grandson, her only grandson, from her for so long? Who was this man she had married, married in England, that she now brought to meet her poor, sick mother? They returned to speaking in alacritous Italian.

I'm going to, scusami, he tried to interrupt. *Scusami, I'm just going to*, but it was no use. He walked back into the living room, dead eyes ever watching, and into the hallway, where even more paintings waited. Outside, Andrea was kicking a stone about the cobbles. Anthony approached, his hands in his pockets.

That's my nonna, he told Anthony, though there was something of a question in it.

Yes. Yes, that's right.

She has cold hands. Her breath is funny.

You shouldn't say a thing like that, not about your grandmother.

She smells old.

Now that's rude. You know not to be rude. Anthony sat on the windowsill, Andrea continued to kick his stone about.

Are we leaving soon?

We're going to stay for a few days. Your mother hasn't seen your grandmother in a long time. As long as you have been alive. This stopped Andrea in his tracks. He looked around at this place he found himself in, at the vehicle that had got them here, and the man who had come with them.

But I've been alive forever.

Anthony lit a cheroot. *Were you alive when I was born?*

The boy thought about it. *That was a long, long time ago.*

Then how could you have been alive for ever?

I don't ever remember not being here.

But at some point you weren't. Anthony thought of the Big Bang, of God creating heaven and earth. *What do you think came before you?*

Andrea seemed to have lost interest. He went over to a creeper, climbing the worn stone face of the building. After pulling many of the leaves from the plant, he said, *I can't remember. I can almost remember but then something stops me. Maybe nothing. Maybe just nothing.*

But I remember. I remember twenty years ago, forty years ago. I remember being a baby myself, in my cot.

The boy held the leaves he had collected and smelt them. He scrunched them up in his palm and smelt again. *You can't remember all that. I can't remember being a baby. Maybe you had all these things put in your head and really you're only four too.*

Anthony laughed. *Come. Let's have a walk.*

He picked a direction and they set off, the boy running ahead and climbing on the brittle-looking walls, Anthony smoking, following behind.

Andrea said, *Why does she have so many pictures of my mother in her house?*

They are not of your mother, they are of your mother's sister. Your aunty.

Where is she?

She died. Before you were born.

Andrea eyed him suspiciously. *Did you know her?*

No, I didn't know her. Her name was Grazia.

He thought for a moment. *Why did she die?*

It was an accident.

Did she really look like that?

Like the paintings? No, she was very pretty. Like your mother.

Is your mamma dead?

Yes, he said, *she died a very long time ago, when I was younger than you are.*

Was it an accident?

No, no it wasn't an accident. My mother died of Spanish Influenza. The boy pulled a face, mulling the words over. *She was very poorly, lots of people were. My sister died too, she would have been your aunt as well.*

How old was she?

Very young. She was just a girl.

Were you sad?

No, I was too young to be sad, I was a baby.

What about now?

Now? He pointed the boy down a wide street off to their right. *Sometimes, I think about them. My mother mainly.*

What about my mamma?

You shouldn't worry about that. Your mother is very much alive and well.

Where is your papa? Did he die too?

He did, but much later. He was an old man when he died.

The boy had another question to ask. He stood still, his foot kicking at the cobbled street, trying to form the thoughts in his head into words.

You want to know what he died from?

No, the boy replied.

They found themselves in a square with a bar at the far corner. He ordered a gin and tonic and a Coca-Cola for Andrea. He spotted, in the back room, an upright piano. *Through here,* he told Andrea.

Placing his glass on top of the piano, he opened the lid.

Are we allowed? the boy asked.

I will ask. He called out, pointing to the piano; the waiter nodded. Anthony slammed his readied fingers on the keys, making Andrea jump and laugh at the same time. He played big, bawdy chords, letting the strings reverberate. Then he played *A Smile, and Perhaps a Tear,* humming along out of time and tune. Andrea laughed and excitably struck two or three notes himself.

Do you know this song? Anthony asked.

I have heard something like it. Can I play? Andrea asked, hitting another few notes at random.

Would you like me to show you?

No, the boy said. *I want to do it.*

Anthony stopped and stood, giving Andrea the whole seat. The boy shuffled on and Anthony pushed him towards to the keyboard. *What will you play, Andrea?* he asked.

The boy thought and said, *I think I'll play the same thing you played.*

Okay, well, let's hear it.

Andrea slammed his outspread palms on the keys, slapping them down wherever they fell. He played with great concentration, stopping at one point because he had got it wrong and then continuing in the same raucous fashion. The bar owner stood behind and watched, amused by the boy's enthusiasm. After forty seconds he stopped, out of breath and ideas.

Very good, Anthony told him.

Ha un talento innato, the bar owner said, returning to the main room.

Would you like me to show you a few things? Anthony asked, moving the boy along and sitting next to him.

Andrea thought for a second. *No.* He hopped down from the stool and drank his cola through the straw.

This, Anthony said, undeterred, *is Middle C.* He struck the note, poignantly. *If you know where Middle C is, the whole piano is laid out for you.*

I'm hungry, Andrea said, milling between the empty tables.

Are you paying attention, Andrea? I am teaching you something.

But I'm hungry.

But nothing. Come here. My father never showed me any of this. You should be grateful.

I want to go to Mamma, the boy said.

No, you can come back here and learn something. This, he struck the note again, *is Middle C. Now, you show me.*

I don't want to.

Come here and show me.

The boy returned to Anthony's side and struck out at a key. *No, that's E. Middle C, I asked for.* Andrea tried again. *No, B. Try again.* Frustrated, the boy hit out with both hands on the keyboard. *Do it properly, Andrea. Here, watch me.* He hit the note again.

I don't want to. I want to go back.

You're being very disobedient. Here, he hit the note a fourth time. *All I want you to do is repeat after me.*

No.

You will. Show me.

No. I want Mamma.

I will take you back after you've – do you not see, this is meant to be fun!

Andrea hit the note and ran from the bar, Anthony yelling behind him, *Show me again! I didn't see!* He chased after his father, who had gone through to the kitchen and was lifting the cap off a bottle of stout. *Please, Dad, I want to know.*

I've bloody well shown you once, haven't I?

Please.

In the square he could not see the boy and shouted his name loudly. There were four roads leading off the square. He could have gone down any of them. *Andrea!* Anthony yelled. *Andrea, come back!*

Stop mithering, for Christ's sake, Jackie. You're givin' me a flaming headache.

He returned to the piano and stared at the black and white puzzle before him. His teacher had told him Middle C was the door that led to the world of music. There had been no piano in the classroom and he had struggled to contain his excitement on the journey home, jumping from the bus and running down the narrow streets. Fraught, he stumbled about the square, shouting the boy's name. What the hell would he do? He should have never been left in charge of the boy, he told himself. This was not his role, not what they had agreed. He waited for a moment of inspiration. He hit a key, one he thought central, one that might, just might be Middle C, but how could the boy know when there was no clue, when all white keys looked the same and all black keys identical? He circled the square, considered going down one road, but instead sat on a bench by the fountain. And if there was Middle C, was there also Middle A and Middle B? Where were they? Why were they any less important than C? He looked up and saw it would most likely rain soon, it was getting late. The boy had disappeared and there was nothing he could do. She would never forgive him, even though it was the boy's fault. Even though he had only tried to teach him something. Standing at the left-hand edge of the keyboard, he struck the last white key, boom, and the next, boom, boom, boom, boom, changing into bah, into bee as he moved up the keys, changing to dah to dee and at the very end, ting. There was nothing for it but to return to the bar and wait. He would buy another drink, sit outside and wait. In all these paintings, a Middle C, in all these bottles of wine, a Middle C, in the women he had met and the places he could possibly be, each one a potential Middle C. But again he had no point of reference, no clue that might eliminate any of the options before him. Which of these passions, his creative outlets was Middle C? He still had no idea. The boy distracting him while he tried to write his screenplay, while he thought about a new novel, while music battled within him for attention, while reviews had to be written, think-pieces thought, biographies set down and critical texts researched. The boy, the son, the child did nothing but distract, did nothing but question and question. *Why why why why why why why?* And his father said, *For money. Not for pleasure? No, not for pleasure. Not for invention or for ego or for the challenge? Lad, have you been listening at all to anything I've been trying to tell you? It's money, in't it. It's for money. I learned where Middle C was, aye, and where the bloody hell did that get me, eh? Din't want me in the cinemas no more, kicked out, the joanna thrown right after me, din't want me in the pubs n'more, rolling in their fancy fucking Yankee jukeboxes and kicking my bleeding arse out the door. We're selling the flamin' thing, so there ain't much point in learning where anything bloody well is. But here, if you must know, here, ding ding ding, is Middle C. Like the thumb of your right-hand fist, your forefinger and ring finger the black'ens. Do you see? Here it is, on the page*

Here it is again

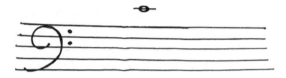

The same, but not the same, do you see that, lad? Keeps itself from the stave, from those lines there that the other notes live on or between.

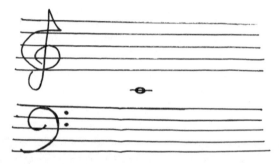

Centre of everything, committed to nothing. Now you know the answer that will unlock all other answers, or so your stuck-up teachers'd 'ave you believe, well, believe me, pianner-playing ain't nothing to do with Middle C, not in my book, anyroad. Not in my book, lad. Music I play, did play, want nothing to be written down and read but was played in like reaction and in responding to the pictures on the screen or the people yelling out for Boiled Beef and Carrots or Two Lovely Black Eyes, only by the time I'm playing one, someone's yelling out for summut else or the picture's changed and I'm avin' to make the joanna do plenty of work and at last orders or when the reel reels off, then it's all gone, all that music disappeared in the night, never to be done the same ever again.

Ephemeral, he replies.

Don't give me none of that big word bollocks, our Jackie. Big word bollocks and a big load of notes on a load of pages, that's you all bloody over. Here, ding ding ding, on the key again, *I'm off out.*

And Anthony sits on the piano stool, looking down at the keys, Middle C in the centre of his vision, and he thinks to himself, now what? *Have you seen,* he begins to say, seeing Andrea on a barstool drinking a fresh bottle of Coke the owner talking to him in broken English.

Ecco tuo padre, the man exclaimed. *Your son,* he said to Anthony, *he came back.*

I can see. Andrea, he said, holding himself together, *come to me.* The boy climbed down from the barstool, eyes downcast. *You must,* he felt he might strike him across the face, *never, never, run off like that again. Do you hear me?* And to the owner, *How much do I owe you? For the Coke?*

Niente, he replied, waving Anthony away. *Little boys are little boys*, he said.

Grazie. Andrea, say thank you. The boy stood rigid, terrified. Anthony snapped and yelled, *Say thank you for Christ's sake! Say thank you. Say it!* The boy said nothing. *Say thank you, say it!* He bawled.

Thank you, the boy's voice cracked.

They walked back in silence, Anthony red with rage, Andrea sobbing, though he tried to hide it. At the door Anthony said, *Your mother does not need to know about this. I will not tell her what you did. Okay?* The boy nodded. *Now,* Anthony said, *wipe your face.*

He opened the door and made sure the boy went in first. Liana came to meet them, exclaiming, *Tell her, Antonio. Tell her we want to take her out to eat. She refuses to let us pay,* she yelled in the direction of the balcony, *she says she will cook.*

In the galley kitchen, no bigger than the ones they had left in Chiswick or Bedford, Liana assessed the ingredients she had to work with. They were limited. She made a list and, taking a wicker bag from a hook, went to the market nearby. Andrea went with her, clinging to her arm, while Anthony took his glass of wine back to the Dormobile and continued to work. The final push to complete *Will!*.

Liana arrived back, weighed down with heavy bags of pasta and vegetables, her face fixed in a scowl. He opened the Dormobile door and gave her a cheery *Buon pomeriggio*.

Liana gritted her teeth and said, *Where is my mother?* She put the bags down, *For Christ's sake, Antonio.* Before he could respond, she had gone in.

He followed her, labouring with so much shopping, saying, *I need to work. I've got so much to finish.*

Liana tutted, grabbed one of the bags and pulled out a smaller bag containing porcini mushrooms. She let them roll onto a wooden chopping board and began slicing.

You should wash them first.

Liana swung round, the point of the knife directed towards Anthony. *Would you like to do it?*

He put on an apron and Liana poured herself a glass of wine. *You should not have left my mother's house like that. You are a guest, you are her son-in-law.* How ridiculous that sounded to both of them.

I need to work, Liana. He poured a great glug of olive oil into the pan and threw in the sliced mushrooms.

Jesus, she cursed, and took the spatula from him, *give it to me.* Anthony took her wine and Liana retrieved the mushrooms from their greasy bath. *You can take a day off to get to know my mother.*

There is no time. The truth was bubbling within him. He watched his wife put a pan of water on and add a loaded tablespoon of chicken stock, which she swirled in the water. *There's no time.*

You have all the time in the world. You do nothing else but write, Antonio. The water began to boil. Liana took a packet and sprinkled what looked like sand into the pan.

Well, I have to bloody write to live, don't I?

Don't speak to me that way. You choose to work so much. She whisked water that grew thick with yellow grains.

You think it's a choice?

Isn't it?

I write to make money, Liana. Don't you—he stopped himself. *Those reviews I've been writing pay for the food we eat.*

Hand-to-mouth writing, Antonio. She continued to whisk, the water boiling and spitting yellow lava. *You get distracted by this small stuff, writing for magazines, for movies. Novels are how you make money.*

He drained the wine in Liana's glass. *Is that what you think?* He knew it was exactly what she thought. *There's no money in sodding novels, let me tell you.*

Shush, you will wake my mother. Liana reduced the heat of the hob and put the lid on.

I wrote, he continued at the same volume, *five novels in a sodding year and didn't earn a penny. If you want money, Liana, if you want things, I have to write for magazines, I have to write for the bloody movies.*

She poured another glass of wine and studied him. *What are you trying to say, Antonio? We have no money?*

He reddened. *Of course that's not what I'm saying. I'm just*—

I think you underestimate your worth as a novel writer. You make bad deals. When we were apart I would often see your books published and think why is this not better advertised, why is Antonio not on the television?

I'm always on the bloody television.

You are on the television talking about everything else except what should be the most important. She lifted the lid and stirred what was now a thick paste.

Anthony peered in. *What the hell is that?*

Polenta. I am no cook, Antonio, but polenta I make very well. She kissed him, the argument seemingly over. He had neither unburdened himself nor kept his secret a secret. He itched with frustration.

Delizioso, Maria said, taking her seat and spooning herself something that looked, to Anthony, like semolina pudding. Thin, watery semolina pudding. It turned his stomach just to sit in front of it. What the hell was he doing here, he poured more wine, in Italy, having to eat whatever the hell this was. He saw his expression reflected in Andrea's face. A little boy sticking his tongue out at the abomination his mother had presented as food.

Eat up, Liana told Andrea sternly. Anthony felt sternly told. He put a forkful to his mouth. It felt grainy and sloppy against his lips. He took a glug of wine for courage and forced the fork mouthwards. It tasted of nothing but the texture was repulsive. It was all he could do to stop himself from spitting the slop out. What fresh hell was this? Liana had made other things, pasta with mushrooms, drizzled in oil, grilled fish, heads still intact. All of this was not right. Surrounded by paintings of – Jesus, no, don't think about her – he was no longer in Chiswick, no longer in Etchingham. Etchingham sold, Chiswick rented out to Terry, his homes were gone. He drank and, distractedly, lit a cheroot. How far away was the nearest lamb chop or rabbit stew? Christ, Christ, oh Christ, how grief came like a falling lift. And then, once you thought you'd hit the ground, how far it fell once more. She was dead and buried, wasn't that meant to be the end?

I've escaped, he wanted to scream. I've fucking escaped, haven't I? Aren't I meant to be bloody free now?

Antonio, put that out. Try this, she stubbed his cheroot out and dropped an eyeballing fish on his plate.

I can't – he thought he might be sick. He stared down at the staring visage of Pisces. My birth sign, he thought, but knew too little of astrology to draw a significant link. *I think I need to get some air.* He got up unsteadily and went into the street.

If he could, he would have driven the Dormobile away. He had no means of escape from his escape, however. He was trapped in his liberation. And, no, he would not eat that Italian filth. He was an Englishman and he would eat pies and black pudding and mince and gravy and peas and she is still with me and I cannot be free and the more I try the more she will find me and drive me mad and curse me.

Music struck again, vivid, arching chords, then the melancholy of oboes and bassoons. He climbed into the Dormobile and searched for staved paper. He tried to write the notes down but found they would not sit on the bars. What he needed was a piano, a piano and more wine.

They left abruptly the next day for Rome. Liana apologised, explaining to her mother they had to get to the capital as soon as possible so she could get a new passport. Liana drove like a getaway driver. Anthony sat in the back, in silence, no crack of typewriter keys, nor humming and drumming one of his one-man orchestras. Instead, with black ink on music manuscript, he carefully plotted a course, charted a journey. They joined the Tiber by night. Anthony saw it running red, the delicious, juicy red of Sangiovese.

You are awfully quiet, Liana called back. But she could not have been further from the truth; he was brimming with noise and bustle. *What do you think is going on, Andrea?* she asked in a comically conspiring tone. The boy looked behind at the old man hunched in concentration. *Why don't you go and see?* But the boy did not want to go and see, instead he fixed his eyes on the road ahead and said *Rome: r, ohm, e,* watching for the corresponding marks on the signs that hurtled past.

They stopped in Caldare; Anthony carefully put away his music and drew his typewriter from the cupboard. Liana and Andrea took a walk by the river. Anthony watched its mighty flow from the Dormobile and knew its significance. The river spurgeoning in his ears, Anthony completed his script for *Will!*;

the finale had him give up the woman he loved in Malaya, and the revelation that a son was soon to come into the world. Will, waving sadly from his departing ship, would never know of the heir he left behind.

By the time his wife started the engine again he had relocated to the toilet cupboard to press on with the *Enderby* script. His head reeled in andantino with dialogue and the reanimation of dead characters. Enderby himself had to be made younger, the cinema being no place for the infirm. Give him a young, glamorous wife, Anthony told himself, it will knock years off him.

Liana held Andrea's hand tight. Rome thronged with people. She drew him through a thousand gesticulating and smoking hands, a ballet of fingers and palms.

Keep beside me, she told him.

Yes, Mamma.

They arrived at the questura, taking their place at the end of a long, meandering queue.

What happened to all of these people? Andrea asked, looking around at faces filled with regret, with rage; a woman in tears, a man holding a bloody napkin to his face.

Different things, she told him. *Don't look at them.*

Andrea looked. He had a sense that this was where he belonged, not in the police station, but in Rome, surrounded by all these lively faces and – *Ve ne andate! Vaffanculo!* – loud voices.

The queue had not moved for some time. Andrea said, *Mamma?*

Liana replied, *Yes?*

What happened to us?

She seemed to hold her breath for a second and then fumbled around in her bag for a cigarette. Lighting it, she said, *When that man stole my bag, he took my passport also.*

It was inside?

It was.

What about me, did he take my passport too? He wasn't sure what a passport was exactly, but for them to be in this queue, surrounded by these people, Andrea knew it must be important.

You have been added to your father's passport. She looked down at him and said, *To Antonio's passport.*

He was not sure what this meant for him but he knew he did not like it. *Antoniole is not my father,* he said.

We have talked about this, Andrea.

Two other boys took it in turns to climb onto the arm of a wooden bench and leap as far as they could. Their mother yelled at them but did not leave her place in the queue. When one of them pushed the other, who fell and cried out as his ankle gave out beneath him, the mother crossed herself and called them *piccoli diavoli.*

His mother gripped his hand and moved him so he could no longer see the other boys.

Mamma, how long is Antoniole going to be staying with us?

What do you mean? They moved forward.

How long?

For always, Andrea. We live together now. He is your father. But when will it just be you and me again?

Sbrigati, per l'amor di Dio, she muttered; and then, *It is you and me now.*

No. Not like this. I mean, when will it just be you and me, only you and me, no Antoniole?

Why are you asking this, Andrea? You know the answer; I have already told you.

He watched an elderly couple, arm in arm, sharing disappointed looks and consolatory words. The queue inched closer to the bank of high fronted desks ahead. He said, *Can I sit over there?*

No, you can stay here with me, she replied, tightening her grip.

He said, *Do you remember when we used to live with Stephen?*
She did not reply.

And he used to take me to the park or to get sweets or sometimes to the toy shop.

Quiet now, Andrea.

And you took me on the boat and let me do the rowing. And you took me to eat lasagne and the woman let me have a glass of wine.

It was not a glass of wine, Andrea. It was only a mouthful. And I told you to drink it very slowly.

And do you remember when I would come and help you do your work and I would put the pages in order and you let me draw on the coloured paper. And you cut out the people –

Signora, come posso aiutarla? came a gruff, disinterested voice from behind the desk.

Il mio passaporto è stato rubato, Liana replied, looking for something in her bag.

Mamma, Andrea pulled on her blouse.

Not now. She handed a piece of paper to the man and spoke in words Andrea did not understand.

Mamma, do you remember when I used to sleep in your—

Andrea, no. Be quiet now. I don't want to hear another word.

Andrea tried to bite back tears. He tried to unpick her fingers with his free hand, but she would not let go, refusing to look at him.

The man spoke aggressively and Andrea caught the word *crimine.* He heard his mother say words he was sure were made up, words that frightened him with their loudness and peculiarity. The man shouted back, his mother slammed her hand on the desk and shouted too. The man shouted again, matching her volume.

His mother rested her head on her hand, watched as the man stood up and left. The people behind cried out, afraid he would never come back and they would always be waiting for him to return. She did not look at Andrea and the boy refused

220

to look at her. He stood still, trying to pay attention as time passed. The man behind wore a watch, which Andrea could see only when he turned around and only when the man's sleeve was not covering the face. This happened every few minutes, and Andrea made it into a game, where he would try, without counting, to guess how long had passed. He turned and the face would be hidden, so he had to wait until the man scratched his arm or twitched his fingers, which he did regularly.

Above him, the man said, *Deve chiamare questo numero.*

One minute and twenty-eight seconds, Andrea thought. He turned his head: correct.

Il telefono più vicino? his mother asked, in a tone he had only ever heard her use with him, when he had been acting up. *Grazie,* she said, pulling his hand, leading him along the crowd and out into the rain-soaked street.

Come on, she said. *We need to go this way.*

He was made to stand in a phone box while his mother talked to someone. It wasn't Antoniole, he knew, because Antoniole didn't speak Italian. Perhaps she was on the phone to his nonna. But Mamma had her serious voice, the one she would use in her office or with Stephen late at night. Finally, she put the phone down and said, *Do you want gelato?*

It's too cold for gelato.

Come on, she tried to pull him close, but he kept his distance. *Okay, we'll have spaghetti.*

Liana ordered for Andrea, who pulled a face at the food put in front of him. *What? You don't like it?*

It smells.

It smells, she mocked. *Eat up.* She took the napkin from the table and tucked it into his t-shirt. His mother laughed to herself and then took a picture of him.

The boy tried to resist, but he was too hungry not to eat. The food was delicious. He couldn't help but return the smile his mamma gave him. After he had eaten as much spaghetti as he thought he could, his mamma ordered more food. The waiter arrived with another plate; it looked like ice cream mixed with jelly.

What is it? He shook the plate with this hand and saw the waiter smiled as he did.

Who knows? Try it. She put her fork into her brown and yellow cake. It smelt of rich coffee.

He took a small spoonful from his plate, so small he could not tell whether it was good or bad on his tongue. The next spoonful was much bigger. It was creamy and sweet and made him feel like laughing. He said, *What is it called?*

Panna cotta, she told him. *Here,* she poured glossy red sauce on top, which tasted like jam. He ate everything on the plate.

Should we take something back for Antonio? she asked, lighting a cigarette.

No, Andrea replied, putting his spoon noisily down on the plate.

He could hear the mechanical tapping before he saw their home. Turning the corner, the sound grew louder. Antoniole, the boy thought, and shook his head. His mother carried a bag with food for him, against Andrea's advice.

How are you getting on? she asked, taking the plate out of the bag.

Very well. The van stank of cigarettes, Andrea hung by the door, taking gasps of air from outside.

Close the door, darling, his mamma said. *I have to go back tomorrow.*

Back?

These police and bureaucrats. They accused me of being a criminal. An illegal immigrant!

Antonio bunched his fists up and said, *How dare they. How bloody dare they! I will go down there tomorrow and give them a piece of my mind.*

Eat, Antonio. I will go, you need to work. There is nothing you can do.

Antonio ate, tomato sauce spattering his blue shirt. There was much work to do.

The next day was much the same for Liana and Andrea. They waited in the queue, then waited in another queue, only this time they were allowed to take a seat. They ate lunch in the cafe and took food back for Anthony. In the afternoon they visited a big church, walked through the open plazas, and Liana showed her son around a huge art gallery. She took photographs of everything. He stood beside portraits of old men and beautiful women, recreating their poses. His mamma took photograph after photograph of him. Andrea and Liana alone again, just the way he liked it.

Don't you, he asked, *wish it could be like this all the time?*

Like what, darling?

Me and you. Just me and you.

She did not reply. They met Anthony outside a different cafe, one that did not look so nice. No one else was eating. The tables were littered with single men who smoked over black coffees or small glasses of red wine. The food was bad. Andrea watched Anthony as he ate it just the same as he had eaten yesterday. When Andrea refused to eat, his mamma did not argue, instead ordering gelato.

How was today?

Good, Anthony replied, mouth full with runny sauce and tough pasta. *I may well have it done by the time we get to Lija.*

Get what done? the boy asked. He stabbed the ice cream with the spoon. It was too cold.

Work, his mother told him. *I spoke to an old colleague from Cambridge today.* It was true, she and Andrea had visited a man, not that Andrea would have told Anthony this. The man had been kind and his wife spoke with an accent he had only heard on television programmes. The wife took Andrea down to the park across the road from their apartment and played on the climbing frame with him. *Bruno offered me some work, translating.* The woman had asked Andrea how he enjoyed his holiday. He was surprised to hear this word; he had not thought of this as a holiday.

It has been, he told her, *hard work.* She laughed and he laughed along, though he didn't know why.

Who's offered you work? When was this? Anthony became animated. Andrea looked to see if his hands had gone into fists yet.

What has been hard about it? the woman had asked him. She rolled the word – *harrrrd* – about her mouth in a way that made Andrea feel happy.

Antoniole, he said.

It's good work, good pay. Bruno is a teacher here now. He has a book he wants translating. The publisher is dragging their heels.

What's wrong with Antoniole?

He's a nuisance, Andrea said, which made the woman laugh again.

Of all the bloody nerve, Anthony yelled. The other men, for there were only other men in the cafe, turned to look at him. Loud-mouth Englishman, they seemed to think in unison, going back to their private thoughts.

That is no way to think of it, Antonio. Who knows how long we will be stuck in Rome waiting for my goddamned passport.

A nuisance?

He's always yelling, or saying nothing, or banging around, or telling me to stop making noise, even though he is the noisiest person in the Door Mobile.

What is that?

It's our house on wheels. It has five big doors and can go very far.

And Anthony makes noise?

And other things. He yells at me.

What about?

About everything. About everything I do.

I'm sure it's not all that bad, Andrea. He smiled at the sound of his name from her lips.

I'm telling you, lady, it's terrible.

Anthony scooped up his cigarettes and matches. He said, *I need a drink. A proper drink.*

Wait and we will come with you. But he was already gone. His mamma went to the door and called, *What about the baby?* She meant Andrea, even though he wasn't a baby any more.

The next morning, the van smelt sweet and sour. Andrea woke first; Anthony's snoring had woken him. The old man lay next to Andrea's mamma, her hair in rollers and a net. She seemed very small beside him, like a child, with her hair hidden she looked like a little boy too. Andrea watched them, trying to remember when it was just he and she, but it was hard with Anthony there to remember anything but the three of them. He tried his best to remember Cambridge, his house with all of his things in it, but Anthony had somehow got into the memory, it seemed like his life hadn't been anything until Anthony arrived.

After cornflakes they went back to the questura. They were taken into a private room where his mamma spoke to two men in grey suits for a long time. She was calm and they were calm. After a little time, the two men left but Andrea and Liana were made to wait. Then a woman came and they followed her, his mamma not talking the whole time. At the front door, the woman said, *Addio*, and Liana repeated this word, so Andrea said it too.

Addio, he said. The woman, who had not looked at him this whole time looked down. Liana said the word again, and they left.

They went to a place called Galleria Nazionale d'Arte Moderna. It was an enormous building, with pairs of thick white pillars. Andrea wanted to climb them to the very top. Inside, there were lots of statues and paintings that his mamma liked very much. She took a great many photographs and was told off by a security guard. Andrea played a game of being very quiet but moving his mouth as if he were talking very loudly. The men and women they passed seemed to think this was funny, so he made even more elaborate head and mouth movements, like a marionette.

Do you remember, Andrea said, eating sugary donuts from a paper bag, *when you took me to the circus?*

I do.

Who else was there?

You mean, like the clowns and the lions?

No, with us. Who else?

No one, she said, suspiciously.

Okay, he replied, licking his fingers. *Okay.*

They ate with Anthony. He had a big piece of meat and lots of vegetables. All the time, he kept saying, *This is more like it. This is much more like it.*

Like what? Andrea asked.

I spoke to Deborah.

Oh yes? What did she have to say?

Anthony put a hunk of meat in his mouth and chewed and said, *Everything has arrived in Lija. She has organised for them to have access to the house. Everything's been arranged.*

That's good news.

The car has arrived too.

Andrea could tell that Anthony wanted to say something else. His mamma said, *Anything else?*

Yes, he cleared his throat. *They, eh, they want me to go to LA. Film people. She's going to organise a flight.*

Soon?

I'm not sure.

What's LA? Andrea asked.

She didn't say when?

They're working out the details. How long do you think this passport business will take?

They say a few more days. But you're not going to leave us here, are you?

I'm not leaving you anywhere.

Antonio, you said—

I know what I said.

What's LA, Mamma?

Quiet for a second, darling. When, Antonio?

Can we talk about this later?

You brought it up now. When did she say?

In five days' time. There's a flight from Malta to London. I'm to meet a man there to discuss a possible film. Then a flight to LA. Bill Conrad wants me out there.

For how long?

A week. Maybe two.

You tell me this now? How long have you known?

Not long. I didn't want to – he pushed away his plate, tired of too much meat. *I didn't want to upset you or make you worry about being alone.*

Because now I am alone.

Andrea said, *You're not alone, Mamma.*

This is not fair, Antonio. This is – how dare you! You make me leave my home, then you make me leave my mother, you make me drive that fucking pezzo di merda all the way here. And you expect me to drive you to Malta, a place where I don't know anybody, where I don't know anything, where I am alone and – how do you think I will survive? Have you even thought about what I will do while you are gone? Cazzo. You are, she gritted her teeth and let out a violent shriek. *You are a selfish man, I knew this. I thought you would show me kindness—*

Liana—

Mamma—

No, I will continue. You think you can act this way? No. No.

We need the money, he blurted. *There is no money. There is nothing. I need to go to London to earn money. I need to go to America so I can earn more money. I have nothing. All of Lynne's money is tied up, the bastard British government have taken half of my earnings. I have nothing.*

We have nothing. She suddenly seemed very calm. *You lied to me.*

I did not lie to you.

You let me believe you were wealthy. You made me believe I would be cared for, I would need no job.

And all of that is true, but I need to work.

How much money do we have?

That's not for you to worry about.

How much, Antonio? Tell me how much.

Anthony was silent, Andrea had never seen him quiet. He appeared like a little boy too. His mother looked at Anthony very sadly, like she was very sorry for him. Finally, he said, *Not much. Maybe enough to last a few weeks.*

His mother put her head in her hands, but quickly sat up straight. She said, *Okay, here's what will happen. I will go and speak to Bruno and take this work with him. There is other work with the publisher, I'll look into it. I will ask for an advance.*

Liana, please—

I'll ask them. Then, I will tell them I can do the work once we arrive in Malta.

Andrea thought Anthony might yell but he stayed very quiet.

When he was meant to be asleep, Andrea listened to them and watched them in the side mirror, while they sat outside, drinking wine. His mother said, *Why the hell are we here, Antonio?*

Anthony looked like he would not reply, but then said, *I had to escape. They,* he fumbled, *they would have taken even more money in tax.*

Why are we here?

I need somewhere to write.

Why, Antonio?

Then, stumbling over his own words, Anthony said, *I needed to escape her. She wouldn't let me live. She wants me dead. We needed to get out of Chiswick, out of England. She haunts me, Liana. I wanted her dead and now she is dead and she won't let me forget my part in it. We had to leave so we could start our lives together. You see that? Do you see that?*

Softly, she said, *You were not a good husband to her, I can tell now, but you will be a good husband to me.*

I will.

You must listen now, Antonio. You will go to London in five days, right?

He nodded.

And I will be with our son in a strange place. Okay, none of this can be helped. But when you return, you will not do this to me ever again. Where you go, I go.

Cara, Liana.

Wait, I want to say more. From now on, I must know everything about the money. I cannot help solve a problem I don't know exists. Okay?

Look, I—

No, Antonio, this is not for arguing. I will not live in darkness, worrying whether my son will have food on his plate or a roof over his head. That is not the life I want for him and it is not the life you promised. From now on, you will tell me.

I'm sorry. He sounded weak.

I'm sorry too, but this is where we find ourselves and we must make the best of it.

He could not say how many days they had come to this same building and waited, but Andrea knew it was many. This day was different. This day Anthony came with them. They were taken into a room when one of the grey-suited men talked to his mother, with Anthony interrupting saying, *What was that? I didn't quite catch that,* and *parli più lentamente.* After a wait, the other man arrived with pieces of coloured paper that he showed to his mamma. There were tears in her eyes, but Andrea could not see what was written or if there were any pictures. The men shook her hand and shook Anthony's hand, saying, *Buon viaggio.*

Outside, Anthony called the men fascists, a word Andrea had heard Anthony use a lot. When they got home, Anthony and Liana packed everything away. Andrea said, *Where are we going?*

We are going home, his mamma replied.

To my house?

To your house, yes.

Andrea was very excited to hear this. He started to pack his things, the toys and papers he had out.

Soon they were back on the road, driving home. Andrea said, *Mamma, remember when we was little boys together and Antoniole was not with us?*

Anthony, who was sitting in the back, not typing or singing, or doing anything really, looked angrily at Andrea, but the boy didn't care. They were going back home, back to just the two of them.

It was late when she pulled up beside 168 Main Street. None of them moved. Andrea kept repeating, *What is this place? Why have we stopped here?* Liana and Anthony looked over at each other, neither wanting to make the first move.

Anthony watched as she studied herself in the rear view. She was thinner, a little tanned, and greasy-haired. He waited for her to jump out, to yell in joy at leaving behind this ugly machine she hated so much. But he realised, watching her grip the steering wheel, it had become something else, in all the madness that had ensued these past few months, it had been steadfast and dependable. And now she must leave it for a future she could barely comprehend. He wasn't quite sure what to do. He knew after they had spent their first night in this new house, he would have to ask Liana to drive him to the airport and he would be gone.

Andrea said, *Are we staying here? Are you getting the bed ready?*

Liana opened the driver's door, saying, *We are staying in there,* she pointed at the green door. *Shall we go and see?*

They all climbed out, Andrea muttering, still unsure what they were doing here. Liana found the key under the pot as had been agreed and, with a short sharp breath, opened the front door. She couldn't find the light switch and then, when she did, it did not work. Anthony went back to the Dormobile and returned with three torches.

Here, let me turn it on for you, he said, showing Andrea where the switch was, pointing the bulb down so not to blind him. Anthony led, pointing his torch down the hallway and following the bannister up the stairs.

We need to find the fuse box, Liana said, apparently to Andrea.

Anthony turned his torch right and came to a door, which he opened. There, gloomily lit by torchlight, was Lynne's chair, her side table, where it had always been. He lost his grip, juggling the torch between his hands.

What is it?

He dared not say. He slowly lifted the torch again. The standard lamp at the side of the door, the bookcases, arranged as Lynne had arranged them, only now completely bare, her chair, her table, the television on the television cabinet, where she had liked it. Their Chiswick living room. He closed the door. He gripped his chest, he could taste thick dust on his tongue, the faint odour of Haji, old books, stale fags, Lynne's stale fags, the smell of stewed tea. Her perfume, her scent, her sweat, her hairspray, her lipstick, he could smell it all.

Antonio, what is going on? Liana's voice came from far away.

She's here, he cried. *She's in there.*

Who is? Her voice further still.

Christ, he yelled, holding his torch at the door, not daring to move it, lest he find this was Glebe Street, a dead zone where Glebe Street stood in perpetual darkness, with Lynne lying in wait.

Help me, he called out. From the corner of his eye he could see candlelight, he could hear her breathing, could smell the sweetness of warm white wine on her cold breath.

John, a voice said.

No, please, he whimpered. His chest stung, he gripped at his shirt, pulling it tight.

John.

I didn't mean to. I never meant to... he struggled to talk, his mouth filling with saliva, his teeth rattling. He dropped to his knees, the torch falling to the floor. In darkness, in this bleakness, he cried. She was dead. She had found him. There was no escape. There was no end. They were bound by more than marriage, they were bound by fate, a shared end that was ongoing, unabated. His chest pounded, his breath ceased, he felt like his throat had been cut. It was death, now. These last few months had been the interlude between her death and his. The piece of string that connected them had not been severed but stretched to its very limit and now it was drawing him back to her.

Antonio, a light shone brightly turning absolute black into blinding white. This was it, then. Dead. *Antonio, breathe, take a breath, my darling. Andrea, Andrea, stop doing that, get down. Antonio, can you hear me?*

The light shifted, white with black, Liana's face peering down at him. He wanted to say sorry, sorry for all of this, but she kept repeating, *Breathe, please breathe, Antonio.*

From out of the darkness, she had breathed new life into him and then she drove him to the airport. Anthony slept on the plane in something like a fever dream, shivering and twitching. All that way by road, a quarter of a year gone by, and now he was returning to London in a few short hours. It didn't quite make sense. He told himself he was not returning to Chiswick, but he dreamt of Chiswick and of Lija, two sides of the same coin. He dreamt of Liana as a kind of sister to Lynne and as, he gasped in his sleep, a kind of daughter. When he woke he asked for gin, drank much, and fell heavily asleep once more.

In the Hilton he was met by John Bryan, who had a copy of the script Anthony had sent from Rome. There was a great deal of red ink.

John said, *Don't worry, Tony, can I call you Tony? Just a few changes, for the studio, you know what it's like.*

He did. He went up to his hotel room, drew his typewriter from his suitcase, and started typing. The next morning, he was met for breakfast by John once more. Anthony ate a full English, his first taste of real food in three months, while John read.

You work fast, he said.

I've got to fly to LA today.

I'll have my guy look over this. It looks good.

Good. He coughed, wiped his mouth with a brown sauce-stained napkin.

Are you feeling okay? You don't look all that well.

Planes. You can't get on a plane without getting ill.

Well, I'll get back to you, Tony. Where are you staying?

I'm not sure. Warner Brothers are putting me up.

He had climbed back into bed, dead tired. Deborah rang and said, *Litvinoff wants to meet you. They've got a director on board, they want you to write the script.*

Meet me? Meet me when?

Now. They're downstairs.

And where are you?

Crickhowell, Powys.

Wales? What are you doing in Wales?

I'm with my family. They only want to discuss the project. Anthony, are you okay? He put the phone down.

In the bar, he met Si Litvinoff, a skeletal man with sunken eyes. Anthony hated this man, who reminded him of foolish decisions made in the pursuit of killing off his dead wife.

Good to see you again, Anthony, Litvinoff said.

Si. A pleasure. A pleasure. So, you have a director?

Yes, but, he looked about to see they were speaking privately, *you must keep it to yourself.*

I have no one to tell, Anthony placated.

Ken Russell. You know him?

I know the name.

He's just done Women in Love. Very sensual, very well received.

Women in Love, as in Lawrence?

A bit fairy for my tastes, but he knows what he's doing. We want you to write the script, of course. It is, after all, your vision. But, Litvinoff stopped himself.

But you want things changed? Anthony was still reeling from the news that someone had put Lawrence on the screen. Why had no one asked him to write the screenplay? He was filled with a bitter jealousy. *Who wrote the script for Women in Love? Do you know?*

Some American kid, I hear. Litvinoff drank his black coffee and eyed Anthony. *We've had a few thoughts that I'd like to run past you.*

I'm sure you have. Go ahead.

We want to make it as a musical. Alex and the Droogs will be the name of their band, and they'll play rock'n'roll.

Rock and roll?

The kids go wild for them, especially Alex, with his bright hair and his catsuit.

Catsuit?

I've had a designer draw up some images. He pulled from his briefcase gaudy sketches of young, lanky men in brightly coloured outfits, red hair in a kind of beehive. The pictures made Anthony's head spin.

He said, *I'd be happy to work on the script. Are you sure a musical is right?*

Sure, sure. Alex loves music, right? So, the authorities take music away from him, make him hate music, make him turn against rock'n'roll. That *'n* sound made Anthony's fillings prickle. *They're lining up to do it. The Rolling Stones, the Beatles, you name them.*

I will write it.

234

Excellent. I'm delighted.

I'm working on a couple of scripts for Warner Brothers at the moment, however. My fee has been set accordingly.

Of course. Of course. We were thinking $10,000. Litvinoff smiled, openly. $10,000 was two hundred times what the bastard had paid for the rights in the first place. That smile, like he was doing Anthony some kind of favour.

I would say $25,000 should cover it, Si.

The smile vanished. He bundled his pictures of young boys, hairless chests revealed, back into his briefcase. *If that's the going rate in Hollywood, Anthony. I look forward to seeing what that kind of money gets us.*

As do I, Si. He stood, feeling light-headed, and shook Si's clammy hand. Back in his room, he resisted the urge to climb back into bed. There were still more planes to catch.

He arrived in Heathrow early and spent several hours drinking, but unable to get rid of the image from two nights before. It was a kind of curse, hantu hantu. But, he thought, the curse had been lifted, broken by his wife, his new wife. His new wife, in their new home, without electricity or a phone line, without gas, without anyone to assist her. There would be a new curse put on him, he was sure. Self-hate is a powerful drug. When he boarded the plane they called him Mr Wilson, but he resisted falling into that reverie again. Little Wilson was dead.

America
1968

He was met at LAX by a car, put on by Warner Brothers. Bill Conrad, waiting at Warner studios, Burbank, said, *Lots of work to do, Tony.*

And don't I know it.

You don't look so good. You sick?

I'll live.

Can't have you sick, Tony. Gotta get this ship on the ocean. Here, he pulled a copy of the script Anthony had sent from Rome. He could already see the red marks of Bill's script fixer.

At least let's get a drink.

Sure, sure. How's the new wife? he asked, the two of them walking into the studio bar, Bill waving over a passing waitress. *What'll you have?*

Something potent.

Two Old Fashioneds, darling. Then, *So?*

Oh, the wife. Yes. I've left her in Malta. No power, no phone. A bit of a debacle.

No power? Christ!

I need to get some money over to them.

That a question?

It's a statement, but I need to talk about my fee.

Fee's been paid, Tony. The fee has been well and truly paid. Thanks, doll, he lifted his drink off the tray and said, *How much we talking?*

Just enough to get them fixed up. A few hundred.

Dollars? Okay, I'll get Joanie to get that together. Cheers, Tony. You sure you're feeling okay?

Bill was a vision of confidence. All that needed to change, all that was required for the whole project to be green-lit was for Shakespeare to stay in merry old England.

But half of the bloody script is him out of merry old England.

And that's what'll have to change. We got faith in you, Tony. He was driven to his hotel and led up to his room, where he was expected to work morning and night until the script was fixed. He wanted to climb into bed and sleep. His nose ran, his body ached. Twenty-four hours passed, the script torn apart and pinned back together. Will and his Dark Lady merrily prancing across merry England. They parted at the port of Southampton. Hiding the swell of her belly, Fatimah sailed to a future without him.

Bill read and said, *We're gonna need to get Marty in on this.*

The fixer?

He'll just give it the once over.

I have to be back in London by the end of the week. I have to get home to my wife.

Don't worry, Tone, he finished his drink, *we'll get there.*

He went back to his room and tried to sleep. Heat and chill seared through his body. His throat was raw, his heart taut and irregular. America would be the death of him, films would be the death of him. There was no sleep here.

He rang room service and ordered a bottle of Scotch. Scotch would chase the sickness away. Half a bottle in, he felt worse. He found himself in a bar, drinking Wild Turkey, watching the Los Angeles Rams, listening to a man tell him this season should have been the Giants', only they managed to screw the whole thing up. Anthony dropped a ten dollar bill on the bar and finished his drink. The bar was light, marble-floored, he'd never seen anything like this in America before, it was reminiscent of somewhere from his past. The bartender said, *Excuse me sir, is everything okay? Can I help?* Very un-American. Anthony followed the sunlight and hailed one of the many cabs that drifted the streets waiting to be mobilised into the pursuit of something or somebody.

Shrill. Shrill. Shrill. A bell struck in rapid succession. He woke back in the hotel room, safely back in the hotel room. He answered, *Burgess.*

This is Burgess too. Her Italian tones unmistakable, but how had she got this number?

Liana.

Antonio.

Where are you calling from?

From home.

He wondered how she had managed to get them, her and the boy, back to Chiswick. *Home? How?*

I got them to put the phone line in. Girgor has been helping me.

She was calling from Malta. They were still there. *Who is Girgor?*

Our neighbour. The electricity is working, gas too. I have a man here fixing some things. Andrea would like to say hello.

No, no, hang on. What things? What's going on there?

Just things. The house is in need of much attention.

He didn't like the sound of that. Houses that required attention also required a good deal of money.

How did you get this number, Liana?

Deborah. I rang her first, so she would have our number and I would have yours. Have you spoken to her?

Today? How are you paying for the work to be done?

I spoke to her this afternoon. She has had an offer from those men who bought the rights to Clockwork Orange. They want you to write a script for a film.

Yes. He knew all this. *I know all this. Everything's agreed.*

Deborah and me, we think you agreed wrong. Deborah is going to ask them for more. I said $50,000.

He seethed, gritted his teeth. *She will bloody not.*

She has. I told her to go ahead.

You can't do this kind of thing, Liana, for Christ's sake. I'll call them now and apologise.

Silence.

Liana?

I'm here. Wait to hear from Deborah. Those two practically stole from you. You are owed, Antonio. Andrea would like to speak to you.

When did all this happen? This afternoon? What time is it there?

Do you want to speak to him?

Fuck, he thought, that money was our lifeline. He would ring and apologise, he would fire Deborah, best not to mention Liana in all this. Why had she not called him herself? He should fire her now, regardless.

Hello? A pitched voice called out as if lost. Anthony looked around his hotel room for cigarettes. There seemed to be none where there should be many. *Hello?* came the voice again.

Liana? One cheroot in a crumpled packet. He lit it.

Where is he?

Where's who?

You. Mamma says you're in America, but I can hear you.

Put your mother back on.

She's talking to Girgor.

Who the hell is this bloody Girgor?

Are you really in America?

Yes. Now, can you ask your mamma to come back to the phone?

What can you see?

See? I see nothing. I'm in a hotel room.

On your own?

Of course. Look, Andrea—

239

I am in the hallway. I can see the front room. We have two sofas now and a big chair that I'm allowed to sit in. The old one is gone. And the kitchen. Rita is making food for us all to eat. Girgor and the master are taking a big cupboard up the stairs. It's very heavy.

And where is your mother? This is totally ridiculous. I have to be at a meeting in fifteen minutes.

I'm going to help them. Andrea dropped the phone, Anthony could hear his little voice asking to help and the replies of a jovial man, most likely the famous Girgor. Liana chimed in, telling Andrea to be careful and not to get in the way when the men were carrying such heavy things. The jovial man responded, he was happy for the boy to help, he was a great help, in fact.

Liana's voice grew closer and closer. *Make sure you stay beside Girgor and do not,* her voice was close now, *go underneath the wardrobe. Andr—*her voice was cut out by the clatter of the receiver being picked up from the floor. *Did Antonio go?* She lifted the phone to her lips, *Antonio? Are you still there?* He said nothing, listened to her breath and the sound of men turning a heavy piece of furniture round a tight corner. *Antonio? Andrea, did you say goodbye to your fa—* She put the phone down. She was about to say, father. It had been the first time he'd heard her use that word in front of Andrea.

He stood for a little while with the receiver at his ear and a crooked cheroot in his mouth. She had bought more furniture and got them to turn the power on. She had hired a cook and who knew who else. This hotel room. That house. There seemed, he held the receiver out to look at, no possible way anything could link the two. He hung up and puffed the last of the cheroot. If he could save the situation, get Litvinoff to see this was a rogue agent acting alone, $25,000 would do them for some time. It would mean no more trips away, not for a while. There were novels to write, as Liana kept on telling him.

He suddenly felt like the punchline to a very sad joke, sitting on his double bed, tying his shoelaces, about to breakfast with Hollywood producers. Foolish old man. They had been married only a few months; Liana in her thirties, in Malta, in the house he had bought for her, Antonio in his fifties, in Hollywood, in a hack's hotel room waiting for the next hack job. He rolled onto the bed, crawled up and wrapped himself in the duvet.

He arrived at the meeting late. Bill said, *Tony, Joe's here already.*

Anthony held out his hand saying, *Very pleased to meet you, Joe.*

Sorry to hear you've been unwell.

Unwell?

Yesterday, Joe said, as explanation. Bill interrupted,

Let's get some coffee and get started. Sit, sit. Anthony sat, glad to be off his feet. Joe returned to his seat, a defaced copy of *Will!* before him. *Coffee, Joe?*

Sure, why not.

Coffee, Tone?

Tea.

Not sure I can do tea.

Bourbon, then.

Bill laughed, saw it was no joke, and went to get his girl to make the order. *Right,* he came back in, still laughing, *Joe's got some ideas.*

Sorry, Anthony said, feeling nauseous, *who is Joe?*

The room fell silent. *You don't remember?* Bill asked, then, *Jeez, I knew you were sick, Tony, but God, man.*

I feel I'm missing something.

We met, Joe said, *last night. We went for a meal, at the La Media Mangia.*

Remember, Tony? You had an argument with the waiter about how to cook pork.

I'm sorry, my... Where had he been? How long had he been in Hollywood?

We've all had nights like that, Joe said. *To recap, I love the project, love the story, but I don't think this film will work as a musical.*

As a... Anthony felt he might pass out.

You agreed with me last night. He agreed with him now, but all of those songs, all of those lyrics, hours on the road, hours after the death of his wife trying to make Shakespeare sing and dance. *I think, maybe, we should rearrange, Bill.*

No, no, I have to go home. I have to get back to my wife.

You're okay? Bill asked.

Yes, yes. He hid his quavering hands. *Carry on.*

Right you are, Joe said. *So the other issue is the length of the thing.* He ran his finger up the side of the script, page after page falling on top of each other.

Too long? he guessed.

Exactly.

Joanie came in with drinks, putting a glass of iced water in front of Anthony. *Hey, Joanie, how long did we clock that last read?*

Last one? She thought for a second, *Six hours. Six and a half, say.*

Thank you, Joan.

We're looking for something around the two-hour mark, Bill said, pouring cream into his coffee.

Of course, Anthony said.

So, you'll go away and rewrite it, Tone?

As a straight script, Joe added.

Back in London Anthony was met by Deborah Rogers, drinking red wine in the Hilton. *It's all been agreed,* she said, trying to hide her delight. *You're getting $50,000 for the initial script and any further rewritings they may require.*

From?

From Litvinoff.

You shouldn't have done that. He pouted and called the waiter over, *Gin and tonic, double.*

I shouldn't have done what? Negotiate? Anthony, that's exactly what I should do. And you should be pleased.

Yes, well, you'll take your ten percent, I'm sure. She did not reply, so he said, *I'd like to get some of that before I leave. Liana has been busy while I've been away. I think she's spending more than we have.*

I'll make sure to get a transfer arranged tomorrow. There's one other thing; I spoke to Bill Conrad.

Yes, they've finally listened to reason. They want another draft of the Shakespeare thing, but without the showtunes this time.

They had a meeting this morning, the project has been cancelled.

Cancelled? But I only met them yesterday.

Studio decision. I'm sorry. Bill will try again, maybe next year. This could be the best outcome, Deborah said, with no hint of sarcasm.

I beg your pardon?

Better to be paid for a good film never made than to see one of your novels forever turned into a terrible one. How many Hollywood adaptations could be truly deemed a success?

She stayed to finish her wine, asked Anthony to pass on her regards to Liana and left. She stopped in the doorway and looked back at hunched and weary Anthony. She had gone with him to clear out Lynne's clothes from their house in Etchingham, and he was still not above implying she wasn't worth her ten percent. She should have made it fifteen.

Lija
1968

A nother taxi ride, another plane ride, another taxi ride.
Was this the house he had left? How long had he been
away? By the looks of things, it had been months, if not years.
The window shutters had been replaced and painted royal blue.
There were planters and plant pots on the balcony. Anthony had
to be let in, as he carried no key. He was eyed suspiciously by
an elderly Maltese woman.

I am, he pronounced, *the owner of this house.* She let him
in with a great show of reluctance and misgiving. The hallway
smelt of fresh paint and varnish. New furniture sat alongside
the things they had transported from London. The woman, who
he was subsequently told was their maid, Rita, trundled back to
the kitchen without so much as a backward glance. The walls
were a kind of off-white, suited to the age of the house. The
stairs had been cleaned, the metal bannister painted black, the
handrail sanded and varnished. There were new lampshades,
elegant and well placed, and new paintings hung on the walls.
In an alternative universe, this was what their house looked
like. And yet, here it was, in this universe, visible and corporeal.
Uneasy, he looked in at the living room. It was alien to him, not
a trace of his own life visible. There were children's toys and a
new television. There was a pale blue sofa, no bookshelves, no
armchair.

He walked back into the hallway and past Rita, who tutted
under her breath. Upstairs he saw a new bed in the master

bedroom, with new bedsheets. In a full-length mirror, he saw the tired old man he had become. He went downstairs into the kitchen, which was now filled with all the equipment and utensils a kitchen might require.

Do you know where Liana is? My wife?

Rita begrudgingly turned her back on the contents of a pan she was stirring and wiped her hands on her apron. *Family go swim. Back soon.*

Family, how that word hit him. He hadn't thought of them being a family before. On a table he did not recognise in the hallway, he took a key from a ceramic bowl. Anthony closed the heavy door, still sticky with fresh paint, turned left and soon came to a crossing. In front of him was a pharmacy and a place called the Three Villages Bar. He went in and ordered a Cisk. He made a joke to the barman, a moustachioed Maltese man with bear-like hands and bear-like chest hair, about the removal of a cyst. It garnered no response. He stayed by the bar and smoked, which the barman appreciated, also lighting a thick cigar.

The family home had rattled him. He cursed himself for this continuing inability to see Liana fully. Even now, he knew he underestimated her. She had made a home they could live in, live in as a, he choked down Cisk, family.

After the third or fourth beer, Anthony felt a gentle hand on his shoulder. *As soon as I saw your bag.* He turned and Liana smiled. She kissed him and, standing up to take a good look at her, he kissed her.

I'll just finish—

No, no. Fonzu, I would like a white wine. She sat beside Anthony and took his hand. *How does it feel to be home?*

He could not answer. This isn't, he wanted to say, my home. It has no trace of whatever home is, whatever home is meant to evoke. But, he realised, watching the smile slowly shift on Liana's face, she does. Being in her presence once more felt rejuvenating.

I feel relief. Relief, he quickly added, *and joy and joy to be here with you and* – he kissed her, holding his lips to hers for a few seconds, aware Fonzu was watching, aware other people were entering the bar, but not caring about any of that.

We are glad to have you home too, she said, the emphasis somehow landing on *we.* She took her freshly arrived glass and raised it to him.

Yes. It is good to be home. I, he told himself, *doubt I will want to leave for some time.*

All is well, Liana said.

Although Anthony had started talking about America and London and Shakespeare and the Rolling Stones and Green Lights and Red Lights, he found himself listening to a grim tale of domesticity. In mid-sentence, mid-flight, mid-air, it seemed his wife had swept him away.

We lived the first night by candle light; the night you left. Liana spoke with no bitterness, only to set the scene. Just as she had in Cambridge, when the sky seemed to be falling in on top of her, Liana reimagined disaster as a great game for Paolo Andrea's sake, and in doing so gave way to a recklessness that kept her from falling apart.

Anthony fell into the house and immediately fell ill. He could barely move, let alone write, let alone fulfil the several commissions he had undertaken. He had cheated death, his wife's life given to save his own, and now death was back to claim its prize. Andrea had given him chickenpox. The child pox, the boy had plotted to make his evil stepfather sick, sick to the point of death. The son, Hamlet-like, would kill the man who had stolen into his mother's bed.

The house was to Anthony a burial place. Lynne's ghost had been purged to make way for his own. She had had the child do her bidding, a twist on the tale. The two, childless wife and fatherless son, were Lilith and Hephaestus. They watched over his terminal billet. He would die in this house. Afterwards, Liana would leave his decaying body in their bed and shut the house, never to be opened up again. Whatever he had contracted would die with him. She fed him chicken soup and spoke to him in gentle, loving Italian. He composed, in his head, a death march to be played at his funeral. A funeral march for his death. Delirious, he tried to dictate the notes to Liana, who had neither music manuscript nor the ability to write or read music notation.

Dum, dee-dee, dum, dum-dee-dee, dum dum, he murmured, as she cooled his brow with a damp cloth. *Da-dee-dum, da-dee-dum, da-da-dur, dur, dur, dur.*

Doctors came and went. They spoke to Liana in Maltese or Italian. In his stupor he heard them discuss the merits of the life he had led, the quality of his work, his abilities as a husband. *I barely know him*, Liana said, *but I know that he is the finest living English writer.*

Living for how long? one of the doctors mused, his colleagues nodding in sombre recognition. He might be the finest living writer but in the ranks of dead writers he was a mere bottom-feeder. There had been no new novels for years. The novel he had recently published had been written some five years before. This man, who on his yearlong deathbed had written five novels, had been idly living, writing quickly for quick cash.

I admit, he told those gathered, *I have not done enough. If I should live*, the doctors again shook their morose heads, *I will do better. I will focus myself on the writing of great literature.* His temperature was taken, the thermometer barely capable of registering the fever within him.

It is, Liana said, *indolent talent that is killing him, I know it. I begged him to write more. He would not listen.*

Now he was fully contaminated, Andrea no longer came to visit. He heard the boy laughing and shrieking beyond the door, for he knew it was only a matter of time before he had his mother once again to himself. The doctors spoke, saying, *To shift so quickly from feast to famine is an extremely dangerous act. More people died after the potato famine from over-indulgence than during from starvation. Unspent words are killing him.*

Give me pen and paper, he moaned, rocking his body from side to side. *Take dictation, one of you, write this down.* But as he began to orate, Anthony fell into a deep, wordless sleep.

There is no hope for him now.

There is an unfinished novel, a village poisoned by polluted water, Liana wept.

The unwritten rest is poison in his veins, his blood polluted. Someone must write all the words he did not or else the sickness will become epidemic. The child is too young, the wife too overwrought. We must retrieve all those latent works from within him. He felt fingers on his temples, running around the circumference of his skull. *Get me my bag, get me my scalpel.*

He felt he could peel the cold sweat from him, as a snake sheds its skin. His mausoleum was decorated with fresh flowers, the smell overwhelming. Very painfully, very slowly, he inched himself into a sitting position. He was terrified that he would look down to see his body lying flat, while he, ghostlike, sat as a translucent outline within himself. The wooden shutters let in warm sunlight, though he felt brittlely cold. The door opened, the sound of unoiled hinges scraped against his inner ear.

You are awake?

He could not speak, his mouth entirely fixed, hollow.

Let me help you. Liana leant him forward, his ribs ached against his skin, and rested him back against plumped-up cushions. *How do you feel?* He said nothing, but she saw it all. She gently placed her fingers between his, barely touching. *I will get you some pain relief. I will be back in a moment.* She went to leave but he grasped her hand, his eyes welled with tears. He had been alone for so long, for years now. They had surrounded him, people, doctors, experts, but it had done nothing to remove him from his absolute isolation. Since he had found her, he had done everything he could to get away from Liana. He did not know why. The black and white still image of his dead mother and sister flickered before him like the slippage between cinema reels. *I will stay*, Liana said, tears in her eyes. She yelled for Rita, who came slowly, crossing herself when she saw Anthony sitting up. *Please get my husband something to eat.*

A response came in Maltese.

No, Anthony wheezed, *no chicken fucking soup.* His head lolled back.

By evening he was ready to take a small glass of red wine and a couple of drags on a cigar. The doctor visited. He spoke no English, simply taking Anthony's pulse and nodding half-heartedly.

What does he say? he asked Liana after the doctor had gone.

That you are better, but you are not out of danger.

I dreamt the beginning of a new novel. I want to make a start. I have wasted so much time.

Rest, Antonio. There is time enough.

Bring me my typewriter.

Rest, she kissed his forehead. But later that day, she brought him his Olympia and a wooden tray with retractable legs to sit it on.

When Liana visited him the next morning he was puffing on a cheroot and typing wildly. *Antonio, you will make yourself unwell again.*

Wait, just wait. He tap tap tapped and drew the paper from the machine. *I'm feeling quite well. Quite rested.*

I am happy to hear that.

Could you get them to bring some tea up, show her how I like it. And some bacon, if there is any. I need to get the taste of soup from my mouth.

Should I open the blinds?

No, no, leave them, he said distractedly, feeding paper and lining it up.

At least let me open a window.

I must get on, Liana. Tea, if you could get me some tea. Thank you.

She left him to it, the sound of clattering keys filling their Maltese home for the first time. The noise continued for three days straight, until Anthony was ready to leave his sick bed. He descended the stairs, Rita, Liana and Andrea watching from the hallway.

Now, Anthony said, *what have I missed?*

What he had missed was the opening of several envelopes addressed to him. Liana, in a panic, had sat with a bottle of wine and a letter-opener. She led him now into the living room and the coffee table where the letters were displayed.

What are they? he asked.

Bills. Tax bills, medical bills, a bill for your wife's death.

He felt immediately sick, immediately delirious. *Let me sit,* she helped him into the armchair. He picked up the letter closest, from Inland Revenue. He had failed to register himself as a Maltese resident and, as such, owed a great deal of money to the very taxman he intended to escape. The sum was enormous, a sum so enormous it could only be part of some mass hallucination.

We're fucked, he said finally, wishing he had died of chickenpox.

Part Four

Manchester

He wakes thinking of his father, though he cannot say he has dreamt of him. He lifts the phone to call Liana. Perhaps there will be a chance to speak to Andrew. The receiver is cold against his ear; the tone modulates from F to Bb, static shifting to melody. The same that played as Lynne lay upstairs in Applegarth, prone and bleeding, as he prepared himself. *It's my wife*, he said, into the dial tone, *I think she may be dying.* Someone had told him, he had read in some book, heard on some panel he sat on, watched on some world service documentary, that trauma must be vocalised, must be shed, to be overcome.

The hotel room is grand. The painting above the bed is of the Midland and Central Library, in faux Renaissance style. The library looks to him like Bruegel's *Tower of Babel*; it's simple cycloidal design has been exploded, the windows large enough to see individual books on individual shelves. A boy and his father forever traversing the circular path. The Corinthian columns lean under the weight of so much knowledge. He thinks of a poem he and Liana had written, from Belli; she the translator, he the interpreter.

> *"We'd like to touch the stars," they cried, and after,*
> *"We've got to touch the stars. But how?" An able-*
> *Brained bastard told them: "Build the Tower of Babel.*
> *Start now, get moving. Dig holes, sink a shaft. A-*
> *Rise, arouse, raise rafter after rafter,*
> *Get bricks, sand, limestone, scaffolding and cable.*

I'm clerk of works, fetch me a chair and table."
God meanwhile well-nigh pissed himself with laughter.

The domed roof half cracked reveals readers sat in the great reading hall. Do they read him? He squints, kneeling on the bed. The phone still in his hand rings a dead tone, *Ab*. That painting, it occurs to him, the one in Chiswick, was a gift from Liana to Lynne. *Please hang up*, a woman's voice repeats.

At the typewriter he starts to make a note but stops himself. *I hadn't met the boy before Lynne died*, he tells the walls of his hotel suite. But that painting, Liana's mother's painting. It didn't add up. He saw the scene, Lynne and Liana together, the passing of the painting, her hand on her hand, a joke at his expense. He tells himself it is fiction. *We had lost touch, four years. She heard I had become a widower.* That is how the story goes.

His thirst is back. Anthony is a firm believer in the medicinal properties of alcohol. Brandy helps to warm his dead extremities of a morning. His father swore by stout for a variety of unconnected ailments. Hot lemon and whisky for a cold, of course. Rita had administered bajtra in Malta to help him in recovery. And, though it had no doubt killed Lynne, he still found curative the taste of a well-made gin and tonic. He pulls his trousers on and buttons up his shirt. No doubt they do a reasonable G&T in the Midland bar.

Your gin and tonic, Mr Burgess, the waiter narrates, sitting the glass in front of him. *On the house.*

I say, he says to the waiter. *Timperley, yes?*

Sorry?

That accent of yours. Anthony lights a cigarette.

Eh, yes. He's a cagey lad, trying to present himself as something he's not. Nodding, a little unnerved, he picks up three empty glasses and returns to the safety of the bar.

Lemon and effervescence lifts him; he enjoys the lad's studied refusal of eye contact. Identifying accents had long been a party trick, though some found it too prying. I should offer to buy him a drink, Anthony thinks.

The bar is quiet, church quiet. A single drinker at the bar, head in the FT. At the far table a mother and daughter sip highballs in their best dresses. Yes, a rare treat for you two, he smiles. They look the part from here but Anthony knows the closer you get, the less elegant the clothes, the more inexpert the make-up. Two couples enter, a husband quietly chastising his loud wife who is loudly telling the room how sick she is to be back in the North. She catches the silence she has entered and takes the other woman off to complain in the bathroom.

He's full of nervous energy. Cheroot lit, he stands and walks the octagonal room. Upon the wall, in ornate frames, is Auden's *Night Mail.* He scrutinises the first four lines. Mail is delivered to the rich, to the poor. Notes, he thinks, are scrawled and stuffed into envelopes.

Moving towards the next panel he sees, in the room beside, a baby grand. Burgess and his gin and tonic make their way over. A Steinway, no less. What his father would have given to play on a piano like this. But no, Joe Wilson would have sneered, would have called it ostentatious, would have called it *la-dee-bloody-da.* Placing his glass on the lip of the piano, Burgess rests his fingers on the keys. The other guests turn in a shared disdain that goes unnoticed. He wrestles with what to play. Wracking his mind, nothing is forthcoming.

Come on, Anthony, he mutters, fingers a paper's breadth away from the sounding of notes. He will play a piece to shimmer off the marble floors, undulate through the stone archways, and resonate with the high Baroque of the building, Wagner or – before he can find a suitable alternative, John hammers on the keys like he's closing up show at the People's Music Hall.

> *I love my little cat I do, Its coat is oh so warm*
> *He comes each day with me to school, And sits*
> *upon the form*
> *When teacher says, "Why do you bring, That little*

pet of yours?"
I tell her that I bring my cat, Along with me
because...

He turns to the bar, grinning Cheshire-like, urges them to sing along,

Daddy wouldn't buy me a bow-wow!

But no, they don't sing. *Bow-wow! Daddy wouldn't,* they're up on their feet, *a bow-wow!* The purse-lipped waiter, he's sure to be an actor, is coming to join him. *Bow-wow! I've got a little cat.* The waiter lifts his uncoastered glass from the piano and the barman lifts Burgess.

Guests are prohibited from using the piano, sir.

Neither looks him in the eye, as they lead him back to his table. The other guests look away, mortified by what he has subjected them to. The mother and daughter stiffen, afraid they too will be seen for what they are. He remains standing, takes his glass from the waiter and necks it. In a moment he is out once more, drenched by Manchester rain.

Bleedin' 'ell, Joe says. *You don't half overdress things, Our Jack.* He's crossing Lower Mosley Street. Behind him is the Midland, all that Manchester could be. Ahead, is Tommy Ducks, all that Manchester is. He follows the tight black of a faux-leather skirt. *The joanna in't hoity-toity, not like you like to make out. I sit at these keys like other men sit at the wheel of delivery trucks.* All this said in front of drinkers in a Manchester pub, all laughing at Joe's scholarship boy. Not this Manchester pub, not that Anthony remembers anyway. Tommy Ducks, famed for its ceiling festooned with women's underwear. The pair above him have a cigarette burn at the crotch, other pairs are beer splashed, tobacco stained, white pants gone grey now yellowy at the edges. A lot of material up there, he thinks. Nymphs appear to him, dressed only in dulled northern knickers. Tommy Ducks is full of longhaired men and short, peroxide-haired women; tough blokes with Salford drawl wear hooped earrings and showy jewellery. They must all smell of stale beer and fags, those knickers. He had held Liana's to his nose and been caught by Andrew, by Paulo Andrea. Caught in the laundry basket, so to speak.

See anythin' you like, love? The woman beside him asked, getting a rise from the throng of men at the bar.

I should think so, he replies, to greater laughter.

She gives him a wink and lifts three pint glasses, held expertly in two hands.

What'll it be?

Piano-playing's a job, Joe says, in some other pub some distant time before. He pronounces it *pee-anna* and Anthony can still feel the quality of keys on the Steinway he has recently been evicted from. When he told the boys in school that his dad played piano, would be playing at the Palace Cinema this weekend, they smirked between them; that'd be right, Wilson's dad being some fruity bloody pianist. How far from the truth of it. Joe saw no artistry in music making. He could make a few quid from piano-playing, just like he could make a few quid from changing barrels in the Golden Eagle or delivering newspapers around Moss Side. John would like very much to blame his stepmother, for whom art was an affront, but the truth is sometimes undeniable. He wanted his father to be, at worst, an artisan, a craftsman. Joe was an odd-jobber. Did he, come to think of it, enjoy music? In the flat above his stepmother's tobacconists, there hadn't even been a piano. Not that his dad was mithered. *I can have a tinkle down the boozer as and when. Anyroad, not much point if I'm not getting paid.*

But don't you, he had asked, *don't you enjoy it? Playing to the crowd?*

You don't do it because you enjoy it, you do it because it pays the bills. You show me someone who gets on stage for the sake of it and I'll show you someone who can afford not to do it.

Facing the bar is a line of three glass topped coffins. Drinkers sit around like mourners or, backs hunched and wheezing, like

257

the dead returned for one final pint. He takes a seat at the central coffin in the line of three. Three coffins, three graves; body, books, ego. Sat at the base of the casket, he raises a glass to his departed self, who in turn raises a glass to him.

His dad had drunk in Tommy Ducks, had played the piano on Sundays sometimes at the regular jazz sit-in. Jack hadn't been invited, being too young and Ducks too rowdy. But he had gone down that Saturday to see him play at the Palace Cinema, providing musical accompaniment for *Metropolis*. His dad smelt of beer and fags that matinee performance. As an older man, Anthony witnessed the film accompanied by an orchestra; they had played over the turning of cogs and machinery with brio and fury. Joe Wilson's rendition had been laboured, the cogs already creaking; one piercing note against the ticking of a second hand. The cogs trudged along and, when they made their appearance, so too did the workers. Joe clattered above their limping gait, a sound that felt all too real. Jack watched as the cinema owner, Jakie Innerfield, waved his hands trying to cajole his father into life. Jack knew his father's interpretation was too close to home; he had turned science fiction into Monday morning outside a Manchester mill. Taking another pull of his pint, spurred on by Innerfield's over-animated expression, Joe began to play comedically, the sound of an old horse meandering down a cobbled track. But even Joe got caught up in the film, the great artistry of it all. *It's only entertainment, Jackie. Grand, aye, but entertainment, mind.* He meant disposable, unimportant, almost a scam, like the sideshows at the fairground, tricking punters out of their hard-earned cash.

Jack had gone to the evening screening and the Sunday matinee and again to the evening screening. Each time, Joe Wilson went at it anew, improvised from scratch. It was some feat. Unrecognisable, playing with all he had to put food on the table. He played with passion, a passion for getting on, for making ends meet. He had tasted poverty, Joe Wilson, and even while he'd married Maggie Dwyer and they lived comfortably above their shop, he still went at life as if he could feel the bailiffs call. What he had was hers. What he had could be as quickly taken away. You don't forget.

And this is what Antonio taught Paulo Andrea, his son. Music is a vocation, like plumbing, it is a trade, like bricklaying, like selling fags. He wanted a cor anglais and so he has one, my son. My son who I only knew about after Lynne's death. He's learning to play well, how to understand the inner workings of music, as his father before him knew it. He will keep the Wilson tradition, Paulo Andrea Burgess, Andrew Wilson.

When Andrew had wanted to become a chef, Anthony had shown him recipes for hare stew with pickled walnuts and his spaghetti formaggio surprise, but these had been dismissed as lacking in cultivation.

It's all a bit rudimentary, the boy had told him.

You what? He sloshed brandy in with the hare and stirred with a thick wooden spoon. *This is real cookery.*

Antonio, Liana said, *Andrea will learn the art of food. Tell him, Andrea.*

But he would not tell him, just sulked in the kitchen corner. *Full bellies and flatulence, that is the art of food.*

Andrew left at that. Liana cursing him for being the father he was. *He adores you*, she said, *and this is how you speak to him?* Anthony had made a phone call and got him a job in London, at the Grosvenor, where Andrew found there was no art in dishing up sides of carrots and peas, no creativity in pouring gravy.

He finishes off his drink and makes his way out of Tommy Ducks. Out of cheroots, he cadges a cig from a woman dressed in biker's leathers. The Midland looms. He should ring Liana. He should ask to speak to Andrew. He should get some rest. There was nothing but artistry to music. What other function did it serve but to elevate the life of the listener? Words had many functions. Written words had sent him to Gibraltar, had taken money he had earned and delivered it to the inland revenue. Words were pernicious in a way music had no way of being. Yes, there were anthems of nationhood and of political persuasion but the notes themselves had no nation, had no affiliation. *Music is all art, for fuck's sake*, he said, halfway down Peter Street. Words carried inherent cash value. The typewriter was not invented for the pursuit of art but for the pursuit of debts and earnings. The piano was invented solely for art's sake.

He had played against *Metropolis* himself, in the metropolitan area of Iowa City, at a film festival hosted by the university. There came an immediate swell of emotion. American students and faculty sat behind while he thrashed at the joanna. There was no payment, not that the university were not paying him well for the teaching of what they stubbornly referred to as creative writing. By the time they transplanted Maria into the Maschinenmensch, his shirt was sodden with sweat, his eyes red, his hands raw. The morning after he gave a lecture on putting words one after the next, the correct and the incorrect way to do so, and was thanked for his creative insights. *Make money*, he told them before he left campus for a plane back to Rome. *Make money and make writing your living.* It was too easy to see himself as his father, but the way those students looked at him, the way Andrew had looked at him that night and so many before and so many after made the identification hard to shake. What he would have given to turn up every evening at a cinema or pub and rattle out music on the piano. What pains it took to rattle out books on the Olympia.

John Wilson had been a sometime pianist in the pubs of Manchester, one down there, in the area they refer to as Hanging Ditch. He had given another player his first symphony to look over. This was during the war and like so much else his symphony did not survive. Blown to smithereens in the back room of a pub whose name he could no longer remember. There had been art there, art in those black marks. On his return from Gibraltar, he discovered the loss and afterwards he could no longer live in Manchester. Lynne said, *Write it all again.* He teared up at the idea. The thought of starting again sent him half mad. All of his art invested into those pages. His second symphony, written fifteen years later, had disappeared with the Malayan heat. He should have made a copy before sending it to the Malayan cultural authorities, before offering it as the first great Malaysian symphony, before it was swallowed up by Malayan bureaucracy. The third symphony – ah! The third symphony – there was a light.

Swimming in all this, he finds himself outside the Free Trade Hall. He's the child again, holding the hand of his father. *If my father had had a choice,* he thinks, walking up the steps, passing the columns, *he would have wished me dead and my sister alive.* What would Anthony wish, had he had the choice of no son or this one, he wasn't sure. *I love him,* he said out loud.

Inside, he can hear, faintly, the orchestra tuning. It lifts him. It has always lifted him to hear strings vibrate towards unity, cohesiveness. This is where my father brought me. The first time, he brought me to hear Wagner. The Hallé. There was no finer orchestra in Britain, not then, according to Joe Wilson. He brought me on the tram and then, when we lived with her above her bloody shop, he brought me on the bus. He meant for me to hear music. The queue moves steadily forward until the barman asks, *For you, sir?*

Give me a bottle of stout, he says, turning to a couple dropping sugars into weak tea to ask if they have a spare cigarette.

America
1969

Liana found him drunk in the kitchen, pouring cognac onto a piece of roast beef. *I've no time for writers who are not willing to write about sex. Fucking is a central facet of life, literature should represent life, fucking included.* Those gathered, many of them faculty members Liana had previously met, looked on in faint horror. They were all members of Chapel Hill's staff, except for the woman who had been cooking, whose kitchen Anthony seized control over.

Antonio, Liana half whispered, not wanting to draw too much attention to herself. He had his sleeves rolled up, an oven mitt on, the top three buttons of his shirt open.

He said, a glass of wine in one hand, roasting tray clutched precariously in the other, *The secret to good meat is booze. The secret to good dessert, butter. Nothing,* lurching towards the oven and clattering the metal tray onto the top shelf, *ever tasted worse for adding cognac, butter, a bit of cream, or all three.* He stood, lifting the oven door closed with his leg. *The tendency is to over analyse or theorise literature, of course. I've been guilty of it myself, but meat and sex and all the rest of it – you know what I'm trying to say – all of it has to be there first, before conceptual whatever, and you come in with your critical...* He drained his wine. A tall man, in a dark brown suit, reluctantly filled Anthony's expectant glass. He raised it, a red bauble in the air, and said, *Meat and sex and wine and cigarettes. Men and women, men and men, women and women. Before all else.* He drank. *Liliana, you've come.*

I have. She spoke quietly against her husband's verbosity.

You've met Len and his wife, eh...

Sally, Sally said, seemingly troubled by the sound of her own name.

Very pleased to meet you.

And this is Tom and—

Antonio, what are you doing?

What does it look like? He asked, waving the mitt about. *I was walking this way and Len said why not come in and,* Len nodded to Liana, somewhat apologetically, but also somewhat put upon, *and you know how I like to cook. You can't cook in our place,* he told Len, *there's nothing to cook on or with. It's a terrible place for a man who seeks diversion in the cooking of things.*

There was some kind of party going on, she could see that, but it was not the party Anthony was having. Most of the guests were in the living room, talking about literature or marking examination papers or the pros and cons of this year's curriculum. She had walked through the house, her husband's voice rattling from room to room as she got closer to the kitchen. There had been several knowing glances her way.

Would someone like to get my wife a glass of wine? White wine.

Red wine, Liana replied, smiling. *Thank you. Antonio, would you like to join me?* She went into the garden and lit a cigarette. Rubin tipped her off to his whereabouts. Something about Chapel Hill had sent Anthony slightly wild. He spent his nights drinking in bars or the homes of other faculty members like these, or in student dorms and frat houses. He was drunk on reverence, their reverence to him. Liana had known it would be like this. Antonio wanted to come alone but she would not be left alone by him again. She agreed to leave Andrea behind and come to America with her husband. Their son remained in Malta with Girgor and his wife, Cikka, all of them living in the house she had brought back to life. A motel was no place for a little boy. Her little boy. Liana had intended to let herself be wracked by guilt. But with meetings with publishers and producers and theatre directors, it was not to be.

She stamped out her cigarette and stood at the back door. Anthony remained in the kitchen, gesticulating, cigarette held in oven mitt. She put her head around the door.

Antonio, she chimed, doing her best to remain light and casual.

The phone rang and Len went off to answer it. Anthony turned his attention to a man opening a fresh bottle of wine.

Sharing Liana's embarrassment, Sally said, *You're more than welcome to smoke in the house.*

That's very kind of you. But I don't like my clothes to smell of smoke.

They both looked at Anthony, cigarette in mouth, ash on lapel, animatedly saying, *I don't consider him a great writer. How many novels has he written?* He waited for the reply. *How many?*

Liana stood in the kitchen doorway. *Antonio, keep your voice down. Come here.*

I'll be back momentarily, he called.

She stepped out again into the garden and, waiting, lit another cigarette.

What's wrong, why are you outside?

What are you doing here?

Cooking, what does it look like I'm doing here?

Eh, Len interrupted, standing at the kitchen door, *Mr Burgess, Max Steele is on the phone, he says he's looking for you.*

Well, here I am.

That's what I told him.

Did he say anything else?

Only that you are supposed to be speaking at Max's event this evening.

Event? When is this?

Now, Liana said.

Yes, Len says, *you were supposed to be there at six.* It was past seven. *What should I tell him?*

Tell him, Liana told him, *that we will be there shortly.*

Right.

Did you know about this? Anthony asked, accusingly.

You told me about it. Come on, finish that and let's go. We can get a taxi.

Anthony finished off his wine, then said, *I've got a roast in the oven.* He went in, calling out, *Larry, what were you saying, Larry? Six novels? That's not even one every five years.* Liana stubbed out her cigarette and followed her husband in.

By the time she got to the drawing room, Anthony, who had failed to find Larry, was talking in the middle of a large group of people. *No, what I'm saying,* he was saying, *is that Shakespeare can't be taken out of context.*

Surely any piece of fiction can be taken out of context, especially Shakespeare.

That it can be is not the issue, the real question is why the hell would you? What do we learn from Troilus and Cressida if we reset it in Belgium during World War One? We lose the subtle allegory to the War of the Theatres, not to mention the very specific attitude of the Jacobeans to the Trojan war. Do you see? They did not see. They seemed to be baffled as to how this had become the topic of conversation.

If you'll excuse me, one said.

And me, said another, following.

A woman, roughly Liana's age, said, *But doesn't our interpretation of Shakespeare say something about contemporary matters? Immigrant gangs on the Upper West Side seemed to be reasonably appropriate. And, of course, when the whole world has been mapped, what better way to recreate the sense of wonder than put Prospero in space?*

In space? Anthony turned to those who remained, two long-haired men, most likely postgraduates, and his wife.

Absolutely. For a generation who no longer find magic and witchcraft a credible distraction, isn't space and space age technology a great analogy for mystic islands and wizardry? She took a deep drag of her cigarette.

Liana said, *He hasn't seen it. I went alone. Antonio would frown on such abuses of his Shakespeare.*

This is a film? he asked. The two men nodded, yes, they could confirm it was a film.

It is, the woman answered. *So, you are Professor Burgess.*

Not yet, not that I haven't suggested they make the offer.

I'm Marsha. Marsha Brooks. This is Lee and Arnold.

Anthony. And this is my wife.

Liana. The women shook hands. The men followed suit.

And you teach...? Anthony asked.

Can't you guess?

Film.

Correct. Drama, Radio and Television to be precise. I used to work out there on the West Coast for a while, an actress and then a script reader, editor, consultant, you get the drift.

What made you move into teaching? Liana asked, lighting a fresh cigarette.

Security. I also divorced my pig of an ex. He's still out there, still convincing wannabe starlets he's in the business of making starlets. I read your book, she said.

Which one?

What's it going to be then, eh? She quoted at him. *My pig ex worked on the failed attempt to make your novel into a movie.*

There have been many, Anthony said, bitterly.

But now, Liana tried to lift him, *they are making Antonio's Clockwork Orange into a movie.*

Then it may not be yours for much longer, Mr Burgess.

If you'll excuse me, I've got beef to attend to.

Something I said?

Antonio has had a lot of setbacks with writing for films. A great deal of promises, a great deal of deception.

Ain't that right. Well, for what it's worth, he's better off out of it.

We're gonna get something to drink, one of the young men said.

Get me a little something while you're at it, Marsha replied.

The men left and Marsha said, *What is it you do, Liana?*

At the moment, I am here with Antonio. Marsha expected her to say more, Liana wanted to say more. Eventually, she said, *I used to teach in England.*

Is that right?

Cambridge.

Wow. Well, that really is a teaching job.

I'm a translator, I suppose, if I had to say what it is I do. Though, my time these days is spent helping my husband.

He appears to be a fellow in need of help.

What is that supposed to mean?

Lenny was telling us about your husband's faux pas. Right time, wrong party. Translator, you said. What sort of thing?

You know Pynchon?

Thomas? Of course.

I translated his V.

I love that book.

Another one your husband wished to film?

Ex-husband, and no, David did not introduce me to Pynchon. You write yourself?

No, no, Liana said, *I leave that to Antonio. I take care of his business.*

You're his manager. Huh! Marsha laughed. *Which came first, marriage or management?*

We need to go.

To see Max, yes.

Enjoy your evening.

In the kitchen, Anthony was carving meat, smoking a cheroot, pontificating on the pleasures of butchery. *Antonio, we must go now.*

Yes, yes, in a moment. At least let me try the damn beast before you steal me away.

I am not stealing. We must go.

In a moment, he continued to carve. *You must work with the grain of the meat. Many a good bit of beef has been blighted by botched butchery. There, see, perfectly pink in the centre. Sally, if you want to serve this up.*

Sally, apparently on the verge of some sort of breakdown, said, *Dinner, everyone. Dinner is ready.* She lifted the plate of beef from the counter just as Anthony was taking a slice as reward. He rolled the whole thing up in his mouth.

There you go, he chewed, *delicious. Liana, try some of this.*

We can eat when we get there. She turned to leave, almost bumping into Marsha Brooks.

It was nice to meet you, Marsha said.

Yes, very nice, Liana replied, sidestepping Marsha and her two friends before heading out of the front door. Anthony followed in no hurry, somehow in the middle of a conversation about whether it was right that Longfellow and Kipling should be considered children's poets.

Chapel Hill breathed new life into Anthony. He felt himself taken seriously as a writer, yet could not help but wish to be taken seriously as an intellectual. He gave lectures on Shakespeare, when he was meant to be teaching creative writing. For an event celebrating his novels, Anthony gave a long and detailed lecture on pornography. It was a subject that weighed heavily upon him.

Rome
1972

He smashes, bang, the letter down and, bang, his drink down. He clutches at the letter and in a kind of daze, turns on his heels and reads it once more. *I shall start off by saying I don't really know how to write this letter, and that it is a task which is as awful for me to perform as it may be for you to read.* Anthony felt lightheaded, as though hallucinating. The ire rose in him once more. *You are far too brilliant and successful a writer* – he choked the words down – *and I am far too much of an admirer of yours to patronize you with a listing of what is so obviously excellent about Napoleon Symphony.* He swooned at all the wasted time. *At the same time, I earnestly hope that our all too brief friendship will survive* – a fraud writing in a fraud's language. Anthony pictured that last day of writing, the ease at which the words flowed, the joy of writing them, the beauty of the sunrise, the satisfaction of the sunset. All tainted, tainted by – *me telling you that the manuscript is not a work that can help me make a film about the life of Napoleon.* He felt himself spiralling.

Anthony stormed along the hallway into the drawing room. The sound of his shoes hitting the tiles echoed one atop the other atop the next in booming resonance. He lifted the bottle of brandy in something like exultation and poured a thick, murky glass and stared into it with desire and loathing. All that time. How much time had the writing of the goddamned novel cost? Days spent watching Andrea from his study window, the child growing before his very eyes. A year passed. More than a year. He turned and went back into his office, into his place of work, his haven, which Kubrick's letter had infiltrated. *Despite its considerable accomplishments, it does not, in my view, help solve either of the two major problems* – how dare he damn me with such faint praise as this?

I never wanted to write a damned novel, anyway, he yelled, draining his brandy glass and marching back into the drinks room for more.

He returned with the bottle. He considered rolling the letter up and forcing it down the neck of the bottle, using it as a Molotov cocktail, setting fire to this typewriter and desk and study and house so hexed by Kubrick. Anthony grasped the letter once more – *that of considerably editing the events (and possibly restructuring the time sequence) so as to make a good story, without trivializing history or character* – and poured himself more brandy. It would have made much more sense to write it directly in script form, the *Eroica* being only about forty-seven minutes long and a Kubrick movie being around two hours. But no, Stanley had requested a novel to work from, so he could claim authorship of another screenplay, no blasted doubt.

In the Algonquin, he merrily drank with Malcolm McDowell, surrounded by beauties only too pleased to be in their company; Malcolm the youthful star, Anthony the enigmatic writer. A glorious night of excess and gratification. Richly deserved after another television interview where they were coerced into hailing Kubrick's invisible divinity, the bloody bastard.

Anthony, a few glasses in, confided in Malcolm that he had been tacitly barred from set. Kubrick would not return his phone calls, would not discuss the film or the content. It was only when the press called Kubrick a degenerate sadist had Burgess' phone begun to ring. Only then had he met the man himself. The master would not explain himself to the world's media, so Burgess had been given a nice little sum of money to explain for him.

Malcolm told Anthony, both well-oiled by this point, cast and crew had all been given copies of Burgess' novel, from which dialogue was taken verbatim. There was no bastard script written by sodding Kubrick, just the novel he, Anthony blasted Burgess, had written. Now he knew why he had been exiled. *Nor does it provide much realistic dialogue* – actual meaning: nor does it provide dialogue I can lift and claim as my own.

Deborah tried to get a fee for the writing of the Napoleon novel and Anthony put a stop to it. Kubrick made all talk about fees and money uncouth, even though Anthony had seen his big bloody house and had heard about the big sodding fees Kubrick demanded. All that time and nothing to show for it. He had been forced, through trickery, back into novel writing. The fucking, he screwed up the letter and shoved it into his mouth, bastard. He ground his teeth and supped down brandy too.

He fell into his armchair, still chewing. They would never let him in, he saw that now. All those interviews with the movie press, talking to him as if he were Kubrick's spokesperson. Recently back from venerating his holy Kubrick at Cannes, he knew none of them had read the book, none of them would. They were convinced cinema was the only medium, Hollywood the only place that mattered. He had nearly convinced himself too.

He remembered Liana's words. Bitter pills, every single one. He remembered meeting Alex North in a bar in Hollywood. Drunk and getting drunker, North had told Burgess to watch his back with Stanley. *A year of my life he took from me*, meaning the writing of a discarded film soundtrack. To be discarded for Beethoven, for Mozart, for Brahms, was nothing to be ashamed of, Anthony had said at the time. Those words sat sulphurous on his tongue now. How he wished he had listened harder. North's music had great qualities, a modern composer, a man of artistic integrity. I don't even have – Anthony chew-chewed the soggy page – a script to sell. Novels had offered little in the way of money, which was the only barometer of success. The only novel he had made any money from was the one Kubrick had stolen and called his own. The publishers fell over themselves to get those bastard rights.

Liana said something at the time. She had had much to say after they saw Kubrick's film. *Claiming this is Kubrick's A Clockwork Orange is like Warhol claiming he invented tinned soup.* He didn't quite get the reference, but had seen soup tins in newspapers since and thought he understood.

The film will age badly, she told him. *Where you,* she ran her fingers through his hair, naked in bed together, *sought to make the book timeless with language, Kubrick's vision dates every day. The fashion has already moved on, his future already looks like the past.*

She was right. She had to be right. He put his own fingers through his hair, pulling and yanking. He would have to find a publisher for the Napoleon novel. He would have to finish the bloody thing first. He would have to be a novelist once more. Deborah would earn her ten percent.

Anthony cried. He had already started working on the score to the film. A great partnership: Kubrick director and producer, Burgess screenwriter and composer. The film would contain the whole of Beethoven's *Third*, but there must be more and he had begun to put down what felt like Beethoven and Burgess, the past and the present. He cried like a child. The sheer disappointment was too much to bear. Napoleon's failure, Burgess' failure. The difficulty in putting music into words, setting themes and melodies and instrumentation and composition into sentences and paragraphs and dialogue and – he swallowed – chapters. Not that Kubrick gave two shits or a fuck. The act of writing had become the act of composing, the dissection of writing and composing and the building of something entirely new. The novel had not been written but composed. The words placed on a stave. How could an act of such creation not help him make a film? The man was a fraud.

On his desk sat the music manuscript he had been working on, ideas to show Stanley when they met. Fool, he told himself.

Here lay a sonata and half a novel and exactly nothing to show for it. The score charted Napoleon's sailing from Corsica to Marseille. The notes rolled like the Ligurian Sea. It was a theme tucked somewhere at the back of his mind for some years. A seafaring theme, written aboard a boat to Malaya or Russia, a subtle hint of adventure in it, but also of reluctance and trepidation. He thought about swallowing down this too.

He walked out of the apartment and into the Rome rain. They were still playing *Arancia Meccanica* in the Catholic capital. The young lapped it up as one of their creations. Which it was not. It was created by an old English man and a bastard middle-aged American.

At a table in Da Meo Patacca, he ordered a gin and tonic. Where was Liana, that's what he wanted to know. Off somewhere with Andrea. Not that he wanted her to hear the news. She would give it the old *I told you so*. And she would be right. He breathed smoke into his glass and sucked down his weak cocktail.

Più gin, he called to the bartender.

The young Italian brought over the bottle of London Dry and poured a healthy amount into Anthony's glass. He smiled toothily.

Grazie, Burgess muttered, biting on his cheroot. Writing the rest of the Napoleon novel was a vast undertaking. It was already some two hundred pages and would most likely be double that when finished. There was still much research to do, much thinking and processing. The bastard. He would need space and time to write, no more trips to America and elsewhere. The fucking bastard. Kubrick had not only destroyed any future of the endeavour but had ripped the joy from writing it. He had, once more, felt like a man of music, a man of literature too. But, no, music had been the catalyst and the engine that drove him on. The music of Beethoven, yes, and his own music too, the music of Anthony Burgess. Why not? Why not the music of Anthony Burgess? These two-bit Tin Pan Alley songsters knocked out rip-offs of the old classics. There was no artistry in film composition, in the same way there was no artistry in banging out a he said/she said script to the specifics of ten contradictory studio executives. Kubrick had all but agreed his music would be used. *Who would know better than you, Anthony?* Fuck. It was one thing to hear his words spoken on screen. But to hear his music... He tried to stem the tears that were welling up, great tears of shame and tiredness.

He drank down his gin, ice and all, and left quickly. In bitter Roman rain, he wept. He wept for the time he had wasted and the flights of fancy he had allowed himself. And all of the rotten deals he had made these past few years. Giving away the rights to books, losing advances, working his fingers to the bone for free. His agents did nothing except take ten percent of what eventually came in. They were to bloody blame, all right. He would fire everyone. He would leave all of his publishers and tell them all to go to hell. And those arrogant movie-making bastards, he was once and for all done with them and their dirty promises and casual betrayal. Back in the apartment, Liana was still nowhere to be seen. He lit a cheroot and thought about burning the entire manuscript, a half-written novel never to be fulfilled. He grasped the top pages with violence in mind. The unwritten poison remained in his veins.

The Directory must be removed, he proclaimed himself King, and now the war was almost at an end. With it finished, he delivered his manuscript to Jonathan Cape to muted response. They would have preferred something more sellable. One of the account managers suggested he write a sequel to *A Clockwork Orange*, which had Anthony balling his fists.

Liana had already decided his next novel would be published elsewhere, there was good money to be had from Hutchinson and McGraw-Hill over the pond. The decision was congruous, his next novel would deal with the replacement of one wife with another. It would be set in Rome, in the very apartment they were living in. It would be about a haunted writer, haunted by his dead Welsh wife. Haunted by his old life, desperate to renew himself so he and his new life might coalesce. It would lay her to rest, he thought.

But as he wrote, he received a letter.

America
1975

Liana attended events where Anthony was introduced as a singular talent. He liked to think so too. They talked to him about novels and journalism and scripts and poetry and declared him a Renaissance man. And a composer, she heard him say before he said it, *Firstly, a composer.*

You could be, she told him, drunk in a Toronto hotel room, *the greatest novelist of this generation.* He thought it a compliment. It was not.

In Pittsburgh, she rubbed sleep from her eyes and pulled the living room blinds, blotting out what felt like midday sun. Her head pea-souped as Anthony might say; the migraine felt apocalyptic. She had begun drinking out of worry around noon, continuing into the evening out of sadness. Liana wanted to return to Malta for Christmas but the house had been confiscated by the Maltese authorities. She wrote to them and, somehow, made the situation worse. The house had been empty for three years; she wept for their first real home together. They were demanding payment for money Liana did not believe they owed, for gas and electricity, for workers who claimed to have been unpaid. She broached the subject with Anthony on the plane. Anthony had made it clear he had enough to think about, but she could not get it out of her mind. Her mother in that tiny apartment of hers, Liana in her Cambridge dosshouse, she had sworn it would not be like that again, and Antonio had sworn it too.

In the kitchen, littered with dirty glasses holding the remnants of wine and brandy and gin, she fumbled with the coffee machine. From somewhere in the apartment, there came a click-clicking, like a retractable pen in the hands of a child. Click-click. There was no one else here but Liana and Anthony, had been no one else here since they took the place some six days ago. She moved back to the kitchen, pouring water into the top of the machine, the clicking became a shunting, a mechanism firing back at itself. Clack clack, click. Liana gathered herself, her hands at her temples, eyes closed, moving back into the room to locate the ever-increasing noise. The clamour of the city fell away, the click-clicking amplified. Crack crack crack. *Christ Almighty.* The coffee began to percolate. The whole of last night weighed upon her, sharpened itself against her. She pulled her housecoat close, although she was too hot, sweat dripping from her pores.

Running her hand at shin height, she checked the plug sockets. Smash smash smash. The noise is gunfire, a final shootout in a building built of breezeblocks. Liana reached the tape machine and watched as the mechanism continued to push against the terminated reel. Crack, she hit the stop button.

She poured coffee and swallowed two pills. In the living room she rewound the tape, Anthony still snoring noisily in the bedroom. The tape whirred. She looked over the ever-growing pages beside Anthony's Olympia. A new novel. Her head was sore but her heart swelled with pride. Beside pages of prose sat pages of music. He worked on the two together, novel and symphony, often shifting between a line of one and a line of the other.

When they had first married, she had had notions of being his muse. Not in a girlish, romantic manner, but in practical ways. He would have space and peace, she would take from him the problems of the real world. It crossed her mind, occasionally, that his muse had been and gone. One novel in five years, from the man who had written five in one. They did so much moving, it was not hard to see why he had got so little done. When they were not arguing about the strain on his work, they were arguing about the strain on their family. When they lived in Malta, Andrea would be left in Malta, when they moved to Bracciano, they left him there instead. Now they lived in Rome and Andrea was to be left in Rome, at the boarding school he detested, while they travelled between Indiana and Pittsburgh. You could not drive a Dormobile from Rome to New York and so writing and family had all suffered.

The tape spooled to a stop. The recorder had been a present for him. He and Andrea would often play small pieces he had composed, pieces for piano and cor anglais. She recorded a singing lesson they gave her, which they played back again and again, roaring with laughter. It did not bother her; she hid her delight, to see them sharing a joke, even at her expense. Anthony had not taken to the new contraption; Liana used it almost compulsively. If they had guests, she would record the dinner party; if they were watching television, she would record their commentary. Above all, Liana had taken to recording their arguments, labelling them with titles such as *Anthony Burgess, In Conversation.* She rarely listened back, archiving the cassettes for posterity. But last night she had been drinking and the argument sat somewhere in the fog of alcohol and too many cigarettes.

She poured more coffee, opened a window, and pressed play.

Eh, so you said it was fairly interesting? Or a bit useless?

She shuddered at her own voice, so thin and sharp.

Well, you see—

But it was useful, only from the, purely from the psychological viewpoint yes?

He had promised her they would visit the Carnegie Museum, but had gone with one of his students. Anthony was not interested in photography and yet went without her. She spent the whole day on the phone to sort out the mess in Malta, to push his British publisher for a larger advance, to organise

Andrea's return for Christmas, and he had gone without her, with someone else.

It meant nothing at all. Absolutely nothing.

He came in late, ready for a fight, expecting her to be battle prepared. He had taken the boy to the exhibition and on to a Cassavettes' film they were showing at the museum: *A Woman Under the Influence.*

Right. For them it was the psychological.

He had taken the same boy drinking the night before. He was, according to Anthony, a burgeoning talent.

Was the exhibition good or bad? She heard the fire rise in herself. They spent so much of their time talking around the subject. *Is it good or bad? It's the second time, eh? Is it good or bad?*

From the speaker came the sound of typing and she watched his typewriter as if watching a ghost. Liana stood and attempted to place the two of them, Anthony at his desk, continuing with the novel, disappearing in plain sight. She was – where? – in the kitchen, fixing another drink. She can hear herself, faintly. The typing stopped, she held her breath, waiting.

No bloody good, he barks. *I've been told that once by one wife, now I'm being told it by another.*

Liana comes back into the room,

You asked me, what is the trouble, and I said, it's not much.

They are both drunk, far too drunk to form a path towards reconciliation.

What are you being so bloody enigmatic about? You say that and then you bugger off. What did you say? He begins to type again, pounding at the keys.

I'm not enigmatic, Liana says. *Not enigmatic, you're just not interested.*

She struggles to follow it. They are pouring all of their arguments into one glass.

I've had a bloody lousy life and I don't want another one like it.

You're able to work in the midst of many, many things. You're able to ignore—

Alright, I'll stop it now; I'll stop it now.

He smacks at the keys and then silence.

You're able to work in the midst of all sorts of things, eh. No matter, because to you they don't exist. What am I going to do?

The argument had been raging back and forth for months. For years. While Anthony was wined and dined by movie producers and wrote think pieces for *Rolling Stone*, Liana had several houses to manage, had him to manage, had book deals to obtain. And there was Andrea, another of Liana's responsibilities. It had always been this way.

I've let you down, oh dear! I've let you down. You've been thoroughly let down by me. Well, there you are, you are alone, poor little woman.

He could be so cruel when he drank. Anthony had told her all about the blazing arguments he and Lynne used to have and, for a time, she had believed it was Lynne who was the unreasonable drunk, who was the perpetuator of violent discourse.

Oh lord. This isn't that beautiful Irish, eh, Irish, sort of, eh – she paled at her inability to speak, willing herself to go to bed – Irish, what? Oratory. You certainly don't do anything for Andrea.

And though she can remember nothing of the evening itself, she knows everything that is about to be said.

I've done fuck all for Andrea and I've done fuck all for you. I've never sworn like this in my bloody life, 'til I met you. Never in my bloody life have I used filthy language the way I do with you. I'm surprised at nothing. But you force me to it.

Probably, your first wife did not allow you to swear as much as you do with me.

Well, the first wife, dying as she was, had a bloody sight more responsibility than you have.

Yes? Then it must be a different story than what you told me. You had to do the shopping, you had to do all sorts of things, pay all the bills. But now, everything now, it is turned upside down.

At least we were a bit more organised than you seem to be. We were a bit more organised.

Well, why don't you organise?

We didn't have too many bloody establishments.

You don't care at all about the other houses.

She cannot make out what he says, but she thinks she can hear him urinating. She wants to turn the damn thing off but lights a cigarette.

What did you say? What do you say? I didn't hear a word of what you said, her past self called out.

Said to whom?

I don't know, to the wall or perhaps to me. Your only responsibility is to write, my responsibility is everything else.

You leave everything to me and I'm not able to cope with these things.

You say, we have too many houses. What does that mean?

I need time to write, do you not see? Not worry about bloody bills and bloody eviction bloody notices.

My god, you write a fugue every day.

You don't read a bloody thing I write, unless you can translate it.

God Almighty, we had no money 'til now. Any money whatsoever in the bank? It may be your work, but believe me, it is money I have made for you.

The tape goes silent. She has heard enough now and must have heard enough then. It all felt incoherent. He wanted only to write his symphony, to talk to her about it, to show her black marks on a stave and for her to nod and say, yes dear, it is beautiful. He was right, she could not translate the music he wrote, could not begin to decipher it. And it paid nothing, though he liked to crow about this great commission. The novel sat waiting, bills sat waiting to be paid, and he wanted to discuss the oboe.

From the silence, Anthony says, *You're always going on about wanting to enjoy life.*

Absolutely, absolutely.

I'll tell you, nobody enjoys life less than me.

And less than me, believe me.

Well, go to a bloody hotel and enjoy yourself. Go and pick up men, do what you like. I don't care. Go and dance, go and dress up. Go and lay who you like, go and drink, get drunk.

Fortunately my idea of enjoying life is very simple, like going to see an exhibition.

Well, go and see it. Go and see the exhibition, what the hell is stopping you?

Liana pressed stop, once and for all.

She had gone back to Rome, leaving him to live in motel rooms alone. Whatever music had haunted him, tried to seduce him, had filled him, it was all gone now. The squeak-squeak sound of the inkwell as he unscrewed it were the only notes in his head. A single G squeaking in 3/4 time. The pen hovered once more, the size of his task already revealed in a hundredweight of paper. When he wrote novels, the pages piled up; only when he had finished did he know what size and shape the thing would take. Music worked in the opposite way. A symphony has a temporal existence which must be held in a physical space on pieces of well-presented paper. He rationalised that the first part of the symphony would be around nine minutes long, which meant around sixty sides. There he had it, empty staves that represented the beginning and the end of his first movement.

Inspiration was unable to penetrate a shithole motel in North Florida. Even prior inspiration shrank in the sickly humidity, in the faux wood hut décor, in the greyscale bathroom suite. He sat on the miserable bed, staring at the miserable ceiling and cursed the good ol' US of A.

Inspiration had arrived back in Rome, the piazza outside their home playing its own chaotic score, reducing his internal music to static notes, suspended in mid-air. The more he tried to blot out the honking and shouting and bell rings and all else, the louder it grew. It grew to deafening.

He had left the apartment to see the bones of Cecilia, who had replaced Francis de Sales as his patron saint. Inside the basilica, the stave hummed. Odd that the patron of musicians should rest in such a quiet tomb. He walked to the back of the church where the organ sat silent. There were very few visitors; two young women who were checking their watches and looking to the door. He sat. From the corner of his eye he watched them leave and made his way to the organ. He struck keys. Pent up for days, for weeks, he pressed hard on keys and pedals, filling the space with a sound thick and full. He expected to be stopped immediately but no one came. He thought about his Catholic family, if they could see him now, blaring out discordant phrases in this sacred place. They would not have cared for it, not only the modernity of his playing but the instrument itself. His family had endured the organ rather than embraced it as God's accompaniment. Give the Dwyers and the Wilsons a penny whistle and a bodhrán any day. They were somehow Pagan Catholics when it came to their choice in holy music. The fiddle could commune very well with our Lord.

He moved quickly back to his desk and wrote the theme down, carefully, in ink. A row of notes at once Celtic and austere. He played it over in his head

283

and found it spoke to the other parts of him gone so still. He threw everything at it, left nothing out. Every note would be played, every moment of his life commemorated. One hundred instruments representing sixty years of life, sixty years of repressed expression. He charged at the task. The brass clambered over each other to be heard. The strings would not relent. He filled in every gap. Anthony was desperate to fill in. By Christmas he had made himself sick with it, blacking out again, waking on Boxing Day and returning straight to the job in hand.

He threw in *Merdeka!* and notated the sea swells of journeys past, waves crashing overboard, drowning notes, notes floating above the waters, riding the skies to the new world, and in that Florida motel he felt the flush of creativity, replicating Manchester terraces in the key of C.

Within two weeks, he was looking out on Lake Mendota. The literary of Wisconsin were left waiting as Anthony began the scherzo, a wild jaunt, notes from the Old World, notes from the New, ricocheting between the two. *Andantino*, he wrote, and *Allegro. Molto vivace* would have written twice as much. By the time he got to New York it was almost finished, yet he had not heard a single note played.

Liana said to him, *I want to become a photographer, a real photographer*, and so that is what she became in his novel. He wrote of her in Rome, just as she had been when they first met, when they first made love; their Roman apartment carefully recreated. He a successful screenwriter, Liana a successful photographer, he gave them both success in his novel. But the phone rang there too. Lynne would have her moment. And she would appear in the opening of his second movement, a stab of strings and brass.

Jim Dixon came to collect him from the English department of the University of Iowa, where they had been explaining his timetable. Anthony would teach creative writing, whatever that meant, to final year students. *A good group*, they had told him, suggesting he might talk to them about composition, narrative voice and the perils of writing historical fiction. He waved this all away; he had been in enough American writing departments, had heard them talk this way about writing, as if it was some science, somewhere between chemistry and physics. He would teach blood and guts, he would teach lineage. If they wanted to learn to write, he would teach them Joyce, he would teach them how to read Shakespeare.

Jim Dixon was around the same height as Anthony, over six foot, but seemed bigger. It was all in the frame; he walked briskly for a man of his size. They went through the usual pleasantries: *How was the flight, where are you staying, we've been looking forward to your visit.*

Jim said, *Have you visited Iowa before?*

I feel America is my second home these days. America grew out of extension of my own country, grew out of a rejection of British hypocrisy and British oppression.

Is that so? Well, let's get you a cup of coffee.

The university had wanted him as a visiting lecturer, to teach their American students how to write international literature. There was an extra note from the conductor of the University Symphony Orchestra, James Dixon. He had read *Napoleon Symphony* and recognised the hand of a composer. The note read, *If my assumption is correct, I would be delighted to present some of your musical works here in Iowa, should you visit.*

Should he visit. Anthony followed Jim's cowboy gait as he strode towards the music department. Many students were sitting out on the grass, flicking idly through novels, textbooks and music manuscripts. Anthony wanted to see if any were his, but his eyes were too poor and the students too far away.

Where'd you fly from?

New York. I've had work up there too.

You're a busy man. Won't you follow?

Jim led him through the building and into the cafeteria. On the way, fresh faces smiled and said *Hello, Mr Dixon*. To some Jim replied, to others he only nodded. Anthony recognised the great delight of the students who had been addressed directly. In another life, Anthony had also experienced the pedagogical admiration of students.

I trust the scores are legible and complete?

What'll you have? Cup of coffee?

Tea.

No tea. One of my staff suggested getting some English tea for you as a welcome gift; I thought that was sort of an English cliché. But you guys really like your tea, huh?

Coffee is fine. Three sugars, plenty of milk.

Okay. Smiling to the woman behind the counter, *Hi Dolores, give me one cup black and one with cream and sugar.* Turning back to Anthony, *The manuscripts arrived no problem. I'll go through the changes I've made when we get into my office.* Jim did not pay. *Thanks, Dolores.* He handed Anthony a large mug of coffee, slightly lightened by some kind of dairy product. *We're this way*, he pointed, and Anthony followed.

Have rehearsals begun? He asked.

They have, Jim said, opening a door and allowing Anthony through. *They are still getting to grips with it, but nothing we need worry for.*

And how does it sound?

Raucous, Jim said.

Well, I'm sure whatever you've amended –

Morning, Mr Dixon.

– will be with good reason.

Hello, sir.

I wrote it without –

Good morning, Mr Dixon.

Morning, Julie.

– without hearing –

Hey, Mr Dixon.

Here we are, Jim said, reaching a door that read: JAMES DIXON, and underneath, SYMPHONY CONDUCTOR. Jim rustled keys in the lock and invited Anthony in.

Piled up on a desk at the back of the office was the music manuscript. Anthony moved towards the score, overwhelmed to see it here in the office of a symphony conductor. *It is strange to think all this exists because of a piece of literature.*

Here – Jim pointed at a group of notes on the manuscript – *we've tried this all ways around and it just falls apart. I'd suggest we repeat this section*, he lifted another page from the stack, *here, you see?*

Anthony had not had an editor for some years, not in the sense of an editor working with drafts, suggesting cuts, demanding rewrites. He flushed at the suggestion he change things, that he had got it wrong.

Don't feel you need to answer now, Mr Burgess. We can look at it when you're better acclimatised.

It's Anthony, or Tony, he said, not for the first time. *I will look at it tonight; here you say?* He pointed at the cluster of notes, marked up for strings, got in close peering down and humming it back to himself. Straightening, he said, *It was bound to happen, of course. The whole thing was written without my hearing a note – it's all up here,* he tapped at his head with the butt of his cheroot.

You haven't heard it?

Not in the sense you mean.

Why on Earth not? Jim looked at the manuscript anew, a little repelled by it. *You play, don't you?*

All this was written in hotel rooms, hotel lobbies, departure and arrival lounges.

Well, you'll hear it this afternoon. What we have of it, anyway.

He was brought through the main doors, the auditorium much larger than Anthony had anticipated. Jim's assistant showed him to the back of the stage where he sat behind the orchestra. She pushed two desks together so he could follow the score as they played. She smiled and nodded, fetched him an ashtray and a coffee from the cafeteria. Jim spent a great deal of time going between the players, conversing.

When Anthony asked him why he must sit at the back, Jim said, *I don't want them distracted.* And then, *Everybody. This is Anthony Burgess.* Anthony had not expected applause but was surprised when it did not come. *He will be joining us in the run up to the performance. Mr Burgess is here to help me with ironing out any issues there may be with the score; you are not under surveillance!* They laughed. Anthony could not help but scowl.

He stood up to say a few words, a quick, *I would like to say what a pleasure* – but they turned to face Jim, who stood behind the podium. He tapped his baton and they started up. Anthony wasn't ready. He was still leaning over the desks they had given him, cheroot in hand, the last few words of his ill-prepared speech still in his mouth. The music hit him like the waves off the Maltese coast as he tried to teach Andrea to swim, hit and sunk by wave after bloody wave. He grasped at notes, at the swell of music as it hit him. In the music he saw a horde of Lowry bone machines, tramping along a cobbled backstreet of Harpurhey; monochrome bees with clipped wings. It all came to an abrupt stop, Jim waving the musicians into silence. He talked to the young assistant who stood close, looking over the manuscript.

If I can be of any assistance, Anthony said, still standing, still wondering if he should finish his little speech.

Okay, Jim said, *from the top again. Let's see if we can get through to* – he shuffled pages – *the top of page four.* He counted them in.

Anthony sat. He peered at the score, notes he had set down, notes now freely sounded, reverberating through the room. It was as it had sounded in his head and, equally, nothing like what he had written. Andrea had had, hanging above his bed, cardboard planets making up a cardboard solar system. At some point, Liana had bought him plastic spheres to replace their circular counterparts. The music in his head had existed on only two axes; what he heard now filled him up, great gas giants in orbit; then planets came crashing down once more. He leaned over his desk to see the harpist push her instrument away and run her hands through lank brown hair.

What's the problem, Catherine? Jim moved from his podium and strode towards her.

Is this some kind of trial? How am I meant to— her hands again ran through her hair. *Does he even know how a pedal harp works?* She flashed a look up to the composer, who strained to hear.

Maybe I can— Anthony stood, but Jim waved him back to his seat.

That's fine. This is, he turned out to speak to the whole orchestra, *a new work. You are the first to play it and the first to test its capacity. We are collaborators in this, not just players.* He stooped a little. *Now, Catherine, you do what you can, and we will work through what is and what isn't possible.*

Back at the podium, Jim looked up. *Mr Burgess? You're happy to revisit whatever isn't working?*

Anthony turned to him, looked down at pages and pages of manuscript, months of work, no: years of work, a lifetime's work. *By all means,* he said, aware that Catherine was still talking to herself. *I am here to help however I can.*

There had been more problems, missing notes, confusion over the tempo of one section, more dissatisfaction from the harpist. Jim let the musicians go early. Only after they left was Anthony invited down to the stage, to Jim's own score. They sifted through notes, Jim made vague reference to a section in need of attention and Helen, his assistant, made the exact place within moments.

Here, Jim said, lifting a piece of manuscript up and turning it, looking at the page beneath. *This is all over the place.* He held it out to Anthony like a wanted poster in a spaghetti Western.

He studied the page, the reverse side and the page that followed. *There's been an error,* he said. *Not,* he added, *mine. There should be a violin solo here.*

Jim studied the pages, Helen over his shoulder.

An error by the copiers, no doubt, Anthony said, lighting a cheroot.

We'll have to work something out. We can tie these sections together, Jim pointed vaguely.

I can write it out again, Anthony said, offering a cigar, which was accepted.

You remember it?

I should think I do.

Jim seemed impressed; Anthony basked in it. *We'll need new copies,* Jim said, Anthony aware he was looking to him.

Anthony had paid for the first lot, sent over from Italy. Now he would have to pay again. *How much?*

We'll need, what? Jim turned to Helen.

One hundred and sixteen, seventeen copies.

Let's call it a hundred and twenty copies.

Anthony had already agreed to cover the costs of copying. He winced when Helen said she expected it to cost $1,200. Liana would baulk at the fee, would be indignant that he, the composer, should have to pay. *If new copies are required,* he said. This pleased Jim and Helen.

Very well then, Jim said. *There's some finer details to go over.* He took his glasses and placed them on the desk, *I swear I can't see the notes any longer. Let's call it a day, Helen.*

I'll get the changes in order for Mr Burgess.

Make sure everyone gives back the version we have now. God knows we've got enough against us.

And I, Anthony said, *will write out the violin solo this evening.*

Not this evening, Jim said. *You're the guest of honour.*

Anthony had almost forgotten about the welcome meal, given for him by both the English and Music departments of the university.

In any case, I will have it for you tomorrow.

Conductor and assistant shared a doubtful look. Then Jim said, *Will your wife be joining us this evening?*

Not tonight, Anthony said. *She is in New York, but she will be here tomorrow, or the next day. My son too, if he chooses.*

Anthony was collected by John Leggett, the head of the writing department and a novelist in his own right. Leggett's wife drove, while the two men discussed literature, the writing of literature and the teaching of the writing of literature. When they got to the restaurant, Jim Dixon was already seated, talking distractedly to a colleague. Anthony was to be seated next to John, so that John could introduce him to other writers on the faculty. Before taking his seat, Anthony excused himself, crossing the table to where Jim sat. Jim invited him to sit.

You've crossed the line in the sand, Jim said, nodding over to the writers across from them. *We're all illiterate this side; though we can whistle a tune.*

Well, Anthony said, looking over the wine list, *then I'm in the right place.*

The meal was a dull affair. John Leggett rose to make a speech, as did Himie Voxman, a student of chemical engineering who had gone on to be the director of music at the University of Iowa. Anthony made a speech too, about the coalescence of music and literature, though there had been no coalescence that night, music and literature refusing to mix as do oil and water. Jim was strangely quiet and, walking out into the cool October night, he seemed to grow once more, as if being surrounded by colleagues and superiors had reduced him.

Anthony refused a nightcap with the writing department, hoping Jim might make him a better offer. *What does one do in Iowa on a Thursday evening?* he asked.

They were already walking together down one of the wide main streets, Anthony huddled in his tweed jacket, smoking another cheroot. He looked up at the expansive Iowa sky as it began to rain.

This way, I suppose, Jim said, lighting a cigar of his own.

Something wrong? Anthony asked.

Jim released a billowing puff of smoke, said, *I need some R and R after shop talk all night long.*

They came to a bar, deep red in décor, that played jazz through a sound system. Anthony recognised some faces, violinists and tuba players, the harpist whose hands still twitched through her hair.

Look who I found, Jim said, presenting Anthony to the group. They played along, cheering his arrival, though he noticed some looked away or rolled their eyes.

What's everyone drinking? Anthony said, over the sound of Thelonious Monk. The group turned to him, even those who had dismissed him smiling and nudging one another.

The first round cost almost as much as the recopying of his symphony, the second even more. He wrote the second cheque through half-closed eyes. Anthony had garnered a reputation for frugality. Less a reputation than a notion of self.

He found Jim talking to a young man; not a student, he guessed.

I supposed I should introduce you, Jim said, after Anthony had joined the conversation. *Richie, this is Mr Anthony Burgess.*

Anthony is fine, he said, shaking the man's hand.

He wore a short sleeved white shirt and pressed denim jeans, his hair sun-kissed blonde though it was autumn, and turning quickly to winter. *This is the writer?* he said, a little sniffy.

The composer, Jim said. *Isn't that right, Tony?*

Anthony said, *I've always been a composer who also writes, I've always...* but he fell quiet, looking at this sulking youth, stuck with this old fart of an Englishman.

Richie was perhaps in his late thirties, more or less the same age as Liana. He looked over to the other end of the table where people somewhat closer to his own age talked animatedly, no doubt about the free form music that filled the room.

I'm writing a book, have been writing it alongside the symphony. It's about an old man who fucks young women.

Richie smirked, continued to look away but couldn't help eyeing Anthony.

They come into his apartment like nymphs, pin him down and defile him. I came up with it as I was writing the scherzo.

Is that what you write, he asked, *dirty books?*

Oh yes, Anthony said, pouring himself more of the bad American wine. *They're all dirty. You haven't read any of my work?*

He shook his head.

Richie doesn't think much of literature, do you, Richie? He's a music snob. Jim smiled. *Excuse me,* he stood and walked to the bathroom, leaving Anthony and Richie alone.

In the absence of anything else to say, Anthony said, *I'm writing a film script too; at least, I've been commissioned to write a film script.*

What's it about?

I'm not sure yet. They want a disaster movie.

Richie spluttered out a laugh. He was still half-turned away from Anthony, and now he turned his face from him fully.

Something funny?

No, no, he said, still laughing. *So have you,* he straightened up and turned his eyes back to Anthony, *got any ideas about what the disaster might be?*

I have in mind an asteroid crashing into Earth. They send a spaceship with the great and the good on it and leave the rest to perish.

And are you on that spaceship, Mr. Burgess?

Not me, no. Richie's attention drifted again, and Anthony said, *You teach at the university too, Richard?*

Richie, he corrected. *No, teaching doesn't suit me. I used to teach privately but, you know, kids.*

He was younger than Liana; up close, his skin was clear, his hair thinning a little. *And how do you know Jim?*

We're friends, Richie said. *I used to be his student, a long time ago.*

What do you play?

Piano. I was his star soloist for a while.

My father was a piano-player. Me too.

Pianist and composer. Quite the change of career.

I have written twenty novels in twenty years; I may very well write twenty symphonies in as much time. Less, even; I enjoy it far more.

And what about your books?

I might not write another.

Richie finished his drink. *You should carry on with books.*

Jim was talking to some students at the other side of the bar, Anthony aware of Richie trying to get his attention.

You've looked at my symphony?

What? He turned back again. *Oh, in a way. Jim had me play over some of it.*

And?

I'm going to need another drink.

Anthony went to the toilet, chatted to a saxophonist about jazz, and waited at the bar to be served. He expected to find Richie holding court with a group of students or perhaps gone home, but back at the table Richie was waiting.

Thank you, he said, taking a sip of the whisky he had asked for. *Well?*

You are a hobbyist, Mr Burgess. Just as I would be a hobbyist if I were to take up a pen and paper and write a novel.

I don't accept that.

Richie shrugged. He could accept whatever he wanted.

If you knew nothing of me, knew nothing of my life as a writer, do you think you would come to the same conclusion?

294

They moved on to another bar, the group growing smaller, Anthony feeling that bit older. The new place was all bare bricks and bar stools, an upright piano against the back wall. On the piano, a bright-eyed white-toothed youth was playing an American pop song, something about lovers and hotels, emptiness and fate. The singer put on an affected voice reminiscent of the crackle of autumn leaves. The group cajoled and Richie went up next, performing a piece of jazz Anthony was unfamiliar with, but he could appreciate the skill, the musicality. He watched Jim watching Richie and felt a pang. Liana had always seen music as a pastime, what Jim would call 'R and R'; Lynne had refused to listen. After Richie, others played; a whole range of styles, blues and country, rock and roll.

Anthony, having bought yet more drinks, sat at the piano now. The bar emptying, it was that time of the night. Behind, someone said, *Is he going to play the whole symphony?* The table laughed. Anthony was too much in concentration, but he did catch the word *disaster*.

He put his fingers on the keys and played Dutilleux's *Piano Sonata*, the second movement: *Lied*. Its notes dropped like pennies from the pocket of a drunk. Anthony played well, drunk enough to lend true meaning to its simplicity and unsteadiness. He thought of his father performing in front of the Eight Lancashire Lads, saw his fingers Chaplin-like stumbling down a Lancashire street. Would he have been a concert pianist if his father had taken an interest, if Maggie had put her hand in her pocket for lessons? How much had Richie's father spent on tuition and school fees? He hated to guess. Better to have a son out of music, for whom instruments and lessons and ever more expensive instruments and lessons were superfluous. Best not to have the obligation when there were bar bills to play. He played fifths down the keyboard and struggled to keep himself upright.

They applauded him. Anthony put his cheroot back in his mouth and found they really did applaud. Perhaps they thought this some kind of abstract jazz, newly invented in Europe. Even the bartender applauded. Anthony nodded and went back to the table. There were only four of them now, Jim, Richie and the harpist; he had forgotten her name. They were still clapping when he sat down.

Wonderful, Jim said.

Richie raised his glass and clinked it against Anthony's. *So, you are one of us.*

They shared a taxi and dropped Anthony off at his hotel room, where he poured himself a glass of brandy and got on with writing out the missing violin solo.

She felt foolish sat there with her luggage – two suitcases and a large carry bag – but Anthony told her to meet him at the auditorium, they would be rehearsing all day. She had gone in, the door opening loudly, the orchestra in the middle of what she later found out was Brahms, the conductor shouting out *Can I help you?* It had been half an hour and she was readying herself to walk back to the reception, to ask them to call a taxi, when some of the musicians came into the lobby, lighting cigarettes. She found musicians fascinating, in the way Liana had come to find many of Anthony's interests fascinating. It was love, she thought.

You know, they forced it on him.

Who?

The writing lot. They'd been trying to get the starry chelloveck to teach for the longest time and then someone had the bright idea of asking him to write a goddamn symphony.

No!

You ask Laird.

Bullshit.

You've heard it. The whole thing is a mess, a joke.

Liana stayed quite still, watching the four of them talk. The girls were tall and fair-haired, the boys rangy and wore their hair long and curly.

You should have seen him last night, buying everyone drinks like he's some big shot composer now.

She steeled herself. They were young. Yes, they were young and they were stupid, uninformed. Liana had seen the letter for herself, signed Jim Dixon.

They noticed her now, sat alone at the table, surrounded by bags, and smiled at her. She smiled back mildly, letting no hint of her true thoughts pass across her face. She was good at this now; it was part of being Anthony's literary agent, to listen to people's opinions of him and, smiling, make them see things differently. It had become a great talent.

The group stubbed out cigarettes and went back into the auditorium, the girls nodding, one saying *ma'am*, as they passed. It was another ten or so minutes before Anthony arrived. He looked dreadful, and when he kissed her she smelt all the drinks the big shot composer had bought the night prior.

Shall we go in? she asked.

He sat at the table and held her hands. *I am very happy to see you*, he said.

And I you. I have good news from New York.

Yes, yes, that can wait.

She was piqued at his dismissal, but said, *You are enjoying life as a composer?*

With all my being, he said.

Liana sat at the back of the auditorium, watching Anthony at the back of the stage. He looked oblivious to the music around him, as if he were struggling to read the small print of a newspaper.

At lunch, Anthony introduced her to Jim Dixon. She told herself she would not mention the students but when Anthony excused himself to go to the bathroom, she cut right to it.

I'm sorry you had to hear that, he said, genuinely.

He said it was a joke.

Kids, he said, by way of an answer, and then, *They take a while to warm to anything new. This is the problem with kids; they think they're great innovators, but really they just want the familiar, the undemanding.*

He would be very upset if he knew.

Mrs Burgess, your husband is a fine composer. These musicians are lucky to be a part of this first performance. If you want me to speak to them...

No, she said. *No, I am satisfied.*

After lunch, she took a taxi back to the hotel alone, Anthony having a class to teach. She walked in on a room littered with music manuscript and dirty clothes, bedsheets strewn. After clearing up, she got on with the job of looking after Anthony. She called Gianfranco De Bosio's office to arrange a visit. He would bring Burt Lancaster out to the concert to discuss a film they wanted Anthony to write. She would arrange a party; they would expect to be wined and dined, and their attendance would make the event even more prestigious, even more of a spectacle. Liana was determined to make their time in Iowa a great success.

Anthony sat on the toilet, aware that his lesson started in less than ten minutes. He felt overjoyed; Liana was with him, the new score would be ready shortly, and he would soon be recognised as a composer. He'd barely slept from working all night. His stomach was turning in on itself; he expelled gas loudly. They recognised him, recognised the music he held within. Richie had. In the taxi he told Richie he would compose a piano sonata, and Richie had been pleased. This was just the start. They all knew him as a composer now. Though he felt heavy with last night's spirits, his own were lifted, joyous. Here, in Iowa, he could be Anthony Burgess the composer, the musician. He would have to teach creative writing, yes, but students rarely knew who he was, not unless they had been drilled by their lecturers, not unless he was at pains to tell them himself. If they asked, he would tell them, as he had told them last night, he was a composer who dabbled in the literary trade. He held his hands against his stomach and felt, not for the first time, the disunion between body and mind.

Walking to the classroom, he found he had nothing to say about the short story. He would talk about the use of myth in modern literature, would talk about how myth had been a great influence on music. Berlioz, Elgar, Stravinsky, of course. He would soon be back in the auditorium, soon be back listening to his own music. He thought, opening the door to the classroom, about telling the students he was someone else. He might pretend to be Philip Roth or, better still, Graham Greene.

The applause startled him. He let out an unexpected belch and scanned the room of standing, clapping, cheering students. They beamed at him, delighted in his presence. He waved their applause away, but they kept on; that was when he noticed it. On that desk, and that one over there, and held in that lad's hand, were copies of *A Clockwork Orange*, some untouched, some dog-eared. One student had *MF* in front of them and he had never been so happy to see one of his books.

Thank you, he said, again motioning them to take their seats. *That's quite enough.*

Mr Burgess, sir, will you sign our... A young woman held her copy of *A Clockwork Orange*. Pristine, he noted, a newer edition.

If there is time at the end, yes.

Back in the corridor, he supped from the water fountain, the ground firm beneath him. He spoke about myth, about James Joyce and his retelling of Homer. *As writers, we are in conversation with writing,* he said.

Don't you, a girl at the back spoke up, *want to talk about how you wrote myths into your work?*

My work?

Sure, like MF and Napoleon Symphony, right? They're basically the myths of Oedipus and Prometheus, aren't they?

Yes, he said, standing. *Well, it's not as straightforward as you would have it.*

Is there, another girl at the back of the class raised her hand, *a writing exercise in all of this?* He noted she did not have a copy of any of his books on her desk.

You want a prompt? He asked.

I want to know this is going somewhere.

Write, then, a myth reset in the present day.

Like what? another student asked.

Like whatever you like. The Minotaur might be a mob boss, the labyrinth his vast empire. Theseus would be a policeman or vigilante, out to rid the city of crime.

Wouldn't it work better if Theseus was a sheriff and the Minotaur was a kind of, I don't know –

An outlaw who preyed on prospectors, a slab of a boy interrupted.

But the Minotaur had his victims gifted to him. He wouldn't be in charge, a girl with tightly swept-back hair added.

You're not here to solve the problem of resetting the Minotaur. I have asked you to come up with your own idea. He sat at the desk and looked at the class.

So, is this meant to be like a short story or something? someone asked.

I suppose so. Or an outline, or the opening of a novel, of a play, whatever you think best.

Hey, I got this idea about a girl who can't take her eyes off of her compact mirror.

I had the same exact idea.

That's all too simple. It doesn't go anywhere, Anthony said, exasperated. *Why not,* he stood, *Bellerophon and Pegasus?* The students looked between them, confounded. *Bellerophon is tasked to capture Pegasus. On the journey, he sleeps in Athena's temple and dreams she has come to him. When he awakes, he has in his hands a bridle for a horse and knows exactly where to find Pegasus. He captures the horse and flies back to the King who offers his daughter as prize. This is just a small part of the story, but how could we transform this into the narrative of a modern novel?*

They sat there stumped, stupefied. One said, *Pegasus is the unicorn, right?*

The flying horse, someone corrected.

I will leave you to contemplate. Anthony collected his things and left.

Andrea arrived the morning before the performance. Though he had been expected at rehearsal, the concert ever looming, Liana insisted they both meet him from the airport. His son looked older than his eleven years as he climbed into the front passenger seat.

How was the flight, Andrea?

Andrew, he corrected.

How was the flight, Andrew?

Long, he replied, in his jumbled accent.

Tell him about school, Liana said, squeezing her son's shoulder.

What's to tell? Liana kept this to herself, whatever it was, held back information so Anthony and Andrew could have a moment, could share in something face to face.

He's started to learn the recorder, Antonio. His teacher says he has a natural gift. Like his father. She squeezed the boy's shoulder once more. Anthony caught the boy's embarrassment in the rear view mirror.

He made sure to tell everyone he speaks to that this is, in fact, his third symphony. But Anthony knew the truth: it is his first. His first two novels did not count until someone had read them, until they existed outside of himself.

Anthony, I'd like you to meet, says everyone he knows, introducing him to everyone he does not.

Anthony Burgess, I'd like you to meet Gianfranco de Bosio, said Burt Lancaster.

A pleasure, shaking the director's hand, wary of directors.

We're very keen to talk to you about a new film. We're putting the money together, Burt said, grinning with brilliant teeth.

I am a great fan of your work, Gianfranco told him. *You are a wonderful writer.* He had heard these words before, from another director. He was about to reply when Liana placed her hand under his and said, *Antonio, this is not an evening for talk of movies. You are a composer tonight. Will you excuse us for two minutes, gentlemen?* The men bowed, charmed by his charming wife.

Jim smoked a cigar and talked to Ritchie, well-groomed, in an expensive looking suit. Jim said, *How you holding up there?*

I have been better. But I have the utmost faith.

Jim's wasted here, Ritchie said.

No one's wasted anywhere. Everyone deserves great art, every place deserves to hear great music. Don't you agree, Anthony?

He moved on, in something of a daze, Ritchie kept his elegant eyes on him. Anthony found himself alone in the centre of the room. It felt like a wake, a wake for the author Anthony Burgess. He was offered and accepted a drink.

Someone said, *I wanted to come over and introduce myself. I am a huge fan of yours.*

Oh yes? Anthony said, uninterested.

I've read a great deal of your work. I'm trying to get through them all, but you keep writing more.

I will have to put a stop to that.

And now a composer too!

I have, Anthony said, *always been a composer. Only now are people listening. Are you on the faculty?*

I am a researcher, though not in Iowa. I have come especially to hear your symphony.

Then I am honoured. Where have you travelled from?

I have brought my wife and my son to hear your work. There they are, in the corner. You see? Beautiful, aren't they?

Charming.

I cannot wait to hear your creation.

Neither can I, Anthony said, shaking the man's hand.

You said once, he said, *MF is the only work you're proud of. Did I?*

It's not true?

It's time, Liana said, and took Anthony by the arm, leading him through the crowd.

How do I look? he asked Andrew.

Better, his son replied. *Look, they're going through.*

Anthony reaches out his hand to his son. His dad takes his hand and says, *Stay close, Jackie.* His son pulls his hand away, *Dad, what are you doing?* He is eleven, but older, somehow ancient, as he was as a boy, that boy who was pulled, hand in hand with his father into the Free Trade Hall. The ceilings! He'd never noticed ceilings before. After the Free Trade Hall, he always made sure to look up. His dad queued at the bar, mumbling to himself about the people 'ere, Jackie. He cadged fags from the couple beside, and his dad ordered a pint of bitter, quickly draining the top quarter.

Where do we sit? he asks.

This way, Mr Burgess. A girl leads them down the steps. Her teeth are a touch splayed, she has a heavy metal brace, the kind only Americans wear. Anthony turns as the door closes behind them, his father showing their tickets, the usher tearing them at the centre and handing them back.

What'd 'e do that for?

Stops people sneakin' other people in.

The hall is huge. Jack gasps at the size of it. He says, *Dad*, too loud, his voice reverberated round.

Joe says, *You're not to piss about 'ere, mind.* He looks at their stubs and at the row numbers. *This way, gobby.* He follows his father, is followed by his son, is sitting and ready to listen, was sitting with his heart beating in his chest, listening to the fizzing hum of expectant voices, beating with anticipation that swelled in the silence. All around them the audience whispers, the energised drone of a bee hive. The background noise, those five unwavering bars, come into focus. It is, he listens closely, the human equivalent to an orchestra tuning up. The low murmur of the boys behind them, the higher register of the girls down the front, the mid rustle of those waiting on the platform, all converging to A 440 hertz.

Jim Dixon makes his way to the centre of the stage. Anthony's hands are shaking. He's trying to open the bag of sweets his dad gave him, but he couldn't get the bag to break. He said, *Can thee 'ave a go?*

Giz them 'ere, he replies, giving the bag a good yank and handing it back, taking one for good measure.

Eh, them are mine.

Cost of admission, Joe says.

When he chews, he can hear his heart beat in his ears. *What will they play?* he asks.

Wagner, his dad tells him.

Wagger?

Wagner, he emphasises the *n*.

Thur starting, he shouts, watching the musicians lift their instruments. He hears the air in the room become charged. Particles held in position wait for the striking moment.

Tap, tap, tap.

His heart is full, he squeezes his son's hand, his father's hand, his eyes are already wet. Then, with a flick of a wrist, the whoosh of a million, billion atoms and particles shifting in one fluid motion. In the slipstream he sees the faces of the crowd, filled with the living and the dead. He can barely make out the music itself, the feeling of it, the sense. The sound of this many instruments, of this many human bodies moving and breathing and beating as one is just too bloody much. He's never heard it before, only in his head, only what he'd heard on the radio, which was tinny and was the sound of just one man as far as he could make out, buzzing out of a tiny speaker by his ear by his bed. There's nothing to prepare you for the force with which music, people playing music, can attack you. They don't need guns in wars, John thinks, they need flamin' trumpets and tubas and timpani and all of them like a wall playing all at once. He wants to ask, *Dad, has anyone's head ever blown off by music?* But his dad is entranced, teary-eyed and transfixed.

Andrea squeezes his leathery hand, he can't remember holding hands with Anthony. There must have been a time, but he's not sure when. He can't focus on the music because he's too absorbed by the man beside him, the man he has known his whole life, yet who he does not know at all. They had taken him to see *Cyrano* when they were living in New Jersey. Andrea fell in love with music then, but had been told by Anthony it was derivative claptrap and not really music at all. Andrea had seen it again and loved it even more, and Anthony's rage against it increased proportionally.

But while he sat stony-faced, sneering almost, during those performances, here he wiped his face with a handkerchief, eyes straining to stay wide open and then, wavering, blinking away tears that streamed down the crags of his face. He had not seen his dad like this before. Music was a job, something to pay the bills. *The piano is a bitch,* he'd heard his dad say. *Joanna, the old bitch.* To see such pleasure on his dad's face disturbed him. It was not his dad, was not what his dad was, couldn't ever be like, he felt himself fill up, he listened hard, like his dad was listening and he could hear, through the power of it, the absolute force of it, he could hear the delicacy, the way certain players played opposite and against each other, but not in a battle, in a kind of dance, swaying between one another like trees by the river, all branches intertwining and pulling apart as the wind blew. He wanted to be overrun by it, for it to fill his every sense, for it to push out every other thought until all there was was this and the moment of every note struck, of every string bowed, every breath breathed.

If there is a god, a higher power, a god that is pure and concentrated, then it is this. People believe in magic, in the reading of words in a certain order, an incantation to make the rains fall or a man drop dead or the future expose itself. He had spent his life toiling with words, in a constant war, and he knew the only true incantation was the playing of notes on a page. They lay there, unmoving, static, incomprehensible, abstract, artless, these black notes and yet a person with an instrument, a hundred people with a hundred instruments, could bring these inert marks to life where they moved and sang and caused the human mind and body to react in a way totally unexpected, totally beyond what the marks hinted at. Music could bring life and end life and, yes, it could reveal the future, it certainly immured the past. Not the past of a previous performance, for all incantations were entirely unique. No, this was the past where the notes were set down, the past the composer wanted to be petrified on the page. Played, these pages contained childhoods and love affairs and deaths and the fall of countries, of entire empires, the end of everything, the start of everything. And that past was fortified by the present, was only possible because of the present, meaning the past was alive in the people who played it, meaning the past was not dead, was not irretrievable, quarantined, inaccessible.

The past lives.

Acknowledgements

First and foremost, thank you to Rosie for your unending inspiration, patience, love, and investment in a project that has accompanied us (for better or worse) through the start of our marriage to the birth of our two children, Finbar and Ray. I love you.

I have been supported in many ways by my dad, Rob, and mum and step-dad, Shirley and Rob, and by our kid, Toni, thank you. Rosie's parents, Christine and Adam, have given unwavering encouragement for which I am profoundly grateful. Thank you also to Adam for reading and always being ready to talk Burgess.

Bluemoose have been wonderful to work with. Thank you to Kevin for recognising a Manchester from the past (Anthony Burgess walking tours of MCR could be a money spinner) and for believing in this book. Huge thanks to Annie Warren, the editor of *Three Graves*, whose influence I see on each page. This has been a real collaboration and I appreciate your investment in it. My thanks too to Hetha and Lin.

My deepest gratitude to Judy Kendall who has advised me from my earliest contemplation of this project to its completion. Thank you for your insight and guidance.

My appreciation to the faculty at University of Salford, particularly Ursula Hurley, Glyn White, Jane Kilby, Jo Scott, Scott Thurston, and Maggie Scott, for their support and advice. I owe Frances Piper a debt of thanks for first suggesting an investigation into Anthony Burgess and his works may prove profitable.

Thank you to Caroline Hodgson, for early reading and proofing, and for being an ally in writing. And to Heather Woodstock and Stebben Bracewell for insightful reading and being lovely, lovely people. Many of the breakthroughs in writing this novel have come, unsurprisingly, in the pub, so thank you to friends and family who have shared their time.

I am grateful to Dr Andrew Biswell, Burgess' biographer and director of the International Anthony Burgess Foundation, who has always been open, giving and, in the earliest stages of writing, helped focus my approach to Burgess. I would also like to thank Anna Edwards, archivist at the IABF, for her interest and kindness.

Chris Thurley's research into Burgess's time at Chapel Hill offered great insight, thank you for sharing your work. My gratitude to Laird Addis, who passed away in 2018, for kindly shared memories of Jim Dixon and the University of Iowa Symphony Orchestra's performance of Burgess's Symphony in C.

My thanks to Chairul Fahmy Hussaini, who proofed the Malay language sections of the novel and offered insightful suggestions.

During my trip to Malaysia, I was fortunate to meet Sharon and Abu Bakar, who shared invaluable insights into Burgess' time at the Malay College, Kuala Kangsar. Gareth Richards, director of Gerak Budaya Bookshop, and Impress Creative and Editorial, Penang, revealed connections between Malaysia and Manchester. I am also indebted to Akos Farkas for his perspective on Burgess and the time he offered.

And, of course, thank you Anthony Burgess. Malcolm Bradbury once described your work as an unstoppable monologue, but I have always seen in it a demand for dialogue.

Quoted Material

All quoted work by Anthony Burgess © The International Anthony Burgess Foundation (with thanks to David Higham)

Epigraph: *Little Wilson and Big God* by Anthony Burgess (Vintage)

p.20: Lines from 'The Crab that Played with the Sea', in *Just So Stories* by Rudyard Kipling

p.69 & 158: Extracts from *Time for a Tiger*, in *The Malayan Trilogy* by Anthony Burgess (Vintage)

p.77: Line from *Ulysses* by James Joyce

p.95: Lines from 'Relativity' by Arthur Henry Reginald Buller

p.104: Lines from 'This is Remembered', in *The Notebook Poems*, 1930–1934 by Dylan Thomas (Orion), by kind permission of The Dylan Thomas Estate

p.106–107: Lines from 'Deaths and Entrances', in *The Collected Poems of Dylan Thomas: The Centenary Edition* by Dylan Thomas (Weidenfeld & Nicolson), by kind permission of The Dylan Thomas Estate

p.111: Line from *Why I Write* by George Orwell (Penguin)

p.123: Line from *Othello* by William Shakespeare

p.167–168: Poem from *Enderby Outside,* in *The Complete Enderby* by Anthony Burgess (Vintage)

p.253–254: Lines from 'The Tower', in *Collected Poems* by Anthony Burgess (Carcanet Classics)

p.255–256: Lyrics from 'Daddy Wouldn't Buy Me a Bow Wow' by Joseph Tabrar

p.283: Music notation from Symphony in C by Anthony Burgess